THE ULTIMATE STONEMAGE

A MODEST AUTOBIOGRAPHY

THE ULTIMATE STONEMAGE

A MODEST AUTOBIOGRAPHY

BY DUNCAN MCKENZIE

Issued in print and electronic formats
ISBN 978-0-9949409-0-2 (bound). ISBN 978-0-9949409-1-9
(Kindle)

Cover design © Duncan McKenzie

MKZ Press
2538 Waterford Street
Oakville, Ontario, Canada L6L 5E7
mkzpress@mkz.com

"My name is writ in stones."

—*Henry Eagles,*
Stonemage of Antiquity

CONTENTS

INTRODUCTION

In Which I Explain How To Write A Great Autobiography

I WAS GOING TO TITLE THIS book *My Name is Writ In Stones*, from a quote by the great Henry Eagles. But then I thought to myself, "This is the story of *my* life and accomplishments, not those of Henry Eagles!" So instead I have named it *The Ultimate Stonemage*.

On seeing the title, some have said to me, "Friend Yreth, we are puzzled. Do you mean your book will teach the reader to *become* the ultimate stonemage? Or do you mean the stonemage is the ultimate mage and stands above all others? Or do you claim you personally are the ultimate stonemage?"

It is a difficult question.

I do believe this book may teach the reader to become a better stonemage, for I have revealed many magical secrets within its pages.

And it is certainly true that the stonemage is the ultimate mage. Oh, the curser inflicts diseases on the skin of his victims, the fire-mage lights his sparkling candles, and the mage-of-the-kitchen makes meals for our pleasure, but what are these professions compared to the fearless stonemage, who casts his magic to sculpt huge castles with towers a thousand feet high? I think we can all agree that using magic to construct a mighty castle is a much greater thing than using it to cook a tasty egg!

I am reluctant to claim I am the ultimate stonemage, for humility is a virtue. And yet honesty is a still greater virtue, and, if I am to be honest, I must confess I have never met a stonemage who is more skilled than myself, nor heard of one either.

All in all, I think it is best if I remain silent on this issue, and you may reach your own conclusions after you have read this autobiography. You may decide, "Yes, Yreth is clearly the world's finest stonemage." That is a valid opinion, certainly. Or you may decide, "No, Yreth is not the ultimate stonemage." And that is also a valid opinion—although I would then encourage you to reread the book, perhaps paying closer attention the second time.

So much, then, for the title. But what of the words between the covers?

There are many rules for writing a great autobiographical work, which this one most certainly shall be. The authorities tell us, for example, that such a book must never have pictures, because the pictures should be created in the reader's mind by the author's words. And it is agreed the writing must be in prose, or in rhyme of no less than fourteen syllables to the line.

Of course, it is widely known that life stories of all sorts, and particularly those recounting great adventures and accounts of travels should contain exactly twelve parts, for twelve is the number that resonates most perfectly with geographical principles (twelve empires, twelve seas, twelve great rivers, and so on).

But there is one point on which the experts are divided—the question of where to start the tale. Some favour the Retrospective Method, where the author begins by describing his current circumstances, then works backwards to recount the events leading to them. In this way, they say, the narrative remains rooted in the present and is therefore bound faithfully to reality.

On the other hand, advocates of the Chronological Method say that, since life itself begins with the moment of birth, any account of that life must also begin there, and the story must proceed systematically through childhood, adolescence and adulthood. By following this sequence, they claim, the story more truly reflects the order of nature.

Countless writers, embarking on their life stories, have chosen between these extremes, using either the Retrospective Method or the Chronological Method. As a result, their stories are flawed from the outset; for, in choosing the merits of the Retrospective Method, they eschew the advantages of the Chronological, while a preference for the Chronological Method throws away the benefits of the Retrospective.

How, then, to begin a story which is to be perfect and without flaw? Why, the answer is simple. Strike a balance between these extremes.

Today, as I write this, I am seventy years old. When I was born, I was a young lad of no years. It follows that the ideal place to begin my story is at the centre point of these ages—specifically, at the age of thirty-five. And this is precisely where I shall begin.

The First Part

In Which I Tell Of My Arrest In Luthen And Of The Towers I Built There

IT WAS THE MORNING OF my thirty-fifth birthday, and I had received a sorry gift. It was an invitation—at the point of a spear—to appear before Gavor Hercules, the murderous Spanish sealord who was the terror of the Mediterranean. With four myrmidons around me, escorted like a common criminal, I was taken from my room at the inn and marched through the town, finally ascending the road of oaken steps which rises up the hillside to Luthen castle.

I was filled with fear. I am not ashamed to confess it, either, for it is not shameful to feel fear. Indeed, the mark of true bravery is to feel fear and to face it well. As I passed under the dark gateway of the castle, I determined in my mind that, if death awaited me here, I would die spectacularly well, with my eyes shining like those of the eagle, my nostrils flared, and a gentle smile upon my lips. I took care to maintain this proud visage, as the soldiers pushed and jostled me through the castle's dark corridors and through the black doors leading to the presiding room.

The room was constructed like a ship, with oppressive oak beams looming overhead and small shuttered windows. All around, the wall hangings showed themes of war, gold, and murder. In the room's centre, upon a dais bench, sat Gavor Hercules himself, clothed all in black and surrounded by guards. He was an old man—in his eighty-third year at the time I am describing—but his expression was ferocious, and the beard on the tip of his chin thrust forward like a white dagger.

He glowered at me over drooping lower eyelids, and growled, "You are Yreth the Stonemage?"

"I am," I replied.

"They say you are a Cypriot?"

"Yes, and proudly so."

He snorted, and said, "If you are so proud of it, why did you not remain in Cyprus?"

I answered him frankly. "I learned the magic arts at the School of Eopan. It is the tradition of my school that, after some years of work, we should travel abroad, to be inspired by the great building styles of other lands."

"Hear! Hear his words!" said the sealord to those around him, slamming his fist upon the arm of his dais bench. "He comes to learn from our great buildings."

I was pleased by his tone, for it was clear to me now Gavor Hercules did not plan to kill me; but his words also made me cross, for they were wholly untrue. I had stopped in Luthen to await a ship to Ireland, where they say the towers glitter like diamonds upon the hills; whereas, here on the south coast of Spain, the architecture was a sorry collection of rough hovels grouped around low and squalid castles.

Still, I said nothing and waited for the sealord to continue.

"I understand," he said, "you are trained in the repair of buildings."

I said yes.

"Certain of my towers are in need of work," he said. "Would you be capable of performing a task of this magnitude?"

Now, this question was absurd. I had noticed his towers as soon as I arrived in Luthen. The structures were twisted and bent. Obviously, the wefts and enchantments supporting the stone walls had decayed and distorted with time. Repairing them would be a simple task even for a stonemage's apprentice—a few days' work at most.

Still, when the powerful speak to you, it is good to treat their questions as weighty ones, so I appeared to calculate and think over the matter for a few moments before I replied.

"My lord," I said, "I believe the task you describe is within my capability. However, these are old buildings, and the art of construction has come far since they were built. Let me replace them with new towers, made from white onyx, each more than five hundred feet high."

He shook his head. "The towers please me as they are," he said. "I do not want to create a gaudy monument to myself, but wish merely to preserve these ancient buildings in their original form. I will pay you two hundred arrans for the task—seventy here and now, and the remainder when you have completed the work."

Two hundred arrans! In the provinces of Cyprus, a stonemage who received just thirty arrans for such a job would consider himself richly paid. And it is said the Long Wall of Tennet was repaired by the great Henry Eagles for nine arrans and two grotecs. Clearly, two hundred arrans for such an elementary repair job as this was gross overpayment.

Many an unscrupulous stonemage would have accepted the job on the spot, saying nothing about the excessive fee, but not I! My integrity cannot be bought at any price, and I knew I must speak my mind.

"O, great Gavor Hercules," I said, "such a sum is far more than I would ever ask for this task. If you wish me to repair the towers in the way you have asked, I can take no more than fifty arrans for the work, and even in this payment I will consider myself indulged beyond my expectations."

He looked at me then for a full minute, saying nothing. Finally, he shook his head in disbelief. "Yreth the Cypriot," he said at last, "it has been many years since I encountered such integrity. Your words gladden my heart. And so I shall now pay you not fifty, but five hundred arrans for the work I have described."

I answered this quickly enough, saying: "My munificent lord, if I have brought pleasure to your heart, that is reward in itself for me and needs no golden bonus. Fifty arrans is all I have asked, and with that sum I shall be well satisfied."

"Yet I, Gavor Hercules, have commanded that you shall receive five hundred," he said—and now there was anger in his voice. "Do you spurn my gift?"

They say there is a time to speak and a time to plug the mouth with cotton. So, I said nothing, but merely prostrated myself on the wooden floor, shaking my head and moaning as if in pain.

At last I raised my head and gazed up at the fierce old lord. "O, great Gavor Hercules," I said, "I am trapped by your terrible largesse. I implore you, if you would pay me this sum, let it be for such work as deserves it. Let me transform these old towers into jewelled spires that shall be the wonder of all Spain."

"No!" he replied. "I wish the towers to remain as they are. Your task shall be only to repair them."

"Then, great lord, I decline!" I replied, shaking my fist at him. "Though you throw me into your jails and have me killed for my insolence, I cannot accept so great a wage. For a bitter enemy I would charge but seventy arrans. To accept more from you for my work would be an insult to your honour, and *my* honour will never allow me to give such an insult. There, have it then. My piece is said, and I now throw myself upon your mercy."

At this, Gavor Hercules was amazed. "*Friend* Yreth," he said, "I said it has been many years since I have encountered such integrity as yours. I now retract my words. I have *never* encountered such integrity. Since you will not accept five hundred arrans for your work, I shall give you what you asked—fifty arrans. But I shall insist that, during the course of your work, you shall dine at my table every night. And you shall receive a chest containing seven hundred arrans as a gift from me. Do not shake your head so, for this is a lordly gift and cannot be refused! Moreover, I make you a gift of a fine ship, the *Moray*, which sits now at the docks of Luthen. Its value is close to six hundred arrans. That is all!"

And with those words, he raised his arms, signalling the meeting was at an end.

This, then, well shows the generosity of Gavor Hercules. It also shows the value of integrity, for, by declining the lord's initial gift, I received both his friendship and a wage five times greater than the one he first offered.

Later, I went to the harbour to inspect the *Moray*. This was a proud vessel, such as a noble or a wealthy merchant might use in the east. It was constructed not of wood but of a white substance known as chank. This is the same material from which Virenian warships are built, and Ered's death barge, and it is the sign of a very superior construction. Indeed, I have talked to many seafarers, and all are agreed in saying ships constructed of chank have no equal upon the sea, and they would choose a single such ship over ten ships whose hulls glitter with gold and diamonds.

Inspecting the interior of the ship, I was impressed by the fine carvings and the bold decoration of the cabins. The slave crew were well trained and strong, and the general upkeep of the vessel spoke well of their dedication. The slaves were not common Trags, either, or even Lopers. They were Pakes of the most expensive variety—the ones with the blue stripe over their eyes and the elongated fingers. Such Pakes are almost as tall as a man, and very strong for their size.

As I walked about my ship, I was filled with joy at the magnificent gifts I had received. I saw I had been wrong to fear and despise Gavor Hercules. I knew now that, despite his fearsome reputation, he was a man of wisdom. He had made a generous payment to me, and I vowed to give my new patron the full value of his coin.

That evening, as he had promised, Gavor Hercules invited me

to his dining room. At least twenty people sat at the table. At the head, of course, was Gavor Hercules himself. At the other end was his consort, Chryse, and between them the guests were arranged in the usual way, which is to say, according to the degree of their favour with the lord. Those most highly regarded were seated closest to him; those least regarded were furthest away, although, of course, their presence at the table at all was nonetheless a great honour.

As I entered, I made to take a seat at the most distant chairs, but the lord called out to me and said: "None of your modesty, Yreth! You must sit on the chair closest to me, on my right side."

The dinner itself was delicious, and the foods seemed all the more succulent to me when Gavor Hercules told his other guests about the strange negotiation he and I had undertaken, and how deeply he was impressed by my character. As I heard his appreciative words, I could only nod and weep with joy.

The next day, I went to the tallest of the towers and examined the binding wefts of this ugly structure. As I expected, it was held together by a few cross-bindings. (If you do not know, these are invisible gossamers of force which function like a sturdy beam between two walls or like a pillar between floor and ceiling.) The cross-bindings had been badly placed when first created, and had also become bent and decayed with age.

Yet as I examined the enchantments more closely, my scorn changed to puzzlement for the composition of these spells was unfamiliar, and I could not identify their type. They were clearly very ancient, and I wondered if this was some powerful enchantment whose secrets were lost in antiquity.

At this point, an impatient stonemage would have laid down new bindings, to reinforce the ones that were failing. Indeed, I had several times raised my arm to cast new spells, but each time I did so an inner voice spoke to me, saying, "Yreth—stay your hand! Solve the mystery before you! Understanding must precede action!"

Suddenly, in a flash of inspiration, I realized the bindings before me were that contemptible type known as the Struts of Atlas, but so badly distorted their form was barely recognizable.

From the grand name, you would think Strut of Atlas a strong enchantment, but it would be better named the Bane of Atlas, for instead of holding your world aloft, it is more likely to bring it tumbling to the ground! It is a crude, treacherous and unstable spell, given to collapsing in a violent manner, and its use is the sure mark of the untrained builder.

But woe to the stonemage who thoughtlessly tries to replace or remove the Strut of Atlas!

I knew one boastful fellow back in Cyprus who had learned a spell or two and fancied he could amaze the world with his powers. He had little training in the arts of the stonemage, but he set about repairing a certain feast hall—against my advice. He detected the presence of a distorted Strut of Atlas. The strut supported a ceiling, and he decided to shore it up with a second beam of greater strength. But he had no sooner placed the preliminary runes than the Strut of Atlas collapsed, its ends snapping powerfully together. Instantly, the ceiling above him was pulled down with great force, and he was crushed and killed by the huge stones. As they say, live a fool's life and you will die a fool's death.

No, be counselled by me, replacing the Strut of Atlas requires the utmost care and caution, and it is often better to leave the wretched enchantment in place and do what you can to repair it than to try replacing it.

I am sure if I had tried to cast new cross-bindings in that tower in Luthen, the precarious struts would have collapsed, destroying the tower and killing me. But my wisdom, insight and restraint saved me then, as they have often done since.

I set to work repairing the vile Struts of Atlas. With great care, I used an ivory turning wheel (together with the resonating whistle) to twist the coils, bringing the strut's central wefts back into alignment. A little dab of acorn oil upon the base rune ensured the roots of the treacherous spell would stay firmly within the stones for the present.

The tallest tower contained fifty-one Struts of Atlas. I tightened them one by one. In just a few hours, I was able to reverse the warping effects of centuries.

As I worked to make these adjustments, the stones of the old tower rumbled and scraped, the walls twisted, and pieces of dust and grit showered down from the exterior walls onto the streets below. Of course, these are the usual signs of a stonemage at his craft, but the townspeople of Luthen were not used to such work, and the transformations caused them the greatest alarm and wonder. When I emerged from the structure, I found a crowd of several hundred waiting outside, gazing in slack-jawed astonishment at the tower and its newly straightened walls.

As I walked down the steps, the people moved aside to make a path for me, and from their faces you would think I had changed their tower into an onion or caused a rain of dragons or some other such miracle, rather than adjusting a few invisible struts inside an old stone ruin.

I proceeded to the next tower—the short tower in the wall. The crowd followed me inside the building, lining the spiral staircases and watching my every movement as I carried out similar repairs to those I have already described for the tallest tower.

I had originally estimated the repairs would take four days or so, but it soon became clear to me the job was simpler than I had first supposed. The small wall tower, for instance, contained just ten cross-bindings, and no other bindings of any kind. Can you imagine a great structure here in the east being held together by just ten bindings? I have seen children's play huts with more sophisticated work! In any event, it took me just half an hour to finish work on this tower—and this despite the presence of all those jostling bystanders on the spiral stairs. By the end of the day, I had repaired all five towers.

That evening, I dined once more with Gavor Hercules. By then, news of my work was all over town, and, as you can imagine, it was the only topic discussed over dinner. Gavor Hercules and his guests repeatedly asked me to explain the procedures I had used to carry out the work. Their interest pleased me—although they seemed to understand few of my answers, and I soon grew fatigued by their slow-witted questions.

Hercules congratulated me on the speed with which I had completed my work. I quickly explained my work had hardly begun, and there were numerous and complex structural modifications which must be made to the towers.

He told me then about the very ancient history of the building, and of their superb, solid construction. You can imagine well enough what I thought of his opinions, and the age of the towers was no excuse for their extreme ugliness. Still, I said nothing, but merely listened politely as his lordship, and then his various fierce captains and warriors spouted their tiresome theories about "good, solid stone."

I politely gave them half an ear, but in my mind I was considering another matter. For I was determined to carry out a far greater transformation than merely straightening the towers. I wished to turn them into objects of true beauty. My problem was that Gavor Hercules did not want extensive changes, because such warlike men have no architectural vision and cannot imagine how a finished structure will look. The moment I started demolishing the stones of his towers, he was certain to object and stop my work. But I knew he would be delighted once he had seen the completed towers. So how to proceed?

As I sat at dinner, deep in thought, a unique solution occurred to me, in the form of three omens.

First, my eyes fell on a design in a silver goblet in front of me. The pattern was of a butterfly. Then, a few minutes later, I noticed Gavor Hercules's consort, Chryse, looking in my direction, and as I thought of her name, I was reminded of the word "chrysalis."

There was a third omen, too, but I forget now what it was. Something or other to do with metamorphosis or butterflies I think.

In any case, the image came into my head of a butterfly emerging from a chrysalis, and this was my inspiration! The towers would undergo a secret change, one which would remain invisible to all until the work was complete. I know this sounds impossible, but an ingenious method had occurred to me. The thought of it excited me so much it quite spoiled the rest of the meal. I yearned for the fine feast to be over, and for the night to pass, so I could return to my work in the morning.

The first thing, of course, was to remove those terrible Struts of Atlas, for I did not want them contaminating my work. It took me weeks of delicate labour to disassemble them safely, and in their place I cast Quater's Firm-Beam, which a fine spell, very stable and durable.

On each of the towers I placed a temporary facade—a thin layer created using the spell Spicesheet. It creates a white shell upon a surface, as thin as eggshell, but very strong.

As I completed each area of gleaming Spicesheet, I placed a second enchantment upon it—the Persistent Mural, a well known illusion spell. The Spicesheet had the precise shape and texture of the granite stones underneath, and was hard and cold to the touch, while the Persistent Mural gave the exact appearance of the stone.

I placed similar facades along the inside walls of each tower, and connected the outer and inner facades with cross-bindings.

If can picture it then, the thick walls of each tower were now sandwiched between an outer and inner facade which closely resembled the appearance of the original tower. Within this facade—this "chrysalis"—I could make sweeping improvements to the towers without being detected.

If you wish to know how perfect these facades were, mark this: on the second or third week of my work, I was standing on a low scaffold, rubbing powdered cloves into the stones to create an area of Spicesheet, when Gavor Hercules passed by.

He said: "Have you altered this stone somehow?"

I replied in the only way my integrity would allow: "Yes, sire, I have."

He said: "It seems to me it is slightly cleaner. And it has a lustre and a depth which before now it had lacked."

I said this was certainly the case.

Then he placed his hand against part of the facade and smoothed it, saying: "How I love these old stones. Since boyhood I have known them, and in all my voyages I longed to return to them. I am well pleased with your work upon them now."

You may be sure I was encouraged! If Gavor Hercules could take pleasure in what he thought was a slight "cleaning" of the old stones, his pleasure would be increased a hundredfold when he beheld the magnificent spectacle which I was working underneath.

Let me now reveal to you the nature of my work.

In the first place, I had applied many fire spells, heating the walls of the towers until rock melted and fused, turning ugly and irregular bricks into a smooth sheet of a glasslike material. I then placed hundreds of powerful spells through the walls of each tower—cross-bindings, Sheet Walls, Peregrine Clasps, and Lasser Spheres in abundance—creating a surface as strong as the finest armour.

For further strength, I bound the towers each to the other with Firm-Beams, so even if one were subjected to so much force it might fall, it would be solidly supported by the other four towers. Finally, I placed invisible Seizure Lines radiating out from the towers and attached to other buildings all over the town. Through these spells, my mighty towers would bestow some of their strength on the surrounding structures.

Having thus established the strength of my towers, I set about industriously fashioning their beauty. But in this, take note, I did not merely impose my own taste. It is important, when doing such work, to bear in mind the tastes and inclinations of the patron. In this case, Gavor Hercules was clearly a man of conservative taste, and the colours placed upon the materials of the towers had to be similarly conservative. With five towers, the choice was obvious: the five primary colours. Simple, elegant. One colour for each tower. So, the square tower in the castle I made a gentle green. The two round towers on the east corners of the castle I made yellow and peach. The small tower in the town wall I made beige. And the great tower in the centre of the town was a soft shade of purple.

I had decorated the interior of the towers, floors, walls, and ceilings with a deep red fur, spun, if you can credit it, from the rock itself. The making of this fur, which is called mashena, is not really a stonemage's skill, but is a little trick I learned from an old instructor at Eopan. Unfortunately, it has become something of a lost art. Correctly spun, the fur is not only far softer than any animal fur, it is infinitely more durable, and also completely fireproof.

Even with no further changes, these towers would have been a worthy addition to any city in Cyprus, and certainly the wonder of the west. But I desired more than this: I intended to make these towers the wonder of the whole world.

To the outer wall of each building, then, I applied a range of transmutations, adding tubes and filaments of gold in a weblike pattern. Within the areas enclosed by this web, I created large glass jewels of all colours, so curved as to catch the rays of the sun and reflect them about the town, and so placed that, at any given time of the day, every area of the town would be bathed in beautiful colours. So you see, these towers would share not only their strength with the dull stone buildings of the town, but also their beauty.

Finally, and most wonderful of all, I had fashioned the walls of the towers so they were narrower in some places than others, in much the same way the sounding board of a well made violin is carved thinner in some parts than others. The slightest vibration on any of the buildings (caused, for example, by a light breeze, or the natural hubbub of the town) would set all these towers into a rapid vibration, producing a pure musical tone from each tower, and a lovely five-note chord from them all. Never, to my knowledge, had so delicate a construction been attempted.

As you may guess, this work, so simple in theory, was mind-taxing in its complexity. For the jewelled reflectors, I was obliged to make careful observations of the sun's movements, ensuring my adjustments left no part of the town unlit. And the tones of the towers were so exquisitely interconnected that every slight tuning of one would send the others into a state of discord. And all this, working by touch beneath the stone facade I had laid. It was many months before these two jobs were completed.

In the meantime, I dined nightly with Gavor Hercules and quickly became a favourite within his circle for my tales of life in Cyprus. Frequently he would ask me about the wars being fought there at that time, or ask me if I knew of certain Cypriot sea captains. A strange aspect of this, which I have since observed in other warriors, is that Gavor might ask a question like, "Tell me, do you know of a fine commander by the name of Illian," and from the tone of his voice I took this man to be some old comrade of his, and I would tell him what I knew of the warrior in question, and he would nod and laugh and make some remark such as "That rascal killed my son, you know," or "Ah yes, he is a worthy enemy indeed." On one occasion during my stay, one of these enemies actually came to visit Hercules, and I saw him treated with all the civility and generosity the lord extended to any of his merchant friends.

I could expound at great length upon various aspects of Gavor Hercules's court, and upon the town of Luthen. I witnessed a thousand marvels and curiosities during my stay. However, I fear this would take me from the proper drift of my historical account, and these fascinating tales must be saved for some other time.

Finally, the jewels in the towers were perfectly placed, and the music of the towers was exactly tuned. The work had taken me, from start to finish, just over ten months, and was by far the longest commission I had yet completed. I was more than pleased with the detail of the work, but I found myself now facing a new problem. My work, you see, satisfactorily paid off my gift-debt to Gavor Hercules; however, if I were present when the true beauty of these buildings was revealed, it was likely he would bestow some further gift upon me. After all, this lord had paid me well over one thousand arrans for a simple repair task. How much more would he reward such elegant and scrupulous work as this? And if he gave me further payment, I would once again be indebted to him.

I resolved upon an ingenious solution. First, I placed Wefts of Sympathy on the facades of all the towers. Then I placed a matching weft on a brick to which I had also added a Spicesheet facade. I took this brick onto the ship which Gavor Hercules had given me as a gift and left it there.

Over the next few days, I made my farewells to all, explaining my work was now finished and I would be leaving shortly. Gavor Hercules implored me to stay, but I explained I had urgent business to attend to further south. He thanked me graciously for my hard work on the towers and made me a final gift of a fur cap and cloak. This, of course, was a token gesture only. The lord had seen no further improvement in his towers in nine months and naturally assumed the remainder of my work had been minor details. My debt was paid, then, and I was free to leave in good conscience.

Very early the following morning, I went to my ship and departed Luthen, bound for the city of Ubari in the kingdom of North Africa. When we were a mile or so from shore, I dissolved the magical facade on the brick I had taken with me. At once, the Wefts of Sympathy on the towers caused their facades to vanish, and at last those structures on which I had laboured so long were revealed.

The experience of seeing those dull chrysalises fall away to reveal the beautiful butterflies beneath is impossible to describe. The towers were ten—no, one hundred times more lovely than I had anticipated. Even the early rays of the sun were enough to catch the jewels of the towers, flooding the town in a brilliant pool of ever-changing hues. And the sound of their music was like angels singing from heaven—a perfect, unwavering chord. Though we were a mile from shore, I could feel the vibration of that divine chorus upon my chest.

I instantly fell upon the deck of the ship, reduced to tears, and my weeping continued unabated until the town of Luthen was just a shimmering spot upon the horizon, and its song was nothing more than a faint pulse, growing and fading with the wind.

We sailed on at a gentle pace, for, having completed such a great and arduous labour, I wished to relax for a time and felt no need of haste. We meandered along the African coast, and I whiled away the hours delighting in the variety of exotic birds and animals I could see among the trees, and sometimes shooting them with my bow.

After five days of this pleasant life, we came upon a fishing boat, and I called out our greetings to them. The pilot answered in kind, then asked us where we were bound.

"Ubari."

"Ah, it is but a few hours further. And whence do you sail?"

"Out of Luthen."

"Could it be," he asks, "that you are a builder from the east?"

"I am," I told him.

"Then I advise you to steer clear of Ubari, for twenty fast warships lie in wait for you there, with orders to catch you and to hang you."

This was scarcely to be believed! I asked the fellow: "By whom were these orders given?"

"By Gavor Hercules. It seems he is angered by certain singing towers."

You may imagine my dismay at this news. I paid this fisherman twelve arrans to keep his silence, then we quickly turned north and west, at full sail, away from Ubari.

As we sailed, and my shock faded, I considered the unfolding of events, and soon the truth of the matter struck me with such clarity it could not be doubted. If you will consider the following scenario, I think you too will appreciate its validity.

It was early morning on the day of my departure from Luthen. Gavor Hercules was sleeping in his chamber, when a soft and lovely sound filled his ears. He rose, on those ancient, noble legs, and walked to his window. There before him he saw such visions of beauty as he, with his warlike disposition, had not the words to describe.

In the streets below, he saw the townspeople were assembling, clutching their hands in wonder at the shimmering array of lights which now bathed their once-drab town. Even as he watched, the townsfolk spontaneously started to sing the praises of their lord, and perhaps of myself for being the creator of these lovely buildings.

Gavor Hercules was overcome with childlike serenity, his old heart bursting with joy and love.

But his followers, murderers and pirates all, were horrified at this change in their master. They said, "The old man is so filled with love he will lose the will to fight, and we will lose the gold and booty we gain from our wicked acts."

They secretly set out in their ships to take their revenge on me, claiming Gavor Hercules had sent them. And they attacked the towers with siege engines, and when these great weapons did nothing to harm the structures, they hired corrupt wizards to remove their mighty bonds. No sooner had one tower collapsed than the bindings between the towers, intended to strengthen them, caused the others to collapse, and this in turn destroyed the scores of surrounding buildings to which I had so carefully anchored the towers.

In the meantime, they murdered sweet Gavor Hercules as he slept, but told everyone he had died of old age.

I have since found numerous witnesses who have sworn to me the events which transpired in Luthen at that time were exactly as I have described, or, at the very least, they could not prove otherwise.

Gavor Hercules did die, and it was indeed claimed he had died of old age, even though he was obviously murdered. I have consulted seers and augurs, and they all confirmed my interpretation of events was the true one.

As I sat aboard my ship and realized the danger facing me, I knew it would be mortal folly to remain in the Mediterranean, for there were close to a hundred raiding ships in his force, all looking to take my life. I knew, too, I could not hope to round the west coast of the Spanish peninsula, for the sealord's largest warships travel those routes in order to exact tribute from ocean traders, and I would surely be sunk long before I reached Ceol.

No, only one option remained: I must set sail to the continent of America, where I might take refuge for a time. So, westward I sailed, and by night my vessel slipped silently beneath the great Gibraltar Bridge which separates the sweet waters of the Mediterranean from the cruel Atlantic Ocean.

The Second Part

In Which I Tell Of My Visit To The Duck Islands And My Victories There

AFTER SOME FIVE DAYS OF westerly sailing, in good weather, we sighted land. I was concerned at this, for I knew it was at least six weeks' voyage to the continent of America, and I feared we might have made some navigational error and turned once more to the Spanish coast. My slaves, however, assured me in the most earnest tones this was not so and said we were approaching the Duck Islands.

Few people have heard of these islands, and some people have expressed to me their disbelief the islands even exist, for they can be found on very few maps. I can understand such scepticism, for I had never heard of the islands before I encountered them. Nevertheless, I will tell you the Duck Islands most certainly do exist and lie some four days' fast sail due west of Askar. If you read Nethercott's account of her travels, you will find them mentioned peripherally on two occasions, and they are also listed in the Lotus Compendium, although I do not remember the precise citation.

And if still you doubt, I can only advise you to hire a ship and follow my route, and you will certainly see them for yourself.

The slaves told me the Duck Islands would be an excellent place to pick up further supplies, for, as you will remember, my intended destination had been Ubari, which is but a few days' sail from Luthen, yet I now faced a much longer route.

You may think me foolish for attempting the onerous voyage to America without first giving heed to the state of my supplies. Why, you may wonder, could I not have quickly put in at one of the small ports or islands along the coast of Africa? And in the normal way of things, this would indeed have been a wise strategy. However, during my ten months in Luthen, I had learned much about Gavor Hercules and his fierce captains. They were craftsmen of sea warfare, merciless and resolute in their pursuit of their enemies. My ship was fast, it is true, but his warships were still faster, and it would have been reckless of me to delay even a few more hours before making my escape to the west.

In the second place, I should point out my ship was well prepared for a long voyage: it had been designed as an ocean trader; the crew were familiar with the routes; and my larders were stocked with enough food for six months or more.

Now, I imagine, a second question will come to you. Why, you will ask, did this man Yreth take a six-month supply of food for a journey of just a few days?

I will explain. When I decided to leave Luthen for North Africa, I carefully considered the various conveniences and inconveniences my destination would afford. In most ways North Africa is a civilized land, but in its food customs it is little short of barbaric. Much of the local diet consists of roots, or leaves, or seeds, with precious little meat. And on those rare occasions when meat is served, it is usually such a base kind as mutton or goat, and is flavoured with herbs of the most disagreeable nature, which hide the poor quality of the meat and impart to it a fiery and mouth-numbing taste. By contrast, the meals I received in Luthen (and elsewhere in Spain) were usually of the highest quality—tender, bloodied meat, with rich, thick sauces—and certainly as good as anything you will partake of in the feasting halls of Cyprus.

So, before my departure from Luthen, I purchased large quantities of various salted meats, dried fruits, and some of my favourite preserves. I took enough for my intended stay in Ubari—in all, about six months' supply. I had also purchased six vats of wine, five vats of strong Spanish ale, and one vat of wince, a delicious fermented drink made from onions. I had intended these for trading, as I am not given to take large amounts of strong drink, but now they were assigned to the provisions for my voyage.

So, in most respects my ship was well fitted for an ocean journey. In most respects, save this one: I had only a few days' supply of fresh water. We had left Luthen with but a single barrel, and, since I place a high value on cleanliness, I had already used most of this in the natural course of my washing regimen.

However, there are many in Luthen who drink nothing but ale, and I believed I could subsist in the same manner during the weeks ahead, provided I drank only moderately and was willing to endure a week or so of light-headedness (for after that long, I am told, the constitution adapts naturally to drunkenness, and the ill effects are no longer felt).

The slaves also required small quantities of water. In their case, however, they could happily survive on sea water for a month or two. As for food, they needed only small quantities of the acorn paste which is favoured by their species, and I had plenty aboard.

Therefore, my first instinct was to turn away from the Duck Islands and continue west, for it was possible enemy ships might be waiting for me there, as they had been at Ubari. But the head slave said that, for an ocean voyage at this time of the year (it was then late in the autumn), the ship's chank hull should be treated with willow wax. This wax could be bought on the Duck Islands, and at a good price too. It comes not from the willow tree as you might suppose, but from a species of fast-growing fern, and protects the chank from blistering in the cold water.

"Could such blistering cause this ship to sink?" I asked.

"Indeed no, sire," he replied, "but the damage is unsightly, impossible to repair, and will certainly reduce the value of the vessel."

"The ship will have little enough value to me if I am caught and hanged," I replied. "No, let us continue west."

"I am yours to command, sire," he said. "Finally, I have recently been examining the dispositions of the clouds and seabirds, and these portend a great tempest, of the most powerful and destructive nature, within the next two days."

It is very typical of slaves to leave the most for the last. Since I had no wish to venture on in a storm if this could be avoided, I yielded and ordered the slaves to steer towards the Duck Islands. It was well I made the choice, for the storm struck just a few hours after our landing, and it was one of the most furious I have ever witnessed. It tore the roofs from houses and wrenched large trees from the ground, roots and all. Even sheltered down in the harbour, my ship suffered a broken mast, and I am quite certain that, had I not decided to seek shelter, we would have been destroyed at sea.

As to the place itself, there is little enough to tell. The islands are small and rocky, with just a few hundred inhabitants apiece. From my conversations with the local folk, I learned that most were fishermen and fisherwomen, and the fish they caught were sold for a high price to those who lived in the lands to the east. However, since the trading ships from those lands arrived at the Duck Islands at the rate of perhaps one ocean trader every two or three months, and since the inhabitants of those islands never ventured more than a few hours' sail from their own shores, I am at a complete loss to explain how this trade in fish took place.

The chief citizen of these islands was an astronomer by the name of Yorke who had come there from the Ten Mountains. Upon my arrival, he invited me to his mansion, and from there we watched the furious storm unleash itself. The next day, he set himself completely at my service, ordering for me a suitable quantity of willow wax, making me a gift of a great-sail, sending to my ship ten barrels of fresh water, and also sending helpers to inspect the broken mast on my ship. I, in my turn, made certain structural improvements to his mansion, and also gave to him my vat of wince. It was a gift he received with much joy—as well he might, for the onion vineyards of Luthen are among the finest anywhere.

The head slave told me the damaged mast could not be repaired in this port, and Yorke's helpers confirmed it. They advised me to sail a few miles to the north, to the town of Leaf-of-Mint on the island of Tip. (Tip, of course, is one of the Duck Islands. The others are Tenatee, Rass Sholloy, and Trubear. We had put in at the last of these, at its only town, which bore the amusing name of Lyce.)

You may guess I was very reluctant to further delay my escape to the west by taking another side-trip; however, Yorke told me it would be at least another day, and perhaps two, until the large quantity of willow wax which my ship required was ready. Further, the head slave told me, if we were to sail with the broken mast, our voyage would take twice, or perhaps even three times as long. Naturally I was not anxious to sail west in a crippled ship, especially with fast warships in pursuit, so, once again, I capitulated, and we sailed the short distance to Leaf-of-Mint.

Tip is the largest of the Duck Islands and heavily wooded. After docking at Leaf-of-Mint, we found a community of carpenters, who agreed to carry out the necessary repairs in exchange for ale. Of course, I stipulated the ale should be delivered only after the mast was crafted and installed, since I did not want drunken carpenters shaping my new mast. After initial resistance, they finally acceded to my terms, and a tall pine tree was selected and cut down for the mast.

I will not describe more of the island of Tip, nor of the town of Leaf-of-Mint, since these places do not rate an important place in my tale, save only for the fact that, while I was there, I was removed from the dramatic unfolding of events back at the town of Lyce.

Suffice it to say I remained in Leaf-of-Mint only long enough for the repairs to be negotiated and completed. This came to three days. I mostly remained aboard my ship in my cabin, since no suitable accommodation was available in the town. The buildings were chiefly huts, made of logs or stones, and there were few features of note, save for a long wooden pier, to which my ship was moored. There was also an old white church in the centre of the town. The town itself is built in a natural inlet, and is surrounded by cliffs on three sides. Steep roads are cut into these cliffs to allow the transportation of lumber from the forests above. You may be sure watching this lumber being moved is the only entertainment you will find in this desolate town, unless you enjoy standing on the rocky beach and throwing pebbles out to the sea.

But there, I have said more than enough about Leaf-of-Mint and we will now leave the subject behind.

After three days, then, at Leaf-of-Mint, the mast was completed and installed. For this task, the local people assembled large cranes, made from pulleys and long beams, and the mast was hoisted from the cliffs, over the town in stages, to my ship. During this process, the beams supporting the mast were variously swung forward, or tilted forward through the use of ropes. By this method, and by alternating which pairs of beams held the weight of the burden, the mast was carried to the ship as if on giant legs.

During the first stage of the conveyance, the mast was "walked" over the graveyard near to the church. From there, it was taken over several houses, and, at one point, when the workers on the ropes decided to rest, they gently lowered the mast so it lay on the roofs of two huts. I should rather say, on the remains of the roofs of two huts, for the town had suffered damage during the recent storm. Then, after the workers had rested for a time, the great mast was raised once more, and continued its walk towards my ship.

On reaching the pier, the "legs" were brought very closely together, and, swaying precipitously, the mast was walked down the pier and alongside my ship. Next, the two forward legs, which had been notched at their base, were fitted over the edge of the pier, and lowered towards the ship, while the rear legs were swung around at ninety degrees, then pulled in the direction of my ship. This action had the effect of tilting the mast.

Little by little, the mast was moved towards the hole which the damaged mast had occupied. Try as they might, however, the labourers were unable to fit the mast into the hole at an angle steep enough to allow the mast to slip in. This was because the mast was very much taller than the legs which supported it. Finally, the workers took the mast away again, using the same wooden legs, and proceeded slowly back across the town. When they reached the cliffs once more, they stopped to reassess the situation.

The enthusiasm and vigour of these people was certainly noteworthy; however, I was pressed for time, so at this point I sent out my slaves, telling them to remove the mast from the complex assembly of beams and ropes, and to transport it back by carrying it in the normal way. This they did, carrying it through the town with the greatest of ease. We quickly installed the mast into the deck of the ship, then set sail back to the town of Lyce, our efficiency bringing astonishment and perplexity to the people of Leaf-of-Mint.

As I write this now, it occurs to me I did not remember to give the townspeople the ale I had promised them in payment for the mast. The oversight, however, was an honest one.

When we arrived back in Lyce, we found our tubs of willow wax waiting for us. My crew instantly set about smearing the substance on the ship's white hull. Since I found the smell of the fresh wax disagreeable, I used the time to pay a farewell visit to the astronomer Yorke.

On entering his mansion, however, I was met with the most mortifying sight. Sitting with Yorke, apparently as guests, were a number of seafarers wearing the colours of Gavor Hercules. The leader of these I knew well, for he was the nephew to the lord, as well as being his lieutenant-in-chief. His name was Panka, but he was known to all as The Spear, and he had been a regular guest at the lord's dinners. Of course, he recognized me immediately, and cried out to his men to seize me, which they promptly did.

At this, Yorke protested, telling The Spear that, according to custom, we were all bound by the laws of guest-peace while we were upon the Duck Islands, for we were both of us equally his guests. He then requested The Spear to release me, and to forget our enmity until we had left the islands.

The Spear was completely receptive to this suggestion, not merely because he respected the laws of guest-peace, but also because he found the business of hanging and skewering men unpleasant. "It is a gruesome end, and barely worthy of a warrior to inflict," he said to me. "I should far rather sink you at sea and be done with you that way." These words he spoke to me with the utmost good cheer and camaraderie, although I had no doubt of his sincerity, for, as I have already told, I had heard his uncle speak in much the same manner of his own enemies.

I responded: "If you will do me no harm while I am here on these islands, then I will happily stay."

To which he said: "I'll warrant you would. But I tell you now, we navigators are a patient lot. I will gladly wait here for years if I must."

As you will see, these last words, spoken in jest, were prophetic. And I will now explain how this prophecy came true.

Naturally, I had no real intention of remaining on the Duck Islands, but it was clear to me that, for the present, I was safe here, whereas, if I were to chance an escape over the waves, my life would be in the direst peril.

Over the next few days, I surveyed the area thoroughly. The Spear's warships were anchored away from view by an inlet on the far side of the island. And fortunate for me they were, for had I seen them in the harbour at Lyce, I should have fled immediately, and it is likely I would have met my end being hunted down on the seas.

There were three warships in all, each about twice the size of my own ship, and built for great speed. Each ship was armed with a large and formidable harpoon. This is a type of rocket spear whose tip throws out sharp barbs upon striking its target, gripping its mark with a tenacious hold. It can be fired great distances into the side of a ship. If aimed low, it will sink the vessel. If high, it will clutch onto the hull, and then, by means of a line fixed to the shaft of the harpoon, the ship may be slowly hauled towards its attacker. When fighting large ships, the practice is for several warships to fire harpoons from a number of directions, slowing the ship, and pull themselves in close enough that their myrmidons might board it. Harpoons are also used against a smaller ship, but this time they are fired below the waterline, so as to sink the ship. Later, the vessel may be pulled to the surface by means of the harpoon's line, and its contents seized.

I observed the warships carefully from a nearby hill. Upon each warship I counted some forty slaves, perhaps twenty myrmidons belonging to one of the spiny or chitinous species, and two or three men. By contrast, I had just eight slaves and a head slave, giving me little chance even against a single warship in a sea battle. However, I had not the slightest intention of engaging these vessels in a sea battle, for a far better plan came to me as I studied the ships, and I will now explain my execution of it. I shall, however, conceal my plan's goal, for you will be surprised and delighted when you discover it through the natural course of my narrative.

My first manoeuvre took place at Yorke's mansion on an evening soon after. He had invited me to dine with him, and I suggested to him he should invite The Spear also. At this, he was much pleased. I believe the presence of such enmity upon his island was a great trial to him, and he wished The Spear and I should forget our quarrel and become fast friends forever. As I have already mentioned, Yorke was an astronomer and had little comprehension of the realities of the hard world that unfolds beneath those shining stars of his.

The Spear was invited to dine with us—an invitation which he accepted. At dinner, we talked congenially enough, and during the course of the conversation, I brought up the subject of eels, saying: "Oh, how I miss the taste of fresh, black eels. In my homeland I used to enjoy fishing for them. There is nothing like the taste of a black eel, caught by your own hand." The Spear was slow to catch on to this, and spoke about the many fine dishes which he had eaten at this place or that.

Still, I continued: "Ah, but these are as nothing compared to black eels. Such fish are a meal fit for a noble. They are about this long, and this wide..." and so on, until at last he nodded.

"Yes," he said. "I believe I have seen such creatures as you have described. In fact, they swim in large numbers near the inlet where my ships are anchored."

I knew this much, of course, for I had noted the eels during my observations of his ships, but, when he spoke the news, I feigned great wonder and excitement, saying what glorious and happy tidings these were, and imploring him to catch me a few of these eels as a gift between enemies. "For I realize you would not suffer me to approach your warships to catch eels by my own hand."

"Nonsense," he replied. "While we are both bound by the laws of guest-peace, I shall treat you with honour. If you want to fish for eels, I invite you to come tomorrow to my ships. I shall show you around the vessels, and then you may fish as you please from the decks."

Yorke was gladdened by this cordiality and pressed me to accept the offer. And, after much head-shaking and hand-waving, I did.

So, the next morning, I made my way to The Spear's ships equipped with a line, some weights, and some hooks. The Spear met me at the shore with a boat and took me aboard his ship. He offered to take me on a tour of the ship, but I declined at this point. "While this would be a great honour," I said, "I see those eels wriggling in the water and cannot wait to catch a few. But when I have done so, I am keen to examine your magnificent ship." And so I cast my line over the side of his ship, and he waited by me as I fished for eels.

Unfortunately, he was very observant. "Why," he asked, "do you send your line so deep? I can see numerous eels swimming near the surface."

To this, I replied: "Those are young eels. The oldest and most delectable specimens lie close to the bottom. But it seems they are not biting, so I would be as well to finish here," and so saying,

I pulled my line out of the water. He commented on the slow and careful way I wound the line back onto the frame, and I told him it was to prevent the line from tangling.

I then asked The Spear to show me more of his splendid ship. He gladly consented. "This ship," he told me, "is my own, the *Silver Ray*. It was given to me when I was just seventeen years of age. It has served me faithfully through many battles."

"It is truly a masterpiece of the shipbuilder's art," I said. "Please, show me every deck."

This he did. I then requested to see the hold, and he took me there too. I examined the ship with great care, paying special attention to the beams which formed the floor of the hold, and the bottom of the ship.

With this done, I started talking once more of eels. "Truly," I said, "it breaks my heart to have so many eels close at hand and not be able to catch them. Perhaps I would have better luck aboard the warship which is anchored nearby."

"Very well," he said, "I shall take you there." And so he took me there in a longboat. From the side of the warship, I once more undertook my eel-fishing. Again, alas, I caught nothing and was compelled to carefully wind up my line once more.

I then turned my attention to the design of this second warship. "This one," I said, "seems to me slightly smaller than the first."

"In this you are mistaken," The Spear replied. "The ships are identical in size. This ship, however, which is named the *Remora*, is the property of my uncle."

"I would be interested to see the lower decks of this ship too," I said, "for your own ship certainly possesses a grandeur which this ship lacks, and yet I cannot say quite from what feature this property derives itself."

The Spear was flattered at my words, and once again took me all around the warship, while we exchanged views on the baseness of this feature or that compared to its fine counterpart upon his own ship. (To speak frankly, the two ships were quite identical in every respect, and I could see absolutely nothing to distinguish one above the other in any way.) Again, I showed great interest in the hold, and when he took me there I examined the floor with diligence, expressing at last my opinion that it was these beams, above all others, that were so regally placed on the *Silver Ray*.

When we returned to the deck, I requested we examine the third ship too, to see if its workmanship matched that of The Spear's own craft, or whether it was of inferior construction, like the *Remora*. He readily consented, and we walked across a plank which connected the two ships while at anchor.

Immediately upon boarding the third ship, which was called the *Seahorse*, and was, again, indistinguishable from the other two ships, I gave a cry of excitement. I told him I had just sighted an eel of the most piquant sort swimming off the ship's starboard side. At once, I set to work with my tackle. Once again, however, I was forced to abandon my efforts and wind in my line. "These old eels," I explained, "are cunning beyond measure. I fear this one has made his escape."

We then inspected the *Seahorse*, and I showed The Spear those aspects of the ship's hold which rendered it so much subordinate to the hold of the glorious *Silver Ray*. "Feel" I said "how coarse the boards of this ship are, and how the wood lacks in the property of delicately hued smoothness which we stonemages call "velvescence." And he examined the boards, and agreed the "velvescence" of his own ship was, even to his own untrained eye, slightly superior to that of the two ships owned by his uncle.

We returned across the plank to the *Remora*, and from there to the longboat. The Spear invited me to join him in luncheon aboard the *Silver Ray*, but I declined, saying I had planned to pay a social call upon Yorke, so he rowed me back to shore, and gave me his commiserations for my failed fishing exercise.

I quickly ran back to my ship and instructed the head slave to prepare for departure that day, but to ensure the preparations were made with discretion and subtlety. I then paid a visit upon Yorke and told the old astronomer how successful the previous night's dinner had been in cementing the bonds of friendship between

The Spear and me.

I said, "I suggest you invite him to your dining room once more, and his men too, for I would like to know them better." Yorke thought my plan an excellent one and immediately sent invitations by paid messenger (for he owned no slaves).

That evening, I made my way to the hill overlooking the inlet, where I lay and watched The Spear and his men leave their ships and march across the island to the town. Meanwhile, I had arranged for one of my own slaves to deliver a message to Yorke's mansion I had been unavoidably delayed but I would join them shortly.

I kept my gaze upon those warships. There were now only slaves and myrmidons aboard. The sun had set, and lamps had been lit, but there was still light enough left in the sky to see the vessels clearly.

Now, you will have guessed my eel-fishing and close inspection of the warships earlier in the day were ploys of some kind. Certainly The Spear's men thought this, for they gave me distrustful looks, suspecting, I imagine, that I was spying out the ground for some elaborate attack. But my visit was no spying exercise—it was the attack itself.

Here was the method of it. Each time I cast the line over the edge of a warship, I let the weight fall to the bottom of the inlet. Then, when I wound up the line, I counted how many times it wrapped the frame, for I had built this frame so each circuit of the line was exactly one half of one builder's measure in length. By counting the windings, therefore, I was able to determine, with the greatest accuracy, the distance from the side of the ship to the bed of the inlet. During my tour of each ship, I measured (by eye) the interior height of the ship from its side to its keel (for these warships are round-bottomed, and the boards beneath the hold also form the belly of the craft); then, during my close examination of these boards, I used my finger to place a Tarn rune, then placed an enchantment connecting the keel of the ship to the rock on the sea bed, for you see, by subtracting the two measurements, one is left with the distance between the keel and the bottom, although I added a few inches to account for the width of the wood at the keel, and the accumulation of silt on the rocks far below the ship. And along this precise length, I placed a Strut of Atlas.

Now, you will say, "Strut of Atlas? But did you not complain about the instability of this ancient spell?"

Indeed I did! The spell is old and unreliable. Every apprentice who learns it is warned to construct the three straight parts of the binding evenly, for otherwise the strut will contract away to nothing, pulling its two sides together.

Worse, I had drawn the rune with my finger, instead of using a chisel or stain. And I had used the Tarn rune, instead of the correct rune for the Strut of Atlas, which is Tessel. Oh, Tarn will work, but not for long! My Struts of Atlas broke every strict rule or dire warning ever spoken about them. I knew they would endure no more than a few hours.

For my work aboard the warships, then, I had created struts of the weakest and most violently unstable character, carefully constructed to collapse after approximately nine hours. Moreover, by their nature, they were sympathetically tuned, meaning the collapse of one would trigger the collapse of the others.

As I watched now from the hill, I felt a tingling in my fingers and neck and could sense the ships' wefts were straining. The sensation grew stronger and stronger still until at last, with a sound like thunder, the binding beneath the *Remora* gave way, and the ship was snapped to the bottom with such force and speed that, for an instant, it looked as if a deep well had been dug in the water and the ship had fallen in. And, in the next moment, great masses of timber and chank, which had been dashed into pieces by the rocks at the bottom, were thrown hundreds of feet into the air. Even as this was occurring, the binding gave way beneath the *Silver Ray*, and this ship too was wrenched below, then spewed up in a great white explosion. Then the *Seahorse*'s binding broke. Here, however, I had not been so accurate in my measurements, and had perhaps failed to take proper account of the depth of silt on the bed of the inlet, for instead of taking the ship to the bottom, the collapsed binding merely brought up a huge quantity of silt and dead weeds, which showered over the ship.

Fortunately, the extreme violence with which the other ships were destroyed worked to make up for my error, and as I watched, I saw the wreckage from those ships, which had been thrown into the air, come crashing down again with tremendous force. Some of the chunks struck the *Seahorse*, smashing through the ship's decks and cracking the hull almost in two. A few seconds later, the *Seahorse* tipped on its side and sank.

You will imagine the joy I felt at witnessing the success of my plans—and the emotion was intensified by the fact that not only had I deprived The Spear of his ships, but also of all his slaves and myrmidons. Still, I did not dally at the scene but rather ran, as fast as I was able, to my own ship, which was waiting in Lyce. As soon as I reached it, I gave the order to cast off and set sail, and as we pulled away, I observed The Spear and his men emerging from Yorke's mansion, doubtless to investigate the source of the explosions they had heard.

We then proceeded west, away from the Duck Islands. I stayed up a few hours and kept watch from the stern to make sure my enemies were indeed stranded. In this fact, incidentally, I felt some regret, for The Spear had kept honourably to the guest-peace (as I had done myself), and not every navigator would have done the same.

These sentimental feelings, however, were quickly dispelled when I finally went to my cabin very late that night. There I met with the most disagreeable smell you can imagine. I found a large quantity of eels had been placed in a bucket on the floor. These, my head slave informed me, had arrived earlier in the day as a gift from The Spear. An accompanying message read: "I regret I cannot give you eels caught by your own hand, but I hope you will take some small pleasure in these eels, which I caught from my longboat using a deep-net."

Of course, I would no more eat a black eel than I would eat a leech, and I promptly tossed the bucket overboard, but the smell lingered for many weeks and made me feel quite ill at times. I was, however, soon afforded the opportunity for revenge, for, two days later, we encountered an ocean trader bound for the Duck Islands and then Alican. I told the captain a terrible plague had broken out on the Duck Islands, and, if he was wise, he would stay clear of the place.

As it happened, he did better. I found out long afterwards that this captain had spread the word of the plague among the other sailors of the Atlantic Ocean, and vessels avoided the islands from then onwards. Since no ships are built upon the islands, only tiny fishing boats, I imagine The Spear and his company were trapped there for a good many years.

As for me, I continued my westward voyage towards America. I felt much relieved, for I had a sense I was safe at last. After all, the lands of my enemies were far behind; those who had tried to pursue me were stranded; and there were surely no creatures aboard my ship that might harm me.

As you will see, in this last assumption I was grievously mistaken.

The Third Part

In Which I Describe My Voyage
To America, The Visions Which
Accompanied It, And The Various
Actions I Took Because Of These Visions

W E SAILED THE ATLANTIC FOR a week without event. The weather was fair, so I spent most of my time upon the upper deck sitting in a long chair and wrapped in a cloak (for even in the sunshine, the winds made the air cold). For entertainment, I read books or watched the sea, and when it came time to eat, I had the slaves bring a table out to me, and I ate in the fresh air to the sound of the waves. It was a very pleasant time in all, marred only by the fact that, every night, I was obliged to retire to my cabin and sleep amid the smell of those terrible eels. This odour is not strong, not in the way the odour of the stinkweed, or of rotting cabbage is strong; however, the aroma seems to increase with the length of one's exposure, and even though the cabin door and the portholes were left wide open throughout the day, which aired the room very thoroughly, I would nevertheless return to my cabin each evening to find the portion of the smell still remaining had become doubly offensive to my nostrils.

The smell was so bad that one night I abandoned my cabin entirely and slept in the large cabin with the slaves. This did not suit me, for slaves, too, have a smell. On the next night, I tried to sleep in the hold, having placed my mattresses upon the wooden floor, but it was an uncomfortable bedchamber, as well as being dark and oppressive. Moreover, I was no sooner sleeping than I was awakened by a minute sound, and upon shining a lamp around I saw a mouse scurry behind my barrels of ale. On seeing this, you may be sure I gathered together my mattresses and blankets, and climbed the ladder back to the top deck, and thence to my own cabin, and I slept there, smell and all.

You may perhaps think it cowardly of me to be afraid of such a tiny thing as a mouse, but I know something of the ways of these animals, which have a vile disposition towards climbing into the mouths of sleeping persons in the belief the orifice is a mouse hole. Inevitably, the sleeping person will inhale or swallow, and the mouse will be drawn into his or her innermost parts, whereupon the creature, seized with a fury born of panic, madly bites and scratches in all directions, doing such damage to the internal organs that the unfortunate victim dies a vile and excruciating death. Scholars now agree countless people are killed in this way, although rarely is the cause of death accurately identified, because the mouse, following its natural instinct, retreats deep into the intestine, where it is swiftly digested by the fluids still resident in the body of its victim.

I write these words knowing full well the nauseating effect they will have upon many readers. Yet surely it is better to speak frankly about the true dangers of the mouse, though it is horrendous to hear, than to tame the warning, thereby ensuring it carries no force and many more people fall victim to this gruesome creature.

Now, I do not tell this tale of the mouse merely to illustrate the hazards of my voyage, for, as I lay in my cabin, this matter of providing a warning about the dangers of the mouse started to tap upon my mind, and I began to address myself to the challenge. Soon, a very wonderful idea came to me, almost as a vision. I saw before me the image of King Thyatus, who died after his victory at the Battle of Neppo Sound. It is now widely accepted that Thyatus died from intaking a mouse as he lay recovering from his battle wounds, and in my vision I saw the great king, sitting in his bed, naked except for his war helmet, pointing skyward with his right arm, and leaning on his left. His legs were swathed in satin sheets, and from his mouth, causing him the greatest alarm, protruded the tail and hindquarters of a mouse as it scrambled towards his throat on its deadly mission.

The vision filled me with the utmost awe and dread, for consider, this glorious king, whose war victory had brought him all Asia as its trophy, now lay conquered himself, and by nothing more than a common mouse. And yet, is this not the capricious nature of all life's victories for every one of us?

You will certainly appreciate, then, this vision of mine was a very remarkable one, and would have made a fine sculpture or a painting—and this would by no means have been beyond my talents, for I have created many paintings and sculptures, and all who saw them, including many of the finest artists in Cyprus, wondered I had not made the pursuit of these arts my life's work instead of playing with them merely as a pastime, for it was clear to them I had the makings of all the greatness of a Ranascawan or a Tybalt. Indeed, the great Azelian artist Chiamo Threedeem said of one of my paintings that it was "finer than any created by Tybalt." Naturally, I give these words little heed, and I quote them here merely as an amusement. Nevertheless, it is worth considering that Threedeem's reputation as a great artist went hand in hand with his standing as a critic, and he was not wont to give praise idly.

To realize my vision in this way, though, would have been to betray it. For, as it came before my mind's eye, I saw tiny mites crawling upon the sheets of King Thyatus, and a green lawn around him. Then, as I examined the vision more intently, I saw the mites were people, and the lawn was a vast forest. In short, the image I had seen was not merely a statue, but a great tower cunningly wrought into a statue's shape. I named the work *The Grief of King Thyatus*, or the *Grief* for short.

Upon realizing the extent of this inspired vision, I was filled with the most intense excitement and zeal, and was no longer able to sleep, for fear some detail of the conception would vanish before I woke. I therefore spent all night drawing plans and writing notes, and even as I wrote, more ideas came flooding into my head, until at last I called for the head slave and spoke ideas aloud for him to capture in writing, while I wrote further ideas by my own hand. The sun was rising before the visionary deluge finally subsided, whereupon I retired to my bed and slept very soundly until late the same afternoon.

During the next day, the weather worsened, so we were constantly sailing through sleet and drizzle, and my reading upon the deck was brought to an end. With my wonderful new mission, however, this mattered to me not a jot. I remained in my cabin, now suddenly caring nothing for the smell of the eels, and I prepared detailed plans for the construction of the great colossus I had envisioned.

A further week passed in this way until the plans were, in most respects, complete. When I say "plans," I refer not to the appearance or layout of the structure—as in Luthen, this work had been completed in a few inspired hours—rather, I mean the placement of the myriad bindings upon the building.

This reckoning of the enchantments was no trivial task. Indeed, for most stonemages it would have been well nigh impossible, for most rely upon mathematics to calculate the proper stress points, a procedure which greatly slows the reckoning time and leaves in its wake a spell scheme that is exact but mechanical and unexciting. I have not used mathematics since my schooling, when I found I did not care for the method. Therefore, I place my runes and wefts following my instinctive connection with the buildings

I plan to create, which exist in the picture of my mind in a form as real as any castle or house that should fall before my eye. This is to say, then, this planning, while it would have been overwhelming for most stonemages, was a trifle for me.

However, there were two aspects to the structure which presented a formidable challenge. The first was the right arm of the statue, which I had decided should be raised at an angle of forty-five degrees. The second was to give this great statue the property of speech. Both these problems posed a level of difficulty so great it would be over a year before I fully solved them, and even this time represented work of the most astonishing swiftness and inspiration, because either one of these tasks might well have represented a lifetime's work for an ordinary stonemage—or even for a very great one.

But let me say no more here. It is not the proper time to explain my remarkable solutions, and I fear my words might be misinterpreted as a display of vanity. This is not so, however, and you may rest assured that, in many cases, I have considerably *understated* the many challenges and difficulties which I overcame, for, although I believe in speaking truly, I often find myself racked with an almost crippling humility regarding my own talents.

So then, I had finished my plans, yet I knew it would still be several weeks before we sighted land. The weather remained foul, so reading upon the deck was impossible—and in any case would have been unappealing to me, for I was alive with the enthusiasm to begin construction, and yet, aboard my ship, I could do nothing but wait. Oh, those weeks were a very wearisome time, and even now, in my memory, the period seems to me longer than the several years of building work which were to follow. And yet the unendurable boredom of those days had a happy and remarkable consequence, for it put my mind in such a state it became receptive to many visions. Often, in fact, as I pored over my plans, looking for some alteration which might occupy my thoughts, I would fancy I heard a noise behind me, or would feel a presence above me, and I would turn to see a great frog, or a hole with tentacles, or a shining weasel, or some such vision. And although these hallucinations were often horrible, and seemed to me to be completely real, yet I felt not the slightest alarm or fear upon beholding them.

Such visions, I am told, are not unusual—and indeed are a commonplace occurrence among those who are forced to maintain a state of solitude for a lengthy period—nevertheless, they provided me with many striking designs which I have since used upon the walls of buildings as grotesques or gargoyles.

However, one of these visions was truly singular. I was staring at the wall of my cabin when I thought I saw a movement through the porthole. Then a great, dark figure rose up from the waves. It was a giant, covered with barnacles and seaweed, with a sunken wreck for a body. He reached out and seized the porthole, tearing it from the side of my ship. In my mind I thought, "Ah, my ship will now sink, certainly." But no. Instead the sea vanished, and I found myself looking upon a jungle. The giant still stood before me, but now had a beautiful and radiant appearance and wore a silver cloak. At his feet was a fox, feeding upon a long-dead carcass, and above him was a peacock in flight. The giant then spoke to me, saying: "Yreth, heed this—what you must lose to the fox, you will gain one hundredfold from the bird." He said this three times, then the scene vanished, and I found myself staring once again at my cabin wall, with nothing but empty ocean beyond the porthole.

Within an hour of this last vision, we finally sighted the shores of America. We sailed south, following the shoreline for a time until we reached the mouth of the mighty river Ram, then we sailed up this river to Ramport.

I had selected Ramport as my destination some weeks earlier, for my head slave had told me the people of the town loved fine buildings and had plenty of arrans to pay for them. In this, he was correct, for the town was attractively plotted, with buildings of every colour, bearing numerous spires, domes, and towers, all decorated with gold and silver. In addition, almost every building in the town had a mast upon its roof, of the sort you would find upon a small sailing boat, and at the top of this mast was fastened a rectangular banner of coloured fabric called a "flag."

These flags worked as follows: each was fastened at two of its corners by a rope, much as a sail or banner is, except the flag was fastened vertically to the mast, without the benefit of booms, arms or stays. Further, the remaining two corners of the flag were left unbound, so, when the wind blew, the flags were pulled out, displaying their designs and making a beating sound, like the wings of a large bird. I was much taken by these flags, and later I purchased a large number to trade in the east, but the fashion has never caught on here, since American ways are unjustly considered crude, and I was quite unable to sell them again.

I spent some two weeks exploring this town and acquainting myself with its buildings and its people. During this time, I roomed at the most expensive inns, staying no more than two nights at any one, and at each inn I let it be known I was a stonemage from Cyprus with a plan for a great construction. Naturally, word of my arrival soon spread among the rich, and before long a letter arrived inviting me to take luncheon with the town's magistrate-in-chief.

During the meal, this gentleman informed me that, while he had no power to authorize constructions (except for work of a trivial nature which would be beneath my skills), he knew of a project that would shortly be open to the bids of builders. The northernmost section of the town, he told me, had been destroyed by fire ten years previously, and it was now desired that this area be rebuilt. "If you feel the task to be worthy of your talents," he said, "then I will mention your name to our principal watchman."

Of course, I assured the magistrate-in-chief that this commission was exactly the sort I had been seeking, and I thanked him very copiously for his kindness.

For the next day or two, I wandered around the area which was to be rebuilt. Most of its buildings were burnt-out shells, although some retained sections of roof, and these served as homes for the impoverished and for thieves. The area was situated far from the river, and this, perhaps, was why the fire had done such damage, there being little water nearby to douse the flames.

As I beheld the ruined houses, I marvelled at the opportunity providence had given to me, for it was clear this would be an ideal site for the construction of my *Grief*.

Some days after my dinner with the magistrate-in-chief, a second invitation arrived, this time to take dinner with the principal watchman, whose name was Eon Vulpine. On seeing this name, certain doubts were immediately aroused in my head, for vulpine is a very ancient word meaning "like a fox," and in my vision I had been warned I would suffer losses to the fox.

Still, I dined with him anyway, and I was favourably impressed by his knowledge of the builder's art. And, I must admit, I was impressed by the man himself. He was perhaps in his fortieth year, with a large, open face, and intelligent eyes. During the meal, I showed him my plans for the *Grief*, and he was overwhelmed by its loveliness, saying it was the most beautiful plan for a sculpture he had ever seen. When I explained this was to be no sculpture, but was a mighty tower, he was astounded beyond belief.

"But I fear," he said, "that we have no need for such a tower. Our town is adequately protected."

"You hear tower and you think warfare," I said. "Yet this need not be a mere fortification. The tower's interior is divided into a multitude of rooms, and these might serve very nicely as dwellings, or even as small shops. Thus, this statue will replace the damaged section of your town."

On hearing this, Eon Vulpine was overcome with joy, saying: "Then indeed, this must be built! It must! It must!" He drooled, and he clapped his hands together uncontrollably, so much was he enthralled by the prospect of this magnificent edifice becoming a part of his town.

Then he asked me why the king had a little tail sticking out of his mouth. I explained to him this building served not only to shelter and to beautify, but also to warn all who might behold it of the dangers of the mouse.

"What dangers?" said he.

I then explained the dangers to him as I have already told it here. He was much alarmed to hear this news, for he, being ignorant of the threat, had given a gift of two caged mice to his children some months earlier.

"If you will take my advice, sir," I said, "you will kill the creatures without delay, for not to do so will certainly bring about the untimely deaths of your own dear infants."

This he promptly did, and he later told me he would be forever grateful to me for saving his children from so terrible a death. So, you see, even before it was built, my *Grief* was already fulfilling its worthy mission, although Vulpine's gratitude brought me precious little reward, as you will see.

We met many times over the following month and discussed every aspect of the building. Vulpine's excitement was hardly diminished since his first glimpse of the plans. And his pleasure was greatly increased when he asked me what it might cost to create such a wonder.

"For my last commission," I told him, "I received gold and gifts totalling more than one thousand three hundred arrans. Though the nature of that task was very much simpler than this one, yet I would be willing to work for the same sum, provided I might be given assistants to help me with the more rudimentary elements of the construction, together with a quantity of slaves to carry stones."

"One thousand three hundred arrans!" he exclaimed. "Come, sir! I may be no stonemage, but I know enough of architecture to know such a price would greatly undervalue the genius of your design alone. To ask such a pittance for both the design and the construction is absurd. No, I will insist you ask no less than five thousand arrans for this commission. In addition, I will see to it you are given builders of the highest skill to work under you."

I was well pleased by these terms, for I had indeed set my price very low in my enthusiasm to win the commission. I was pleased also by this fellow's recognition of the importance of my work. Nevertheless, I remained constantly mindful of my vision, and I watched Vulpine carefully for any sign of trickery or false dealing.

A few days later, I had picked out several builders who would help me with the job. Vulpine approved my choice, assuring me of their considerable talents and urging me to begin work without delay. But then he said a very curious thing. He said: "And if the citizens of this town are outraged that our time-honoured customs have been broken, let us care nothing for it, for we would do a far greater wrong by jeopardizing the construction of so worthy an artwork."

These words disturbed me, for we folk of the Cyprus Horn place a high value on custom, and so I asked him: "To which customs do you refer."

"Oh," he said, "it is the usual practice, for any great building such as this is, that the many stonemages of the area be summoned together and given the chance to submit designs of their own. Then a competition is held, and the winner's design is used for the construction in question."

"Well then," I said, after some thought, "if that is the custom, let us abide by it."

"No no," he said, "I could not allow it. What if some other stonemage's work were chosen? No, the *Grief* must be built."

"Is the competition a fair one, unsullied by corruption or by prejudice towards the local stonemages?" I asked.

"Why certainly," he said. "The submissions are judged solely on their integral beauty, with no thought for the background of the works' creators."

"And are its judges such people as would appreciate greatness in a building?"

"The judges are the members of the town's council," he replied. "None are stonemages, but I have shown sketches of your proposal to them all, and they were unanimous in declaring the *Grief* a work without equal in this land."

"Well, then, there is nothing to be feared by this course of action," I said. "I am confident no stonemage might create so lovely a structure as my own. And if, by some miracle, one should create a work still more marvellous, why then, let that person take the commission, for he or she will certainly have earned it."

"I see you are a man of the most perfect integrity," he said. "And perfect judgement too! Very well, then—we shall have the competition as you suggest. And I shall sleep soundly in the secure knowledge your mighty *Grief* will win the contest and be built." And at this we both raised our glasses and drank a toast to my *Grief*.

So the competition was announced, and several score stonemages of East America were summoned to Ramport for the purpose. On the assigned day, which was eight weeks after the conversation I have just recounted, exact models of the various designs, cast in plaster or lead, were placed in the Great Hall of the Round Fortress, which houses the administrative chambers of Ramport. Each model was placed upon a separate table, and the stonemage responsible for the design remained in front of its table in order to answer questions from the many people who had come to view the proposals.

Truly there were some attractive designs—although it is one thing to create a pretty model, and quite another to execute the plan on a grand scale—and I watched carefully as the townspeople wandered past the tables, nodding or smiling at the miniatures, for they were pleased by them. But as they reached the *Grief*, which I had sculpted in platinum and gold and then painted in lifelike flesh tones, and which stood more than twelve feet high, all were astounded and impressed beyond measure.

There were many high officials of the region present, and I spoke to some of them. A powerful merchant by the name of Ildreth told me he thought the design remarkable. The governor of North Pocern was there, and he nodded at me in such a way as to convey, without any possibility of doubt, that he thought my *Grief* to be one of the new wonders of the world. Also, I spoke with the Bishopa of Quebec, who had toured the hall with an entourage of several bishops and some thirty huge myrmidons. We talked very pleasantly, and she expressed her admiration for my daring model, saying that, in her opinion, it was certainly the finest design in the room, and she added that, if I ever sought work, I might presume upon her patronage.

Some hours later, before a large assembly, the winner of the competition was announced by the magistrate-in-chief. You will be astonished to hear that the council had selected not my design, but the design of a local architect. The work was a gaudy pastiche of the Far Western school, incorporating a fat central thimble-hall, surrounded by numerous nested towers, and various small houses, shops, and inns. As the magistrate read the decision, one could sense a great tension in the room, for it was clear to all present that a heinous injustice had been committed.

As you may imagine, I was outraged and insulted, and a mighty wave of fury rolled over me, for I knew who was behind this villainy—not only because of the warning in my vision, but also because Eon Vulpine was the only member of the council not present when the decision was announced, and this, I knew, was because his shame would not allow him to face the one he had wronged so grievously.

Therefore, I took my throwing-razor, which I carry always in my boot, and I placed it in my sleeve, then I quickly made my way to Eon Vulpine's chambers, determined that, if his explanation of matters did not suit me, I should certainly take his life.

There I found him pacing back and forth in a state—so it seemed—of the utmost agitation. "Alas," he said, as I entered the room, "what a disaster has befallen the town! To think we should have lost such a beautiful work."

Now, this confused me and blunted my anger slightly, so I put aside my idea of killing him. Oh, what a cunning creature he was, for in speaking my own thoughts to me, as though he believed them himself, he made it seem as if my interests and his were one and the same.

I then asked him to explain why the competition had been won by a work which was so clearly inferior to my own. Could it be, I asked, the other officials had not in fact been as enthusiastically disposed towards my design as they had first pretended.

"Indeed, no," he said. "The magistrate-in-chief, the purse warden, and the bishop all felt your design to be by far the finest. And as to my own feelings, you know them well."

Here he broke into a powerful fit of weeping, so I was actually moved by sympathy for him, fool that I was, and I said: "This is a disaster for all. And yet, how do you explain this final verdict?"

"Our decision was overruled by a higher official," he said. "The sentiment was expressed that it would be unwise to give so handsome a commission to a foreigner, particularly when many of our own stonemages, who have served us well, might relish the task.

"However," he went on, "I was able to persuade the council to give you a commission of your own, a smaller version of the same magnificent design. It could be erected upon Paddle Island, which is the little island you see in the centre of the river. There it will serve admirably as a lighthouse, warning ships during foggy weather."

A lighthouse! As I think back on the suggestion now, my anger rises, for I see Eon Vulpine was mocking me, extending the indignity of my defeat. Would that I had strangled him then and there with my bare hands, for his blood was not worthy to be spilled by my throwing-razor. Yet at the time, my own anger and disappointment were tempered by compassion for this treacherous, miserable creature.

"This is very much less than I had hoped for, and indeed, than I had been promised," said I. "For you told me the competition would not take into account the nationality of its participants."

"I share your disappointment," he said, and he was all sympathy and comforting arms. "And yet, consider this: once people see the beauty of the lighthouse, they will clamour to have greater structures built by your hand—and with such popular support, it will be impossible for any higher official to oppose the construction. Further, I shall personally see to it that you are paid handsomely for the work—let us say, one thousand arrans."

Now, in my state at the time, this seemed a generous price, for

I knew a small lighthouse would be very much simpler to build than the great statue-tower I had planned. I accepted on the spot, requesting the funds be paid to me in advance, as a token of good-will.

"Alas! With the limited power I possess, it is quite impossible for me to pay you this sum from the town's treasury without further delays," he said. "Therefore, I shall pay you this sum immediately, and from my own purse, for such is my great trust in your genius and your talent." And with that he opened a trunk and thrust into my arms a great bag of coins, containing the requested amount.

I was moved by this gesture—fool, simple-minded dolt that I was!—and thanked him profusely, with bows and touches to the head and kind words which dismissed as nothing the great work of which I had been unjustly deprived.

But then, at last, a measure of sense came to me, for I remembered once more my vision. Therefore, I determined to investigate the details of the account as he had relayed it to me.

"Sir," I said, "may I be so bold as to ask you the precise identity of this higher official of whom you have spoken?"

"I fear I cannot say," he said. "The details of conversations held at council meetings must be kept in the utmost confidence. I have perhaps breached that confidence already even by telling you what I have."

"You may rely on me to keep my peace on the matter," said I. "And, since you have already told me most of the tale, it would certainly do no harm to fill in this one small detail."

"Yes, yes, that is true," he said. "And perhaps you have a right to know, particularly considering the unusual nature of the decision. Very well, then—the truth of the matter is we were all most impressed by your glorious plan and were on the verge of putting the issue to the vote. Then the Bishopa of Quebec entered the room, which is her right, for she is bishopa of all East America. Do you know of this woman?"

Although I had met her that very day, I said I did not know of her, for I wished to see what he would tell me.

"Oh, she is a treacherous creature," said Vulpine. "And though she is a bishopa, yet she is evil and calculating, and much feared and despised throughout the continent. Upon hearing we were about to approve the expenditure, she spoke, insisting a local stonemage receive the commission, and commanding the bishop to reject your own application. This, naturally, he was obliged to do, although it was with the greatest unwillingness. But even so, the rest of us stood firm, for we believed yours was the finest of all the entries. Then the bishopa said she had made her views clear, and if we wished to oppose her, we would reap bitter consequences indeed. You may be assured the bishopa's threats are not to be taken lightly, for she commands a great army, and it has often been used to wreak destruction in the towns of this region. Indeed it was that very army which burned the north section of our town, in retaliation for a previous offence against her. Therefore, we had little choice but to reject your proposal."

Now, Eon Vulpine spoke these words in tones that seemed earnest, and his eyes too expressed honesty—so much so, in fact, that I resolved, as a result of this encounter, never again to trust the honesty of people by their faces or by their words. For you see, my dream had predicted he would cheat me. Also, the bishopa had told me how much she had admired my building and even expressed her desire to employ me herself, so it was inconceivable she should have cancelled the construction.

At last, through the power of pure reason, which shines upon all statements like a great beacon, the truth had been revealed: Eon Vulpine was lying. Unfortunately, I reached this conclusion only after I had left his office, and the mood was no longer in me to return and to kill him.

In any event, I knew how to deal with the situation: I sent word to Vulpine that I would have to take a few days to begin plans for the lighthouse, then I boarded my ship and set sail for Quebec, a few score miles west down the river. I took my sack of arrans with me, and I have not returned to Ramport since.

Now, Eon Vulpine had wronged me, that is certain, but you

may wonder whether my act of making off with the money was just, for, while it can be an honourable act to kill your enemies, it is never honourable to rob them. Yet consider this: I was originally promised five thousand arrans for the commission, and yet, thanks to his treachery, I received only one thousand. Therefore it was I, not he, who was robbed, and to the tune of four thousand arrans, even after accounting for the sack of coins which he had given me. You can see from this that my actions were honourable.

And they were prudent too, for, while I suffered the loss of a large fortune to the fox, I nevertheless managed, through heeding my vision, and through skilful timing, to minimize the degree of those losses.

The Fourth Part

In Which I Tell Of The Many Good
Things Which I Received From The
Bishopa And My Execution Of Certain
Duties In Quebec

I ARRIVED AT THE DOCKS OF Quebec the next morning and made my way through the city in the direction of Quebec Cathedral, which glittered like a jewel before me.

Quebec is a principally a port for fishing ships and ocean traders. Its industrious people also produce very fine leatherwork. The architecture in the city's centre is attractive but unremarkable, save perhaps for the Abbey of Saint John the Weak, a long building, which spirals inwards within a great circle, symbolizing his holy vacillations. This abbey houses more than five hundred monks of the New Carolingian Order, the most ascetic in the Eastern Gnostic Church, although you will also see many other types of monks and clerics about the city.

For strategic reasons, Quebec Cathedral lies a half-mile outside the city's centre. It is a heavily fortified structure, and yet its design displays the utmost grace and delicacy. The walls are a deep blue mineral fusion, laced with platinum tubing enclosing religious scenes of unsurpassed beauty and artistic accomplishment. A magnificent central tower rises six hundred feet above the building, and here are situated not only the bells, which are plated in gold, but also a military lookout post. Four more towers, each three hundred feet high, occupy the corners of the cathedral. These are coated in sheets of purple amethyst, and atop each tower stands a great golden crucifix, cunningly worked so the cross can be quickly pulled down upon a pair of hinged arms, strung, and transformed into a powerful and accurate ballista, capable of hurling an explosive javelin many miles upon the enemies of the church. This I learned only much later of course.

I made my way to the cathedral's propylon, where I requested an audience with the bishopa. To my surprise and pleasure, the audience was granted within mere minutes. Upon entering the building, escorted by two myrmidons in tunics of red and gold, I was instantly struck by the sumptuous and tasteful decoration, which included rich carpets and a plenitude of fine artworks—including an impressive collection of war scenes by Tybalt.

I was escorted to a great hall, much like a king's throne room, where the bishopa herself looked down from a richly upholstered dais bench placed more than twenty feet above the floor, topped by an exquisite red baldachin. There were many bishops in attendance, and priests too, and along the walls stood more than fifty myrmidons, with an equal number standing guard on a great balcony which surrounded the room.

As to the woman herself, I was immediately struck by her great beauty and serenity, which seemed to have increased since our previous brief meeting in Ramport. I was also impressed by the great wisdom in her face, something I had not noticed before. Upon her forehead, she bore a few faint lines, which denoted her deep and charitable concern for the many wards of her spiritual domain. She wore deep purple robes, modestly adorned with jewels of all colours, and with fine gold thread, and trimmed at the collar and cuffs with what I first took to be ermine, though later I learned it was the far more precious fur of baby albino sea otters.

She then asked me my business, in a soft voice which carried a lovely vibrato quality.

I then said, "Your Excellency, I had thought my business to concern some financial matter, but now I find this has been swept from my mind as trivial, for, as it strikes me now, the only business which seems of import is to tell Your Excellency how struck and overcome I am by your great beauty."

Now, at this the bishops who stood in attendance upon the bishopa began exchanging disapproving glances. It was clear, however, the bishopa herself was well pleased by my words, for she gave me a radiant and lovely smile, saying: "Come closer—I wish to see you better."

I obeyed and climbed the steps to come closer, and she looked upon me for a few moments and then nodded approvingly. "You have a sweet tongue," she said. "Such language is not normally considered appropriate in addressing me, but I see from your face you spoke in earnest and from your heart." And then she raised her voice so all in attendance might hear her better and said: "I only wish everyone who addressed me would speak with such sincerity, for I am very often forced to hear false and hypocritical words." Then, speaking once more to me: "But tell me, Yreth, what was it that troubled you before you entered my hall?"

"Truly, Your Excellency," I replied, "as I stand now, so much closer to you than before, it is hard for me even to remember my first business. And yet I am loath to waste your time. So, if you will pardon the action, I will close my eyes as I address you, for only in this way will I be able to speak coherently."

To this plan she gave her assent, and then I closed my eyes and explained to her of the way Eon Vulpine had cheated me of my commission. "Further," I said, "he claimed it had been Your Excellency who gave the order to cancel the work. Naturally this seemed inconceivable to me, for you spoke to me yourself of your feelings for my modest plans. Therefore, I was forced to conclude that Eon Vulpine had lied to me. This conclusion was supported by a prophetic dream I had in which I was told that what I would lose to the fox I would gain one hundredfold from the bird—though naturally I do not follow such visions blindly."

She laughed at this, for I unwittingly spoke these words with my eyes still closed.

I then told her how I had minimized my losses by escaping with Eon Vulpine's payment to me.

She nodded, saying: "Your actions do credit to your integrity and your judgement both, for indeed, you are correct in your suspicions about this man's lies. It was very proper you should come to me and seek my advice in this affair, for I fear evil is frequently spoken of me in my absence, and such words are all too often believed. Yet now I shall see to it that this Eon Vulpine is sought out and punished for his crime against you and for his slanders against my name. As to your vision, I am certain this was a divine revelation, for my full name is Lenata ad-Hern, and a hern, as you will know being from the east, is a type of bird. Moreover, you will find I am indeed in a position to compensate you for what you lost to Vulpine, although not one hundredfold. But then again, perhaps I am mistaken, for prophetic dreams often contain truths beyond the imaginings even of a bishopa."

I said, "If I may serve Your Excellency in any way whatever, it will be my privilege and my honour to do so. You have only to state the task and I shall do it."

"Hear my will then," she said. "Yreth, I wish you to build for me a second cathedral, for this one has grown too small for my needs. For its design, you must use the plans which you had intended for Ramport—your statue has all the properties of greatness and spirituality which are required for a cathedral, and in any event was far too grand a structure to be wasted on Ramport. I shall pay you five thousand arrans for this task, as the town had promised you, and you shall be given such assistants as you may require."

Upon hearing these words from this lovely lady, I fell to my knees and began to gnaw upon the base of her dais bench, my tears of joy blending with my own saliva and pieces of wood, until at last the bishopa commanded several bishops to escort me from that hall and to another great chamber, the Ambassadorial Suite, which I was to have as my own during my stay in Quebec.

Now, the bishopa was very anxious to have the *Grief* built, but, unlike that swindler Vulpine, she had the arrans to pay for the job in full. As you may imagine, she and I spent many weeks in close consultation, for, while she was awestruck by my original design, there were also certain practical alterations which she felt desirable—for instance, she wished the walls to be heavily armoured, so the building might be protected from attack. Also, she wanted a great worship hall placed at the ground level, and within this hall were to be placed dreadful weapons of war, so sinners might be reminded of God's terrible wrath. And she asked that the building's many rooms be sized and equipped in such a manner as to make them suitable as a barracks for myrmidons—for she had nearly six thousand myrmidons at that time and most were housed in and near to the cathedral.

Of course, when I understood her desire to make the *Grief* into a military as well as a spiritual stronghold, I had many ideas of my own. I modified the plans so the eyes of the statue housed ballistas, and I added subtle machicolations to the ears, and from them could be poured great vats containing Oil of Aenu, which would then flow down the body of the statue-king and along the stone sheets, engulfing and destroying any attackers. The *Grief* concealed other traps and hidden weapons too, but for various reasons these must remain a secret.

We decided to situate the edifice beside the original cathedral, just to the south, and connected by a road of gold, so the bishopa might easily use both buildings for her religious duties.

These few weeks were a time of remarkable plans then. But they were remarkable in another way too, which I will now explain.

The rigours of my work required that I rose before dawn each morning and made my way downstairs from my chamber, and thence across the cathedral's central courtyard, which was covered in snow, for it was winter. I then walked to the bishopa's chambers to show her my work of the previous night. She would examine my plans and changes as she sat in her bed, clothed in her purple nightrobes and night-cloak, and during these early hours we would discuss further changes, and details of the building, and so on, for, as you may imagine, the appointment scroll of a bishopa is a very busy one during the rest of the day.

Well, one morning, as we examined the plans, the bishopa asked me to come closer to explain some minor detail or other. I sat upon the bed to do so, talking for a time, and then suddenly I felt a great silence fall upon us both. For you see, I was suddenly overcome with a feeling of the deepest and most profound love. Slowly I turned and looked into the face of the bishopa, and it was clear she too was overwhelmed by the same strong feeling.

You will understand me when I say both modesty and my great respect for this beautiful woman prevent me from describing the details of the hours that followed. Suffice it only to say that the bishopa sent word her appointments of the day were to be cancelled, and you may be sure this lovely lady proved herself more capable than the finest harlots of Cyprus.

During the following months, our romance continued—at first in secret, as I continued to visit her chambers under the pretence of having further modifications approved, but later openly, for it was the bishopa's desire that I should dine with her at all her meals and accompany her on many of her trips around the region.

Now, this caused a great commotion in many quarters. In the town, the people said I sought only rank and power through the match, for they said I surely could not be drawn to a woman of the bishopa's age. This, of course, was nonsense, for I have already spoken of the bishopa's great beauty.

It is true she had passed a little over eight decades upon the world, while I had passed only three, but when a woman has such spiritual radiance as was possessed by the bishopa, you may be certain that such matters as her age, and the colour of her hair, and the quantity of her teeth seem trivial indeed.

And in any event, few would pass comment if a wealthy man of eighty years—or even ninety—took to himself a mistress who was a half-century his junior. Why, then, should the great and holy love between the bishopa and young Yreth be the cause of such enmity? But cause it was, and there was great unrest in the town, stirred largely by the many monks who lived there, who were bitter and frustrated by their vows of celibacy.

Within the confines of the cathedral, the hatred was of a different kind. All the male bishops detested me with a great passion, for there was not a man among them who would not have gladly taken that lovely bishopa for his own, had the opportunity arisen. And as for the women bishops, I believe it was my attentions they craved, for I was a handsome devil in those days, very tall and strong, with black hair, so when those women saw I had been taken by the bishopa, they hated me out of jealousy. Yet the bishops and the priests dared not insult the bishopa by mocking her age, so instead they selected a different pretext for opposing the affair, speaking many words about the impropriety of a romantic liaison between a member of the clergy and one of her congregation.

However, the bishopa, in her wisdom, very quickly put an end to this debate, for she raised me to the rank of archbishop, which is higher than a bishop, though lower than a cardinal or bishopa. She placed other honours and ranks upon me, too, giving me the post of Bath Protector, and Keeper of the Golden Fig, and Head Whisk, which assured me the pick of the larder for my meals. Each of these posts carried a large stipend, so I was now receiving more than one hundred arrans per month, in addition to my salary for the construction.

Soon, however, problems arose from a new source. The Archbishop of Ulph, who was a senior administrator for the bishopa, came before her, saying:

"Your Excellency, it is perhaps unwise to give to this one man so many positions of high honour. These posts involve little work, save for very occasional inspections of the kitchen and orchard staff, and I fear, to those not familiar with Your Excellency's wisdom, the appointments might appear an overindulgence of our dear brother Yreth, and this could lead to dissent."

"Of what dissent do you speak?" asked the bishopa.

"It grieves me to report the lies of others," said the archbishop, "Yet there are evil rumours spreading to the effect that our beloved Yreth is merely a kept plaything of Your Excellency and contributes nothing to the church yet places a great burden upon its treasury."

Here he spoke truly—there were indeed such rumours, and it was none other than he who was spreading them, but I said nothing, for it would not have been fitting to enter a crude debate in that holy place.

Still, the bishopa was concerned at the accusations, for, with her gentle and trusting nature, she put much faith in the Archbishop of Ulph. Therefore she asked me to commence construction of the *Grief* without delay, so all might see the value of my presence in Quebec.

"Your Excellency," I said, "though it is my one desire to serve your every want, in this case I regret to say I cannot. The climate of the season (it was now midwinter) makes soil hard and difficult to excavate. Also, and more importantly, enchantments placed by cold hands are more liable to be faulty than those placed in warm weather. No, I fear we must wait until the spring before construction can begin."

On hearing this, I could see the archbishop was pleased, though he feigned concern, while my dear bishopa was distressed.

"I shall accede to your expertise in these matters," she said. "Tell me though, Archbishop Yreth, are there any other skills you possess with which you might usefully and visibly employ yourself in the months before the thaw?"

"Your Worship, I have many skills," I said, and here we exchanged smiles, and a minute pursing and licking of the lips, though in a subtle way, so it might not be detected by those others present. "As well as being a stonemage without equal, I am an accomplished painter and a passable cook. In addition, I have experience as a commander of myrmidons."

"Ah!" she said. "In that capacity I can well use you. I hereby make you Commander of the Northern Guard, and with the post you shall receive a further sixty arrans per month."

Ha! So, the Archbishop of Ulph, who had tried to deprive me of my posts, merely succeeded in winning for me another post, a still greater salary, and a great increase in my powers, for now I had myrmidons in my command.

Let me tell you something of the Northern Guard. The body numbered eight hundred and thirty myrmidons and ninety-three slaves. These latter, while they were called merely "slaves" were equal to all the tasks of a head slave, and would have gone by this description in the east. In ancient times, the Northern Guard patrolled the lands far to the north of Quebec, providing the first line of defence against the Eager Tribes who once ranged the area.

Of course, at the time of which I speak, the Eager Tribes were long dead and buried, and the main function of the Northern Guard was now to seek out spies and heretics and enemies of the church. I undertook this mission with great zeal, reading many books on the methods whereby spies and heretics and enemies of the church might be discovered. If you read on, you will learn my method, which I devised by taking those elements of the other methods I had studied which seemed to me the most prudent, and combining them with my own insights into the nature of the human animal.

When my studies were complete, I gathered together sixty myrmidons and went marching into Quebec, following the Cathedral Road, past the foul-smelling fields used by the leather workers, and through the market, which is in the centre of the town, close to the abbey. I ordered the myrmidons to march slowly, making a great stamping sound, so all might be aware of our approach.

When we were into the market, I bade the myrmidons stop, then narrowed my eyes and fixed my gaze upon various people, observing their reaction to my observation. There was one man, a fishmonger, who looked nervously about and refused to meet my gaze, whereupon I pointed at him, and upon this signal several myrmidons ran at the fellow. He took to his heels, his attempted escape merely assuring me my suspicions of his guilt were correct. Of course, my myrmidons were very much swifter than he, and they soon overtook him and brought him back to me as a prisoner.

We marched on for a short way, along a narrow street, where many people sat outside their houses, wrapped in warm furs, and playing dice in the snow. Here we stopped, and once again I narrowed my eyes and examined every face. Two people, a young woman and a boy with spotted skin, seemed to me the most suspicious, so once more I sent the myrmidons after them, and they took flight. The woman ran here and there, screaming, and was quickly caught. The boy, though, was much faster, and might have escaped if, by God's grace, he had not slipped on the ice and broken one of his legs. So, in short order, the guilty pair were my prisoners.

Travelling on, we arrived at the harbour. I fixed many people with my gaze here, but none showed guilt. Yet two of these people were monks, and suddenly my powers of reason raised a suspicion where my intuition had shown none, for why should two monks have come to the harbour? Should they not be in the abbey, praying? Or in the market, buying goods or begging? It was very dubious, so I sent the myrmidons to seize the monks, and the men did not even bother to run—for doubtless they realized the futility of denying their guilt—and were brought back to me. After this, I returned, with my prisoners, to the cathedral.

Now, when I recount this story, I am often asked whether the behaviour of these people might not have arisen purely out of a fear of wrongful arrest. Well, it is true I quickly became widely feared in Quebec—although I was respected too, for my former critics soon saw I was no caged bird, but a hard-working man of honour, and one to be reckoned with. However, it is not fear that identifies an enemy of the church, but another, less tangible property. Therefore, while many of the townspeople I encountered would indeed show great fear, and might quickly make themselves scarce, or hide their heads when I was near, this was no proof of guilt, just as a lack of fear was no proof of innocence. Rather, I looked for a certain, subtle difference between the behaviour of a guilty person and an innocent, which one may recognize with the passage of time, and which is impossible to describe, but equally impossible to mistake.

And if you doubt the accuracy of my methods, hear what we discovered when we interrogated the prisoners upon the wire.

The old fishmonger confessed he hated God and all His works, and had plotted to overthrow the church, and had conspired with others to kill the bishopa and myself and many other good and charitable people. Also he confessed to consorting with demons and goblins. Here he lied, for educated persons know that goblins are mythical, but he clung to his story despite my protests, and so, in lying he committed perjury, which is another very grave offence.

The woman confessed she hated God and all His works, and had plotted to overthrow the church, and had seduced virtuous men, and virtuous women too, and had conspired to create war, and had placed noxious fluids from diseased animals into wells, and had, on many occasions, eaten human flesh.

The boy confessed he hated God and all His works, and had plotted to overthrow the church, and had committed many sins so terrible he did not know the names for them and was incapable of describing them with a mortal tongue. Also he confessed to the sin of stupidity, and to the sin of sloth.

The first monk confessed he hated God and all His works, and had plotted to overthrow the church, and had plotted to burn the abbey and the cathedral, and then to set ablaze the whole town, intending to dance naked amidst the flames, while eating human flesh. I interrogated him no further, for it was clear he was not only dangerous but also completely insane.

The second monk was very stubborn and initially confessed only to desiring bony old women. This, I knew, was a vicious insult directed at me and my love of the bishopa, yet I did not let my anger affect my duties as interrogator. Therefore I proceeded slowly and patiently, returning to him every day, until at last, after ten days upon the wire, he confessed he hated many of God's works, and planned, if he escaped, to overthrow the church and to kill certain archbishops. This was all I needed to hear, and you may rest assured the fellow did not survive to achieve his fearsome ambition.

Now, these five were merely my prisoners from one afternoon of searching. During the following months, I would go into the town every day or two. I always returned with prisoners, and, upon interrogation, there was not one of these who had been falsely arrested. Indeed, so proficient was I at seeking out the enemies of the church that I became popularly known as the Bloody Archbishop, and Yreth the Bloody, because those who watched my infallible instinct at work thought it was Christ's own blood that flowed within my veins, giving me my perception and my wisdom.

There were others interrogators too, mostly bishops, who sought out enemies of the church, but I did not care to associate with them or to watch them at work, for they were bloodthirsty and cruel, using blades and coals—and worse—to torture their prisoners. One of them said to me once, "You are too slow about your interrogations, and the wires are always taken up by your prisoners, leaving little room for ours."

I said, "I take exactly the time required for each interrogation. I do not accept the first words from the lips of the prisoner, but rather I continue until I hear confessions which are the truth."

Then this fellow said to me, "What does it matter whether the confession is true, as long as a confession comes?"

"A false confession taken to be true," I replied, "could lead to the death of an innocent, and it our duty to persecute the guilty for the sake of the innocent. As I interrogate my prisoners, I do so with the constant hope in my heart that my first suspicions might have been mistaken and they might prove innocent after all."

"You deceive yourself," he said. "Once a person is upon the wire, he will confess to anything, true or not, and he will keep confessing until he is believed." And then he laughed a vile laugh.

Although I turned my back on him and left, still his words disturbed me greatly, for I could not carry out my duties in good conscience if I thought I was making the innocent suffer. Therefore, I decided to test the properties of the wire, to see if it would make an innocent man admit to crimes he did not commit; and, two days afterwards, I ordered the strong priests who assisted me with my interrogations to place *me* upon the wire. This command horrified them, and at first they refused to do it, but I was adamant, ordering them a second time, and also explaining my reasons for the request. Astonished by my great virtue, they obeyed.

The procedure by which a person is placed upon the wire is painful. My robes were removed, and the tip of the wire, which is very sharp, was inserted into the skin of my left arm, just above the wrist. It was then pushed along a few inches under the skin, then back out to the surface. A few inches further along the arm, the wire was pushed under the skin once more, proceeding, above and below, like a thread through cloth. The wire went across the left arm, then across the shoulders and the back, across the right arm, and finally emerged at my right wrist. At this point, it was pulled tight, so several feet of wire extended beyond each arm.

When this was done, I had the priests suspend the wire across the beams, so I was hanging like a prisoner, with my feet dangling above the ground and my arms outstretched. I ordered them to interrogate me, as they had seen me do to others. First they asked me whether I hated God and all His works. I answered that I did not. Then they asked me again, but I remained firm. Then they asked me whether I had plotted to overthrow the church.

"Yes," I said. "I have done so on many occasions."

"Is this truly so?" they said. "We do not believe you."

I was pleased at this, and I admitted I had merely been testing them, and that, in truth, I had never plotted to overthrow the church.

"Let us take you down now," said the priests. "There is blood dripping from your heels, and we cannot bear to watch it."

But I told them to continue, for I was suffering only as much as any other prisoner. So they asked me whether I sought to make men suffer. I said no. Then they asked me whether I taught heresies to the gullible. I said no. Then they asked me whether I had ever committed a sin.

"Yes," I said. "But what sins I have committed, I have repented of."

By now, I was well satisfied that the wire did not produce lies, and besides I was growing uncomfortable up there, so I commanded them to let me down, which they did. Then the wire was carefully removed, and surgeons were called to place soothing unguents upon my wounds.

I told the surgeons and the priests not to tell anyone of what had happened, but they disobeyed me, and soon the whole town knew of my virtuous act. Then the townspeople came to love me dearly, for they saw I would not inflict on others any punishment which I had not first tested upon myself. And you may be sure that when the bishopa heard of my act, her admiration for me was heightened still further, and she gave me rewards in private which only a woman can give, and only to a man.

The bishops and the monks, though, now hated me more than ever, for they were jealous of my excellence and my rectitude, as well as of my intimacy with the bishopa.

The bishops continued to look for ways to bring about my downfall, hoping I would perform some shameful act, bringing disgrace upon my position. So they laid traps for me, sending whoreboys to my room, or giving me gifts of strong wine. But I kept my honour: I gave arrans to the whoreboys, then sent them away without accepting their services; the wine I gave to the beggars of Quebec, who love such drinks. Then the whores and the beggars came to love me, and so, once again, in setting out to degrade me, my enemies merely made my virtue still more famous.

Their next trap took a different direction. As an archbishop, it fell upon me to be present at certain religious assemblies, and here I learned much of the One Religion, as I sat at the back behind the pulpit of the cathedral dressed in my archbishop's robes. These garments—for suddenly I realize I have not yet described them, yet they were extraordinarily beautiful—were made of a strong, yet delicate purple fabric, lined at the cuff and collars with ermine. The lining was not so wide, however, as that upon the bishopa's robes, nor was the stuff so thick, for her garb comprised numerous layers, giving the impression of tremendous bulk and solidity, although the bishopa was actually a very thin woman, and her ribs and hips jutted out against her skin.

Now, a part of every service was the recitation, in which a bishop would say a part of the Holy Code, speaking from memory. One day, on the Festival of the Eight Saints, the bishop responsible for the recitation said:

"This worthy festival reminds us that holy men, of great learning and worth, may come to us not only from our own land, but also from overseas. With this in mind, I would like to withdraw from the recitation, which is from the Book of Exodus, inviting that great archbishop who came to us from overseas to take my place." And he gestured to me.

I realized at once that this was an attempt to trap me, for if I refused, it would appear I was incapable of giving the recitation, and therefore was not so worthy and learned as the bishop had said. Yet if I accepted his invitation, everyone would see I was unable to recite any lengthy passage from the Book of Exodus, for, although I had read the tales in that book, which is to be found in the First Testament, I preferred to study the meaning and general content of the stories, rather than committing their words to memory and mindlessly reciting them.

Still, it was one thing or the other, and since I had great faith, and was not one to shrink from a challenge, I immediately stood and replaced the bishop behind the pulpit, while he retreated to the back. There were a great many people in the congregation—at least a thousand and a half, I should say, for the cathedral was very large, and it was at least three-quarters full—and they looked upon me, waiting, for some moments, while I tried to recall the story of Exodus. I remembered there was talk in it of the prophet Moses, who had a great staff which could turn to a snake, and this prophet led the Hebrews, and was a prisoner of the Egyptians.

"From my lands," I said, "comes much learning that is lost or forgotten here. You have all heard, and perhaps memorized, the book of Exodus. Yet the tales I tell now, as divinely inspired as the Code you all know, are not told in your version of this great book. Hear the Holy Code, and be terrified."

I then waited a few seconds, and in my mind I prayed the knowledge I needed would be given to me. Sure enough, my faith was rewarded, for God placed in my head a mysterious missing part of the Book of Exodus. Many present, misinterpreting my introduction, believed this came from a version of Exodus used in my own land, but it did not, for although the story was divinely inspired, it was given to me at that very moment, and placed into my head, piece by piece, even as I spoke. Yet, it was God's will that they believed about the story what they did, and it was not my place to contradict God.

I do not remember the exact wording of the tale, for as I have said, I am not a believer in rote learning. Yet I will share with you now the essence of the holy yarn.

While he was in Egypt, Moses had a magical staff, which could be transformed into a serpent by speaking a certain holy word. This serpent was more than fifty feet long, and its mouth could swallow a man whole. In colour it was a sickly yellow, and it smelled of vomit and dung.

Now, the Pharaoh spoke to Moses, saying: "If you wish to be free, show me some magic." Then Moses threw his staff to the ground and said the secret word, and the staff turned into the deadly snake. But then all the Pharaoh's magicians, and there were more than a thousand of them, threw down their staffs also, and these also turned into snakes. But the snake of Moses attacked the other snakes, and though there were a thousand of them, it killed them all, and, with its powerful head, tossed their bodies this way and that, ripping them open, and sending their poisonous blood in all directions.

The blood from the dead snakes landed on the magicians, and where it touched them, their skin began to blister and bubble, then it formed a hideous black scab, which quickly spread over their bodies, until each magician had turned into a writhing mass, covered with a single giant scab, and in the middle of the scab was a human mouth, which screamed in horror and pain, spitting blood and bile, until at last it fell silent in death.

(On hearing this, the congregation gasped, and twisted in their seats, for the holy words struck at their very souls.)

When the Pharaoh saw what had happened to his magicians, he was afraid, and he ran off, telling his soldiers to stay behind and kill the snake. But when the soldiers approached the snake, it bit their heads, crushing their skulls between its strong jaws, then it slithered off after the Pharaoh, and Moses ran after the snake to watch what would happen.

The Pharaoh's palace was made of seven jewelled towers, each made with a thousand Sheet Walls, and a million cross-bindings, and each was more than twelve thousand feet in height. In the centre of these towers stood a great statue-city in the shape of a golden calf. Beneath this statue was a huge labyrinth, and the Pharaoh ran there, hoping to escape the snake. But the snake's tongue tasted the ground where the Pharaoh's footsteps had been, and it followed those footsteps, step by step. Moses, in his turn, followed the snake's slimy trail, hoping now to save the life of the Pharaoh, for Moses was a virtuous man.

Suddenly, as Moses turned a corner of the labyrinth, he came across a terrible sight. It was the body of the Pharaoh, whom the snake had caught. There was a hole in the top of the Pharaoh's head and a hole in the bottom of the right foot, for the terrible snake, on capturing the Pharaoh, had chewed into his head then burrowed through his body, emerging at his foot. The snake itself was nowhere to be seen though.

Then Moses heard a loud hissing behind him. He turned and he saw the snake, which had climbed the walls of the labyrinth and was ready to jump on Moses, for, having eaten the flesh of the evil Pharaoh, the snake itself had become evil and now wanted to kill Moses.

Moses knew he must say the secret word, for this would turn the snake back to a staff once more. But he realized with horror he had forgotten the word, and he would instead have to fight the snake with his bare hands!

Then the snake jumped on Moses, but Moses smote it with his fist, striking it in the belly. The snake was stunned for a moment, and fell back, but then it regained its strength once more and jumped at Moses' leg. Moses kicked the snake with his other leg, and the snake gave a hiss of pain. Then, as Moses prepared another kick, the crafty snake moved aside, so Moses kicked his own leg, and he fell to the ground in pain.

Thereupon, the snake reared up above him, preparing to strike with its poison fangs. But Moses used the same trick the snake had just used, and he moved aside at the last moment, just as the snake's great head was darting towards him. The snake hit the ground with tremendous force, and its fangs broke off.

Moses quickly grabbed these fangs and tried to stick the snake with them, but the snake whipped at his wrists with its tail, binding his hands together and forcing him to drop the fangs.

Then Moses bit the snake's tail and freed his hands, but as he did so, the rest of the snake, writhing this way and that as if in agony, placed itself in ten great loops around Moses, one loop for each commandment. Then suddenly it pulled tight, wrapping itself around him, squeezing with all its power.

The snake opened its great mouth, and Moses could see far down its throat, where lay the rotting bones and flesh of dead people. Slowly, inch by inch, the snake squeezed Moses towards its mouth. Moses struggled, but he could not break free, and soon he could feel the snake's foul breath over him and could feel its cold lips brushing against his head.

(When I told them of this, the congregation were most distressed, and many cried out words of encouragement to Moses,
saying, "Quickly, Moses—place your thumbs into the serpent's
eyes!" or "Hold its mouth closed with your strong arms, Moses!"
as though the story I was telling was real before their eyes, which,
thanks to God, it was.)

But then Moses had an idea, and he prayed to God for help. The
next instant a shining figure appeared nearby, and Moses recognized the man as Christ. Then Christ said to the snake, "O, snake,
which God has created, stop what you are doing!" Then Christ
spoke the magic word, and the snake once more became a harmless staff, which fell upon the ground.

Moses then took the staff and escaped from Israel and from the
Egyptians, because the Pharaoh was dead, and for this Moses gave
thanks to God in the highest degree.

Amen.

Now, this was the story as I told it before the congregation, except the fight between Moses and the snake was very much longer,
and so was the fight between the snake and the soldiers, and the
fight between the snake and the other snakes. The whole tale ran
for nearly an hour, and I used all my storytelling skills, producing
the terrible hisses of the snake, and the sound of the punches, and
making faces which showed the expressions of terror on the victims of the snake.

When I had finished the story, the congregation rose up, cheering and clapping their hands together in joy and appreciation, for
they knew this was indeed an inspired story from God. But the
bishops were angry, for they thought the story was too violent for
the common person (as if the stories of the First and Fifth Tes-
taments are not violent!), and some dared accuse it of being he-
retical, saying Christ could not have appeared to Moses because
Moses lived before Christ was born. To this I replied, in the first
place, I did not care for years, only for truth; and in the second
place, since Christ is immortal, He must have lived not only after
his physical death but also before his physical birth, and therefore,

in denying my story, they were denying Christ's immortality. And so those who had accused me of heresy found the charge suddenly upon their own heads, and those who did not retract their words paid dearly for it, you may be certain!

One very pleasurable task which fell upon me as archbishop was to hear the confessions of sinners. It was the custom, you see, for all the members of the assembly to come, one by one, to me, and to admit all the evil acts which they had committed. You would be astonished to hear the scandalous deeds which were performed in that small town. I found the admissions so fascinating that, after a time, I began to keep detailed notes, which I still show to my friends and acquaintances for their edification and amusement.

But do not think I approached my duties frivolously, for, having been made an archbishop, I determined to become a master of the craft and spent much time in study, learning all I could about the Holy Code, and memorizing two long passages, so the bishops would not be able to trap me a second time. One passage, which is from the First Testament, describes the symptoms of a terrible skin disease. The other, which is in the Fourth Testament, is the entertaining praise-poem *The Six Thieves and the Four Whores*. This poem I know by heart even to this day, for my memory is very retentive. If you do not know the poem, you must seek it out and read it, for it is a diverting piece; and yet it also tells us much of God's grace, for, at the very end, after the thieves and the whores have committed many shameful and sinful acts, they repent, and are forgiven by God, and surely, if they can be forgiven for such outrageous conduct, so can we all.

In fact, all the books of the Holy Code are well worth the reading, and I recommend them to everyone. Within their pages I learned of the one all-powerful God, the God With No Name, who is an indomitable ally and a fearsome and terrifying enemy. Those who befriend this great God may call upon him at any time to give them wealth or to destroy those of whom they disapprove.

There is much practical wisdom in these writings too. For example, they teach the warrior to love his enemies. And this is perceptive, for in loving his enemies, the warrior will be able to understand them; and in understanding them, he will be able to predict them; and in predicting them he will be able to conquer them and win their lands for his own.

In any event, I have now told you of the way in which I became very virtuous, and how my virtue engendered hatred in those jealous bishops. Next I will tell you of how their hatred at last resolved itself against me.

The Fifth Part

In Which I Tell Of How I Left Quebec, Leaving Two Griefs Behind

BY THE SPRING I HAD selected two stonemages who were to work with me on the *Grief*. One of these was an East American named Quebble Steech, and the other had come from Germany and was named Asken Hote. They had originally been employed by the bishopa to carry out repairs to the old cathedral and to other buildings around the town of Quebec. They worked very diligently, I will confess, but they did me a grave disservice, which I will describe in due course, so I have nothing good to say of them here.

I will tell now of the building of the *Grief.*

The first stage was setting the wall roots or foundation. For this, I had my myrmidons and slaves dig a great pit, fifty feet deep, delving out the area which the building would occupy. I then encapsulated the floor of the pit in Sheet Walls, shored with Seizure Lines, and heated it so it was fused into solid rock. I carried out the same procedure upon the walls of the pit—after installing pipes for the drainage of rainwater, of course, for I did not wish to create a reservoir!

Upon the floor of this pit, I set out a pattern for the interior and exterior walls, which corresponded to the shape which might be seen if the finished building were sliced horizontally in the middle of the lowest level of cellar chambers. The myrmidons brought rocks and earth, placing them upon the outlines, whereupon either I or one of my assistants would encase the rocks in Sheet Walls and fuse them at a great temperature with various incantations of fire and furnace, as I had done with the floor and walls of the foundation. An endless stream of carts and wagons from the alchemical merchants brought supplies for the enchantments—waxes and sepia inks and jay feathers and reticule leaves and horse chestnuts, all in such great abundance that the land was stripped of these resources for miles around.

All this, of course, is standard stonemage technique. What was more remarkable is that we used no winches or pulleys during the construction. Instead, the building proceeded slowly upwards, in two-foot segments, with each segment forming a cross-section of the entire building. I had made the walls very thick, so they might not only add strength to the *Grief*, but also provide a suitable surface for walking during the construction—so, if you can picture it, each cross-section of the building formed a maze of pathways, these being the tops of the partially completed walls. In a similar fashion, the great central ramp, which spiralled up through the tower, gave us access to the higher floors as we proceeded slowly upwards.

Now you will wonder how, using this method, it was possible to create the ceiling of a level—which, of course, served also as the floor of the subsequent level. The answer is very simple. When the walls were of a sufficient height, I would place a large and powerful Sheet Wall across the surface to be covered, save only for the central ramp, through which we gained access to each level. Then the myrmidons brought large quantities of rocks, evenly covering the area. I covered the rocks with a second Sheet Wall, applied more spells of fire and furnace, and fused them into a solid surface. The bindings were removed, and—piffeta!—the finished surface would drop a fraction of an inch onto the supporting walls.

Although I was anxious to complete the building, I was determined it should be perfect in every regard and the task should not be rushed. Therefore, after completing each floor, I spent several days decorating it, carving beautiful sculptures in the rock. I also added a fine carpet made from mashena, very like that which I had placed in the towers at Luthen but crafted in purple rather than red. Only when a level was as perfect as the abilities of mortals would allow did I permit myself to move upwards to the next stage.

Upon the outer walls, I bonded quartz in various colours—shades of pink for the skin of the king, and shades of blue-green for the sheets. All the exterior surfaces were then covered in a type of permanent sheet binding known as a Blind Veneer, which armoured the walls very effectively.

The *Grief* emerged slowly from the ground like some huge plant. Thus I had heeded the words of the great stonemage Henry Eagles, who wrote, "As a tree from the earth does the great tower grow forth."

The work proceeded in this manner for nine months or so, and we fused hundreds of walls and placed countless thousands of cross-bindings—although the design was so sturdy in itself that I believe it would have stood firm even without these enchantments. At last the winter came once more. The statue was now complete up to the centre of the chest, and yet I still did not know how to solve the building's two great problems, these being its property of speech, and the difficult angle of the right arm.

During the winter I turned my attention once more to the duties of my various posts, while simultaneously pondering the construction problems.

The speech was a secret feature, and so nobody knew of it, save only for the bishopa, whom I told in an intimate moment. The arm, however, was clearly detailed in the plans, though without the binding scheme, and, throughout the winter, my two assistants would frequently ask me how I planned to set the arm at such a pitch. When I told them I was still working on the plans, they shook their heads, telling me the angle was too steep, and no binding would reliably support the great weight of the arm. This, you see, reflected the inflexibility of their minds and their training. On hearing these objections, I assured them that, yes indeed, the arm would be constructed and in exactly the way I had drawn it.

Towards the end of the winter, my assistants saw my mind was still set upon building the arm in the way I had first planned, so they changed their tack, suggesting I could build the arm from some very light substance, such as paper over a wire frame, so it might be supported by the bindings over its full length,

I said, "No, I plan to make the bindings so powerful that the arm would remain in place even if it were made of solid lead."

They said, "Then you must resort to a cantilever design?"

I said, "Perhaps that is the method where you are taught, but I am a stonemage, and I did not study my craft at the great school of Eopan in order to use cantilevers."

At this they wondered greatly, knowing of no other way this task might be accomplished. And indeed, I knew of no way myself, but I had learned God cheerfully gives to His servants anything they might need, and since I was an archbishop, and therefore a servant of very considerable rank, I remained confident the answer would come to me, which it did, in the manner I will now describe.

I am in the habit of taking meditative walks from time to time, and one night I was walking around the streets of Quebec. I had just visited the newest floor of the statue, and I was contemplating the problem of the arm. I had not taken my myrmidons along, for the sound of their marching disturbed my thoughts. In place of their protection, I disguised myself, wearing my purple robes with the hood over my head. Yet my disguise must have been inadequate, for suddenly I heard a cry: "It is he! It is the Archbishop Yreth!" and before I knew it, twenty or thirty monks came running at me, and I was sure they meant me ill.

I was poorly prepared for a fight, carrying only my throwing-razor, but I noticed the leader of this mob was running some yards ahead of the rest, and he carried a great staff with a heavy gold top-piece such as senior monks carry in those regions. I quickly pulled my blade from my boot and flicked it towards him. It hit him square in the face, and he dropped the staff, screaming in pain. I instantly leaped forward, seized the staff and set to work on the rest of the monkish villains.

Now, they were confident, for they were many in number, but I had great faith in God and fought with a fury that astonished them, swinging left and right with the staff, and punching and kicking at their throats and groins. At last, those who remained took flight, calling me a demon in human form. Yet I knew it was God and not demons who gave me my strength and skill in combat. By contrast, they, who were weakened by Divine indifference, could barely fight, for instead of punching, they had only been able to slap at me with the palms of their hands or pull at my hair, such as children might do.

I then turned to the monks who lay upon the ground and examined their injuries closely. This was not because I am morbid, but because, like most people, I am both repelled yet fascinated by gruesome injuries, for they remind us how precious is the gift of life, and how close every one of us is to horrid death.

Some had received mortal wounds, and these I mercifully dispatched with my throwing-razor. As I went from monk to monk, I saw one lying on his back with his head tilted back into the gutter. I went over to look at him, but when I lifted up his head, I saw the back of his skull had been crushed and malformed. I had struck him several times around the head with the staff, you see, which had killed him instantly. Amazingly, there was no blood upon his bald head, which made the appearance of his wound even more horrible, for it made the skull appear like that of some hideous monster.

Of course, I shuddered to look at the sight, but it also made a strange impression on me, although I did not realize the meaning of it at first.

My myrmidons arrived soon after, and took the rest of the monks away. The treacherous monks were then given to the care of surgeons. When they were recovered, I committed them to the wire for their crimes.

A few days later, I once again returned to the problem of the *Grief's* right arm. As I was working, the image of the monk's head appeared before me once more, and suddenly I saw that, just as the monk's skull had been crushed into a new shape, so might a certain type of binding, which is called the Lasser Sphere, be malformed to follow the contour of the right arm of my *Grief*.

The procedures involved in this transformation are very complex, but the principle is simple enough. The Lasser Sphere is the strongest of the twelve essential gossamers, but it is also the most difficult to construct, because it will distort if other bindings are placed within the volume it encloses. In the normal way of things, it is an inviolable rule that no other binding should be placed within a Lasser Sphere, save only for another Lasser Sphere placed symmetrically around its centre. Yet my plan now was to defy the common wisdom, placing other types of binding through the centre of the Lasser Sphere, thereby pulling its surface inwards so it might assume, more or less, the shape of the arm.

Experimenting with this method, I soon found that, with a little effort, the Lasser Sphere could be distorted into a vast array of forms, and working on a small scale I distorted the gossamer to resemble a potato, a turnip, and a sort of cactus shape. Later I used this novel method, which I named Yreth's Transformation, to create countless architectural marvels.

Hear this, though: on my eventual return to Cyprus I explained my method to Pycan of Inteda, who was the master thaumaturge at the great building school in Eopan, where I myself had studied. I said to him that, if he wished, he might teach the method to his students, providing only that he respect the name I had given to the new binding. You may be sure he was grateful for the technique, yet so jealous was he of my ability that he changed the name

I had given to the method, calling it not Yreth's Transformation, but "Spherical Synthesis," and he later claimed it was a traditional technique and had been used for centuries. So, even to this day my divinely inspired method is known in most parts as "Spherical Synthesis" (may the name rot the mouths of all who speak it).

In any case, Yreth's Transformation was the technique I used to bond the right arm to the statue. I carefully applied interior bindings of various sizes until the outer binding conformed precisely to the contour of the mighty sculpture. That arm stood firm at an angle of forty-five degrees, exactly as I had seen it in my wonderful vision. And, as I had stated to my disbelieving assistants, the enchantment was indeed strong enough to support the weight of many tons.

As for the statue's speech, I considered a number of ingenious solutions. One involved placing two slaves in the head of the statue, and having them speak the message through a great horn which led down to the mouth. While one slept, the other could repeat the message, and vice versa.

Another solution involved training large quantities of starlings to speak the words simultaneously, for these birds have a remarkable ability to mimic human speech. My idea was that breadcrumbs and lard should be left about the *Grief* at all times, providing food for a great flock of these trained starlings, and their natural chattering would sound as if the mighty king's voice was coming from all directions. In addition, since these birds are quick learners, other flocks of starlings which might fly to the *Grief* seeking the food would learn the words from the native flock. This concept, however, carried one obvious flaw: at night the birds would fall asleep, and King Thyatus would then fall silent, whereas I wished him to speak always, through all hours of the day and night, providing an eternal statement on the dangers of the mouse.

In the end, I settled upon a third solution, and this was to imitate the works of nature. That is to say, I would give my statue vocal cords and a tongue of sorts.

Thus, within the throat of the statue, I placed great reeds which vibrated when air rushed through them from many holes I had hidden beneath folds in the stone. This deep sound was then carried to the mouth, where it was further modulated by a series of wooden tubes, each tuned and shaped in order to produce a certain syllable when a lever was depressed. So the first tube made the sound of "Oh," the second made the sound of "Hhhh," the third the sound of "Ooo" and so on, with the action of each tube tripping the mechanism of the next.

For the mouse, which I wanted to speak also, I used the same technique, but employing smaller reeds, so the voice of the mouse would be high and squeaky, while that of Thyatus would be low and majestic.

This then was how I solved the final problems of the *Grief*, and a few months later, the structure was complete, to the utmost wonder and admiration of all who beheld it. On that day, people ascended the central spiral ramp, and then the wide staircase leading into the head, and looked down in awe as they saw that even the great towers of the cathedral were far below them.

Then, when there were many people gathered in the head of the statue, including my dear bishopa, and as many more people watched from below, I opened a trapdoor and climbed down the stairs into the Wind Room, which housed the speech mechanism. There I set the apparatus in motion, and instantly the great king and the fearsome mouse began to speak.

The speech was an absolute success, and even though only a soft breeze was blowing, everyone could clearly hear the king as he said, over and over, "Oh, who will relieve me of this mouse?" and the mouse replied, "Ho ho. Thyatus—victor over men, but conquered by me."

The bishopa, the dignitaries, and all those present marvelled at this mechanical speech, and agreed I was not only a great stonemage, but also an engineer without parallel.

For some reason I cannot explain, the voice of the mouse turned out to be very much deeper than the voice of the king, but this only served to make the creature appear more sinister, and I was delighted this accident came about, even though it was contrary to my original intentions.

Some people claimed the speech was unintelligible and sounded like the moaning of an agonized elk, and these cruel rumours have followed me back to Cyprus. But you may rest assured there is no truth to them. Any truly careful listener could easily hear the words, and the speech of the *Grief* was frighteningly natural, as if God Himself was speaking down from on high.

During the months which followed the completion of the *Grief*, there was more unrest among the monks. At the roots of this dissent were the events of a half-year before, when I had killed several monks in self-defence and killed a few others upon the wire. Well, the other monks of the New Carolingian Order took umbrage at these deaths, forgetting that the victims had first tried to kill me. The monks provoked riots among the townspeople and blocked roads, and they tried to set fire to the *Grief*, which they said had been a shameful waste of the church's money.

Still, I am not easily moved to violence, and so I endured their insults for a time, for it is written in the Holy Code that, if you are struck upon the cheek, you should turn your other cheek to your attacker and let him strike it also, and only then should you let forth your fury.

Yet my restraint did not impress the monks by so much as one grain, and mindless hatred continued to swell within their ranks. Many priests and bishops joined their movement, and they often formed huge crowds and marched upon the cathedral or the *Grief*, chanting words of hatred for me.

They became so troublesome that I was forced at last to seek the bishopa's advice. She told me—reluctantly, for she was a gentle woman—to let the myrmidons settle the matter. And so I did, taking twenty of the most troublesome monks, five priests, a bishop, and an abbot and hurling them from the cliffs at Quebec Peak.

So ended the revolt. But the other bishops, instead of being grateful peace was restored, complained to the bishopa that I had handled the affair too roughly and the rebels should have been arrested and not killed, and so on. They said justice must be observed and I should be tried for murder.

Once again, of course, the truth of the matter was simply that they hated me and wanted me gone, but I cared nothing for their views, since I commanded a strong army, and I also had the protection and support of the bishopa. We were still very much in love, she and I, and would spend, I estimate, one-third of our waking hours taking delight in the joys of the bed.

Then, one day, a terrible tragedy occurred. During a moment of the greatest intimacy, the bishopa gave a gasp, saying: "Oh! I cannot see!"

"Shall I bring you your magnifying glass, bishopa?" I asked, for she had very poor eyesight.

"No," she replied. "I truly cannot see. Everything has become brown and my head feels dizzy."

"I shall call a surgeon," I said, and I jumped from the bed—I was very fit and virile—and dressed myself, instructing the bishopa to dress herself also. But she did not move, saying there was no sensation in her limbs.

Now at this I was alarmed, for, although the bishopa suffered from a swelling of the joints which often made movements difficult, I had never before seen her in such a state as this. Then I realized she was dying, and she needed not some surgeon to prod and cut at her body, but a divine who could administer to her spirit.

I knelt down and began to speak the special prayers which one of God's representatives must speak when a person is dying. And the bishopa smiled sweetly and nodded as she heard me saying these words, for she knew she would soon be in heaven. A few minutes later she said: "May those I have killed forgive me." And then her breathing became very shallow as I pronounced more of the magical prayers. Then she passed wind with a great sound— which was no common flatulence, but the passage of her soul from her body—and suddenly she was dead.

I quickly opened the window, so her soul might have egress from the room, then I dressed the bishopa's body in her night-cloak and her robes and set her in her bed, covered by sheets and supported by cushions.

There were many treasures in the room, and I quickly set about gathering some of them together. I forgot to mention that, in her last moments, the bishopa had also said to me: "Yreth, I would like you to take all of my treasures and my myrmidons and keep them as your own, or sell them if you so desire, and leave this place as soon as possible."

Contrary to her wishes, however—and may God forgive me for this—I did not take them all, but rather claimed only a few jewelled ornaments, some rings, a gold book stand, and a few other items which had sentimental value to me. I wrapped these things in a bed sheet, so they might be more easily carried. In addition, I took the bishopa's pendant, which was part of a tusk set in gold and which she wore always around her neck.

I knew I was in great danger, for, once my enemies discovered the bishopa was dead, they would try to have me killed. Therefore I locked the door to the bishopa's chamber, and, dragging the bed sheet behind me, I made my way to my own quarters. I then summoned some myrmidons from the Northern Guard. I instructed one group to carry all my possessions and chests of money to my ship, which was still moored down at the shore. I gave them orders to stay with the ship and protect it, and I sent written instructions to the crew to sail south to the Passage of Zebedee, then north along the western coast of America to the port of Great Tasker, at which town I would eventually arrive by land. I picked this site, incidentally, because I had heard Great Tasker is a fine, rich town, and very far from Quebec.

I ordered the rest of the myrmidons to find their comrades, and to assemble on the road beyond the northwest side of the city, which was the area furthest from the river. I told them to go there in small groups in order to attract less attention.

Next, I sought out the bishopa's bodyguards, who were known as the Behemoths. Huge and fearsome myrmidons they were, eight feet tall, and completely black in colour, with chests like bulls

and hides as rough and hard as stone. They were formidable fight-
ers and cunning in all martial affairs, yet simple-minded in their
loyalty. They served the bishopa not for her rank but because she
wore the tusk pendant around her neck. This, then, was why I had
removed the item from her dead body, for the Behemoths held
the pendant in great reverence and would serve any person who
wore it.

I showed them the pendant, which I had placed around my
neck, and commanded the bodyguards to follow me and protect
me. Then I walked from the cathedral, through the outskirts of the
city towards the northwest road.

The Behemoths guarded me well. Their movements through the
streets appeared chaotic, yet this was deceptive, for, as I watched
their frantic running, I noted, at all times, at least five bodyguards
stayed very close to me, ready to take my orders. Also, no matter
where they ran, each bodyguard would look back at me every few
seconds, to make sure I was safe.

We were almost out of the city when a bishop spotted me. His
name was Gyappo, and he was a great friend of the Archbishop of
Ulph—who was a great enemy of mine. Gyappo had command
of the Winter Guard, a body of around two hundred myrmidons,
and he was very smug about this post. Twenty of these myrmidons
were with him. When he saw me with the Behemoths, he was immediately suspicious, and called out:

"Archbishop Yreth! Where are you going with the bishopa's own
bodyguards?"

"That is not your concern," said I, and I kept walking.

"It is indeed, Archbishop Yreth," he said. "Now come here and
explain yourself."

I ignored his impudence and still kept walking.

Well, he was having none of that, and ordered his myrmidons
to stop me by force, which was very foolish of him, for he must
surely have known the power of the Behemoths. In any event, his
myrmidons came running at me with spears raised, whereupon
my bodyguards, instantly spotting the danger to me, gave terri-

ble screeches and rushed into battle. Some charged headlong at Gyappo's myrmidons, while others leaped upon them from the rooftops.

Even in their frenzy, though, five Behemoths stayed by me, forming a circle around me, and looking in all directions for any ambush which might be planned, yet also twitching in their eagerness to join the battle. Meanwhile, the rest fought with a strength and ferocity which Gyappo's guards could not match. I saw one Behemoth scoop up a myrmidon in his arms, then smash him upon his knee, dispatching him with one blow. Another bodyguard leapt upon a myrmidon, who collapsed under the weight, then stamped him into submission with his huge feet.

Gyappo's myrmidons fell one after another. Soon the Behemoths were fighting two or three against each smaller myrmidon. Now they used different tactics. Instead of delivering hard blows, they circled their prey at a distance, using their greater reach to inflict damage with their claws, while remaining out of the myrmidon's striking range. They seemed almost to take pleasure at the myrmidon's futile efforts, and little by little they tore at him, until he was dead upon the ground.

In a few short minutes, all the myrmidons were destroyed, and our friend Gyappo had long since fled. My Behemoths had received only minor scratches in the fray, and were barely winded by their strenuous efforts. Indeed, by the time we joined up with the Northern Guard, who were waiting by the road some miles from Quebec, their energies were completely recovered.

I marched away from Quebec with a powerful fighting force under my command, as well as the fortune in treasure the bishopa had paid me or bequeathed to me in her dying breaths. This fulfilled the holy vision I had seen nearly two years earlier, for I had now received wealth from the bishopa which was at least one hundredfold that which Eon Vulpine had taken from me, and when I considered my situation, I was delighted beyond measure.

That is to say, I would have been delighted beyond measure if I were not so overcome with grief at the death of the one I loved so very dearly.

In her sweet memory, then, I will end this part here, and I ask of the reader that he or she might share my sorrow by remaining silent for a few moments before turning to the next part.

But then we shall forget her, as I was forced to do, for fear that the continuous contemplation of my tragic loss would drive me insane with the terrible heartache it brought.

So it was that I left two griefs behind at Quebec—my great statue, and my near-inconsolable sadness over the death of the bishopa. I have often thought this coincidence would make a fine poem, and one day I will write it down.

But enough—let us all now bow our heads in respectful silence for a time before we continue.

The Sixth Part

In Which I Tell Of My Travels Through A Great Forest And The Events Which Followed After I Left It

A S WE TRAVELLED AWAY FROM Quebec, and darkness fell, we saw great flashes coming from the sky behind us, and lights streaking overhead. Then came huge explosions from the road miles ahead of us, and we saw tongues of flame leaping up halfway to the zenith.

At first, I thought this to be a heavenly omen, but then I realized the truth of the matter: the Archbishop of Ulph, who was second in power only to the bishopa, had ordered the ballista gunners in the cathedral towers to fire their explosive javelins and rockets in the direction of my escape. The barrage continued for many hours, with javelins exploding ahead of us at first, and later both ahead of us and behind us. Fearing the javelins would eventually strike the middle of my host, I ordered the myrmidons off the road and into the Mississauga Forest, which extends for hundreds of miles.

We continued marching throughout the night, staying within the forest, for I knew the following day it would not be javelins the Archbishop of Ulph sent after us, but myrmidons, and even my mighty force was no match for the five thousand troops the archbishop now had at his whim. In the forest, though, I knew my army would be very difficult to find; and if we were found, my Behemoths could use the location to their advantage, leaping up into the trees, and then down upon the enemy.

To further increase my safety, I had the slaves follow up the rear, brushing leaves over the tracks left by the myrmidons. So meticulous was their work, that, in my opinion, not even a master tracker would have been capable of detecting the passage of my great army.

The next day it began to rain, and this shower turned, in the course of hours, into a thunderstorm of exceptional violence, which persisted into the next night. I was not afraid at this, for it seemed to me that God was sending a fearsome warning to my enemies, but nevertheless I became very wet from the rain as it splashed down from the trees.

The storm subsided the following morning, but the rain continued to fall, and it made our marching a very miserable affair. I was exhausted, for I had taken only a few hours of sleep in the night. I was also hungry, for, while my army carried a good supply of the foods a myrmidon eats, there was nothing there for me. I had only a small satchel of food, consisting of three churney cakes, a wedge of cheese, and a few pieces of white-raspberry, wrapped in a grape leaf, and those provisions which my myrmidons carried for me were meats and foods of such a sort that must be cooked before being eaten. As you may imagine, in such weather as this, making an ordinary camp fire was impossible, while an uncontained magical furnace would send plumes of steam and smoke wafting above the tops of the trees, providing my foes with a marker to my location which could be seen for many miles.

So, then, I ate very little, wore heavy wet clothes, and marched for long hours. Soon, this strain made me weak, and an illness fell upon me. At first, I felt very cold, although at times I felt hot, and the heat seemed a pleasant relief. I thought these feelings would pass as we continued our march.

We were still marching west, but then a great foreboding came over me, and I sensed my enemies were close behind us. Therefore, I ordered my troops to change directions, and for the next day we marched north at double speed. During the course of this travel, my illness grew worse, and I felt terrible cramps in my bowels. Also, I developed a fever, and I felt very hot, (and this time the sensation of heat was unpleasant) yet the cold rain which fell upon me seemed to provide no relief.

My memories of what happened next are indistinct. I remember tripping a number of times and then being carried in the arms of one of my Behemoths, and I remember being attacked by a great flock of a ten thousand huge ducks, and shouting orders for my myrmidons to take to the trees, because the ducks, with their webbed feet, would be unable to perch there. The ducks were some fevered hallucination, certainly, yet I believe my orders were real enough, for I remember my frustration when I saw the myrmidons were not fighting as they should, but instead were milling around in confusion.

I do not know if I told my Behemoths to seek help, or whether they did so on their own initiative. Neither do I know exactly how much time passed between the onset of my sickness and the events I am about to describe, although on thinking the matter over later, I calculated it must have been at least two days, and perhaps as many as six. In any event, I will tell you my next clear memory.

I was lying in a hut, upon a bed made from sticks and moss. Several Behemoths were around me, crouching, for the ceiling was low, and two men were feeding me with herbal soups. These men looked very strange, for they had dark skin, and narrow eyes, yet even in my sickly state I knew at once that they were Chinese!

You may think this very improbable, for even such open-minded authorities as Libbins declare that no Chinese remain upon the face of the world, but if you talk to Americans about the matter, as I later did, you will learn that small bands of these magical folk still live upon that continent, hiding in remote places, far from the towns and cities.

In just a few days, my sickness abated, and I was able to walk around. The hut was situated in a small encampment, consisting of five dwellings constructed from earth and pine tree branches. Here there lived a total of perhaps fifteen Chinese. The women were beautiful and wore robes of woven flax, dyed in earth tones. The men wore paint of various colours and patterns upon their faces, in the way we might do during Nutmeg Week.

Their language was strange and amusing, and resembled the chattering of squirrels. I was enchanted by these gentle folk. I examined their lifestyle meticulously, comparing my observations to those written accounts of the Chinese with which we are all familiar.

We are greatly misinformed on many so many aspects of these people. For example, the stories say the Chinese eat with sticks. They did nothing of the kind, but rather ate with hands and knives as people do everywhere. Neither were they at all fearsome, but, on the contrary, were very gentle, kind and sweet-natured, and they lacked the capacity for anger.

Their food consisted mostly of roots and berries and leaves and herbs and other things from the ground.

Their tools and utensils were primitive: their soup pots were made from strips of wood, with a circle of stone for the bottom. Their knives were chipped stone.

They also kept little wooden cages, within which were numerous small, plump birds. The Chinese were a very happy people, and often laughed and pointed at the little birds, as they hopped around, and they fed the creatures from their own meagre food supply, which was mostly nuts and berries as I have already said.

However, despite my amusement at their simple ways, do not think I looked down on these folk. I knew that beneath their simple clothes and tools, the Chinese were a wise and magical folk with much to teach me, if I could only find a way to learn from them.

I listened carefully to their talk, hoping to pick up their language, but I could make out no word I understood. There were many questions I wished to ask them, and I tried to talk to them many times, shouting as loud as I was able, but they understood nothing of our speech, always using their squirrel language in its place.

I tried imitating their sounds. They listened to my words with interest and pleasure, laughing and replying with their own sweet exclamations. But, as yet, I could understand nothing.

Later, as they sat around their fire and sang a song, an inner voice seemed to speak to me. "Yreth," it said, "listen with your heart." So I listened in a different way, closing my eyes, letting the sounds waft over my ears and allowing general impressions to form.

Instantly, visions appeared in my mind. I knew with certainty they sang the story of their people. In my mind's eye, I saw Chinese emperors and wizards from long ago, and mighty armies clashing.

I realized I had discovered the secret of the Chinese language. Its words are a series of emotional exclamations which speak not to the mind, as our language does, but instead exert a direct and magical influence upon the feelings and the soul.

A short time after the song was over, I tried talking with one of my Chinese friends, who was now scraping at a piece of bark with a stone knife. I used my new method, *feeling* my words rather than thinking them, and selecting the sounds that, in my opinion, best captured their mood. After I asked my questions, I pointed to him and made gestures with my mouth and hands, indicating I wished to hear his reply. Again, once I ignored the sounds of his speech, a translation of his meaning came clearly into my head, and I found we could now communicate perfectly.

I asked first, "Who are you and why did you save me?"

He said, "I am known as Drem the Great, and I am a sorcerer. Our group are among the last Chinese in all the world. We are powerful wizards all, and we use our magic to travel from king-dom to kingdom, seeking out righteous persons who need help, such as yourself."

"How do you know I am a righteous person?" I asked, making such sounds as I thought would convey the message.

"We know much about you," he replied, still working his piece of bark. "We know your name is Yreth, and you have been wrong-ly treated by others who are jealous of your great talent and ability. And we know you have created glorious buildings of unmatched beauty in Quebec, and far-off Luthen, and Cyprus too."

When I heard that, I knew all he said about being powerful wiz-ards was true, for how else, except by magic, could this man, living here in the forests of America have known of my works in Spain?

I asked him no more questions. I thought it best to begin my communications slowly. And, in any case, he had taken his piece of bark and walked away from me. I anticipated further dialogues, where I might learn the long-lost magical secrets of the Chinese, which are reputed to have been very great.

But, alas, it was not destined that I should learn the secrets of Chinese magic, for the next day, when I awoke, I was alone in the hut. The Chinese had silently departed.

Had they gone into the forest, blending into the trees? Had they used their magic to transport themselves across the world? I do not know. But I felt privileged to have seen these mysterious, magical folk and spoken to them.

Just a year ago, I sent a letter explaining my discoveries about Chinese to that great philosopher and linguist Ducambe Aletto. He replied that my rapid and successful decoding of the myste-rious Chinese language was "incredible, in the truest sense," and he doubted whether he or any linguist alive "could achieve such a total understanding of an unknown language in the course of a few short minutes," as I did. He even urged me to take up the study of linguistics. I am too busy to do so, but I was flattered at the suggestion.

After my encounter with the Chinese, I travelled west with my army, and we continued in that direction, in good weather, for a week or so. We encountered no enemy forces, and I was eventually emboldened to strike south once more, in order to join the road. So I left the Mississauga Forest and East America behind and entered the vast land of Manitario.

Only one thing remains to be reported of East America and its capital of Quebec, and that is the cruel fate which befell my *Grief*.

In my haste to leave Quebec, I had left behind a copy of my plans for that magnificent structure. Now, you will remember I had two assistant stonemages who worked with me. Well, those scoundrels kept my plans and used them to build further statue-towers which, in form, were virtually identical to mine, save only for tiny details of styling. First they built a woman, who was supposed to be the wife of Thyatus, a few miles along the river from the original *Grief*. She too had a mouse in her mouth, although there is no record of any wife of Thyatus dying from a mouse. Then they built statues, in various colours and sizes, of Thyatus's various children and relatives. Again, all had mice in their mouths. Subsequent statues depict more relatives, and some of Thyatus's close friends, and some of these have mice in their mouths, while others have bats or serpents, and the most recent structures show men and women eating grapes, or pears. To this day, they are known as griefs, although most depict figures in poses of elation or relaxation without any hint of the anguish for which they were named. I have seen pictures of the region as it appears today, and the proliferation of these works greatly diminishes the effect of the original *Grief*, which was intended to stand alone, staring hopelessly out across the land.

I have read, in Burnell's *Architecture of America*, that the area along the river Ram near to Quebec is now known as the Giants' Picnic, and Burnell says the designs are the invention of two brilliant East American architects, which as you know, is not true. He also says the reason the statues are eating such unusual foods upon their "picnic" is in order to convey the valuable message that "we must all sometimes consume things which disagree with us."

It makes me very angry to think of this, because that was not the meaning at all, and I fear such foolish words lead innocent people away from my dire warning about the mouse.

I will say no more upon the subject, for I grow red-faced with rage even as I write this, but I will ask this of the reader: if you should chance upon a copy of *Architecture of America*, and it is a common book to be found, turn to Chapter Eleven and find this offensive and thoughtless comment by Burnell, then strike it out with a pen, writing in the margin: "Beware the Mouse!" This is what I have done to every copy of the book I have yet encountered, and perhaps, in this way, the ignorant untruths spread by Burnell may yet be quelled.

In any event, I had left the *Grief* behind me, and looked now only to starting some new work.

Now, I will tell you this. A stonemage who seeks work with persuasions and entreaties is far less likely to receive it than one who enters a town with an army at his back. You may say all you will about the value of courtesy—and I prize it highly myself—but sweet words are no match for the eloquence of marching feet and glittering blades. This, at least, was my experience.

The next town I came to, after my adventures in the forest, was Molys, which lies on the river Flite, a minor tributary of the Ram. As I crossed the Molys bridge with my army, I saw the gates of the town closing, and spears appearing along the outer wall, but then, it seemed, they further considered the great size of my army and the gates opened once again.

When I entered the gates, the town officials came forward to meet with me, and they told me what a great pleasure it was to have an archbishop of my stature pay a call upon them. These words, of course, were insincere: theirs was no pleasure at all, but a great terror, for every town tries to cheat its church of its rightful tithes, and all live in dread of the day when the church discovers their dishonesty and extracts payment by the blade.

In any case I quickly assuaged their fears.

"I come not as a tax collector, but in my capacities as a

stonemage," I said. "Your town, while clean and brightly coloured, lacks the spiritual element which a great cathedral would confer."

Now, here they were full of promises that such a cathedral would certainly be built, and they sang the praises of the idea, saying: "It will be a sight to behold. By this time next year, a mighty cathedral will grace the very centre of the town."

I said: "Next year can fly with the geese! The cathedral shall be completed by next month. Further, you will pay me two thousand arrans for the task."

At this they were astonished, but they agreed readily enough, asking me if they might see the plans for the structure.

"You may not," I said. "The cathedral will be built by divine inspiration. I shall use no plans." Then I commanded them to set aside a suitable area in the centre of the town where I might commence my work.

Now here they hesitated and fussed about the difficulty of finding such a site, and they told me of the great value and age of, so it seemed, every building in the town. So, finally, I simply picked a building (which, as providence would have it, was the great mansion of one of those town officials, with its surrounding grounds) and I commanded my myrmidons to tear it down and dig a great pit in its place.

I instantly began my next construction, the design for which did not yet exist, although as I placed bindings and had my myrmidons move soil and stones, the shape slowly formed in my mind. I decided the cathedral would be in honour of Saint Elifax the Mariner, and would be formed in the image of a great ship, complete with billowing sails and mighty crossbows. It would be more than three hundred feet long, with masts two hundred feet high.

Now, you are probably wondering why I wished to create such a wonderful structure in so short a time as a month.

Well, there were two reasons for this. First, I wished to challenge my talents. I was beginning to feel as if there were no design I might not transform into a building of some sort, and the challenge of attempting to complete the work in so absurdly short a time seemed to make the task more worthwhile.

Second, I was concerned the Archbishop of Ulph might still be pursuing me, although it was more than five weeks since I had left Quebec, and, technically, the town of Molys was fifty miles outside his diocese. I reasoned it would take at least a month for word of my presence to reach the Archbishop, and for him to send an army of sufficient size to tackle mine, so I had that long to build my new cathedral in safety.

As it happened, I need not have worried, for, after the death of the bishopa, the archbishop was faced with more troubles from those terrible monks who lived in Quebec. He needed all of his myrmidons to keep the peace in Quebec, and he dared not send a large army in pursuit of me and my little band.

Only a few months later, I heard, there was a great uprising in Quebec, and Ulph had many people killed—not just monks, but also many innocent townspeople who did not deserve to meet an early end.

The following year, Ulph was made bishopa, and not long after, I am told, there were diseases in Quebec, and a sudden plague of big black flies, and also a fire which destroyed the famous egg shop near to the fountain.

Truly, then, it can be said that God left Quebec when I did, and if you go there today, you will find only the shell, the broken ruins of a once-great city. For while the place may be large and prosperous, with rich crops and many more people, yet any bishop who is honest (and these are a rare breed!) will tell you Quebec has lost its soul, and the great religious paintings and sculptures which are so common there today are merely a mask to hide the corruption beneath, as the corpse-painter's pigments make skin appear to be pink and healthy, hiding the ghastly pallor of dead and rotting flesh. So it is, then, with Quebec, for God's curse fell hard upon it.

And that curse fell also upon my enemy, the Archbishop of Ulph, now Bishopa of Quebec, who was forced to live a long life in these cursed surroundings. And if uneducated folk thought well of him, it is only because, as he sat shadowed from God's love, he sought the love of people, sending paid rumour-mongers far and wide, spreading word of his good and charitable deeds and his great statesmanship. Yet those who knew the man personally must surely laugh at these tales, for the character in these stories is very far removed from the real man.

But this talk is mere flotsam, and bears little weight upon the true thrust of my account—unless it is to show that not only were all my actions just, they were also divinely guided, and those who opposed me placed themselves also in opposition to God.

So, there I was in Molys, and I believed pursuers would soon be close upon my heels. Therefore, I wasted not an hour before setting to work.

I will not explain the details of the construction, for I have already told much of my methods. I will tell you this, though: to look at the complex shape of the ship and its great billowing sails, most stonemages who understood my methods would guess hundreds of bindings had been used in their construction. In fact, I used only five Yreth's Transformations and eleven Eternity Stakes for the principal structure, but these were used with the utmost efficiency.

Economy is one of the highest virtues any stonemage can attain in his designs. How easy it is to set massive grids of wefts, enchantments and bindings and toss rocks upon them like sand upon glue paper! Yet how much more elegant is the design which accomplishes the same end with but a few well chosen gossamers. And it is for this reason I hold the stonemages of the new school in such low regard, for they lay their enchantments like butter, and while their works are huge and impressive to the untrained eye, yet there is little real craft in it, as any true stonemage will tell you.

Now, an interesting thing happened while I was in Molys. One day, I felt thirsty, and, seeing a pail of water at a nearby doorway, I picked it up and took a drink. At this, the door burst open and the owner of the bucket came running out to challenge me.

At once, my Behemoths, who always travelled with me, gave roars of anger, and bared their great teeth, but this fellow cared nothing for them, and walked towards me as bold as you please. He had a hunk of cheese, which was his luncheon, in one hand and a large stick in the other.

"Put down that pail," he said. "Who do you think you are!"

"I am the Archbishop Yreth," I said. "And you would do well to stop where you are, my friend, for these stalwart companions of mine have short tempers."

"So do I," he said. "And I should give you a thrashing for stealing my water." Then he tried to push past my Behemoths.

Well, they were having none of that! A Behemoth struck him with the back of its hand, and threw the fellow back a good six feet. But this just made him the angrier.

"So, Archbishop, you think you can steal the drink from a man's lips!" he said. "Well, why not take my food too." Then he threw his cheese at me, and it struck me hard upon the face, giving me a bloody nose, and causing my right eye to swell up.

When my Behemoths saw this, they instantly leaped towards this man, their claws out, desiring only to kill him and to tear his body into pieces.

I quickly bade them stop, and I walked to this man and spoke, saying: "But for my intervention, you would certainly be dead now. Do you wish to know why I spared your life?"

And he said, in a surly way, "I think you will tell me, whether I wish it or no. Why, then?"

I said, "Because, although your actions were foolish, driven by such false rumours about me as you may have heard through idle gossip, yet they were also most brave, and this is a quality I witness all too rarely in these sorry times. So, although I am a great archbishop and you are but a humble townsperson, I greet you now as an equal. You have earned my respect, and my friendship."

On hearing these words, he was amazed. He said, "I had heard you were a greedy coward with no morals, Archbishop Yreth. But I see now these rumours were false, and you are actually great and compassionate. Well then, if you give me your friendship, I will give you mine. I am Lyvell the merchant."

Here we shook hands, both right and left, and we entered Lyvell's shop, where we consumed much wine and ate much food. I soon discovered he was a good and honest man who had been cheated by many of the people of Molys—for this is the way of the world.

I realized his earlier anger at me, and his desire to injure me with the cheese, was born of an unsatisfied desire for vengeance. So I compiled a list of names of those who had done him wrong, and that very evening we paid visits upon them all, Lyvell and I and my army, and we punished them for their wicked deeds, tearing down their houses, and confiscating their property, and breaking knees and arms and even necks, according to the severity of each injustice.

It was a long and profitable night that passed before Lyvell's desire for vengeance was finally satiated. In all, more than eighty people had been punished (or several hundreds, if their families were also counted) and the morning sun rose upon that sinful town to greet the sound of moaning and the smell of burning wood.

Now, you may say, "Yreth did right there, for it is good to help others who are in need." Or perhaps you will say, "Yreth dealt too harshly with those townsfolk." Yet, in either case, perhaps you wonder why this incident is worth the telling, for you have already heard, from other events I have recounted, that I am a righteous man, and a fierce man, and sometimes a bloodthirsty man, and above all a man with a great and charitable love for all people, be they distinguished or humble.

Well, here is why it is worth telling. It was because of that evening's work that I made a great discovery. I became aware of a subtle yet irresistible force, a destiny guiding my life.

I realized, through my meeting with Lyvell, that the unfolding of my fortunes seemed to be following a great scheme, and every event was a part of some great tapestry, in which the removal of even a single thread would have caused the pattern to be ruined.

Some people may scoff at these ideas, yet I tell you, with the utmost certainty, a great destiny is at work in the world, although few people are as fortunate to see its effects in their own lives as I have been.

But enough. I will say not another word about the conclusions I reached only after much contemplation and bewilderment, and instead I shall reveal to you the facts upon which these conclusions were based.

I shall do this in a new chapter, since the matter is important enough to merit the break. And indeed, some might say the matter merits not a chapter but a book, and they are right, for this revelation is one of the reasons I am writing this very book which you are now reading.

The Seventh Part

In Which I Show How Every Single
Event In Life Is Ruled By A Great Plan
And Tell Certain Secrets I Have, Until
Now, Hidden

AFTER OUR NIGHT OF VENGEANCE, Lyvell and I break-
fasted together, and we told stories about the places we had
been and the people we had met. I was astonished to discover this
man Lyvell was no ordinary merchant, but, in the course of sixty
years, he had travelled to all parts of the world, and knew many
persons of great rank.

Naturally, then, I asked him whether he knew anyone from my
own homeland, Rowel, on the Horn of Cyprus.

He said: "Rowel? No, I never went there. But on the Horn I
knew Huriband, the Duke of Oaster."

Well, here I gave a cry of surprise, saying: "That duke was my
first patron! I built for him a shrine outside Chattan, the city of
his birth."

Lyvell, in his turn, marvelled at this, for he had by chance visited this very shrine. He remembered it well, for he thought it a pretty thing, and now here he was talking to its builder.

I then told Lyvell of my career with the duke.

I was just eighteen years old, fresh from the school at Eopan, and I had gone to the duke to offer my services. The duke had stonemages of his own, but he magnanimously gave me the task of repairing the old shrine to the sprite Denn. It was a crumbling ruin, visited by nobody and tended by a mad old priest. I set to work with great energy. I dismantled the old shrine, replacing it with a domed building, decorated in blue and white glaze, with narrow gold piping and delicate stone roses. It was a just a small structure, you understand, and the only real difficulty was the interference of the priest, who uttered vile curses and imprecations as I worked and tried to strike at me with his stick.

When I was done, it looked very pretty there in the heart of the woods, and pilgrims started to visit anew.

When the Duke of Oaster saw the shrine, he was so delighted with my work he set me to decorating his castle wall with gold tubing. I completed this task, too, to his utmost satisfaction, and so, quite naturally, he desired I should remain with him, building such other structures as he might desire.

During those happy years, I built the baths at Oaster, and the hall for the Ropemakers' Guild, and the new barracks, and the eastern watchtower. And in Chattan, in addition to the shrine, I built the well-house, and the famous North Bridge, and I improved the sewers, widening them and adding many statues and decorations. All of these structures still stand, except for the watchtower, which fell during a storm.

The duke paid me a fair salary for these tasks (five arrans a month), and he also granted me a commander's post, setting me in charge of a body of myrmidons. I worked hard to learn the arts of war, and it has served me well ever since, as you have already seen.

The duke made me Commander of the Night Watch. I had twenty myrmidons under me, and my duties were light, for the myrmidons were keen and disciplined, and they needed only occasional instruction.

When I was a little over thirty, the uprisings began in Pheyos. Of all the regions of Cyprus, the Horn lies closest to Pheyos, and because Oaster lies upon the tip of the Horn, I began to find myself spending more and more time tending to the demands of my military post, and less time working on my construction projects.

One night, a stranger arrived at the gate. When I asked him to identify himself, he spoke rudely and impertinently to me, ordering me to admit him at once. I told him if he did not identify himself, he would not pass the gate. He said, in a brusque tone, "I am the Prince of Piapa."

I said, "You are certainly ill-mannered enough to be the prince."

Then he called me a scoundrel and a lover of whoreboys, and he told me to win a woman for myself, if one would have me.

I said "I have a woman, and a beautiful one too," and this was true, for I was secretly courting Setina, the Duke of Oaster's second-youngest daughter.

He said he knew my woman, and he said that, even as we spoke, she was sharing her bed with a lively black hog.

This remark angered me, for he had insulted not only my own honour, but the honour of the woman I loved, and of the duke, her father. I instantly told the myrmidons to seize the gutter-mouthed scoundrel and to toss some sense into him. This they did, and they threw him from one to another, while he screamed the foulest insults I have ever heard.

Then, quite suddenly, the flow of insults ceased, and his body became loose as they threw it around. I commanded the myrmidons to stop, and, upon examining the body, I saw the man was dead, although his neck was not broken, and he had only a few small bruises from his ordeal. I was greatly mystified.

Of course, in the light of my later learning, I know his death at that moment had simply been God's will—for He sets for each one of us a precise term, which may not be exceeded—and neither I nor my myrmidons were in any way responsible.

In any case, we threw the body on the dung hill by the west wall.

The next day, the duke came to me and told me to keep my eyes open for a man travelling alone and claiming to have business with him. This man, he said, was the Prince of Piapa, brother of King Bellay. He was travelling incognito, and his arrival was expected very soon.

Here I was most afraid, and I told the duke I thought I might have killed the prince by accident.

With great trepidation, we went to the dung hill to look at the body and saw, to our dismay, that the stranger from the previous night had indeed been the Prince of Piapa.

The duke was very angry at me and said he would kill me, but then I told him what the prince had said about his own daughter, and how my actions had been in the defence of the duke's own honour and of his daughter, and I told him of the love between myself and his daughter (for until that moment I had kept it a secret from the duke).

When the duke heard the truth of the matter, his anger was no longer towards me but towards the prince, and he said the prince's rudeness had earned him death many times over, and it was fitting he should have ended up as a corpse on a dung hill.

Then the duke clutched me to him, saying, "My dear, loyal Yreth! What a wicked day this is. In my heart, I too wished you should marry my daughter, but now that is impossible. You must flee, my man, for the king will have a terrible end for you if ever you fall into his hands."

"Could we not tell the king that the prince has simply disappeared?" I asked, for I was naive in those days.

"Ah, this would be my dearest wish," said the duke, "but life is not so simple. For you see, honour demands I tell the king the truth."

Then I asked him what would become of Setina, and he said he would never allow my love for her to be sullied by that of another man, and instead he would marry her off to some wealthy merchant. (And I heard later he had kept this promise to me.)

Then he gave me ten arrans and let me escape to the west, while he delayed the king's pursuit of me.

Now, if you think back, you will remember, when I spoke of my first arrival in Luthen, and at the court of Gavor Hercules, I said I had travelled west seeking inspiration for new works of architecture. And this was true, but my travels were also inspired by Bellay, the King of Cyprus, who had offered a bounty of one hundred arrans—and later, I have heard, six hundred arrans—to any person who would deliver me to his justice over the death of his brother.

You will perhaps think I should have revealed my status as a fugitive at the outset of my tale. But I reasoned—wisely, as it seems to me—that, had I spoken of this at the start, such a tale of princely murder might have prejudiced any reader against me, making me appear brutal and ignoble. Yet now you have learned so many other things about me, it will be plain my involvement with the death of the Prince of Piapa and my hasty escape afterwards is by no means a reflection upon my own virtue or upon my strict code of honour.

The accidental killing of a royal personage is merely one of those events which happens, from time to time, to every one of us.

So there it is. The darkest secret of my early years is told, and now I may continue to tell of my meal with Lyvell.

As Lyvell and I discussed my adventures with the Duke of Oaster, I became nostalgic, for I owed the duke a great debt of gratitude. I wondered aloud about events in Oaster, and about the fortunes of my first patron.

Here Lyvell was wonderstruck. "It is very strange you say this," he said, "for not a week past I happened to meet a merchantwoman of my acquaintance who has lately returned from those very parts. The news is bad, for the duke was recently stripped of his title and driven from his own lands by the king."

(Now, I should point out here that my companion had been misinformed. It was not the Duke of Oaster who had been driven from his lands, but that rogue the Duke of Imandello. Still, I believed it was the Duke of Oaster, and it would be many years before I discovered the truth of the matter.)

"How did this horror come to be?" I asked.

He said he did not know, but it was often the way of kings to dispossess their most loyal nobles in this way.

Then I said, "It is very wrong for any king to dispossess one as noble as Duke Huriband. For I will tell you, that duke would make a better king than Bellay."

Lyvell laughed here, saying, "Then go there with your myrmidons and see it so. You are already a builder of churches. You might become a builder of kingdoms. And a toppler of them too, if you desired it."

Now, although he spoke this in jest, and we did not talk more upon the subject, still his words stayed in my mind, ringing like great bells, and they set me to thinking.

I spent the following days in meditation. Slowly, I began to become aware of a pattern behind the events of my life. I will explain this.

As a stonemage, I must work constantly from a plan. Even when I was young and newly out of school, I could look at a plan and see, in my mind's eye, the image of the final construction. Of course, this is the very essence of my profession, and there is no good stonemage who would not be capable of the same thing.

As I became more experienced, however, I learned a new skill. I found I could look at a building and, even though I might have no previous knowledge of it, I would quickly understand the plan behind it. For example, when I first saw the newly finished Arch of Lechittes, I saw not the great stone columns, nor the jewelled keystone, but the intricate network of bindings which holds the structure in place.

With the passage of time, this ability, which is based on keen observation, intelligent analysis, and divine guidance, became more acute. Gradually, I gained the ability to see the "plan" behind other things. So, if I was staying at an inn and the cook spat upon me while I was eating, I would not just shrug it off, but would instead think to myself "Ah, there is a reason for that!" and would instantly set my mind to analysing the cook's motives. Only when these motives were clear to me would I settle the score with my throwing-razor.

Given my unusual abilities in discovering the plan behind all things, I suppose it was inevitable I would eventually attempt to deduce the plan behind my own life, and the great plan behind Life Itself. The first stages of this analysis are based in pure logic.

Let me now share with you my reasoning, and, since I am educated in these matters, I shall do so in the classical form demanded by the finest logicians. So:

The First Proposition: There is a reason to all things.

Proof: For the proposition to be false, either there is a reason to nothing or there is a reason to some things but not all things.

The first of these options we know to be false, for in everyday life we perform certain activities for which we can give good reasons. So at least some things have a reason.

Therefore, for the proposition to be false, there must be a reason to some things and no reason to others. A thing that happens for a reason can be said to have that reason as its cause. But what is the cause for a thing that comes about for no reason? We say it has "no reason" as its cause. It follows that "No reason" is itself a reason, so even a thing that happens for no reason in fact has a reason.

Since nothing can be reasonless, there must be a reason to all things. So the First Proposition is proved.

The Second Proposition: Every person's life unfolds according to a single and coherent purpose.

Proof: We know from experience that life consists of a single series of events, and though we may profoundly wish some-and-such a thing had not occurred, or may wish some other fortune had fallen upon us, yet these wishes cannot be granted, for at each juncture where a decision must be made between several alternatives, there is only one alternative we can choose, no matter how we might desire them both.

This simple truth is summed up in such common phrases as "You cannot be in two towns at once."

Secondly, we know that, in life, the passage of time is continuous. It is not possible to leap across the years, as the hero does in *The Adventure of Toe the Mariner*, going from one's third birthday to one's thirtieth. Neither can a portion of one's life be omitted, even though this may be desired (as it is, for example, by the victims of torture). Even while we sleep, time continues to pass steadily, and when we wake it might be the next morning, but it is never the previous morning.

From this we learn that every life has two important properties: it is single (consisting of only one series of events) and it is coherent (it is unbroken in time).

Since life itself is fundamentally single and coherent, it follows that all its attributes must also be single and coherent. One of those attributes is life's purpose. Therefore life unfolds according to a single and coherent purpose, and this proves the Second Proposition.

(It has been suggested to me the above argument might be misapplied, so one might say since life is violent, its purpose must also be violent. Or since an apple is green, its purpose must also be green. Such reasoning must be ignored, since its intention is not to enlighten but to confuse, for who ever heard of a "green purpose"? Let no one use the precious tool of logic for such flippant entertainment, but let it rather be used to uncover eternal verities, as I have used it in my reasoning, so people everywhere shall be enriched.)

The Third Proposition: Through the analysis of the events in life, one may discover life's single and coherent purpose.

Proof: This proof is very elegant. Think about the first and second propositions. Now think about the fact that you are capable of thinking about them. Because we have analysed and thought about those propositions, it follows we have the ability to analyse and to think.

Is there, then, a reason we should have this ability? Of course! We know from the First Proposition that all things have a reason. Why, then, do we have the ability to think and reason? There is only one possible answer—so we *can* think and reason. Therefore, since the ability to analyse exists for a reason, it is only proper we should use that ability.

Next we must ask ourselves, where must the ability to reason be used? Why, in life, of course (for I doubt there are any dead people reading these words!).

But remember: according to the Second Proposition, life is single and coherent. It follows that the analysis of any event in life is identical to the analysis of life itself. And, since life's purpose is a part of that life, and life is, by its nature, singular, the analysis of life's events is identical to the analysis of life's purpose. Therefore, in discovering the purpose for any event, we come closer to discovering the purpose for life as a whole. Thus, the Third Proposition is proved.

The Fourth Proposition: Those persons capable of discovering the purpose to their life must do so, thereby enabling them to achieve that purpose with greater efficiency.

Proof: If a person has the ability to discover his or her life's purpose, then it follows (from the First Proposition) that there is a reason for the person to have that ability.

Since there is a reason for the ability, the ability must be used, for if an ability is possessed but never used, then it exists for no reason, and this, as we have seen, is impossible. Note that the requirement to use this ability is not a moral obligation but a logical one. It is a logical necessity that an ability which is possessed should be used, and not to do so is to the detriment of reality itself.

Yet let us now take a step back. For we have shown the utmost necessity of using those abilities of analysis which we may possess to analyse the events of life in order to understand its purpose.

But what is the reason for this activity? (For, like all other things, it, too, must have a reason.) For the answer, I might easily turn once again to the stark rules of logic, but in this case I do not think it necessary, for the answer is very obvious: we must understand the purpose of life so we might attain the goals required for that purpose with greater speed; for, just as a sighted man may find a doorway more immediately than a blind man, so a person with greater awareness may achieve the goals of his life more readily than one who lacks this awareness. This, then, proves the Fourth Proposition.

Now, the foregoing reasoning was carried out over several days, while I sat in my chamber in a large house I had occupied, together with my myrmidons. During this time, I ate little, and drank only watered ale, for I wished all my faculties to be focused upon the intellectual battle which I was waging. I did not leave my room during those days—not even to relieve my bowels or bladder (I accomplished this task from the side window, which is the custom in most of America). Nor did I take any interest in the events of the town, nor in the great cathedral I was still designing.

When I had finally finished my pondering and had proved the Fourth Proposition, I was well satisfied, for now, at last, I saw how perfectly the events of my life had led to that moment.

For example, it was necessary in the scheme of things that I should have trained as a stonemage, for, as I have said, this gave me an understanding of plans and designs, even those which formed the design not to a building, but to a life.

Also, it was necessary I should have been forced to leave the service of the Duke of Oaster, for this drove me to greater glory with Gavor Hercules. And the unfortunate events which occurred after I left the employ of that great man raised me to still greater heights, because my escape across the Atlantic resulted in my command of a great and powerful army, and this would certainly never have occurred had I stayed in the kingdoms of Europe.

All of these remarkable insights were fresh and buzzing in my head, and I was anxious to share them with another person. Although there were many people in the town who treated me with great courtesy, there was only one I had come across who I considered a friend—the brave merchant Lyvell; therefore I swiftly made my way from the mansion which was my home to the shop where Lyvell carried out his business.

On arriving there, I found the shop to be gutted, the insides burned, the door broken off, and the windows smashed. When I asked the neighbours to tell me what had happened, they said that, two nights earlier, a mob of all Lyvell's old enemies and their families had come to the shop and destroyed it, and had then beaten and strangled the old man, leaving his body in the gutter.

It was distressing news, you may be sure, yet it also brought me a strange satisfaction; for I now knew that the purpose of the life of the merchant Lyvell was to give me the news of the duke, and to set me reasoning upon the purpose of my life. It was only natural, then, that his life should end once it had achieved this worthy goal, which, in God's mercy, it did. And this, in turn, provided yet further evidence of the truth of my new theories.

I returned to work on my cathedral to Saint Elifax the Mariner, and quickly finished it. It is a construction whose simplicity and elegance doubtless brings admiring gasps even today, for, as one approaches the structure from a distance, it seems very like a real ship upon the waves, and it is only upon closer inspection the waves reveal themselves as tiny hillocks, upon which grow blue spinewort.

The ship has no entrance door from the ground, for I built it to be entirely watertight, exactly like a real ship. Those who wish to gain access to the great interior hall must climb one of the long ladders of rope which dangle from the sides of the vessel, and then enter by the deck. Neither does this render the building useless for the old or the crippled, as some have speculated, for those cripples who truly wish to enter will frequently find the strength to climb those ladders is bestowed upon them by God, and, upon reaching the top, they discover they are entirely cured of their maladies, so, instead of entering the cathedral to pray for the restoration of their health, they pray instead to give thanks to God.

As I had planned, the cathedral was built in exactly one month. This would not have been possible but for the great size of my army, for I set every one of them to working on the cathedral. Some went to chop trees and gather rocks and magical ingredients, others transported the wood, while others hauled it into place and fixed it with pegs, which I later reinforced with bindings. I do not think I would have spent more time upon it even if I had had twenty years at my disposal, for although the wood (which was the principal material for the structure) was rough-hewn and splintered, yet this places in the mind the image of the sufferings of Saint Elifax as he drifted upon the waves. It is the same for the sparse interior of the building: it is like a great ship's hold, with neither rooms nor windows, but merely a wooden staircase descending from the deck, and it reminds us of the saint's privations during his voyage (for it is written: "he had not grain nor drink nor any soft thing for his head to rest upon"), and the ladders remind us of the path to heaven.

As to the sails, in this I made a minor error, for I set local workers to make real sails of canvas, which were then lashed to the masts, and held in a billowing state through the use of the binding scheme I described earlier.

Unfortunately, a storm struck a few months after I left Molys, and the strong winds wrenched off the sails and broke the masts. (I heard about this years later) And yet it seems to me this is a very trivial loss, for the same might well have happened to the real Saint Elifax, just as it happened to me at the Duck Islands, and the lack of masts and sails reminds us of the terrible storms which he must have endured—and not merely the storms of rain and wind, but also the storms of fury which later fell upon him from Uss Naygler and the so-called Legion of Toads.

When the month was up, I left Molys, and though I was given my two thousand arrans for my builder's fee, yet I left the town carrying a much greater treasure, which was the treasure of Knowledge, and an understanding of the way in which my destiny was meant to unfold. And I am sincere in saying that this knowledge is worth far more than two thousand arrans, and more even than five thousand. In fact, I would gauge its worth at close to ten thousand arrans, yet it was given to me for the price of a few bruises inflicted by a piece of cheese.

This thought I find a very remarkable one.

The Eighth Part

In Which I Tell Of My Travels West From Molys And My Coming To Learn Of The Principle Of Directional Exhaustion

I F YOU DID NOT READ the previous chapter (and I am speaking here of the four great proofs contained in it), but skipped over it, because its contents seemed too tedious or difficult, I urge you to turn back to it now, and work through it, with a pen and paper in hand, if it is necessary. Work slowly and steadily, absorbing all the arguments I present, for they are very important, and they will certainly change the course of your own life, as they did mine. But more, you must understand these arguments if you are to understand my motives for the decisions I made at that time.

When you consider the matter a little, you will see my four proofs show the existence of destiny and providence, and show the value of prophesy, and of omens, and dreams too, *for there is no thing that does not happen without there being some reason to it.*

There are those who will say attending to dreams and omens is mere superstition, but this is too narrow a view. Heeding dreams is not superstitious—only heeding them foolishly. So, to pick an example which befell me just weeks ago, if you dream of a pig wearing shoes, and draw from it (as a fool would do) that you will have both food and footwear in abundance, then this is no more than superstition.

Yet, examine the image intelligently and you will find within it a profound message, or even many profound messages. In order to determine which message is the true one, it is necessary to apply the same good judgement you would extend to any important matter. For example, my dream of the pig conveyed five possible meanings:

First: That it would be an act of piglike greed to buy a new pair of shoes.

Second: That, if I were buying shoes, I should seek out those of pig leather, and not ox leather.

Third: That I should be wary of bacon or pork for the next while, for it is apt to be as tough as shoe leather.

Fourth: That I should beware of animals which might steal my shoes.

Fifth: That I should be careful not to splash my shoes in the mud because it might give them a foul smell, like a pigsty.

On considering these options, I reasoned the first and second to be inappropriate, for I was not considering the purchase of shoes. The third also I rejected, for pork and bacon give me the burps and I eat them only rarely. The fourth message seemed to lack relevance. The fifth message, then, was the true one. I therefore took great pains to stay away from puddles, and my efforts were rewarded with a pair of shoes that are clean and dry today, even though it has rained several times during the past weeks.

Truly, I would no sooner ignore a dream than I would walk along the cliff edge with my eyes closed, and this belief in the importance of dreams and omens is not superstition, but logic, proved with logic and reason, and those who deny this also deny reason, and thus, if they do it consciously, they are clearly lunatics, and if they do it unconsciously, they are clearly fools.

I will return to my tale now, and you will see how I applied my reasoning in the field, as it were.

On thinking about the news which Lyvell had given me, I realized it was my destiny to restore the fortunes of the Duke of Oaster—for if this were not so, then why should I have received news of the duke when I did? I realized also that, with my great army, I had the means whereby I might attain this destiny. Still, questions remained: What route should I take to find the duke? And how urgent was his need for my aid?

First, I considered the question of urgency. I reasoned that, since I had heard the news of the duke's dispossession quite soon after the event had occurred (within a year, I guessed), I should therefore hurry to his aid. This line of thinking, unfortunately, was wrong, as you will see later.

Next, I considered the route, and here my reasoning was much more inspired. Was it ordained, I asked myself, that I should scuttle back to the River Ram, find ships, and cross the Atlantic Ocean once more? Clearly not, for providence had left many enemies in my wake, and this can only have been in order to discourage my return along the route I had taken. What is more, I had sent my own ship to sail around the coast of America to the western town of Great Tasker. I had planned to travel overland, meeting the ship at that faraway port, and now it seemed that destiny supported my plan, for were I to do otherwise I would lose a good ship and large quantities of gold and jewels.

So, I must travel west across America. But how, then, was I to help the duke, whose lands were an ocean away to the east? The problem was vexing. Nevertheless, I resolved to place my faith in God, and to travel west, though it might fly in the face of reason, for I knew, somehow, an answer would be given to me.

My faith was soon justified. I was no more than a few days from Molys when I came to a river with a wooden bridge and a bridgehouse beside it. I banged upon the door of the house with my staff, and a short time later the bridgekeeper answered it. She was an old woman dressed in shabby robes. Her hair was white and very long, but the wisdom in her eyes reminded me of the pictures I had seen of saints and prophets.

I said to her, "I wish to cross the bridge with my myrmidons. Is your bridge a strong one."

"Strong? Yes indeed," she said.

"How many myrmidons do you estimate it will support at one time," I asked.

"Six," she said. "But perhaps eight. Although if they were my myrmidons, I would send no more than two across at a time, and if I were in a cautious frame of mind, I would send only one, and I would tell each to step carefully with it, avoiding those planks which have a spongy feel to them."

These words did not inspire my confidence. Since it was past nightfall, and it is not wise to cross an untested bridge in the dark, I ordered my myrmidons to put up camp on the near side.

Now, the bridgekeeper's name was Cayglee, or Caglee, or one of those American names. Her given name, in any case, is unimportant. What is important is, thanks to my great faith and all my recent contemplation, I was filled with goodness and humility, and I decided I would invite this simple bridgekeeper to dine with me in my tent. I had intended this as no more than an act of charity, but once again, just as it happened with Lyvell, great truths were revealed to me during the course of the meal.

(Truly, around that time, hardly a month seemed to go by without my receiving a great revelation or making an astonishing discovery. My good fortune was quite remarkable.)

We were eating a fine meal of wined lamb, which the slaves had prepared, when I decided, on the spur of the moment, to tell this woman of the problem I faced.

"How," I said in my frustration, "is it possible for me to travel west but return to the east?"

She replied, in a strange, faraway voice, that I might do so through the knowledge of Directional Exhaustion.

I knew at once that this old woman had been possessed by the ghost of Saint Elifax the Mariner, who, I instantly perceived, was grateful I had built a beautiful cathedral in his name in Molys and wished to help me in my travels. Some people, upon realizing they were talking to a ghost, would have become afraid, but I stayed quite calm, and simply asked those questions which I wished answered.

"I have never heard of Directional Exhaustion," I said. "Explain the principle."

Here she shook her head and said she could not do so. "It is a great secret which was imparted to me long ago when I was initiated into the Navigator's Guild, long before I became a bridge-keeper."

I pressed her to confide in me, but at first she would not be persuaded, saying she had sworn never to reveal the secret to another soul.

I said, "You are clearly a woman of great honour. But tell me, by whom did you swear this oath of secrecy."

"Why, by God," she replied.

"Then, as an archbishop, I command you to tell me," I said, "for it is God's will you share your secrets with his closest servants."

"That is reasonable," she said. "Yet I also paid a high price in gold to learn the secret."

Here I knew the saint's ghost was testing me, so I offered him, or her, gold if she would tell me the secret. We negotiated for some minutes, and finally agreed a price of two hundred arrans was fair. I gave her the money, and she told me the secret.

Naturally, since I paid a high price for the secret myself, I do not intend to share it at no cost in this book. Therefore, I have reproduced the secret only in the most expensive edition (which, as I plan it, is to be bound in cream deerskin with gold lettering). If that is the edition which you, the reader, are now reading, you will be pleased to know your edition was well worth the additional expense, for it contains this extra secret, worth two hundred arrans, and you may rejoice in the fact that the following paragraphs are reproduced only in your edition. The cheaper editions will not contain the secret at all, moving instead to the next leg of my travels.

The bridgekeeper (which is to say, Saint Elifax) began by telling me that, in life, the most important qualities are those of persistence and tenacity. "With these two traits," she said, "all obstacles may be overcome. Do you agree with this?"

I told her this view certainly tallied with my own experiences, and she said "Ah, I see you have a good mind. Many people stumble upon that first part."

She then went on to talk about the nature of travel. "If you travel westward," she said, "you believe, perhaps, that you are moving further and further west."

I said, yes, this indeed was my understanding.

"Your belief is mistaken," she said. "The truth of the matter is that you are always in the same place. The name we give to this place is 'here.'"

This made complete sense to me, and I told her so, for I had often wondered how people could speak of "here" as a single place, when, apparently, its location changed as the speaker moved about. But almost instantly a question entered my fast-moving mind.

"How, then, is my apparent motion to be explained?" I asked.

She replied, "What changes is not your position but the quality of your surroundings, the 'here' you occupy. Every place has a unique quality which is a mixture of the properties of north, east, west and south. Points further west have more 'westness' to them and less 'eastness.' Points in the south have more 'southness' and less 'northness.'"

"Therefore," I said, "there must be some point on earth which has none of these properties."

"That is certainly true," she said, "and what a terrible place it must be."

I agreed with her wholeheartedly there, and we sat for a few moments shaking our heads and thinking about this nightmarish place before she continued with her explanation.

"When travelling in any direction, the traveller changes the properties of the 'here' he occupies. So, if he is travelling west, the place gains in westness but loses eastness. Is that clear?"

"Completely clear," I said. "But tell me, is there a limit to how much westness a point can have?"

"Ah, you have cut to the very nub of the matter," she said. "Such a sharp mind! Yes, indeed there is a limit. And this is where the personal characteristics of perseverance and tenacity come into play. For, if the traveller has sufficient perseverance, and the tenacity to endure hardship, it is possible to travel so far west—or, for that matter, so far in any other direction—that the point he occupies becomes saturated with westness. In other words, it is not possible for the point to become any more westerly. If, upon reaching that point, the traveller goes but a single inch further west, a very remarkable thing happens. By the grace of God, all the westness of the point will instantly drain away to nothing, leaving room for thousands of miles of continued westward travel."

"Where does all the westness go?" I asked.

"An intelligent and perceptive question, to be sure," replied the bridgekeeper. "All the westness is poured, as if through a siphon, into the property of eastness."

"The traveller, then, is transported in an instant from a point of utmost westness to a point of utmost eastness."

"Exactly so."

"The moment of this transference must be a very jarring one," I said.

"In fact, it is not," replied the bridgekeeper. "Indeed, the passage from the limits of western travel to the limits of eastern travel is barely perceptible, save by the most astute and delicate perception."

"It follows, from what you have told me," I said, "that a traveller proceeding west from a given city, must, if he travels far enough in a westward direction, return to his starting point."

"Yes! Yes! You understand perfectly!" she said, delighted at my intelligence.

"Let us consider this phenomenon from a practical standpoint," I said. "I wish to return to my homelands in the east by travelling west. The question is, how long would such a journey take? Ten years? Twenty? A hundred? A thousand?"

She said, "The Western Extremity lies in the Pacific Ocean, approximately three thousand miles west of the American coast, and just a few score miles beyond the island of Sira Tereen. From there, you will be transported to the Great Eastern Sea, at a point some five thousand miles from the eastern coast of Dranseet, and from there, if you wish, you may travel overland to Europe. In any event, the journey from the west coast of America to the eastern coast of Dranseet, passing through the Western and Eastern Extremities will take ten weeks, if your ship is fast and the winds are favourable."

"It seems remarkable," I commented, "that by applying one's efforts in one direction, one may be taken into another. Yet perhaps the process is like kneading dough: through the constant pressure upon the dough, and strong will of the baker, the bread will compress no more, and becomes not smaller, but much larger than it was to start with."

"I have heard numerous people try to explain the underlying principle many times," said the bridgekeeper, "but never has anyone expressed it so exactly or so simply."

There you have it then. This was the secret of Directional Exhaustion which Saint Elifax imparted to me.

The next day, when it was light, I crossed the bridge with my myrmidons, which took some hours, but which was accomplished without the loss of any myrmidons or slaves. The bridgekeeper was nowhere to be seen during this time, but as we marched away over the hills beyond the river, I happened to look back in the direction of the bridge. To my astonishment, I saw it had vanished, together with the house. Also, trees had appeared at the spot where the house had been, and the shape of the river had changed. Furthermore, I saw a grey bird flying over the trees, and the appearance of this bird in many ways resembled the old bridgekeeper.

Now, a sceptic might say I simply looked back in the wrong direction and saw some other part of the river, but this was not so, for my sense of direction is excellent, and even though we took a winding route over the hills, I do not think I would have become confused in this way, and if I had become confused, I would have admitted it. As proof of this last fact, I will tell next of a navigational error I did make, and the tragic consequences of it.

The Ninth Part

In Which I Describe A Series Of Terrible Calamities Which Befell Me

For three months I marched westward across the continent of America with my myrmidons. I was filled with a great energy to return to my homeland and to unleash my myrmidons upon the enemies of the Duke of Oaster, who, as I believed it, had been greatly wronged by the king.

My plan was to march across the continent until I reached Great Tasker, upon the western coast, where I would once more take possession of my ship (since I judged it should arrive ahead of me by several weeks).

So, I marched for a month or so, and at last I came to a great body of water, which I took to be the Pacific Ocean. I followed the coast, and then inland a little, until I came to a town, which I believed to be Great Tasker. It had been a very tiresome journey, and I was grateful it was finally at an end.

You will imagine my dismay, however, when I entered the town and discovered this was not Great Tasker, but the town of Sudbury, and this body of water, which I had taken for the Pacific Ocean (for it certainly seemed very flat and peaceful) was merely one of the huge lakes in the region.

And if you do not have a sense of the geography of the world (for in this ignorant age, many people do not), this means, instead of crossing the entire American continent, I had crossed only a fifth part of it, and was sitting in the heart of Manitario, with thousands of miles of travel remaining to me.

Upon making this discovery, I was filled with a Sad Mood. I left the town again, and for many hours I sat on the shore of the huge lake, surrounded by my soldiers as I gazed out at the waves and splashed my feet, and, it seemed, the longer I sat, the sadder I became. I felt I would never return to my homeland. The way behind me was blocked by my cruel enemies, while the march ahead seemed impossibly slow and wearisome. And at the end of the march would come not rest, but a long and dangerous ocean journey.

It was all too much for me, and I felt close to weeping. I am a hardy soul, however, and not given to emotions of weakness. Instead, my sadness turned outwards, transforming itself like a mighty phoenix into anger. In my mind, I raged at the town whose presence had so cruelly tricked me, lifting my great hopes and dreams, only to dash them upon the millstone of hardship and crush them to the rancid flour of despair.

Then, I fear, my Sad Mood got the better of me, and I commanded my army to lay waste to the town of Sudbury so no trace of it should remain to sadden me further.

Here is how I did it.

I had my myrmidons surround the town, then I sent the Behemoths scaling the walls to deal with the guards patrolling at the top. Those great black brutes were excellent climbers, and were up those walls as quickly and easily as you or I might climb a ladder. Once at the top, they were dangerous fellows indeed, for they ran around the walls, and when they came upon a guard, why, they just gave him a swipe with their long arms, sending the myrmidons flying off the wall and tumbling to the ground.

With the walls cleared, the Behemoths returned to me. We then moved forward together, the Behemoths surrounding me to protect me from arrows or spears. When we reached the wall, I placed my hands upon it and began to remove the bindings which held it up. It took, perhaps, an hour to walk around the entire wall, removing every large binding I found, and replacing them with the same unstable Struts of Atlas I had used to destroy the three ships on the Duck Islands, for I find these bindings are ideally suited to the demolition of buildings. Then we retreated, and, after a few minutes, the bindings collapsed, bringing the walls down, together with a good many buildings which stood in the shadow of those walls.

Next, I advanced my myrmidons, telling them to kill any people they might see, and to remove from the town any items of gold or silver, or any items which contained gemstones, or any other small and valuable items.

This they promptly did, storming through the gates and setting upon the unfortunate citizens with a fury terrible to see and hear. Indeed, at times the spectacle was so horrible I was forced to place my hands over my ears and to close my eyes.

When the myrmidons returned, they bore a great fortune in gold, which I had them place in a large pile before me. We also captured many vats of sweet-oil, which is used in the manufacture of certain metals.

Most of the town was still standing, and, since I did not wish to go through the streets taking down the bindings on every house and hall, I ordered my troops to spread some of the sweet-oil upon the buildings, then to light great fires, so the town might be utterly destroyed.

Many people had escaped the assault and fled into the forest, but when I saw this, I called, "Ho! None of that!" I sent groups of myrmidons to encircle the refugees. The myrmidons quickly rounded them all up, then dragged them back inside the town walls, where they tossed them into the inferno. Some of these folk were nobles, and they pleaded for mercy, claiming they were closely related to the region's ruler. That was nothing to me, though, and they met the same fate as the rest.

The town burned for three days and nights, like a great bonfire. It was a jolly sight, I will confess, and it gave me a very slight, short-lived relief from my Sad Mood.

When the flames had subsided, I had the myrmidons divide up the treasure and place it in their packs. We took the remaining vats of sweet-oil too, for I saw it made a fine weapon. I marched my myrmidons southwest, along a great road which connected Sudbury with Enek Tireal. I could hear the singing of birds as we marched, and in my Sad Mood this was abhorrent to me. I therefore commanded the myrmidons to throw rocks into the trees to hit such birds as they might see. Also, I told them to sing songs of war as they marched, so the town ahead of us might hear our sound and be terrified.

There were travellers on the road. Most turned hurriedly and fled when they saw my advancing army, but some came fearlessly towards us, whereupon my myrmidons seized them and brought them to me, saying, "What shall we do with these innocent travellers?" Alas, I was still gripped by my Sad Mood, and I said "Hang them at once," and although the poor wretches begged and protested they had done nothing wrong, my heart was hard to their pleas, and I watched without pity as they were put to death.

Upon reaching Enek Tireal, I found the town had received word of my approaching army and had closed its gates and set myrmidons upon the walls. These preparations on the part of the citizens of Enek Tireal, while they might seem reasonable precautions to take in the face of such a mighty force, were the very worst thing they could have done for my Sad Mood, for they made me feel I was hated and reviled. Therefore, still under that mood's terrible influence, I commanded my myrmidons to do to that town what they had already done to Sudbury, which is to say, remove the valuables and use sweet-oil to destroy it utterly, leaving no trace. Once this was done, we marched away from the remains of the town, travelling at a leisurely and dejected pace through the forest for many weeks.

One day, while I was relaxing under a crab apple tree, still very much afflicted by my Sad Mood, my myrmidons brought a young man before me who, they said, had been found hiding a short distance away. I interrogated him thoroughly, and, before he died, he admitted he was acting as a spy for various officials of Manitario. These officials, he admitted, wanted to know the size of my army, so they might send a much larger force against me.

Unfortunately for my enemies, my Sad Mood had not diminished my cunning in any way. In fact, if anything, my mood focused my intelligence upon the task at hand.

Without an hour's delay, then, I ordered my myrmidons to march south. We marched for six days, passing, and destroying, many towns and villages on the way, as well as killing cattle, pigs, sheep, goats, geese, and any other livestock we found in those places. I shudder now to think of the ferocity of my Sad Mood.

Then, having left a terrible path of destruction in my wake, I ordered my myrmidons to turn westward once more, but to go with speed and subtlety. I knew my enemies would find the southward path and would think I had continued south through the forests there, whereas in fact I was proceeding west.

We continued west for a week, travelling with great stealth and discretion, although, according to the dictates of my Sad Mood, I was obliged to destroy five more villages, and hang several groups of merchant-travellers.

I thought I had fooled my enemies very well with my cunning stratagem, but, in my naive sadness, I little realized the extent of the treachery which was in the hearts of my unseen opponents. They laid a trap for me which was very wicked, for they knew, although I was afflicted with a great sadness, I was still virtuous, trusting and innocent, and I would not anticipate the depraved nature of their monstrous plot.

I will tell you of their trap now. It is a very gripping tale, and you will very likely sweat with fear as you read it.

As we marched west, I came, with my army, to the town of Grim. You may laugh at this name, for I too laughed when I heard it, yet it would have been better I had heeded the divine warning being sent to me by this word.

I approached the town without fear, my army at my back. My scouts had told me the town was small, with no more than two thousand persons. There were forests around, and mountains behind. The buildings were small and neat, with bright colours and many ornamental gardens. It was a pretty place, although, naturally, in my Sad Mood, I could think only of how it would look once it had been committed to the flames.

Since the town gates were open, I said to myself, "First I will have myself a good luncheon, then I will destroy the place."

As we passed through the town gates, though, we received such a welcome as I had not ever received before, with cheering and music, and with men and women throwing themselves down before me to kiss my feet. They showed no fear of me, as folk from other towns and cities had done, but instead showed only joy.

They set foods before me—even as I marched through the streets—and threw flowers, and placed garlands upon my myrmidons and my bodyguards.

I was pleased at the reception. No, I must be truthful, I was more than pleased—I was deeply moved, and at once I felt the ice melt from my heart, as my Sad Mood began to weaken. I said to myself, "Perhaps I will not burn this town immediately. Rather, I will wait a day or two and enjoy the fruits of the place."

So, I remained there, and whenever I wandered the streets the people cheered, and all about me were joyful faces. When I asked several townspeople the reason for their rejoicing, they said it was because, with my holy presence, I brought good fortune to their little town, at which words I made a holy gesture, applying a blessing of luck upon the crowd, and upon seeing this they cheered still more.

I struggled terribly with my Sad Mood during those days, for a part of me did not wish to see this charming town destroyed. I told myself I was planning a special destruction for this town, and I ordered my myrmidons to gather great piles of wood from the forest, which they placed against the walls.

While this work was going on, an old woman came up to me and asked me if I planned to burn the town and kill its occupants.

I said, "Yes, it is very likely I will."

I expected her to plead and beg for mercy then, but she did not. Instead she said, "Then we are truly blessed."

Naturally, I asked her to explain herself.

"It is inevitable every one of us must eventually die," she said. "Only the manner of the death is uncertain. It seems to me that being put to death by a revered holy man is a very godly death, and one to be grateful for."

I was astonished at her great faith in me, and, the grip which my Sad Mood had upon me loosened still further.

Now, for a time I remained cautious, and although I was soothed by these people, still I went about the town with my bodyguards around me. After a time, though, I began to feel foolish, and not a little cowardly, to go so well protected, so I bade my myrmidons set up camp some distance from the town, and I reduced the size of my escort, keeping only five Behemoths around me, a number which later fell to two, and then to none at all, for there seemed to be no need of it. Neither did any harm come to me from this action, for the people of Grim were all very peaceable and tame, and even without my Behemoths I felt no fear of them. In this, however, I was deceived, for, as you may well suppose, there was false dealing being done in that town.

I was one day sitting upon the steps around a statue which is in the marketplace of Grim, eating a delicacy called summer-and-winter. This is a type of fruit-ice made from fresh strawberries and snow. The snow is collected in the winter, then stored in caves until the summer months when the strawberries are out.

In any case, as I sat, my eye fell upon a very lovely young girl, no more than sixteen years of age, I should say. She was gazing at me, and I saw tears upon her cheeks. I said to her, "What troubles you?" to which she replied, "Archbishop, I wish in my heart to beg a favour of you, yet I know you have not the time to help a common person such as I am."

"Nonsense," said I. "Though you may be small and insignificant, yet I am not so proud that I will not hear your plea."

Upon hearing these gentle words of mine, she threw herself prostrate before me, saying, "Archbishop, my little baby son has died not two hours ago. They say the words of a holy man have powers to heal the sick and to raise the dead. Please, will you say these words to my dead son and raise him up to life."

I was touched to hear this request, and I said to the girl, "Your faith in me is very great, and, if God wishes it, will be rewarded. Lead me to your son."

Thereupon, she led me a short way, talking of her dear son and the untimely death he had met, until we came to a small house. She said her son's body was in the cellar, so I opened the trapdoor and climbed the ladder. But when I reached the bottom, a man seized me from behind, while another threw a liquid in my face.

I struggled very bravely, but the stench from the liquid was so powerful I found myself rendered insensible, and I think I remained in this state for some minutes. When I regained my faculties once more, I found myself lying upon the floor. Iron bracelets had been placed about my wrists, and these were fastened, by means of a chain eight feet or so in length, to a plate set in the floor.

The two men who had attacked me were standing before me, and I recognized them now as two officials of the town, named Midana and Reckdohl. I will describe them now, so you might imagine the scene with greater accuracy.

Midana was the older of the two, and he had thick white hair, which he wore rolled up in bush-bunches. This, indeed, was what had made me suspicious of him from the first time I laid eyes on him, for it is an arrogant thing for an older man to wear his hair in such a flamboyant way.

The other man, Reckdohl, was a few years younger than me. He had a weak chin, which is a sure sign of a treacherous disposition, particularly when its owner tries to hide the fact by growing a beard upon it as Reckdohl had done. Also, he had a high voice, which sounded like that of a woman.

I noticed both these men were wearing white silk sashes which I had never seen them wearing before. The significance of this was not lost on me, for I had seen men and women wearing similar sashes when I was in the bishopa's court. It indicated they were trusted agents of some great lord.

I knew then I had fallen into the hands of a powerful enemy and my situation was very dire. I looked down at my boot, to see if my throwing-razor was still there, but it was not. They had stolen it from me while I was unconscious.

As soon as he saw I was awake, Midana came over to me and helped me to my feet. Then he said, "Did you, Yreth, lay waste to the town of Sudbury, the holy shrine of Enek Tireal, and the towns of Chan, Indril, Diadril and Sleck?"

I thought to myself, "How do I answer him? Do I shout insults at the fellow as he deserves, or perhaps kick at him?" Then I thought, "No, Yreth, cast your dice with care. In such situations as this, it is best to be humble and polite, and to answer all questions with precision and honesty."

So I replied, "I did not lay waste to those places. The task was done by a group of myrmidons."

Midana said, "Were these myrmidons under your command?"

I replied, "In one sense, yes."

Then Reckdohl asked, "In what sense do you mean?"

"In the ordinary sense," I said, and I gave a very sweet and genuine smile to each of them, to show them I was a man of great charity.

Reckdohl asked me then, in his woman's voice, "By whose order did you carry out these destructions?"

"Not by the order of a person," I said, "but by the order of a thing."

"What thing?"

"A Sad Mood," I said. Then I told them all about my Sad Mood and how terribly it had afflicted me. I had hoped they would show sympathy for me then; however, they did not, for they were callous, insensitive fellows. In fact, they did not even believe my story of the Sad Mood.

Midana said, "We know you are an agent of some great prince. Tell us in whose name you carried out these terrible atrocities, or we will extract the information by means of torture."

I thought about this for a time, then I said, "My actions were motivated by my Sad Mood, as I have said. But since you ask me which great prince commanded me to carry out these actions, I will say it is the same prince who placed the Sad Mood within my soul."

They grew excited then, and said, "Which prince is this? What is his name?"

"Why, the Prince of Heaven," I replied. "The one true God."

They did not care overmuch for this answer, and they struck me about the face, then started to chastise me, in a very tiresome manner, for the wicked deeds I had done, and the many close friends and relatives they had lost in the towns and cities I had destroyed, and what a terrible thing it was, and so on.

Now, they spoke as if they were shocked and alarmed I could have caused so many deaths, so they might make themselves seem very virtuous and noble. However, I quickly perceived the true direction of their desires.

I said, "If you seek gold in compensation for your losses, you will be disappointed. What wealth I have, I have earned, and you may be sure my myrmidons will guard it well."

One of the men said, "I would not sully myself by touching your gold, for it is tainted by death."

I laughed at his hypocritical lies, and said, "I am pleased to hear that, my friend, for you may be sure you will never touch it. And do not think you will take it by stealth, either, for I am not such a fool as to hoard it all in one place. Rather, I have divided the gold into numerous portions, which each myrmidon may carry easily in his pack."

I think I was too wordy for their liking, because they then slapped my face three more times, and struck me upon the back with a cane. But I did not give in to the pain. Instead, I just repeated the words, "I shall not give you my gold! I shall not give you my gold!" over and over, which infuriated them, because they saw they would never overcome my great determination, and they pummelled me with their fists, while I, all too aware that a violent response might bring about my execution, was forced to endure this cruel punishment.

Then a plan entered my head. I said, "If you let me send word to my myrmidons, I think, perhaps, I might see my way to making you a gift of a small portion of my treasures. You may use the wealth as you see fit."

Midana pulled at my hair and said, "I have told you I care nothing for your gold. Now, tell us who commands you."

I said, "I will tell you, if you first let me send a message to my myrmidons."

Then Midana said, in a rude tone, "You must think me a very green leaf if you think I will allow you to send a message to your myrmidons. You will just have your forces rescue you and kill us all."

"That is not so," I said. And I thought to myself, "No, I would not have them kill us all, just the two of you."

You will notice how, even in my adversity, I remained honest. That is a very ethical thing, for they say honesty is the highest of all the virtues.

These days, you often hear bandit priests telling of how they have escaped some calamity or other through the telling of a convincing, well performed lie. For myself, though, I would not lie, even though it might save my life. It is much better to die as an honest man than to live as a liar, and somebody should take those bandit priests who boast they have told such clever lies, then slit their throats, so everyone may see how far their lies get them in the end.

In any case, I then said to Midana, "Do not fear my motives. My wishes are very simple. In my message, I will give the myrmidons my good regards." And truly I would have done this, although I would also have told them where I was and ordered them to rescue me, but I chose not to tell this part to my captors.

I went on to say, "Because my feelings for my myrmidons are of a strong and very affectionate nature, I would have to insist you do not embarrass me by reading the message I send, but you may be sure nothing but good will come of it." Which is to say, good for me, in so much as it would bring about my rescue and their well deserved deaths!

Still, despite all my clever words, they would not let me send a message, and they questioned me for several hours more, pretending they wanted to know who had sent me, but secretly trying to discover how they might get my gold for themselves. When they finally realized they were wasting their time, they departed, leaving me chained up in the cellar.

While they were upstairs, they talked between themselves. I have good ears, though, and I heard everything they said, even though they spoke in hushed tones.

Reckdohl said, "Let us kill him. He deserves to die."

Midana replied, "No no. That would be terrible bad luck. He is, after all, an archbishop, and only the prince himself may put him to death. And even the prince may only kill this man with his silver sword of office. To do otherwise would offend the archbishop's God, who is said to be very fearsome."

Then I heard Reckdohl say, "Well then, let us torture him, so his life becomes a living death."

But Midana said, "Even that would be unwise. We might perhaps slap him or poke him, but I think it would be dangerous to spill even a drop of his blood."

I was greatly heartened to hear this, and when the two men returned again a few hours later, and started to prod at me, I cried aloud, saying, "Oh! Do take care! My skin is of a very tender sort, and the slightest jolt is liable to send blood gushing from me."

They tried to pretend my plea did not frighten them, but it must have done, for they stopped hitting me, and started shouting at me instead. Well, shouting is nothing to fear, for it is only words and air. And indeed, if it is loud enough, and near to the ear, it can even be a pleasant sensation, for it tickles the insides of the ear in a highly agreeable way. At least, I find it agreeable, or used to, when I was younger.

So, they were there, shouting at me, saying "Who was the prince who sent you? Why will you not tell us?"

To which I responded, "How can I tell you? For there is no prince who sent me!"

They would not believe me, though, and they questioned me for an hour or so before they went away. The next day, I was visited four times by these two men. They came, too, the next day, and the next, and the day after that, and so on and so on. And that was how my life revolved when I was a prisoner there.

The conditions under which I was kept were very cruel. I will describe these now, so you might have some idea of my sufferings.

In the Category of Company.

The company was very bad during those long weeks. There was Midana and Reckdohl, who I have described already. There was an old woman, Tirbe, who would sometimes come in their place to question me. She was a vicious old hag, and she would scream at me to tell the truth, while she prodded me with her hideous, curled fingernails. Also, there was another man, Giella, who was very fat, and far too cheerful for my liking. He affected a great compassion and friendship for me, which I knew was false, for, as I said to him, "If you are such a dear friend to me, why do you not release me?" Of course, he had no good answer. From time to time, other interrogators would be there as well.

Besides the interrogators, there were two others, whom I shall call servants. One was the girl who had first tricked me into coming to the house, and I grew angry each time I looked at her, although she did not seem to care. The other was a skinny young lad of unsurpassed ugliness, who had protruding teeth, deeply pocked skin, and who was besides afflicted with a mild form of stupidity.

In the Category of Food.

The two servants brought me nothing to eat but rice cake, or nutty bread, or cheese, or sometimes a few pieces of beef. And to drink, I was given only water or ale. This may not sound so bad, but it was a monotonous diet, and it lacked zest. Also, the meals were served on wooden plates which were not always properly washed, so they bore a slight smell on occasions. And they gave me only a spoon to eat my meals with, for they said I might use a knife as a weapon. Neither could I use my throwing-razor to cut my food, for they had taken it from me, as I have said, and they refused to give it back.

In the Category of Bedding.

My bedding was made of reeds, tied together with twine, and placed in a sort of frame. On top of this was placed a long sack, filled with straw, which served as a mattress, and over the sack was a meagre linen sheet, and a woollen blanket which was of poor quality. This was an uncomfortable arrangement, because the sack was altogether too soft, and the reed frame tended to sway and creak when one moved about. Worse, my wrists were still chained, so, if I slept on my side, I would sometimes awaken with reddish dents upon my skin where the chain had pressed in.

In the Category of Rats, Mice, and Other Vermin.

Even though they remained hidden from view, I am quite sure there were many rats and mice in that cellar, and I have already spoken on the great danger posed by the second of these. Also, when I looked closely at the walls, I saw they were somewhat damp, and on more than one occasion I saw a tiny red mite crawling upon the stone. Furthermore, one night, while I tried to sleep,

I saw a creature crawling across the floor, near to my bed. I examined it closely, and saw it was another mite. I do not remember the name for this kind of creature, but he is something like a beetle in size and shape, except he has strips of armour across his back, and a great many legs beneath, and if you poke at him (for example, with a piece of straw) he will curl up into a ball, but then, if you wait and leave him in peace, he will uncurl again, and wander on his way. So, as you can see, the cellar was a filthy place, and was infested with all manner of pests and vermin.

In the Category of Light and Heat.

The cellar, being a cellar, lacked windows, so the only light came from a few hanging lamps, and a floor lamp near to the bed. Often one or another of these lamps would go out, and it would remain out for some hours before somebody thought to change the oil, and during this time, the cellar was not so light as it previously had been.

Given the intolerable conditions I faced, you will surely wonder why I did not use my skills as a stonemage in order to escape—for example, by making the walls collapse. The reason is very simple: the metal bracelets around my wrists interfered with the casting of bindings. In fact, no sooner had I cast a potent enchantment than it would collapse around the bracelets and be dispersed along the length of the chain.

I quickly discovered the only gossamers I could control effectively were those of the most puny kind, like Flap Ridges or Imber Lines or Etched Maisies, which are all cast from the fingertips. These forces were of no use in helping me escape, but they brought me some entertainment, for I decided to use them to create a variety of attractive images. I intended to place these images into the walls and the floor, and the frame of the bed, and parts of the ceiling. In fact, I planned to place images into any flat surface the length of the chain would allow me to reach.

My plan for the design was a representation of the Fifth Day of

Creation. It included all manner of exotic birds and flowers and fish, as well as dancing weasels, and a good fat pig with his head being cut off by savages, and countless other marvellous animals.

I spent most of my waking hours upon this pattern, except for those times when I was being questioned, and, by the time it was finished, I would say I had spent a hundred hours working on it. It was truly an intricate, beautifully crafted pattern. Unfortunately, because my bonds prevented me from creating any of the coloured or shining gossamers, it was completely invisible, even to me, its creator. When I was finished a section, I could not sit back and admire my work. Instead, I had to be satisfied I knew the job to be done, and well done too, though no eyes might ever perceive it. In this way, my self-discipline was greatly bolstered, making my imprisonment easier to endure.

As I have said, my work was frequently interrupted. I was questioned at least twice a day, sometimes for hours on end. The periods of questioning were a difficult business, all in all, for they would ask me the same questions again and again, and if they did not believe my answers, which they usually did not, then they would try to get some answer from me which was more to their liking. It was their strategy, I think, to make me feel very alone and isolated from the world, and for this reason they tried never to engage in casual conversation with me, and instead concentrated on their questions, so these might be all I thought about during their absence.

Sometimes, though, I was able to push my interrogators from their intended course for a few minutes and find out a snippet or two of what was happening outside. Getting this information depended upon taking advantage of the questioner's nature. For example, Midana was sly, and I could never distract him from his dreary questions. However, Tirbe, the old woman, could often be manipulated into bringing me news, especially if it was bad news.

On one occasion, I said to her, "You will get nothing from me today. I am feeling very happy, for I dreamed my army was still waiting for me."

She replied, "You are wrong. We have sent word to your myrmidons that you have died. Hundreds of the uniformed ones have wandered away."

She was pleased with herself then, imagining she had lowered my spirits by telling me this. In fact, though, her words cheered me immensely, for it told me that, while the ordinary myrmidons, who wore uniforms, might be wandering off, my loyal Behemoths were still waiting for me.

When I was being questioned by Giella, I took a different tack, playing upon the friendship which he claimed to have for me. So I would say, "How can you claim you are my friend when you will not even tell me such-and-so." Then he would chuckle, and rub his fat chin, and say, "Very well, I will answer your question, but then you must answer mine," and I would find out the thing I wanted to know.

Now, Reckdohl usually questioned me with Midana, but sometimes he came alone, and when he did he was a rich source of entertainment. He would try to trick me, you see, but he was very poor at it, and I would often turn the tables on him.

For example, I boasted to him that he would never trick me into telling my secrets, for I could never be tricked by the simple people of his town.

He grew angry then, and said, "Nonsense! We have already tricked you. Are you not a prisoner, and at our hand?" Then he revealed to me that all the people of the town had played a part in trapping me, at the instruction of Prince Tiaphan, who ruled Manitario, and whose family and ancestral home I had unwittingly destroyed in Sudbury.

He also told me, while trying to frighten me, that the prince had summoned upon the aid of many other princes and archbishops from Manitario to gather together a great army. This army, I was told, was on the march towards this wicked town of Grim, and when it arrived, all my myrmidons would be captured or destroyed.

He then repeated what I had overheard when he talked upstairs with Midana. He said I would meet my end when the prince arrived, and he told me, "A prince may kill a holy man, if he does so with his silver sword, and this will not bring down the wrath of God."

I replied, "You are in error. The death of Christ, for example, was sanctioned by both King Caesar and King Herod, and yet their actions brought doom to them both."

To my great pleasure, the superstitious fool was very afraid at my words, not realizing it was not the death of Christ which brought doom to Caesar and Herod, but rather the fact he rose from the grave, and then quickly escaped to heaven before either of the kings could kill him a second time.

Another time, I was in the middle of creating a complex part of my Fifth Day of Creation which contained seventeen interlinked baboons. I had tried several times to create this image, but always I would lose track of which arm was wrapped around which tail, and so on. This time, though, things were going exceedingly well. In fact, I was almost finished, when suddenly Reckdohl blundered in to interrogate me, and I completely lost my place.

He started to interrogate me, saying, "What other armies do you command?"

I snapped at him (though with my usual perfect honesty), "I have told you, I command no other army—just the one camped outside your town."

But Reckdohl had a theory of his own. He tried to win my love then, saying, "You are a great and powerful general. Surely a man such as you has other forces, to augment his power and reputation still further. I believe there are other forces hiding in the forest."

"Not so," said I. "The myrmidons you see from your town walls are all the myrmidons I command, although it is true that, under my skilful direction, they fight with the power of a much larger body."

"No no," he said, growing angry. "You have a still greater army somewhere. I am certain of it."

Well, I was still angry from my spoiled work, and I thought to myself, "It is clear, despite what he says, that this man does not want to hear the truth at all, but rather wishes me to tell him a story of an imaginative and fabulous nature. So, if that is what he wants, that is what I shall tell him."

Then I said to him, "Very well. I do have a greater army."

He said, "Ah! I knew it!" Then he said, "Where are these other myrmidons encamped?"

I continued with my entertaining tale, saying, "Exactly one hundred miles to the north of here."

He scribbled this down upon a slate, and said, "One hundred miles! Evidently this distance serves some superstitious purpose."

I said, "One hundred is the number which represents victory in the simple but warlike culture of our people."

He said, "Indeed, indeed. I thought it was something of the sort. Now, will you tell me which prince you serve?"

I said, "I serve Prince Fiathor Fthather, who sent me to win all of America for him."

Reckdohl laughed, and said, "Your prince has much to learn about the world. No army could conquer this great continent. The idea is preposterous."

Then I said, "Do you think so? Well, perhaps you are right. We shall see how well the Puissant Ones fare against your American armies."

"The Puissant Ones? Do you refer to those fat black myrmidons which you command?"

I laughed and said, "No no. Those myrmidons are puny by comparison with the Puissant Ones. The Puissant Ones are camped sixty miles to the north of the first army I mentioned, and comprise thirty thousand winged spectres, who spit vitriol, and cast fire from their fingertips."

He became very fearful then, and started shouting at me. He said, "You are lying! There are no Puissant Ones. It is a crafty lie."

I replied, "It is certainly no lie."

And it was not a lie either. To have said I possessed a hundred additional myrmidons would have been a lie. But to say I commanded winged spectres was merely an entertaining fiction, a fairy tale, if you will, which only a fool would take as fact. However, since Reckdohl was a fool, he took it all as fact, and when he had finished with me, he dashed off to talk to the others of the town about his latest discovery, and also, I am sure, to send messengers to carry the news to his prince.

After that, my interrogators lost their patience with me, and, while they did not dare to torture me, they tried to punish me by withholding all food and drink from me, save for a plain bread roll and a small cup of lemon-scented water.

Also, they would come to me telling me how close their prince was, and saying things such as, "It is now just eight days until you must die," and "In six days the prince will be here and you will die," and so on. To add to the terror of it all, they placed a painting of the prince in the cellar, which showed a young man with red hair and a great sword, surrounded by all manner of his fierce myrmidons.

I would have despaired if not for the fact that I had a great faith within my soul, and the Holy Ghost visited me daily, just after my meagre lunch. Then I saw how wise I had been in creating the beautiful scene from the Fifth Day of Creation, for this work not only showed my devotion and secured my bond with God, but also it heightened my ability to perceive invisible things, including the Holy Ghost.

The Ghost said to me, "Fear not, Yreth. Your troubles will soon be ended."

I asked, "Am I to die then, in this prison?"

Then the Holy Ghost replied, "Perhaps you will and perhaps you will not. That is all pie for the miller, my friend, and not for me to guess at. But I will warrant you this: if you die, I will take you to heaven and introduce you to God himself. You will sit at his right hand, closer to him even than Moses, and you will be the architect for a new heaven, with finer buildings than we currently have."

I was delighted to hear this. Then I asked the ghost, "Will I be paid for my labours?"

The Holy Ghost replied, "In heaven, the needs of all are sup-plied by God. A man needs no money for food or drink, for these things are always present on a long table, and there are no flies to buzz upon the feast, except for the good flies, such as the gentle cranefly, and the delicate false-bee."

"My two favourite flies!" I declared. "But what of shelter? Are there good houses in heaven?"

"To be sure," replied the Holy Ghost. "Although the climate is so soft a man hardly needs a house at all, and indeed, those who do not have one, such as the beggars, exist with the greatest comfort sleeping their nights upon the numerous thick and grassy banks. You can see then, nobody needs money in heaven. The angels, who labour endlessly for God, receive nothing for their troubles. Neither do I, although God and I are very close indeed."

"You are saying, then, that I too shall receive nothing for my work?"

"So you might think," said the Holy Ghost, with a chuckle to his voice. "But God has decreed otherwise. He has said you alone, in all of heaven, shall be paid for your work, and paid handsomely, to boot. You will receive a thousand arrans a day, whether you work that day or not. How does that strike your fancy?"

"With such rewards waiting for me in heaven, I am sure I shall no longer have any fear of death," I said.

"Of that you may be sure," the Holy Ghost replied.

Then the Spirit left me. But he returned every day, as I have said, and he was always good company, for he had a ready wit, and he would talk to me in an ordinary manner, without lacing all his talk with lessons and preaching, as Christ is depicted as doing. This is not to deny the fact Christ was the most perfect man ever to live—I just do not think he would have been such an entertaining cellmate.

The days passed slowly, and with some physical discomfort, for I was very hungry. I continued to work on my pattern with the utmost dedication, and as I worked I prepared myself for the mo-ment of my death which I believed was close at hand.

One evening, I was at my work, putting the finishing touches on the Fifth Day of Creation. I was going at it as well as I could in my weakened state when the boy servant came down into the cellar to bring me a small amount of water. He chewed on a hunk of beef as he went about his work, which was most cruel and inconsiderate, seeing how I was starving to death at the time. Still, it is no more than I would have expected from his type. As I have said, he was somewhat slow-witted, and ugly into the bargain.

As he filled my cup of water, I said, "Listen, boy, I have not taken good food in many days. I am very hungry and would think kindly upon you if you will give me some of your beef."

Well, what do you think? He did! He gave me his entire piece of beef. And he did not knock it away as I was about to eat it (which was a little trick Reckdohl delighted in) but instead stood and watched and let me eat it in peace.

I thought to myself, "Here is a remarkable thing. Let us see what else he will do." Then I said, "Some wine would go down well with this."

He replied, in a voice that stammered, "Th-th-th-ey will not let me t-t-touch the w-w-wine, for th-th-they say it w-w-will make my head even w-w-weaker."

I found his stammer most irritating, but I decided to try to strike up a conversation with him anyway, asking him about my myrmidons. We talked for a good hour, and I learned many things. I had wondered, for example, why my myrmidons had not come looking for me. They were usually very inquisitive when they were left to themselves. So I asked the boy about this.

He told me Midana had sent frequent messages to my myrmidons. He knew this, because he had been the messenger. At first the messages said I was ill (which was true enough, for I was quite weak by that time!) and then that I had died (which, thanks to God, and to my strong constitution, was untrue). Upon hearing this news, my myrmidons became confused, and did not know what to do. Then the townspeople sent more messages, repeating the news of my death, and urging the myrmidons to dismantle their camp and leave. This the myrmidons gradually did, wandering off in groups of tens and twenties, just as that old hag Tirbe had said. At last, almost all my myrmidons had left.

My Behemoths, however, had been less easy to trick. Upon being told of my death, they told the boy they would not leave until The Revered was among them. By this, they meant the pendant which I wore, and which they worshipped, but the townsfolk took their meaning amiss, thinking they desired my return, and, by means of further messages, tried to persuade them that my body had been burned, whereupon the Behemoths, perhaps believing the pendant was destroyed, gave angry screams and shrieks and tried to kill the lad who brought such a disagreeable message.

The Behemoths then took to the trees, carrying much of my treasure with them, and from this vantage point, they had watched the town for many weeks. At night, I learned, they gave out strange calls, which were like the sounds of many bass horns. First one of the creatures would call out, then another, and then others, until the air was filled with their music, greatly terrifying the townsfolk. I had heard these sounds myself, even down there in the cellar, but had thought it to be the sound of some local celebration.

By God's will, even as I was talking to the boy, the Behemoths began their howling. He looked fearful then, and made as if to leave, but I said, "Wait. Do you know what they are singing?"

"I d-d-do not, but I know it is an eerie sound," he said.

"They are singing a prophecy," I said. "For many nights I have listened to it, but it puzzles me."

"What does the song f-f-foretell?" he asked, and his eyes were wide with wonder.

I was very clever then, and I said, "I cannot be entirely certain, but I can guess at it. Perhaps it tells of one in this town who is held in the lowest regard. This man will come to be raised to great rank, through taking pity upon a prisoner. The prisoner, I am certain, is me, yet I do not know the name of the man which they sing." And then I looked at the lad, as if an idea had just entered my head. "Tell me, boy, what is your name?"

"It is Smad," he said.

Here I burst out laughing, for a smad, in those parts, is a word used to describe the leavings of a horse. Yet I restrained myself, turning my roar of laughter into a cry of the utmost delight. "Why," I said, "that is the very name they speak of. They prophesy that you, who are the least of this town's citizens, shall become its lord, and all who live here shall bow down to you and obey your commands."

You will realize, of course, all my talk of prophecy was trickery, for I no more understood the song of the Behemoths than this boy did. It follows from this that I could not be certain the song of the Behemoths was *not* a prophecy, so my trick was not actually a lie. It is important to be aware of these distinctions if one is to live a moral life.

In any case, he believed my words, and he asked how these things would come to be.

"I will make them so," I said. "But first, you must run me an errand. You must go to my bodyguards, and tell them where I am to be found."

He was very afraid at this, and understandably so, for they were fearsome creatures, and they had already tried to kill him once. And, in truth, it was a miracle he had escaped, for they did not usually miss their mark.

Still, I spoke soothing words, speculating as to the kind, wise hearts which beat beneath the ugly hides of the monsters, and the great sadness they must feel at the fear which people had for them. Again, there was little substance upon which to base my speculations, for I believe there is nothing in the world the Behemoths so enjoyed as fighting and killing, and very often, when marching, I had seen them step quickly to one side in order to stamp upon some lizard or shrew by the road, or flick a claw into a tree to disembowel a squirrel.

At last, Smad agreed to my request, saying he would go to the bodyguards the next day, when he went to fetch water from the river.

The next day, Reckdohl came to visit me. He said, "We have consulted experts and can find no record of a Prince Fiathor Fthather. Furthermore, we do not believe the army of winged spectres you have described actually exists."

I explained to him that, in an infinite world, all things must exist somewhere, including an army of winged spectres.

Now, this was good logic, but it made him very angry, and he started shouting at me about how I had no comprehension of the gravity of my sins, and that I was a liar, and so on, which was very tedious.

As he shouted, however, I heard a distant sound, which I recognized as the war cry of my Behemoths. I knew they had just received word of my location from Smad.

Because I wished to distract my visitors from the sounds of the Behemoths, I shouted back at Reckdohl, saying that everybody commits sins from time to time, and, before he passed judgement on my adventures, he should perhaps spend time confessing to me his own imperfections.

Well, Reckdohl grew furious with me then, and he walked up to me and poked me in the chest with his index finger. But no sooner had he done so than there came a series of deafening roars from outside. Then, suddenly, the room shook under a crashing, thundering sound, mingled with the screams of men and women and falling bricks. Above this terrible din came the sound of splitting wood, and, looking up, I saw great claws tearing through the ceiling of the cellar, and pulling it away in clumps, as easily as a dog digs away at a rat-hole. Within moments, the cellar was ablaze with daylight, for the Behemoths, in their determination to reach me had torn down the very walls of the house where I was held captive, leaving the cellar now open to the sky, so I was almost blinded by the brilliance of the light (for I had been many weeks in the dark cellar, and my eyes had seen nothing but lamplight).

You may be sure the Behemoths did not deal kindly with Reckdohl, and, although I am a compassionate man, I dearly wish I could have watched and relished every moment of his death. Yet, although my eyes were temporarily blinded, my hearing was still keen, and I was well satisfied with the sounds I heard, which were those of blows and splashes and breaking bones and tearing flesh, such as you might hear when hacking apart a leg of pork, yet mingled with the man's agonized death-screams.

The Behemoths then released me from my bonds, but I found myself too weak to walk properly. So they carried me above, and then back to the camp.

You will wonder why I did not command the Behemoths to kill everyone in the town without delay, as a righteous revenge for the abuses I had received. Yet the truth of the matter is that, although I had rejoiced to hear my Behemoths arrive, I was no sooner released than a powerful wave of nausea swept over me. I felt no urge for vengeance, but wished only to depart the place.

Still, I did not let my wits leave me, for I knew that later, when I was well, I would exact my revenge and take pleasure from it. Therefore, as the Behemoths carried me away, I commanded them to keep watch over the town, making sure no one might leave the area, either by day or under cover of darkness. Later, I ordered them to guard the water boy, Smad, whose actions had released me from my imprisonment, so the people of the town could not harm him. I also sent other Behemoths out to track the groups of myrmidons which had left upon hearing of my death, so they might be brought back into my service once more.

For a day, I remained at the camp, eating, exercising as much as I was able, and gaining my strength once more. Soon, I was able to walk again, and although I still had wounds, it was clear they were healing as they should. I considered very carefully what form my revenge should take, and decided the proper punishment would be to kill only those who had tortured me. For the rest, I decided I would pay like with like. Since they had imprisoned me in their town, I would imprison *them* there. I will explain this shortly.

The following day, I walked into the town, with my Behemoths around me. We took the townsfolk from their houses, where they were hiding in fear, and assembled them in the marketplace. Many tried to hide in secret places within their homes, but this did them no good, for the Behemoths have a keen sense of smell, and were able to sniff out the villains, no matter where they might be concealed.

Once the townsfolk were all gathered together, I looked over the crowd, searching for the faces of those who had tortured me. I quickly found Tirbe—that savage old woman who had taken delight in mocking me, claiming it was in retribution for the life of her son—and I said to one of the Behemoths, "Kill her without delay."

Well, no sooner had the words left my lips than the Behemoth jumped forward, seized the old hag, and killed her in a way I will not describe here for the sake of those readers who may be weak in the belly.

Although her death was horrible to behold, and many present fainted away at the sight, I was much delighted by the efficiency of the killing. The Behemoth's actions were astonishingly fast. It seemed I had no sooner spoken the command for this woman's execution than she was lying dead upon the ground in two pieces. I then told the creature to use precisely the same methods to dispatch the other interrogators, and also some other folk who had earned my displeasure.

In the course of an hour, I found and executed all of my interrogators, except for Midana.

I said to him, "Where is my throwing-razor which you took from me."

He said it was in his house, so I told him to go and fetch it. When he returned I took the weapon and returned it to its place in my boot, then I said to him, and to everyone, "The killings are now at an end. Midana, I will spare your life, although you would not have spared mine. In this way, the world will see I am the more magnanimous. But although I will let you live, your actions cannot go unpunished, for this would set a bad example to others."

I then issued commands to two of my Behemoths. I told them to take him away to a comfortable, private place and there to tear off his legs, but very quickly, so the pain would soon be over. I also sent the town's physicians to go after him and to care for him so he would not die of his injuries.

When these severe punishments were done with, I addressed the rest of the people as follows: "You have wrongfully kept me prisoner, and done foul deeds to me. Yet now the jug is in my hand, and I shall pour as I drank. All of you shall now be prisoners, and you shall suffer daily indignities, as I suffered them." Then I brought forward Smad, the water boy, saying: "This boy, whom you have mistreated, I will now set above you all. He will command you, and he will whip you as he pleases every day. Moreover, I shall leave four of my bodyguards behind, who shall be in his service and will protect him from those of you who may wish him harm in his new post. Further, these bodyguards will be your gaolers, for if any of you should try to leave this town, they will hunt you down and kill you."

Then I chose four Behemoths, and I commanded them to guard Smad as they would guard me, and to obey his every command. I told them also to kill any person who might try to leave the town of Grim.

And I spoke to Smad too. I gave him a fine leather whip, and I said to him, "Give such orders around the town as may please you, but remember this: for my sake, let no day pass without soundly whipping fifty of the townsfolk, for I wish them never to forget the sufferings they inflicted upon me."

I stayed there a few hours longer, to watch the new order of things, and it pleased me very well, for Smad took quickly to his appointed role, whipping the townsfolk with vigour, and having them wait upon his every need. When I was satisfied all was as it should be, I left the town, accompanied by my Behemoths and also those of my myrmidons who had returned while I was recuperating.

We left the town in some speed, for I knew Prince Tiaphan was close now. As we marched, I sent out scouts to find the other myrmidons that had wandered off, and we sounded horns to summon them. Over the next few days, more of them returned, although not as many as I would have liked. In total, I now had only two hundred of the original Northern Guard to command (there had been over eight hundred when I left Quebec), together with twenty-five slaves, and all thirty Behemoths, less four which I had assigned to the permanent protection of Smad.

You will be sorry to hear that the punishment I inflicted upon the town of Grim, and which seemed to me a very fair and cool-headed one considering my sufferings there, did not work itself through as I desired, and I will quickly tell of this now.

A few days after I had left Grim, the rear observers spotted several figures coming after us at a run. As they approached, we saw these to be the four Behemoths I had assigned to Smad. I was angry to see them, and, when they reached us, I asked why they had disobeyed my orders to guard him. I could not make out their answers at first, for the tongue of a Behemoth is not well suited to eloquent speech (although they can understand such speech well enough), but at last I understood them to say they had abandoned their duties because they had "no love of it." As I understood their meaning, they had no desire to serve any person save the one who wore the pendant, which was to say, me.

Fearing for the life of the virtuous Smad, I sent six of my ordinary myrmidons back to Grim, with orders to take over the duties which the Behemoths had abandoned. Two weeks later, however, these myrmidons, too, returned, saying Smad had been killed in the time he was unguarded, and the people were no longer prisoners in their own town. Worse yet, Prince Tiaphan's great army had reached Grim, and passed it, and was in fast pursuit of me. My myrmidons had crept past the army at night, and they said it numbered many thousands.

I was tempted to double back, past the enemy army, and to punish those townsfolk once more, but, after considering the matter, I decided I had wasted enough time in the town of Grim, and I would leave them to stew in their own sins, until their offences against God himself became so great He would strike them down, as He did in Sodom, and in Gomorrah, and in Tentennal, and in Rhad. I therefore turned to the southwest, and we marched at great speed.

This, then, was how I escaped from my time in Death's Kitchen, and with no serious injuries to speak of. However, I had lost three-quarters of my army, together with much of my wealth, for my treasures were in bags strapped to the myrmidons, and when they wandered off they took thousands of arrans with them.

In my mind, I resolved I would use the wealth that remained to me to buy more myrmidons, and build up my army once more. As you will see, however, Destiny decreed I should turn away from the military life. I will tell next of how this came to be.

THE TENTH PART

In Which I Describe How I Lost My Army And My Exciting Adventures In A Great Pot

A FEW WEEKS AFTER I HAD left Grim, we entered a region where the land was desolate and wild. The trees were stunted, the ground was boggy, and there were no towns or villages to be seen, even though the hills were so gentle I could see for many miles.

We marched across the land for some days. Travel was slow, for there were many pools covered by moss that looked like solid ground—until a myrmidon stepped in. There were quicksands too, and numerous biting flies. Still, all in all I thought this would be a good region to travel, for I had not forgotten the great army searching for me, and I reasoned an army would have a harder time tracking me in a region such as this, where travel was sluggish and where there were no people to report my own army's passage.

One evening, though, I saw a glittering upon the southeast horizon. I was not sure whether this was a distant city or the glint of sunlight upon weapons and armour. Even the scouts, with their sharp eyes, were uncertain, saying sometimes the setting sun plays tricks upon the eye.

The next morning we saw no further sign of an army, but I exercised caution. We changed direction and marched westward at a good speed. We had been travelling for no more than a few hours, however, when the scouts spotted an enemy force to the west, and this time there could be no doubt but that this was an army of great size.

Upon hearing this news, I commanded my myrmidons to change direction once more, marching now to the south. The following day, around sunset, we saw more glinting to the southeast, and again it was clear this was another army and not a city, for, when it grew dark, we could see distant campfires burning.

So then, there was an army to the southeast, and a second army to the west. In addition, I thought it likely another army approached to the northeast, in the direction of Grim, for, as you will remember, my scouts had reported the approach of troops shortly after I left the place. I resolved to march southwest once more, hoping my force might pass between the two visible armies.

The sergeants came to me then, saying, "Commander, shall we lay forward the running spears and sharpen the croves?" and "Shall we dispatch throwers and steppers to eight points or to four?" and "Where do you wish us to deploy nets and spiked traps?" and "Shall we assume a hawk formation, or divide into double wolf-packs, as we like to do against a much larger force?" and many other such questions, which I did not understand and did not care to.

I replied, "Your words mean nothing to me. Simplicity is the mark of tactical excellence. Listen, then, to these simple commands: travel quickly, but not so quickly that you trip and fall. Avoid the enemy, for I do not wish to lose either myrmidons or the wealth they carry. If you come upon an enemy myrmidon by accident, kill him. If the group of enemies you encounter is too large for you to destroy, call others to your aid."

They complained then that my words were of too general a nature and would not help them set the formation, which is to say, the shape the army adopts while marching.

I thought about this for a few minutes, and I came up with a most ingenious plan. I said, "We will march the army in a straight line, single file. Then, if we are observed from the front, the enemy will underestimate our number, thinking the group to consist of only a few myrmidons. The enemy will either ignore such a force, or will attack recklessly. In either case, the day will be ours. On the other hand, if we are observed from the side, our numbers will appear far greater than they are. The enemy will either flee from such a force, or will attack timidly. In either case, once again, the day will be ours."

One sergeant said, "If the enemy numbers many thousands, while our numbers are only two hundred, it will make little difference whether they attack recklessly or timidly, for their numbers will speak too heavily in their favour for us to take the battle."

I said, "Not so. I have a plan to deal with the contingency: if we come close to a powerful enemy, form the army into a great circle, with slaves on the inside, and Behemoths and the strongest myrmidons on the outside, facing outwards. No force, no matter how large, may penetrate such a formation as this, for a circle is the most perfect shape, and its strength and perfection can be proved with mathematics."

The sergeants were sceptical at my words, but I had stated my wishes and they were duty-bound to obey. We continued marching to the southwest, and, the following night we observed that the campfires to the southeast were closer than they had been. We also observed the campfires from the army to the west, which had not been visible on the previous night. Worse yet, we saw other sets of fires, one further away to the south, and one to the north.

I decided further marching to the southwest would be unwise, since at least three armies would converge upon us in that direction. Instead, I decided to change our heading and march north, to meet head-on the army approaching from there.

We had marched north, in single file, for half a day when a new idea came to me. I reasoned that, by marching to the enemy, we were doing more work than was necessary. If the enemy wished to catch us, why then, let him come to us! Without a moment's delay (for I am a decisive fellow), I commanded my myrmidons to stop their marching and to form into the defensive circle I had described. We waited in this formation for some hours. I sat in the centre of the circle, where I had a fine meal of several expensive cheeses, and then I had a nap.

One of the cheeses I had eaten was a sheep cheese, so, not surprisingly, while I napped I dreamed of sheep. When I woke, I thought about this dream, and it put me in mind of the story of the Greeks who one night dipped a flock of sheep in tar, then set fire to their fleece to make it appear as if the sheep were a great army. Well, I did not have a flock of sheep, or I might have tried this trick, but then I thought, "Perhaps my enemy is also very cunning, and has used this same trick against me. Perhaps the armies which I think I see ahead of me to the south and southwest and west are merely flocks of sheep, while the army to the north is the real one." It seemed to me that this might well be the case, and, if it was, I would look a pretty fool sitting here while an army approached.

We quickly set off once more to the southwest, and I left behind a few pieces of firewood and a woollen tunic for my pursuers to find. If they were indeed using burning sheep, and they came across the scraps, they would read it as a message and be disheartened, knowing I had discovered their ploy. On the other hand, if they had not schemed to use burning sheep, the scraps would mean nothing to them, and they would not know I had miscalculated.

As we marched, the armies ahead of us came closer, and I saw they were not sheep but fierce myrmidons. But do not think I was saddened at this sight, for now I saw that my enemies were not so clever as I, for they had not thought to use burning sheep in their attack, whereas I *had* thought of this clever ruse. My pulse quickened with the excitement of the upcoming battle, and, with every minute that passed, six new ideas and plans entered my head. I quickly relayed these to my myrmidons, and instructed each of them to take their pick of the plans that suited them best. "And if you do not like any of the ones you have heard until now," I said, "then listen on, for I have many more plans to guide our actions and win the battle."

The hours passed, and we saw the size of the enemy force was much larger than I had first anticipated, numbering not thousands, but tens of thousands. When they had approached within a mile of us, they stopped and began to spread out, hoping they might terrify us with their numbers and their resolve.

Not to be outdone, I brought my myrmidons to a standstill also, and ordered them into circular formation. We were in an especially boggy place, which seemed to me to be an excellent stroke of good fortune, for I knew it would hamper the enemy as they drew close, whereas my myrmidons, who had merely to stand in one place, would not be affected by it. Further, upon setting up tents in the middle of the circle I discovered the ground was so soft that it made a pleasant bed, as comfortable as the finest mattress, although much wetter.

Now, over the next day or so, the other armies arrived and set up camps in all directions around us, and it was an astonishing sight to be sure. I would say there were fifty thousand myrmidons in all! Certainly, I counted three hundred banners, and their tents were so many that the whole land was made white by the number of them. They assembled war machines too: I saw ballistas, firethrowers, and huge crushing wheels.

The sergeants were alarmed at this sight, and they said, "This force is too great for us to overcome or break through. Should we prepare to fight to the death, or do you plan to surrender?"

I said, "I will tell you when the time comes. There is no reason for you to know this now."

They complained then, saying, "If we are to die, we wish first to carry out certain rituals which are meaningful to us in times of despair. We would like the time to prepare these ceremonies."

"Ah, you simple-minded brutes!" I exclaimed. "There are a hundred crafty plans in my head, and with every hour that passes more plans come to me. Believe me, if you obey my orders, victory will certainly be ours."

They became stroppy then, saying they did not believe me, and pointing out the many superior varieties of myrmidons which could be seen in the enemy camps. They called these species of myrmidon by their own names, saying: "Furthermore, the enemy has several hundred *Gurth*, and a hundred *Illashi*," and so on.

For those who are interested in such matters, my myrmidons were all either Common Wartbacks or Mottled Wartbacks, although when they were in uniform the two types were indistinguishable. My slaves were all Lopers. I do not know the proper designation for my Behemoths, for I have never seen their species described in any literature. They resembled Great Grey Turpins but were very much bulkier, yet faster too. The enemy force consisted of, I would say, two thirds Wartbacks, plus an assortment of Blue Turpins, Great Grey Turpins, Ridgeheads, Giant Dashers, Webs, and various giant types of Soft and Chitinous Spinebacks.

In any case, I said to my sergeants, "Do you forget our force contains thirty formidable Behemoths, which are more than a match for any enemy myrmidon."

One of the sergeants said, "They are strong, it is true, but they smell bad, and we do not care for their manners and their foul tempers."

I replied, "You will like their tempers well enough when it is the enemy they are cross at."

They had other complaints too, but I would not hear their words, and I ordered the sergeants back to their places in the circle.

A short time afterwards, a slave came to us from the enemy camp carrying a message from Prince Tiaphan. The message asked me if I wished to discuss terms of surrender. I sent an amusing message back. I said I would be happy to accept the prince's surrender, but he had better be quick about giving it, for I grew weary of waiting in this lonely bog. The joke of this is, in asking to discuss the terms of surrender, the prince meant *my* surrender to *him*, and not *his* surrender to *me*, but by my reply I indicated that I understood the reverse to be the case, and believed him to be pleading for mercy.

I do not think the prince enjoyed my joke, because some minutes later a great hail of arrows and ballista javelins came flying towards us, and I lost several myrmidons and slaves.

I wished to direct the battle in safety, and I had devised a clever plan to accomplish this. I climbed into a large round iron cooking pot I had selected for its extreme sturdiness and had the Behemoths place it in the branches of a nearby tree. The pot had a lid, which was placed on top, so, by lifting the lid, I might see what was going on in any direction, while remaining safe from arrows and spears. I also had the Behemoths set chains over the top, through the handles on the side of the pot and the handle on the top of the lid, with enough slack that I might lift the lid a small distance, but not so much that an enemy might easily pull the lid away. The chains were held in place by metal loops, which the Behemoths bent around the handles.

Watching from my pot, I saw a group of enemy myrmidons on our north side were advancing. There were three hundred myrmidons, with the most powerful at the head. I called out to my Behemoths then, telling them to bloody the noses of those fine fellows a little. At once, with whoops and screeches, ten of the Behemoths went tearing towards the enemy, leaping and twisting like mad dogs. They ran straight at the centre of the advancing ranks, leaping upon the largest myrmidons with a fury. The enemy surrounded them at once, but the Behemoths were tremendously fast and strong, and their hides were very tough, so it was difficult for the enemy's spears to poke them.

After they had wreaked havoc in the enemy ranks for some minutes, the Behemoths returned at a run, hardly any the worse for their adventures, aside from a few small cuts and nicks, yet leaving forty or fifty fallen myrmidons behind them.

I was delighted at their success, and I called down orders to my ordinary myrmidons to place mud and ash upon themselves, and to pad out their clothing, so the enemy might observe their great black forms and believe my force comprised a much larger number of Behemoths than was in fact the case. This they did, and I am sure it struck terror into the hearts of the enemy.

The enemy commanders must have rethought their plans then, for the group to the north stopped its advance and returned to its previous position. A second, much larger group, at least two thousand myrmidons in number, then moved forward on the north side, while another group, of similar size, began to advance to our south.

I called out to the Behemoths again, telling them to show the enemy, for a second time, what we were made of. One of the Behemoths said, as far as I could make out (for their speech was very bad, you know), they would obey my orders if I wished it, but they would suffer losses by the action, for the advancing ranks were made up of powerful myrmidons with good spears.

This prospect did not please me, so I decided upon a bolder plan. I told the Behemoths to attack the tents of the enemy commanders and kill any princes and archbishops and generals they might find there. I reasoned, you see, that when the myrmidons saw their leaders were dead, they would quickly become disorganized and wander off.

The Behemoths told me they would need all their numbers to accomplish this task. I said, "Very well, step to it then." But they would not obey. Then I realized they did not wish to leave me—or more precisely, the pendant—unguarded in the middle of a battlefield.

Since I did not intend to accompany them on such a dangerous raid, I knew I would have to come up with some other solution, and one came to me very quickly. I called one of the Behemoths to me up in the tree, then I gave him the pendant, saying "I will give you this thing to guard. Take it with you on your mission. When you have finished, return it to me. Will you do this?"

The creature grunted that it would, and so I reached my hand out of the pot and gave the pendant to him.

At once, the Behemoth gave a great howl. Then the others started howling, and leaping, and snatching at the air. They continued this dance for some minutes, ignoring my orders to set about their mission immediately. Then, at last, they heard my words, and they ran off towards the enemy. However, instead of making for the tents, as I had ordered, they veered off to one side, towards an area where the enemy were more thinly spread and comprised the weaker types of myrmidons.

What carnage followed! In the space of just a few minutes, those magnificent black monsters had cut a bloody strip straight through the ranks of the enemy. I was much heartened to see this, for I thought it was their plan next to come around behind the enemy's lines and to attack the commanders' tents from the rear, which, it seems to me, they might have done very easily.

Instead, though, the Behemoths continued running straight, travelling further and further away, howling and leaping and shrieking all the while, until they were far away.

It was clear to me they had misunderstood my instructions, and had gone running off to attack some other set of commanders, perhaps in some distant city.

Most men would have despaired at this sight, but I understood such events are merely the fortunes of war, and one must either accept these fortunes and adapt to them, or face rapid defeat. In any event, when I realized the Behemoths were not returning, I called down to my myrmidons, urging them to form a more perfect circle, for by now the formation had become ragged in places, and many of the myrmidons had turned to face the forces approaching from the north and south, now almost upon us.

In a few moments, under my firm command, my troops were once again in a circle, facing in all directions, with spears at the ready. On the inside of the circle, a second circle of myrmidons stood ready, with spears pointed higher than the outside circle. In the centre were the slaves, who had also been issued with spears. I was also near the centre, perched in my tree.

The enemy troops arrived then. They were of the type known as Ridgeheads, and they were very ferocious, being larger and stronger than my myrmidons (although not so large and strong as the Behemoths, as I have already mentioned).

There were at least three thousand enemy myrmidons there, against just two hundred of mine, yet I fancy we could have taken the day with ease if my troops had followed my instructions and stayed in a circle, for a circle is an indestructible shape. Unfortunately, even though I constantly shouted "Keep the circle perfectly round!", they allowed the formation to become slightly dented in one part, and at once they were overcome by the attackers and quickly destroyed.

With my army defeated, I knew it was time to flee for my life, and it seemed to me that, with my smaller size and swifter feet, I stood an excellent chance of escaping these lumbering Ridgeheads. Therefore, I pushed against the lid of the pot so I might climb out, and jump down from the tree.

It was then I remembered the lid of the pot was still chained to the handles. Alas, the loops of metal which fastened the chains there, and which had been very easy for the Behemoths to bend, were impossible for me to break. For some time, I pushed against the lid with my shoulder, but it would not budge, and I realized I was trapped.

Thinking quickly, I decided upon a second strategy. I closed the lid and remained quietly inside the pot. It was my hope, you see, the enemy myrmidons might not have noticed I had been shouting orders from the pot and would just disregard it, thinking it was just an ordinary cooking pot which someone had placed in a tree to keep it out of harm's way.

I waited there for a long time, listening to the sounds around me—myrmidons coming and going. An hour passed, and the sounds moved away. Then I heard approaching footsteps, and a voice called out, "Archbishop Yreth. Are you there?"

I said nothing, hoping this was merely a trick to discover my hiding place. But then the voice said, "Archbishop Yreth! I know you are in that cooking pot! Will you answer me?"

I lifted the lid and looked down. Below me I saw Prince Tiaphan. I laughed to see him, for in the portrait I had seen of this man, he looked young and fit, with long red hair, whereas the man before me had a pockmarked face, and a bald head which was only red from the colour of the skin. Still, I knew this was Prince Tiaphan, for he wore a white cloak, which in America (or in the eastern and central parts of the continent, at least) is the mark of royalty. Around him were other men, who I took to be his generals and followers.

He said, "I understand you were reluctant to surrender to me. Are you now ready to rethink that decision?"

I do not care for these foolish games kings and princes play, for they do so only to amuse those around them, so their admirers might say, "Oh, he is a witty fellow indeed."

So, I did not answer his question but instead said, "I have lost a good army today, and I feel cross because of it. Kindly leave me in peace." Then I lowered the lid of my pot in a dignified way.

He would not leave me alone though. He shouted, "Oh, come now! Why so glum? Let us do something to raise this archbishop's spirits. You there, and you!"

I heard footsteps then, and I felt the pot being lifted down from the tree and carried for some distance. When I next looked out, I was on the ground in the heart of the enemy camp. I heard the prince's voice saying, "It is said silver can cheer a man up. What do you say, fellows?"

They all laughed, and I could see the prince was holding a silver sword, although I could not see his face, for the lid blocked my view.

I said, "Prince, it seems to me that to kill a man while he is trapped inside a cooking pot is a very cowardly thing to do."

He was very angry at my words, and he put his face down to look inside my pot, saying, "It is also a very cowardly thing to kill a royal family by burning them to death."

I said, wisely, "The present is here and the past has gone. It is folly to dwell upon the misfortunes of yesterday."

Then I spoke more softly.

I said, "I myself have suffered many calamities, yet new opportunities always presented themselves."

Then I spoke more softly still.

I said, "Perhaps you will take yourself a new wife, and have other children to continue your line."

My voice was so soft he could not hear my words, so he said, "Heh? What is that you say?"

I repeated my words in a still softer tone.

Now, as I had expected, he drew his ear in close to the edge of the pot, so he might hear what I was saying. At this moment, when he was good and close, I quickly slashed out with my throwing-razor, hoping to slit the throat of this cruel tyrant. Unfortunately, I succeeded only in cutting his cheek, which made him still angrier.

He thrust his sword between the lid and the pot and waved it around inside, trying to run me through; however, I grabbed the blade with my cloak, and pulled it down sharply against the lid of the pot, snapping it off, and also causing the lid to fall in place.

I knew it was time to abandon my instincts as a warrior and trust to my skills as a stonemage. So, I hurriedly applied several Peregrine Clasps to the place where the lid met the pot, so the two were firmly bonded.

I heard hands scrabbling against the lid of the pot next, followed by angry shouts. Then, I think he kicked the pot with great force, for there was a great sound like a bell and I felt myself rolling head over heels.

Moments later, I felt the pot being lifted and dashed to the ground with great force. This happened several times, and I suppose the prince must have commanded his myrmidons to play with me so, for the pot would have been too heavy for a single man to throw about.

If they had continued, I am certain I would have quickly died, for there was a great length of sword in there with me, and I received several nasty cuts from it.

Luckily, I heard the prince's voice saying, "No, I have a better plan. Place him over there. It is a fitting punishment for his crimes, and in a way he has selected such a death himself."

Once again, I felt the pot being lifted and placed down again. I quickly realized what this wicked prince had in mind, for the pot suddenly started to become hot, and I knew he had ordered it placed it upon a cooking fire. This, however, posed not the least threat to me, for, in a few moments, I had cast a Sheet Wall upon the base of the pot, which protected it very well from the heat of the fire.

I removed my cloak and placed it beneath me, and I lay back in comfort while the prince had me "cooked." I also removed my tunic and wrapped it around the blade of the sword to prevent it from cutting me if I were jostled again. After that, I merely waited, giving out occasional screams as if I were in agony. When I decided I had been on the fire long enough to be cooked through, I let my screams subside.

Some time later, I heard the prince say, "Enough. I am avenged. Throw him in there." Once again, I felt the pot being lifted up, and then I was tossed through the air. I heard a great splash as I landed, and, after I had recovered from the jolt, I realized I had been tossed into a body of water.

I was worried then, because during my time sealed in the pot so far, the air had become very stale, and I feared I would suffocate. Worse, although I could easily remove the Peregrine Clasps which held the lid fastened shut, I could not think of any way of breaking the chains holding the lid on, meaning I had no way to climb out of the pot and swim to the surface. Therefore, by removing the enchantments and opening the lid, I would merely allow the water to come rushing in and drown me.

It looked bad for a time, but happily, after a certain point, the air became so stale my senses began to leave me.

In my sorry state, it suddenly seemed to me that, if I opened the lid, fresh air would come rushing in, carried by certain grateful fish. I realize this makes little sense now, but it made a good deal of sense to me at the time and well shows how muddled one's mind becomes when one spends too much time thinking about getting fresh air to breathe.

In any case, I dismissed the Peregrine Clasps and lifted the lid a few inches, expecting water to come rushing in, along with the grateful fish. Instead, though, a refreshing breeze wafted onto my face. You see, as luck would have it, I had not been thrown into some deep lake at all, but only into a small pond. The bottom of the pot was submerged, but the top was open to the air.

Once I started to breathe fresh air, I quickly came to my senses again, and once more tried to think of how I might use the tools at hand—specifically, a silver sword blade and my stonemage skills, to release myself from this pot. First, I tried to break the links of the chains with the sword, but the blade was too soft.

Then I turned my mind to how I might use unstable Struts of Atlas to break the chains somehow.

I considered applying an unstable strut to the lid and base of the pot, but I realized the collapse of the binding would bring the two sides together with great force and I would be crushed to death between them, which would be a poor sort of escape.

Then I considered applying one end of the binding to the lid and the other end to some external object, such as a tree, so the collapse of the binding might tear the lid off. On further thought, however, I realized the rest of the pot, with me inside it, would be catapulted with the lid, for the chains were very sturdy.

Next, I contemplated applying the binding across the width of one of the links of the chain, in the hope that the sudden con-traction would break the link. I tried this, but, alas, I discovered I could not create a binding of such a short distance, for, whenever I tried, the parts of it would become confused and melt away to nothing. It was like trying to tie knots in silk thread while wearing falconer gloves.

"No matter though," I thought, "I will instead place one end of the strut on the chain on one side of the pot, and the other end upon the chain on the other side. Then the diminution of the gossamer will stretch the chain against itself, wrenching free the metal bands around the handles." Once again, though, this excellent plan proved difficult to put into practice, for, although I could place the strut upon the chain, the enchantment did not stick well to the metal. When the strands collapsed, they merely tore away from the chains and vanished in a flash of light.

After many hours, and much experimentation, I came to the conclusion that I had no means at my disposal by which I might escape from the pot. On the other hand, I also knew I could not stay where I was, for I would eventually starve. It was clear I needed outside help, and, therefore, I must rely on trickery and guile. After some thought, I formulated a clever plan.

I waited until dark, then, after tossing the sword blade out into the water, I sealed the lid of the pot shut once more. I had discovered, by shifting my weight and stepping along the inside of the pot, I could make the vessel move. Now I took advantage of this ability, and proceeding slowly, with frequent stops to lift the lid and check my position, I rolled the pot out of the water and back onto land. This stage of my journey was difficult, but once it was accomplished and I was on firmer ground, further movement was easy. So, travelling with great stealth, I rolled my pot across the camp for some hours until I found an area where the banners were those of some other noble, not Prince Tiaphan, for you will remember this great army was not his alone, but also included the troops of various allies. I rolled around for a while, looking for a cooking pot similar to my own. When I found one, I rolled my pot near to it. Then I set the pot upon its belly again and waited.

The next morning, my pot was discovered by a group of slaves. However, because I was now in a different part of the camp from the one where my pot had been placed on the fire, they did not realize what a treasure it contained.

I had hoped the slaves would try to open it by breaking the chains, which would have allowed me to escape at my leisure later on by removing the point bindings. Unfortunately, these were dim-witted slaves, and, after they realized the lid was chained shut, they merely ran a pole under the chains and carried it between them.

The army dispersed during the day. The force I was with belonged to the city of Stanneck and was under the command of a general named Picren. This city is not a part of Manitario, but lies instead in the little bordering kingdom of Saghena. However, kingdoms are as thick as curds in those parts, and if one of them decides to go to war with you, the others are quick to join the game. This, then, was why an army from Stanneck had been sent to aid the ruler of Manitario.

Now, Stanneck is many miles to the south and west of the marshes, so I travelled with this army for weeks. During the day, I remained quietly in the pot while they carried me, while at night I would roll around on quiet expeditions for food and water. The water was easy to come by, but food was much harder to find, for slaves and myrmidons eat very little, and what they call food provides no nourishment for a man, being such things as stewed acorns and pulped wood. One night I found a roast goose, though, which I pulled inside my pot and made to last several days.

You will perhaps wonder also how I was able to relieve myself during my imprisonment. Well, I will not explain the details, but I will say that, after some experimentation, I discovered an ingenious way whereby even this action could be accomplished with the greatest efficiency and a moderate degree of hygiene.

Finally, we arrived in Stanneck, and there was a great cheering from the crowds as their myrmidons returned home. Soon the slaves who carried me came to a stop and placed the pot upon the ground. At the first opportunity, I rolled the pot away into the streets.

After a short distance, I came upon a carpenter, sitting outside his shop, who was amazed to see this wonderful rolling pot. I called out to him, and said, "You there! Be so good as to remove the chains from this pot."

He looked inside then, and, seeing there was a human face within, and not the form of some ghost or demon, he asked me, "How did you come to be inside this pot?"

I said, "It is a fascinating tale. I will tell you the story at length, if you will be so kind as to remove the chains."

He said, "No, for I fear you have been placed in this pot as a just punishment, issued by some person of great rank. If I were to release you, that person might turn to me for retribution."

I laughed at this, and said, "You are quite wrong. I placed myself in this pot, and gave orders it should be sealed securely with chains."

"Why did you do this?" he asked.

I responded, with great honesty, "I did so for my own safety, for it seemed to me at the time that within this pot I might be safe from the dangers of the world, and yet, by means of this gap beneath the lid, still be able to observe, listen, and talk."

He said, "Do you truly feel the world to be so dangerous a place?"

I said, "Yes surely, for every day men and women are killed by various means, both accidental and malicious, and yet if they were securely sealed in a pot, such as I am here, many of these unfortunate deaths might be prevented."

"Ah, that is very true," he said. "And the terrible massacres carried out in the towns and cities of Manitario give weight to your convictions."

I was worried to hear this, for I did not realize the region to be so dangerous a place, and so I asked him, "What massacres are these?"

"A mad archbishop, by the name of Yreth, waged terrible war against innocent folk," said the man. "His army numbered fifty thousand, and all the brave myrmidons of the Plains were sent against him."

Well, as you may imagine, I chuckled to hear how the facts had been turned around. Then, so he might not grow suspicious of me, I said, "I was laughing as I thought upon that strange name of

'Yreth.' I certainly would never go by such a name, for my name is Glissa." And this was no lie, for Glissa is my peace-name.

He told me his name was Otter, like the animal, although he looked little enough like one, for an otter is lithe and graceful, whereas this man was lumbering and fat. Then he called over a myrmidon who was sitting in his shop, took a hammer, chisel, and crowbar, and, with the myrmidon's help, set to work removing the metal bands holding the chains in place. When he was done, I climbed out of the pot (with some effort, for my legs were weak from my confinement), gathered together those of my possessions which remained in the pot, and wished him good day.

He asked, "But will you not take your protective pot?"

I told him he might keep it, and he expressed his gratitude for the gift. It was a good pot, you see, and worth an arran or so, though I, for my part, was glad to be rid of it, for I had spent enough time in its company.

The Eleventh Part

In Which, Through The Use Of An Entertaining Dialogue, I Describe Various Aspects Of The City Of Stanneck

I WANDERED STANNECK FOR A TIME, enjoying its sights and sounds. It is a wonderful city, to be sure, and there is so much to see there that, rather than merely describing it, I will instead take you on a tour of the place now, so it will seem to you that you are walking on those very streets, just as I was, and you and I are talking as we explore the city together.

I will do this through the use of a Dialogue, for all the experts agree a Dialogue is an excellent means of narrative, as well as being an entertaining way of conveying all manner of important facts. Remember, though, although I describe Stanneck now using a Dialogue, I actually explored the place alone, and silently.

But hush! Let us now listen to the chat as you and I explore the byways of Stanneck together.

You: Friend Yreth, there are all manner of things you may see in

Stanneck.

Yreth: Yes. There is a good arena for dog fights, and several large markets. There are many fine buildings, too.

You: I see there are countless domes (by which I mean abber domes, not pinnacled domes) decorated with gold and silver and coloured enamels of all kinds.

Yreth: Yes, and you will see the towers are very grand, although they are not quite so tall as you will generally find in the larger cities of Europe.

You: Indeed, even the tallest of these is twenty measures short of the celebrated Hen Tower at Bedea.

Yreth: I will tell you the reason for this, for it will surely astonish you. You see, the stonemages of the American plains eschew the cross binding, depending instead upon the ring binding as their principal tool!

You: Amazing. And what kind of cross-section does this technique bring forth in buildings?

Yreth: Why, buildings with a circular cross-section.

You: And will their walls stand firm against both ram and rocket?

Yreth: Yes, surely.

You: I can see their stonemages are masters of piping and shell-scooping, and their choice in matters of jewelling and colour is very refined, even to those of excellent tastes, like you, my friend Yreth.

Yreth: You are too kind. And you are right, too, for these shapes and colours are very much to my liking.

You: Clearly, Stanneck is a huge city, and a prosperous one. But tell me, what is that river I see, upon which the city lies? Could it be the river Demiak, a vast waterway, which connects the city to the Bay of Beans a thousand miles to the south, and, beyond, the great continent of Tara and the kingdom of Brazil?

Yreth: It is the same. A great many trading ships travel up and down that waterway, bringing many goods to Stanneck.

You: From the city's pleasant setting, I speculate it also lies on one of the important overland trade routes, leading both west to Great Tasker, and also east, to Ramport.

Yreth: Your speculations are precise, to the last detail. And, as you may also suppose, such a quantity of trade going back and forth means all manner of merchandise is available here, and at good cheap prices, too.

You: I see a simple merchantwoman there, standing at her stall. Let us see what she has for sale.

Yreth: A good plan indeed. Sa! You woman there! Tell us what you have for sale.

Merchantwoman: Gladly, good master. I have clothes and fabrics; spices; carpets and tapestries; rare oils and medicines; spheres, roots and amulets; needles in wooden cases; gar nuts and white nuts; wheat, barley, lurk and trundle; silver in both raw and crafted form; incense and steams; red peppers, green peppers, pale peppers; laughleaf; dark sugar; more than eighty types of wax; timber of all descriptions; inks of various types; coconut; white raspberry and other fruit cheeses; limpets, sweetsnake, cod and flounder; poultry and rabbit; a vast array of fruits, including apples, honey apples, and sours; fine wines and ales; horses, cattle, pigs, monkeys and other edible livestock; ancient artefacts and statues; and an impressive assortment of fine books and papers.

Yreth: I see you also sell slaves of excellent quality, and all types of myrmidons, which are sold for just a small fraction of their price in the markets of Cyprus, for these myrmidons are freshly taken in Tara, and transported north, directly to Stanneck, where they are trained.

Merchantwoman: And if you do not wish to pay for a trained myrmidon, why then, you may save yourself more money still, for, if you go to the training farms, just outside of the city, the trainers there will be happy to sell you a wild myrmidon, which you may train for yourself if you have the talent.

You: Thank you, good merchantwoman. But tell me, Yreth, is not the ownership of myrmidons a privilege granted only to nobles, as it is in the east?

Yreth: Indeed no. In fact, quite the reverse is true, for, here in the Kingdom of Saghena, the ownership of myrmidons is considered a civic duty. See there, an ordinary tradesman goes about his day's work. Clearly, he is not a rich man, but he has two myrmidons following him about. Let us strike up a conversation with this fellow. Sir, I see you have two myrmidons there. Are they your own?

Merchant: They are, yes. These two fellows give me solid protection, you may be certain, and they also carry my tools. Here in Stanneck, there is hardly a family which does not have a myrmidon or two to its name, and wealthy families may have dozens of myrmidons which are put to work in the garden, or around the house, just like slaves. During wartime, though, every family sends its myrmidons off to be a part of the city's army, which, in total, numbers countless thousands.

You: What a fascinating town this is, to be sure. There are so many things to see and to buy. I think I will now go off on my own, and leave you to your adventures here, good Yreth.

Yreth: May good luck follow you, and goodbye.

More Of The Eleventh Part

In Which I Describe Several Events And Encounters, Some Of Them Good And Others Bad

WHEN I SAW THE BUILDINGS of Stanneck, it filled me with a powerful urge to practise my arts once more, and to build some magnificent structure or other, so the local stonemages might see how tall a tower might go, and how quickly it may rise, when it is built with cross-bindings.

I decided to seek out a patron who would pay me to build a great tower. I had no particular plan in mind, except the tower would be very tall, at least a third again as tall as the tallest tower in Stanneck. Nobles and wealthy persons love to pay for such great structures as these, you see.

After several weeks in a pot, though, I was in no state to present myself to a person of quality. My robes were shabby, and torn in places. They also had black stains from the inside of the pot.

Alas, I had no money to replace these clothes, because all the

gold I had accumulated earlier was placed into the care of my myrmidons, securely strapped to their backs for protection. After my
army was defeated in battle, the enemy wasted no time in picking
off all my hard-won wealth and taking it for their own

(Of course, you will remember, too, I still had my ship, which
held great wealth and slaves and a few myrmidons. However, it
was far away, out at sea at that time, and could be of little help to
me here. But do not forget the ship, for it plays an important part
in my story later on.)

Nevertheless, I was not a complete pauper, for I still carried
a few valuable jewels on my person. I had some fine rings, and
a gold bracelet, and a golden cloak clasp with an emerald in the
centre, and some gold buckles on my boots. I decided I would
sell these valuable items and use the money to buy some fine new
clothes to impress a patron.

I searched around the city for a while, looking for an honest
goldsmith. When I found one, I exchanged my jewels for gold
coins, thirty arrans in all—and you may be sure this was a good
price, for I am a shrewd bargainer.

Next, I found a tailor's shop where the stuff was very thick, and
I said to the fellow there, "Take a look at this fat purse full of gold
arrans. Now you can see I am a man of means and power, give me
the finest set of clothes you can make. Let them be such things as
a true gentleman might wear, not an upstart, and do not try to
furrow me with old clothes which some other customer has sold
you."

"Oh, I would not do that, sir," he said.

"You are a liar," I replied, "for there is not a tailor in all the world
who does not try to sell rags as silk."

He laughed then, and said, "You are very perceptive and world-
wise. And because you are shrewd in the ways of tailoring, and not
to be tricked or swindled, you may be sure I will treat you well,
and will give you a very fine set of clothes indeed."

Then he said, "I have a thought." He pulled a fine costume from
his closet, then whispered to me, "This costume was made for

none other than Matroy, the king of Saghena. It looks as if it will fit you well. Why not try it on, just for the merriment of it."

Well, I tried the outfit, and it suited me very well indeed. It had a black tunic, with red and purple duffs, and a green leather hat, with gold around the brim, just like the wealthy and eminent persons of those parts wear.

The tailor gasped as he saw how perfectly it fitted me. I said it was a pity these clothes had been bought by the king, for they looked most flattering on me.

"You are right," he said. "Indeed, these fine clothes suit you so very well I think I will let you buy them, if you so wish, for you have a discerning eye and a good understanding of this business, and I know you will appreciate these clothes far better than the king."

Then I asked, "Will this not make the king angry at you?"

He said, "Yes, it will indeed. But I will give him some excuse or other, for I delight in vexing him. He dares not injure me, you see, for I am the finest tailor in all of Saghena, and he comes to me three times a week for clothes and such."

Well, this was a tempting offer, as you may imagine. I asked him the price then, and he said, "The king said he would pay me one hundred arrans for these clothes, and they are worth every part of that sum. However, because you show such discrimination towards my art, I feel inclined to make you a gift of them, in exchange for a token sum, let us say, six arrans."

Six arrans is a great deal of money, of course, but when it is in payment for clothing worth one hundred arrans, it is well worth the paying. I handed him the gold on the spot, and I left the shop looking every part the wealthy gentleman of Saghena. Then I looked at the clothing of those around me with a keen new eye, and I quickly saw how bright and colourful my clothes seemed, compared to the inferior garments of Stanneck's other inhabitants.

You can see, then, how important it is to be frank yet friendly with such people as tailors, and to have a little knowledge of how they do their trade, for in that way you can avoid being cheated and instead receive excellent goods at bargain prices.

To complete my outfit, I bought myself a slyte, which is a weapon gentlemen carry in that region. It is like a stiff whip, eight or nine feet in length. At its tip is a tiny blade, called a nugget, which is like a miniature axe blade, and is no more than two inches long. I know it does not sound a very formidable weapon, but in the hands of an expert it is lethal indeed, and can easily crack open the skull of a myrmidon.

For myself, I carried the slyte only for the sake of appearance, and, like many well dressed gentlemen, I walked the street with the whip part folded over double, so I might use it as a walking stick. Still, although I never learned the proper use of the weapon, I dare say I could have done so easily enough, if I had been inclined. In fact, I am sure just a little training would quickly have made me a master of the slyte, and I would have been able to perform the many tricks people do with it, such as flicking fruit from a tree, or chopping a man's beard, or killing a lucifer beetle in flight.

For my defence, I bought a very fine new throwing-razor, with a silver handle and an ornamented blade. I kept this in my other boot, so I now had two throwing-razors at my disposal. I planned to use the old steel weapon for killing thieves and scoundrels, and the new silver one for killing enemies of higher rank.

Next, I paid for a room at a good inn, *The Horse*, and I treated myself to a large supper, then socialized with the various patrons of the inn. This was an expensive inn; many of the patrons were lords or wealthy merchants, and everybody there was exceedingly refined. So, while it was an inn by name, its atmosphere was closer to the court of some king or emperor.

I talked with one man—his name was Travyn Horne, and he was a sheinor, which is something like an earl. We talked a little about the towers in the city, and the various heights of them, and then he asked me if I was a merchant.

I said, "No, I am a stonemage."

He said, "A stonemage, is it? Peh peh peh."

I said, "What do you mean by saying 'peh peh peh'?"

He said then, "Oh, no insult, surely. It is clear from your face and your voice you are from some far land, and I am certain, in that place, the occupation of stonemage is held in high regard."

I said, "That is so. It is an honourable profession, and a well paid one, too."

"In these parts," he said, "we look down a little on our stonemages, for they do not accumulate riches as our merchants do. Indeed, if I wore your boots, and was a wealthy stonemage coming to Stanneck, I would abandon my craft altogether and turn my hand to the pursuit of gold through trade, for it is in that direction a person may gain fame and prominence and wealth for himself, and there is no better place than Stanneck to do it. You can live a good life here if you have plenty of gold to spend."

I saw at once he was right, and I would be a fool to return to building work when I might easily make a fortune as a merchant.

An ominous voice seemed to speak in my head, though, saying, "Do not listen to this man's words, Yreth. You have another path to follow. Remember, you cannot serve both God and Gold."

But I was caught up in my dreams of wealth, for having tasted some of the luxuries it bought, I thought it would be a very fine thing indeed to be a wealthy merchant. So, I ignored my wise inner voice, and I resolved that very moment to follow this excellent lord's advice, and to turn my ambition from the building of a tower to the building of a great fortune. I told myself that, if I became very wealthy, I might even buy myself a new army here, and, when I was ready, I would take it back to Cyprus to aid the Duke of Oaster. Deep in my heart, though, I knew I desired gold for gold's sake, and no good will ever come of that, as any person of morals will tell you.

Over the next few days, I looked around the markets with a new eye, searching for a bargain I might buy at a low price, then quickly sell again for a high one. This, you see, is the essence of the merchant's art, and I calculated, by doing this repeatedly, I could quickly parlay my small fortune into a very large one.

Now, as I crossed the numerous bridges of the city and wandered the various markets, I came upon a group of men playing a curious game. Here was how it worked. One man, who was clearly very rich, sat at a bench in the centre, clutching three wooden sticks. In clear view, he placed a metal pin into the end of one of the sticks, then closed his hand around the sticks at that end, so the pin was hidden. Next, he shuffled the sticks around a little, and the men standing around placed bets on which stick contained the pin. After the bets were placed, he pulled the sticks from his hand one by one, so all might see where the pin lay. Now, as I stood there, the man in the centre called out to me, asking if I wished to play.

I said, "I prefer to watch, for the present, so I might see how the game is played."

He said, "Gladly, friend. Watch to your heart's content. And if you wish to place a wager, why, just say, for you may do so at any time."

Well, I watched the game for a time, trying to figure for myself which stick held the pin. On every round, I was able to guess correctly, for the shuffling of the sticks was easy to follow. Yet the other fellows there seemed to have a hard time of it and always picked the wrong stick.

After watching this for a short while, I became frustrated at the poor play of these unfortunate dolts. One fellow was about to place his money on the leftmost stick when it was clear to me the pin was in the centre stick.

I said to him, "Sir, you would be wise to choose the stick in the centre."

He considered this a little, then said, "No, no, I feel it is on the left this time."

I said, "Hear my advice. I have a keen eye for this game, whereas you have lost repeatedly."

He replied, rather insolently, "Then place your own wager."

"Not just yet," I replied, and I continued to watch the progress of the game. Well, of course, the pin was within the centre stick, just as I had said, and the dolt lost his bet.

At this point, suspicion began to scratch at my shoulder. I said to myself, "How do these fools have so much money to bet upon a game such as this? And why is it that this ignorant fellow, on receiving the advice of one who is dressed very much better than he, and who is clearly very much wiser than he, should ignore that advice and go his own foolish way? It does not make sense.

Then I realized there was trickery going on here. These players, I instantly saw, were in the employ of the man holding the sticks, their purpose being to lure innocent dupes into playing his game. I have heard of such swindles—games and challenges which seem easy at first, but which, when the unwary traveller places his bet, suddenly take on a new level of difficulty.

I thought to myself then, "Ah, walk away from this game, and give it no further heed." And indeed, I was about to do so, but something held me back. I seemed to hear God speaking to me saying, "No, Yreth, stay and play this game. Use your sharp wits and your cleverness to swindle these swindlers, and punish them for their deceptive ways."

And so I did not leave, but stayed, carefully watching the next shuffle of the sticks. It was an easy one, so I turned to the man with the sticks and said, "Very well, I will play." Then I drew out a small sum, just a few Saghenian grotecs, and I tossed them into the pot, saying, "I will wager these upon the centre stick."

Of course, the pin was within the centre stick, just as I had said, and I instantly doubled my money. You may be certain those other players acted as if they were very much impressed by my skill, and they tried to tempt me to play on, saying perhaps it was the luck of the novice, and I should play again, betting all my winnings and a little more besides.

I pretended I was taken in by their words, and I made more wagers, increasing the amount of my bets by a little each time, but still keeping my bets very small. Of course, each time I played, I won, for the game was still very easy. The other players laughed and slapped me on the back, saying I was an excellent fellow to win so much off old Capper (which was the name of the man with the sticks).

"It warms my heart to see you win," said one, "for I have lost great sums to Capper in the past, but now I see he is getting a taste of his own pie."

I said, "I am sure you are pleased indeed. But watch on, for I plan to win much more."

When Capper heard this, he gave a groan and pulled at his hair, pretending he did not like to play the game against such an opponent as me.

I played some more, and won some more, and then Capper said he had lost enough and wanted to go home for the day. Of course, I did not believe this, for I knew he wanted to trick me into placing a large bet.

All the other players said he must not end the game so soon. Those sly rogues pretended to plead on my behalf, saying, "You were willing enough to stay while you were taking our money. Now you must stay while this gentleman takes yours."

"No no," said Capper. "I have had enough. I will play only one more round." Then he placed the pin one last time, and shuffled the sticks once more, while I watched very carefully. This shuffle was cleverer than the ones which had gone before, and the movements of Capper's fingers were more deft.

The other players then said, "It is the last round. Use the hidden pin to stick old Capper for all he is worth."

One of them whispered to me, saying, "Yes, throw all your money into the pot so you might win a great fortune off him."

This plan suited me very well, therefore I asked Capper whether I might place a higher bet than before.

He said I might. (Naturally he said this, for he wished to rob me of all my money!) Thereupon, I poured the contents of my purse, together with all my winnings so far, into the bowl.

Capper cried out at this, and pretended he was horrified. He said, "What! When you asked if you might increase the stakes, I thought you to mean by just a few more crowns, not by this great fortune!"

But my fellow players said, "None of that, Capper! You agreed he might place the bet, and now you must face the consequences, for he has outwitted you with his cleverness and guile."

Capper said then he would accept the wager, although he shook his head at it, and sighed terribly, as if he was very sorry he had been trapped in this way.

Well, Capper asked me which stick my wager was on, and I replied, "The leftmost stick. The pin is there, I am certain."

Now, you will wonder how, when I knew I was playing amongst rascals who planned to use trickery against me, I could be so certain the pin would be where I said. After all, the final shuffle of the sticks was very much more deft and confusing than the shuffles that had preceded it, and old Capper had used all his skill in performing it.

Well, here I will confess I was using a little trick of my own against these would-be tricksters. You see, I did not do what most simple-minded folk would have done when watching the play of the game—following the movement of the pinned stick until it finally came to rest—for I knew this old rogue's nimble fingers would be able to outwit even my keen eyes. No, I used a different strategy. I had noticed that the three sticks, although they were very similar, bore subtle differences each from the other. One, for example, had a slight bend to it. Another had a white mark on one side. The third had a little splinter sticking out of one end. By observing the key feature when the pin was first placed, I had only to find it again when the shuffling ceased and I would be certain of victory, no matter how much dexterity Capper's hands might display.

When the pin had been placed on this final shuffle, I had noted that the splinter-tipped stick was the one which held the pin, and this was the stick which had ended up in the leftmost place. That stick, therefore, was my selection.

When he heard my choice, you may be sure Capper gave a terrible cry of woe. He said, "You have beaten me, my friend. I am certain your choice is the right one. See, I will show you."

And he withdrew the stick, so I might take pleasure in viewing my victory. But then an astonishing thing happened: *the pin was not there!*

Moreover, I could see Capper was as perplexed and astonished as I. Then, wide-eyed, he pulled out the centre stick, which was the one with the white mark, and not the one with the splinter, and what do you suppose? The pin was there, embedded up to the head. This sight brought further astonishment to him and to everyone else who looked on.

Well, of course, all my money was gone! I left that marketplace a pauper, and returned to the inn, where I lay in my bed and puzzled over the strange things which had come to pass.

At length, the explanation of the changing sticks came to me. I realized that, while I played the game, a miracle had occurred. God had interfered with the sticks, so I might not become corrupted by wealth. He wanted me instead to follow the mysterious path which He had laid out for me, and to follow such signs as He might send to me when He was good and ready.

I also saw now that the task of restoring the fortunes of the Duke of Oaster, my old patron (who, I still believed, was exiled by the king) was not something to be completed within a few months as I had thought, but was, rather, a great task, of the sort a hero might take a lifetime to fulfil.

I therefore resolved to stay in Stanneck for a time, and enjoy the fruits of the place until a clear message was sent to me from God that I should move on. I was very tired, you see, of all the hurried travelling I had been doing lately.

I knew I would need money soon to pay for my food and lodging, so the next day, I decided I would set myself in business as a joiner and mender in the marketplace. I knew it was a profession using similar skills to my own, and its practitioners can make a solid wage without having to win the favour of a powerful patron. I am surprised that other stonemages have not thought to use their skills profitably this way from time to time, for it is much easier to stick together broken shoes and pots than to stick together broken buildings.

Of course, before I started I needed a bench and a table, and I had no money for these things. I remembered, though, I had seen benches and tables and all manner of wooden furniture at the shop of Otter, who, you will remember, was that man to whom I gave a valuable cooking pot just a day before.

I thought, "Perhaps he will lend me a bench and a table so I might set myself up in business." So I set out, looking for his shop once more.

The streets of Stanneck were still new to me, and I had not been paying close attention to which street I followed and which street I turned at when I had left Otter's company, so I was tramping the streets for some time looking for his shop.

As I walked, I began to think, "What if Otter does not choose to lend me a bench and a table? What shall I do then, for he is under no compulsion to help me?"

Then I thought, "No, no. I must think well of this man, for he released me from the pot when I asked him to, and I owe him a great debt of gratitude."

Well, I walked on, with this happy and naive attitude in my head for a time.

Yet I felt a nagging doubt, a worry that troubled me, for I felt I had not appraised the situation aright.

I thought through the situation again, about how Otter had helped me.

"Here is Otter, the fat carpenter," I said to myself. "He is sitting outside his shop, lazing away the day, when along comes our good friend Yreth, in a beautiful and valuable pot. 'Let me out,' says Yreth. And so Otter lets him out. And, for the price of a few blows of a hammer, he gains himself this rare pot, whose worth is at least a full arran."

Of course, it was true I had not asked any payment for the pot, but that is my carefree way. More importantly, though, *he had not offered any payment.*

Suppose some stranger came to me and said, "The pin of this precious jewelled brooch is stuck through my skin," and I removed it from the stranger out of charity. In such a situation, I would not think of keeping the precious brooch. Instead, I would give it back to the stranger, and, if the stranger would not have it, why then, I would pay him a fair price for it.

I said to myself, "By rights, that fellow Otter should have offered me a fair price for the pot. An arran, at the least."

An arran, did I say? Well, as I walked on, I thought upon this, and it occurred to me that, in all my travels, I had never seen a merchant selling so large a pot as the one which Otter had taken from me. Mind, I make no claims to be an expert on the price of pots, but I know they are often expensive items, especially the big ones, and most especially those made of iron, as this one was, for iron is a fine, strong metal. So, while I had seen pots priced at an arran, it struck me that those pots were not quite so large and tough as the pot I had given to Otter. That pot had a lid, too, which not every pot does.

After I had thought the matter through carefully, I decided two arrans would be a more appropriate token price for that magnificent pot, although three arrans would be fairer, and it would not be unreasonable to pay even as much as four arrans for such an unusually large, well crafted, attractive and solid cooking pot as that one was.

At length, I found the shop where Otter worked. He was sitting outside, with his myrmidon standing near, and, as I approached, he waved at me and said, "Ah, my good friend Glissa. How goes, then?"

You will remember, I had given the name Glissa when I had talked with him before, so he believed it to be my true name.

I nodded politely in reply, and said, "Well enough. Well enough." Then I walked on, looking casually into his shop as I passed.

There were good benches there, and fancy chairs too, as well as many tables. At the back of the shop, a long folding door was open, so you could see right through the shop into a garden at the back. In this garden, I saw the pot. It was lying in the grass and a child was playing in it.

I walked away then, saying nothing about the pot, for I had not quite settled my thoughts.

I continued through various streets, thinking over this matter of the pot. I felt angry and offended that this valuable item was being wasted, just left to rust in a garden while children used it as a plaything.

I said to myself, "No, this matter must be settled, for otherwise it will twitch at my stomach for nights to come! I must seek immediate and satisfactory redress." Then I turned around and marched to Otter's shop.

He waved once more, saying "Ah, it is Glissa again."

I said, "It is none other." I used a friendly tone, for I thought it would be best to resolve this matter in an amicable way, especially since Otter had a myrmidon guarding over him, whereas I had none.

He said, "Well then, how is Stanneck treating you?"

I said, "The place fills me with ambition. I intend to become a joiner and mender in the marketplace."

He said, "Why then, you will need a bench and a table for that." (As you can see, I had no sooner mentioned my new trade than he starting thinking of how it might benefit his own old one.)

I said, "Yes, and I know the very place where I will acquire these things, which is to say, here."

He was delighted at this news, and told me what an excellent decision I had made, for his craftsmanship was the finest anywhere, and so on. Then he showed me all the tables he had for sale. I looked carefully over a number of them, but they were too large to carry, and besides, I did not need a large table for the work I planned to do. In the end, I decided upon a very fine little walnut table, with an intricate flower pattern around the edge.

As for a bench, Otter showed me a few, but none of them really suited me well, for they were very plain and ordinary. The fancy chairs, however, were another matter.

Otter laughed at my judgement, saying, "These are not for setting in a marketplace. These chairs are such as you might set at a dinner table in a fine house."

I said, "Why is it necessary that a trader or merchant must sit at a plain bench when the same person might sit upon a fancy chair? There is no sense in it whatever." Then, so Otter might see my good taste was nothing to be mocked, I picked myself a very pretty chair, with padded red cloth upon the seat and back, and carving upon the legs.

He said, "Well, you have chosen some good carpentry there. Now, shall we discuss the price?"

I said, "Without delay, for it will be a short discussion. As you will remember, when we first met, I made you a gift of a very fine pot. I have calculated its worth very carefully, which I estimate as four arrans."

He said, "Do you think me so wealthy that I will pay you four arrans for an old pot. No! No indeed! Take it back, if it is so valuable to you! I have no need for it anyway."

I replied, "The pot was a gift, and I asked no payment for it. In discussing its value I am merely pointing out what a generous gift it was. Moreover, I think it very rude of you to make light of my gift by trying to throw it back at me."

He was shamefaced then and apologized for his rash words, saying he had mistaken the angle of my argument.

I said, "I do not insist on any payment for my pot, let me be clear on that point. And yet there are important customs and traditions at stake here. For example, where I come from it is customary, when you are given a gift, to offer a comparable gift in return. Does the same tradition hold here in Stanneck."

Otter said, "Very often it does, yes."

I said, "And it is a very fine tradition, too, for we are all brought closer by the spirit of generosity. In the church the priests use the terms "charity" and "love of neighbour" to describe this excellent state."

He said, "Yes, but let us cut to the sap. If you are saying I should give you this beautiful chair and table as a gift, because you have given me that pot, which is, frankly, an old one, well then, it is simply not fair, for the value of one gift outweighs that of the other."

I said, "Let us not quibble over silver, for such discussions are not part of the true spirit of gift-giving. If we are to measure every gift so scrupulously, we might as well be two merchants haggling over the price of a hen."

Well, he thought about this, and then he laughed, saying, "Very well, take the chair and the table as my gift to you, and may your new business flourish. In fact, I am certain it will flourish, for I see you are a much cleverer man than I, and quick with your wits besides."

I laughed at this, for it was so true, then I thanked him for his gift and we bade each other farewell.

I left his shop, with the chair under one arm and the little table under the other. I felt very sweet and charitable and in love with the world, for my good friend Otter had given me a fine gift.

But as I walked away from his shop, he ruined it all, for he shouted after me, for everyone in the street to hear, "Make me no more gifts, though, or I will be a pauper!" Well, his thoughtless comment instantly made my mood very sour, for it made it seem as if my gift had been no gift at all, whereas his was like alms to a beggar.

I said nothing in response, of course, and merely kept walking. Later, though, I came across the shop of another carpenter, so I went in, with my chair and table, and said to the old man there, "Here, what would you give me for the two of these?"

He said, with barely a glance at them, "Half an arran."

At once, I saw what a paltry gift I had been given—a chair and table worth half an arran in exchange for a pot worth four! Well, I returned to the inn with my furniture, but when I reached my room I had already decided I would settle the score with Otter.

Late that night, I set out once more for Otter's shop. Of course, the shop was locked up by then, but it was easy for me to gain entrance, for the window frames were held in place with just a few of those ring bindings their builders are so fond of. I removed these bindings from one of the windows and pulled it out, frame and all, from the wall. Setting the window frame against the ground, I climbed inside the building through the hole where the frame had been.

I had brought along the little bedside lantern from the inn, and by its dim light I started hunting around for Otter's money box. I searched every cupboard and shelf, but to no avail. Well, after I had searched for half an hour or so, I began to despair, for the hour was late and I was growing weary. I thought to myself, "Ah well, perhaps I shall accept my losses as they come."

I think, though, that God read my thoughts and decreed I should be recompensed fully and fairly, as I had first intended, because, just as I was about to leave, I suddenly felt a piece of the floor wobble beneath my foot. I looked down and saw I had stepped upon a small, square section, set cunningly in among the planks.

"Hoho!" said I. "I will wager this is where he keeps his gold."

I pried up the section and pulled out a wooden box placed beneath. When I opened it, sure enough, it was filled with money— Saghenian crowns, mostly. I counted out eighty of these for myself, which is approximately the value of the four arrans he owed me for the pot.

Then I thought, "Ah, but what of the chair and table Otter gave me as a gift? If I take this money for my pot, I will then be indebted to him for the gift." The solution was simple. I decided to pay him for the chair and table, so they would no longer be a gift from him, but would rather be an ordinary trade, silver for wood. So I took ten crowns from my purse (which is to say, half an arran) and placed them back in the box in payment for the chair and the table.

I left the building exactly as I had found it. I placed the box back in its hiding place and I carefully replaced and repaired the window—for I was not there to do mischief, but simply to rectify an inequity.

And do not think I returned directly to the inn with my money, as a thief might do. No, I made certain that, on the way there, I passed a church. Although it was locked, I knelt at the door and prayed my thanks to God, and then I placed five crowns under the door as a gift to Him to show my appreciation for His wisdom and justice.

Yet More Of The Eleventh Part

In Which I Describe My Practice As A Joiner And Mender In The City Of Stanneck And The Friends And Enemies I Made There

T HE NEXT DAY, I ROSE early and went to one of the better marketplaces. I set up my chair and my table near the centre, and when the people started to arrive, I called out to them. I had a fine cry to bring in the crowd. It went:

> O, you that have things broken or unjoined,
> Come to me, and I will make those things mended or
> joined once more!
> My prices are half those of any other mender or join-
> er,
> And my workmanship is better also!

My cry attracted a good many customers, and they soon found my claims were not idle. Most joiners in the city charged two crowns for each tiny binding they placed, so if you came to them with an urn broken in many pieces, you could pay fifty crowns by the time all the pieces were secured. What is worse, they would take days to complete the job.

I, on the other hand, charged a flat rate of five crowns for all easy repairs, and ten crowns for a difficult repair, and I completed most jobs within minutes of receiving them. What is more, my repairs were so well executed that people gasped to see the high quality and durability of the work, which far exceeded anything the local menders might achieve, for their bindings were weak and delicate, whereas mine were the same powerful bonds I used to strengthen mighty walls and towers.

On one occasion, a woman came to me with the pieces of a valuable ivory statuette which had been broken. She wore rich clothing and had ten myrmidons escorting her, She asked me what it would cost to repair it and how long the repair would take. I said, "Ten crowns, and it will take me five minutes."

She said, "How is that? Yon Crowid said it would cost eighty crowns and would take a week."

I said this Yon Crowid of hers was an unskilled rascal, and I told her I would set to work immediately. "If you do not like the results," I said, "then pay me nothing."

Before her eyes, I assembled the parts of the statuette, with strong point bindings, then, when all was done, I placed sheet bindings and cross-bindings throughout the ivory, for added strength.

Then I turned to her and said, "Is that to your liking?"

She said, "Yes, very much."

I said, "Well watch this!" Then I threw the statuette down onto the cobblestones with all my strength.

She cried out at this, but when she saw the statuette was not broken or even chipped by my violent action, her cries of alarm changed to cries of the utmost delight and pleasure.

She said, "I declare you are the finest craftsman in all the world." Then she paid me twenty crowns, which was twice what I had asked, and said, "My name is Shellith and I have many powerful friends. You may be sure I will speak to them all about your singular talents."

She was true to her word, and many of the city's wealthiest patrons started coming to me, bringing valuable and precious objects in need of repair.

Another time, a young child was crossing through the market near to my table when a group of older children set upon him, teasing him about his fine new cloak. Then they took hold of the cloak and started pulling it, so it tore.

I cannot bear to see injustice done, and I immediately leaped over my table and dealt out discipline with a few good swipes and punches, chiding the youths for their heartless behaviour. Then, so they would all remember the lesson, I took the leader of the group and gave his ears such a boxing that the blood flowed from them and he howled for mercy.

After the other children had run off, I turned my attention to the little fellow who had been their victim. He was very distressed to see such a gash in his cloak, and he wept like a tiny baby, which was hardly surprising since he was barely more than an infant.

I quickly cheered him, though. I said, "What, then? Your cloak is ruined? Let us see what we can do." Then I took the fabric, laid it out flat upon my table, placed the torn parts together, and cast Renny's Plaque upon them. It is usually used to cover a wall, but I scaled it to a small size, just enough to cover the rip. At once, the cloak was mended, and the join was almost undetectable, except the fabric in that small area was now as stiff as steel.

The infant was very much cheered when he saw his cloak was once again restored, and all the passers-by who had stopped to watch the scene gave me a great cheer when they saw the kind thing I had done—and at no charge too.

Thanks to these and other acts of generosity and good craftsmanship, my reputation spread very quickly. I did not let fame swell my head, and I kept my prices very low. Even so, I completed each job so swiftly I was able to accumulate a great fortune in just a few months—hundreds of arrans, in fact. I saved this money in a chest which I kept in my room at the inn. To keep out thieves, I placed powerful wefts and bindings upon the chest, so it might not be moved or opened except by me. I also spent a couple of arrans on a large and ornate tent, which I set up in the marketplace to draw further business.

Naturally, my success did not please the other menders and joiners who worked within the city. This was partly because I was taking business away from them, but they also hated me because I was not afraid to speak out about them. I told everyone who came to me that the other menders were cheats and rogues who lacked any real talent.

After a time, the menders and joiners conspired against me. I started to receive notes which said such things as "Leave this city, or face the consequences," and "Soon you will die," and so on. I merely laughed at these threats, for I am no coward. But those rogues looked for fresh ways to strike a blow against me.

A cat used to follow me to the marketplace in the morning and, during the day, it would often come up to me as I worked and rub itself against my legs. One morning, as I left the inn to begin my day's work, I saw the cat had been killed and placed near the inn's entrance, together with a note reading: "Glissa: Cease your work!" This did not bother me a jot, though, because I had never asked for the creature's affections, and I do not really like cats, although the inn's gardener, who owned the cat, was sad when he came across the creature's body.

They used magic against me then, or rather, I should say, some sorcerer they had hired used magic against me. I cannot say precisely how this transaction was negotiated, but I am certain it went something like this:

They said to the sorcerer, "This fellow Glissa is too fine a craftsman for us to endure his presence in our city, for he makes our work look shoddy by comparison, and he reveals to the citizens that we are cheats, and inept into the bargain, which is a secret we do not wish to spread."

Then the sorcerer said, in evil tones, "What vile service would you have me do?"

And they said, "Kill him! Kill him! It would delight our wicked souls for you to spill his good and righteous blood."

But the sorcerer told them, "There is no magic so strong it may cut a righteous man open or strike him dead upon the spot. But I can weave powerful spells so he will die of fear."

They said, "Yes! Yes! That would be even better! O, what a cruel and unjust revenge we will have upon this fellow!"

So then, as I was in my room one night, I saw a green light at the window. When I looked out at the window, I saw a luminous globe hovering there, with a evil face inside it.

I am no illusionist, but I know enough of such magic to know these spheres are harmless, provided you do not lick them. Therefore, I just nodded, thinking, "Very pretty. That is a nice one." Then I went to bed.

The next night another globe appeared. This time, within the globe, there was the image of a dagger. Well, that is not a very frightening thing, for a dagger is nothing more than a knife, so I opened the window and shouted out, "The face from last night was a more frightening image. Moreover, the detailing upon the dagger is shoddy, for the back of the blade is hazy, as is part of the handle."

I am sure these words must have annoyed their sorcerer greatly, for all those illusionists think their creations are very perfect.

On the following night, I left my window open to see what would happen. Instead of hovering outside, the globe drifted into my room, so I could see it from where I lay in my bed.

This globe contained the form of a beautiful maiden eating fat, juicy strawberries, which she held out for me to try. The maiden vanished then, and all that was in the globe was a bowl of straw-berries on a small, round table. I watched the strawberries for a long time, but they did not move or change in any way. I was puzzled, until I realized the sorcerer expected me to try to lick the strawberries, which would have killed me from the violent shattering of the magic into my face.

I know all this because I once built an illusion house, and I was told to add a barrier between the inner seats of the circle and the stage where the magical globes appear. The purpose of this barrier was to stop drunken patrons in the front row from leaning forward and licking the illusions.

Even if I had been unaware of the dangers of the illusion-spheres, however, I would have been a sad sort of fool if I had tried to lick those strawberries, for they glowed green; and furthermore, the table on which they stood hovered a foot from the ground. Besides, I am not in the habit of licking food while it sits within the bowl. Rather, I like to pick my food up with my hands, and if I were to find my hand passed through it, I do not think I would be inclined to make further explorations with my tongue.

Still, I found I could not sleep with those strawberries lighting up the room, so at last I left my bed and shouted from the window, "Yes, yes. I have tasted those luminous beauties, and they are quite delicious. Nyerm nyerm nyerm!"

My words brought no response, so I took a little water from the jug at my bedside and flicked a few drops at the globe. This action caused the globe to evaporate in a bright flash, and I heard a voice in the street give a cry of pain, so I suppose the illusionist had burnt himself through some kind of sympathetic reaction.

On the next night, the globe showed a group of excellent dancing fiends, then showed a beautiful maiden being devoured by a snake. This was a fair display, and could have been a very good one if the snakes had eaten the maiden starting at the feet rather than at the head, for then I would have seen her terrified face to the last.

On the fifth night of these entertaining displays, I saw a truly marvellous show, which I will tell of now.

It started, as usual, with the sphere appearing at my window, then drifting through the window into my room. It stopped a few feet beyond. It was a little further from the foot of my bed than

I would have liked, but I suppose the sorcerer who was casting the spell could not see my room from where he stood. (He would have stood somewhere in the streets below, for that is the way this magic works.)

Within the globe, which was green, I saw the image of a beetle. "Well," I said to myself, "that is not so frightening. This will not be a good show."

I was wrong, though, for the next thing you know, the beetle began to walk, and it seemed as if he walked towards me, for he grew bigger and bigger. Then I saw the beetle burrowing into something. As the image emerged from the haze, I saw it was burrowing into the neck of a sleeping man. I think the man was supposed to be me. Certainly he had clothes much like those I wore then. His face, though, was a little different from my own, and not so handsome.

In any case, the beetle burrowed into his neck, and then the man awoke, and he clutched his throat. As I watched, his body seemed to rot away, until only the bones remained. His skeleton then started to move. It stood, walked away from me, apparently looking for something. Suddenly, it stopped as if it heard a sound. Then it slowly turned and started walking towards me, with an accusing finger stretched out.

A very remarkable effect followed this. The skeleton grew closer and closer, until its skull filled the globe and became hazy. Then, very suddenly, the globe itself grew and took the shape of a skeleton, hovering horizontally above the floorboards. Its mouth opened wide then, and it actually spoke, saying "Aaaaaaaaahhh."

Well, I jumped when I heard it speak, you may be certain! I had never before seen an illusion that spoke, and I have never seen one since. Or at least, not speaking with a voice of its own, for the voices you hear in the best illusion halls are provided by actors who hide under the treddle boards.

I quickly realized the skeleton was supposed to be hovering over my bed, staring down at me, but, once again, the sorcerer had made a bad guess of where my bed was placed in the room.

Because I was anxious to receive the full effect of the illusion, I pushed my bed over to the part of the floor where the skeleton was hovering, then climbed back under the blankets.

It was very exciting to look up and see a great skeleton hovering over me, although it was now silent once more. Well, I wanted the full effect, so I shouted out, "Oh! That is a horrible thing! By the gods, I hope the skeleton does not once more return to the globe, then emerge in exactly the same manner as before, moaning in the same fearsome way!"

Sure enough, the illusionist heard my words, and, taking me to be almost at my wits' end with terror, he repeated the last few minutes of the illusion, with the skeleton inside the globe walking towards me, then the globe growing and changing shape so it became a skeleton hovering directly over me. When it opened its huge mouth and started moaning once more, I was so thrilled and frightened I pulled my blankets over my face with the excitement of it all.

Then the skeleton returned to the confines of the globe, and it danced around and shook for a time. Then, I saw a kind of story unfold. First, the skeleton was in the marketplace, when it saw a beautiful girl. She looked at it very lovingly, and it was clear the skeleton was in love with her. But when her father, who was a king, saw she was looking at the skeleton, he pulled her back and beat her, then sent soldiers to drive the skeleton away. The skeleton ran off, but later it came back to the marketplace and looked up to the tower of the castle, where the princess could be seen.

There were roses growing on the wall of the tower, and the skeleton picked one of these flowers, then threw it to the ground. At once, the rose changed to a floating shell, and the skeleton stepped on and flew up to the window of the tower. Then the princess stepped out of the window onto the floating shell, and they flew to a distant cave.

When the king saw what had happened, he waved his arms, summoning six huge bats, and, by means of further gestures, he ordered the bats to seek the lovers out and kill them both.

I do not think I need to tell more of this story, for I am sure you have already recognized it as the story of Addo and Corithane. The illusion continued to follow the plot exactly, except Addo, instead of being a handsome youth, appeared as a vile skeleton. This made no sense, of course, for why should Corithane fall in love with a skeleton? And, for that matter, why should a skeleton wander freely in the marketplace without the common folk screaming and running in fear?

What is worse, there is one part in the story where Corithane places an enchanted lotion upon Addo's ears, so he will not hear the death-wail of the witch, but in this rendition of the story, she placed it upon the sides of the skull, for the skeleton, being a creature of all bones, had no ears.

The scenes of their lovemaking were unsatisfactory, and a little gruesome. But as to the rest, it was very entertaining all in all, particularly the fights, and I was generally able to put out of my mind that Addo was a skeleton and imagine he was the attractive lad who had won the princess's heart.

In total, the spectacle lasted the best part of an hour. Clearly, the illusionist had merely taken the standard pattern for casting the story, and added a skeleton so it might frighten me. I am sure he did not suspect I knew the story, because there are no illusion houses in America (or at least, none I ever came across) and neither are any of Obic's tales known there. I deduced, then, that the sorcerer who sought in vain to torment me was from the east, like me.

If you remember the end of the story, you will recall that Addo is killed by a poisonous arrow, and then Corithane weeps over his body, and, as her tears fall onto him, he is suddenly transformed into ten thousand butterflies, which lift her away. Now, this last part did not happen in the illusion I saw in my room. Addo was struck by the arrow and fell, and then Corithane wept over him, but at that point the illusion ended, for I suppose the wizard did not think the sight of a skeleton turning to ten thousand colourful butterflies would be a frightening thing to leave me with.

I was annoyed at this, though, and I rose from my bed and looked out of my window, shouting, "What about the butterflies?"

Then, from down below, I heard a frustrated and angry scream, and a voice shouted out, "Here are your accursed butterflies!" And with that, a large clod of dry earth came flying at me and hit me in the forehead in a painful way.

I determined not to open my window to any more globes on the following nights, but, as luck would have it, no more globes came, so it seemed the sorcerer and I had reached some sort of agreement, for he knew now that I was not the kind of man who might be terrified into leaving the city. I imagine the sorcerer's failed endeavours must have cost the joiners a fat purse though, for the casting of such illusions as I saw is an expensive business.

About a week later, the joiners tried to kill me. It was late at night, and I woke to hear a grating sound at my window. When I went to look, I saw a man, all in green, and with a large metal cutting disk strapped to his back. He was standing on the ledge, slowly waving his arms to indicate I should open the window.

I guessed he had thought to disguise himself as one of the wizard's globes, so I would open the window and let him into my room, thinking I had let an illusion in, whereas he was actually a murderer.

Of course, a man in green smear with a metal disk upon his back looks nothing like a shining illusory globe, and the joiners were fools for thinking I, or any person with eyes to see with, would be tricked by this disguise.

In any case, it was this fellow, not I, who soon fell victim to trickery, for I leaned forward, as if I would open the window on the right, but instead I unlatched the window on the left, which he stood directly behind, then I pushed it open with such force that he tumbled from the ledge and fell to the ground, where he lay dead of a broken neck.

After that, the joiners did not dare to attack me physically, and instead they spread malicious rumours about me, which harmed my business.

The first I heard of this was when one of my customers, a very wealthy man named Bariah, came to me with a little tree carved from moonstone. I recognized this tree, for I had repaired it some weeks earlier with my novel techniques, using bindings powerful enough to hold up a building, yet intricately cast over a tiny area to form an invisible and indestructible repair.

I said to him, "What, is there an imperfection? Would you like me to strengthen the bindings still further?"

He said, "No, indeed. I would like you to remove the bindings you first placed upon this carving."

I was mystified at this, and said, "If I remove the bindings, the carving will fall into broken pieces once more."

He said, "That is what I wish, for I will then take it to a true joiner, who will mend it in the correct manner."

I said, "What do you mean by this? A fool could see the repair is already perfect. Why do you wish to undo this beautiful work and to squander your gold upon some inferior craftsman?"

He said, "I have heard that small objects repaired by you have a habit of exploding with great violence."

I laughed at this, saying, "That is not so."

"Indeed it is," he said. "My good friend Irech Ven brought you a bowl to repair, and a few days ago it exploded, injuring his wife's arm. Also, I have heard a precious brooch which you repaired for Teal the Trainer exploded so violently it took down one of the walls of his house."

The truth of this was immediately evident to me, and I told him so. "These explosions are not the result of poor craftsmanship," I said, "but of a terrible hatred which is levelled against me."

Then I explained how desperately the other menders and joiners wished me to leave the city. Now it seemed they were creeping into houses, under cover of darkness, and placing explosives near those objects which I had repaired so my reputation might be harmed.

Well, this put his mind at ease a little. But then he said, "How do you explain that other items repaired by you, which are worn upon the person, such as rings and clothing, cause welts and blisters to appear beneath the places where the repairs were done?"

I told him, "It is true that contact with powerful bindings can sometimes cause a tingling sensation (and anyone who has accidentally leaned against the wall of some great building only to find his back is against the principal bindings will immediately attest to this), but I have never heard of it causing welts and blisters. If these symptoms are as you have stated, it can only be that the menders and joiners, in their mindless hatred for me, persecute my customers by coming to them in the night and secretly placing caustic substances upon their skin."

He said then, to my great dissatisfaction, "If their hatred for you is as strong as you say, and their ability at committing violence by stealth is so cultivated, then I am by no means sure I wish to side with you in your feud against them."

At length, though, I persuaded him. I said, "What, you are afraid of menders? Tell the myrmidons of your house to keep special vigilance for intruders, and no harm will come to you."

He left satisfied. Unfortunately, the fellow did not heed my advice, and a few days later I heard that a great explosion had toppled his house, burying him beneath it.

My business suffered sorely in the next few weeks, and rumours persisted that my repairs were dangerous to person and property. Those devils the joiners were busy, too, exploding valuable objects I had repaired, and applying caustic substances to the skin of men, women, and even children, just so people would think my repairs were at fault.

I did not know what to do to improve my trade. I considered killing all the other menders and joiners, but there were a great many of them, and most had myrmidons to protect them.

Of course, I might have bought myself some more myrmidons and set them upon my enemies, but, quite honestly, I had taken my fill of leading myrmidons about and having them follow me everywhere. Besides, I had an ally far more powerful than any myrmidon, this being my old friend God, and, one morning, I decided to go to the church, to call upon His aid.

Now, as I entered the place, I surprised two rogues, dressed all in rags, who were kneeling down at the front. When they saw me, they ran out through the rear door.

I walked up to where they had been kneeling, and I saw they had been performing a ritual there, for there was blood upon the floor, and a dead shrew, and pine needles, and dozens of small white stones, arranged in a circle. In the centre of a circle was a human hand, cut off at the wrist and covered in chalk dust.

As I my eyes fell upon the hand, I gasped, for a vision entered my head. I saw a great white hand, set upon green fields, and pointing up to heaven, and I knew this was not some idle musing, but a message, sent to me from God, that I should leave Stanneck now and journey west once more to build this beautiful structure.

This view was confirmed when I returned to my stall in the marketplace. As I approached, I was thankful I had made my pious visit to the church, for I saw that Otter, the thieving carpenter, was waiting there, with several of his friends, and a mixed group of myrmidons, and it was plain he was angry. He was probably telling them I had stolen money from him, while conveniently omitting any mention of the beautiful pot which he had so wrongfully taken from me.

My blood ran hot at his impertinence, and I nearly ran at the group, with a will to kill them all. But then my reason took hold, and I said to myself, "Control your fury, Yreth, for to fight against men is one thing, and you could surely defeat a group of six others, for you are fearless in battle. To fight myrmidons, though, is a different matter. You will be killed, and your death will be unjust. Besides, you are using your peace-name of Glissa here, and it would be ill-omened to set into a great fight under that name."

I decided to leave Stanneck without a moment's delay. I went directly to the inn, and took those possessions I had left there in my chest, including my clothes, a quantity of gold, and a number of jewels I had purchased with my earnings.

While I was in my room gathering my possessions together, I

heard a noise from below. Looking down from the window, I saw a crowd of people and myrmidons, with Otter at the head, striding towards the inn. In the crowd, I saw menders and joiners, and many of my old customers.

"This does not look good," I thought. "Who knows what lies he has spread about me."

I quickly left the inn by the back door and escaped through an alleyway. Then I watched around a corner as Otter and his friends banged on the door of the inn.

I was angry at Otter, and keen for vengeance against him for forcing me to leave the city in this way. Then a good idea came to me. "If the thieving Otter is here with his myrmidon," I thought, "I will warrant nobody is guarding his shop."

I quickly escaped down an alley and made my way to his shop. Sure enough, nobody was there to guard it. So, I lifted up the panel in the floor to see if his money box was still there. However, it was gone. I prayed then, saying, "God, lead me to Otter's wealth, if you deem it right that I should have vengeance against him."

Then I looked up to heaven, and suddenly, there up in the rafters, I saw the money box. I quickly took a shutter-pole and knocked the box down to the ground. It broke open, revealing more than a hundred crowns, together with five gold arrans.

It was clear Otter had done well for himself that summer, but I immediately made sure he would be a pauper in the autumn. I placed all the money in my purse, then I entered his house to see if there were any other objects which I might take to anger him further.

I looked around several rooms, and I took a china spoon and a silver incense tray, but really there was very little worth having. Next, though, I came to his kitchen, and what do you suppose I found there? It was a small child, in mud-stained clothes, who was trying to reach a tray of cream tarts which was laid upon the table.

I am a kind fellow, even when I am filled with anger, and so I took one of the tarts from the tray and passed it down to the child, saying, "There you are, my little one."

As I watched the child eat the tart, I could not help but laugh, for it made such a mess of the meal, and put cream all over its chin and nose. My longing for vengeance left me then, and I was filled with feelings of charity and goodness.

"It is not right," I said, "that a tiny child such as you should have such a cruel and dishonest father. Come. I shall adopt you as my very own."

With that, I lifted the child up into my arm, and took the tray of tarts, together with a fresh loaf of bread.

I quickly left the house, then, walked directly to the city gates and said goodbye to Stanneck, walking west along the merchant's road.

A Further Continuation Of The Eleventh Part

In Which I Describe My Travels West, During Which Time I Educated A Child Until A Sad Thing Happened

THE ROAD LEADING WEST FROM Stanneck is none other than the famous Golden Way portrayed in Tybalt's masterpiece of the same name, and it has changed little since Tybalt's day. The road is very wide, paved with fine white brick, and lined with numerous shrines and statues, although sadly many of these have been chipped or broken over the years.

This road stretches thirty miles, connecting Stanneck with the city of Uot. Many merchants travel the route, as well as farmers, craftsmen, pilgrims, philosophers. All manner of people, in fact, so I was never short of company.

I walked this route, carrying the child in one arm, and the tray of tarts in the other, placed near enough that the child might take the tarts as it wished.

I had thought the child to be a boy, for it had a very ugly face, and I named it Daleth, after the famous falconer. Later, though, I passed a clear stream, and I took the child down there to wash it, but no sooner had I undressed it than I discovered it was actually a girl, and so I was obliged to change the name to Dalit.

Now, from the moment I had taken the child from Otter's house, it had not spoken, and I had soon realized this was because it had never learned how to speak. Can you imagine what kind of father would raise a child in this way, caring so little about it that he did not even teach it to speak? I was disgusted and greatly angered when I thought about this. I knew, too, I must break this barrier of silence if I was to teach the child other, more important things. Therefore, as I walked, I spoke to the child at great length, asking it to speak, and repeating phrases it might learn, such as "My name is Dalit," and "Please give me another cream tart," and "Father, how dearly I love you." (This latter phrase, incidentally, I intended for the child to use in reference to me, not to its previous father, the contemptible Otter.)

As I walked, my efforts attracted the attention of other travellers, and, as people are wont to do everywhere, they started to offer their tiresome opinions, telling me the child was tired and needed a rest, or it was sad and should be spanked to release the tears, or it should be kept out of the sun, and so on.

One woman said, "Those cakes cannot be good for your little girl. You should be giving her goat milk, and good clovebread."

Then I said, "I am sure the child knows better than you what foods it likes."

She said, "Liking is not needing. She will eat those tarts until her hair turns grey, but it is only because she knows no better. If you were a good father, you would be her guide in matters of food."

I replied, "Who am I to force my tastes on this dear child's lips? If I were partial to strong wine and well spiced beef, my preferences would not make these things any more appropriate for a child's digestion. It follows, then, I cannot rely upon my own preferences in feeding this infant, and since I cannot, I certainly will not rely upon the fancies of a stranger, met upon the road."

She said, "These are not my fancies. I can see from the little girl's face she wants goat milk."

I said, "If she truly wants it, let her ask for it herself. Such appetites may encourage her to learn to speak."

The woman became cross at me then. A short time later, she stopped a farmer's wagon which was coming in the other direction, and bought a cup of goat milk. Then she followed close behind me, trying to win the child's favour by making strange faces and pointing at the milk. I ignored the woman, but I found her antics annoying, for she distracted the child from my speech lessons.

The woman's husband followed behind me too. He was a merchant with a cloth hat and red face, and he made frequent comments and criticisms about me to his wife, but in a loud voice so I might hear too, saying such things as, "If that man really wants the child to speak, he should beat it. A beating would gain its attention."

After a time, I became angry and turned upon him. I said, "I will make this child speak, for it is my desire to do so, and I am not easily prevented from obtaining the things I want. Moreover, I will not teach the child through beatings, as a brute would do, but rather shall smother my child with love and kindness, giving it whatever its heart desires, and squeezing all the evil out of its nature."

Of course, they scoffed at me, saying this was no way to raise a child, and boasting of how many children they had raised (although I could see none present, so it was clear they must all have either died or run off). Still, you will be pleased to hear I was publicly vindicated in my views just an hour later, as I will now explain.

I had left the road to relieve myself in a group of trees, leaving the child sitting on a big stone at the roadside, under a tree. It was a fair walk from the trees to the road, and on my way back, a stall caught my eye. There were many such stalls along the roadside. At these places, merchants and farmers sell goods to the passing travellers, usually food and drink, although some offer other services to aid to a traveller, such as repairing wheels or selling you a new pair of shoes.

The stall I had noticed sold pastries, chingo, and all manner of other sweet things. They looked exceedingly good, and I thought to myself, "The child will enjoy those treats," so I spent a grotec or two and bought myself a large assortment of these foods, and bottle of sweet strawberry juice as well, for I knew this was a drink the child would relish.

When I returned to the child, I found a large group of people were gathered around there. That terrible woman and her husband had taken hold of my little one and were trying to make it drink goat's milk and eat bread. They were pulling at the child's lips and trying to place these things in its mouth, saying "Come, my child, it is very good for you," although the child clearly did not wish to be a part of their feast.

I was furious at this sight. I drew my throwing-razor and ran forward, ready for battle. But as I drew close, the child showed this wicked couple exactly what it thought of their food, for it vomited all over them, giving them both a good dousing! I immediately forgot my anger and burst out laughing at the spectacle of these two in their dripping clothes.

Then the child heard me laughing, and looked towards me. When it saw the plate of excellent food and drink I carried, it reached out happily with its arms and said, "More cakes!" in a voice as clear and distinct as you can imagine.

I was excited beyond measure to hear these clear words from the child's own mouth. I walked over to the child then, and picked it up. Then I turned to the others and said, "You see, thanks to my caring love, this child has learned to speak. You would be wise to think upon your actions. Your foolish ways have brought you nothing but a set of stinking clothes, which, in my opinion, is a very fitting punishment."

Of course, they disagreed, but my wisdom was clear to see, and I heard the people who stood around saying, "He is quite right," and "What fools they were to meddle in a good man's dealings with his child," and so on.

After that, the child learned to speak very quickly. In fact, no sooner than a day had passed before the child was telling me stories about the moon, and talking spiders, and all those other amusing tales that children have.

Although the stories were not profound or instructive, I was still very proud to hear the child prattle on so. I have read, in a number of authoritative sources, that it normally takes a child years to learn to speak properly, and yet, under my careful instruction, this child had learned to speak in a little over a day.

I realized I had a natural gift for raising children, and I decided to devote myself to this task for a time, for surely, I reasoned, if I could teach the child to talk in a day, what wonders could I teach it in a month? I would educate this child in so many wonderful skills that people would come from all around to see it demonstrate its talents and to hear its wisdom.

That night, I bedded down in one of the roadside shrine-shelters. While the child slept, I worked by candlelight, formulating a series of rules which I planned to follow in raising the child.

In the first place, I decided the child should be fed only those foods which its natural appetites commends to it. Human judgement may be fallible, but the dictates of nature never are, and if people would only follow their natural drives and impulses more often, they would stay healthy and live long. If the child wanted cakes, then cakes were right for it—"a sweet meal for a sweet infant," as they say—and it would be wrong to give it anything other than cakes.

Secondly, I decided I would not wash the child again, except to remove stains. This was not because I found the task disagreeable (although I did), but because I realized washing is probably not good for children. After all, if you cherished a dog or ferret or cow, you would not wash it. Why then should you wash a child, whose skin is so much more sensitive to the abrasive effects of water than these other creatures? Besides, it is clear children do not enjoy being washed, but rather revel in all manner of dirt and filth, and, once again, because this is a dictate of nature, it must been seen as a wise and useful preference.

Thirdly, I decided the child should not be beaten. Some people maintain that regular beatings teach a child to bear pain, but it is my opinion that precisely the opposite is the case: those children who are never beaten and are permitted to behave in whatever way suits them will ultimately become bold and reckless warriors, whereas those who are beaten learn only to become the slaves and tools of others.

This rule, I might add, is not some vague and abstract philosophy, but a wisdom based on my own experiences. When I was a child, I was never beaten, and far from being made puny by it, I became very fit and strong. One day, when I was 12 years of age, my father had been drinking wine, and he got it into his head that now was the time to begin beating me, so he started hitting me with a stick. It made me so angry I snatched the stick from my father and turned it upon him, striking him again and again until he cried out for mercy. Since that day, I have been widely feared as a formidable fighter.

Fourthly, and finally, I decided the child should not spend its time in foolish or wasteful pursuits, such as playing with dolls or blocks or coloured beans, but, rather, should always be engaged in useful and profitable activity. As an adjunct to this, I vowed to myself not to speak to the child in a foolish way as many parents do, but rather to treat it as an equal, and to address it in the same sober and respectful tone I would use in dealing with any lord or patron. In this way, I knew, the child would develop a noble and refined attitude, and this, combined with the wizardly skills I planned to teach it, would give it an early start in making its way in the world.

What plans I had for this child, and what a great success she would have been! I can remember looking by candlelight at the little face sleeping there and thinking upon the glorious future that awaited her, and the wealthy suitors who would someday bid against each other, offering me large sums of gold for her hand in marriage.

The whole prospect set my mind in such a spin that I was not able to sleep, so I went to the tent of a doctor who was nearby and bought from him a little bottle of wormsblood, and by means of a few drops of that powerful medicine, I was very soundly asleep in a few minutes, and I stayed that way, alas, until well into the next morning.

As you may guess from my sorry tone, a terrible thing happened during the night which utterly spoiled all my ambitions for this child, and removed from her the great opportunities which lay ahead. When I finally awoke the next morning, the child was gone! Moreover, my bags had been opened and their contents spilled out over the floor, indicating that thieves had visited me as I slept.

I cared nothing for the property, of course, for a child is more valuable than any jewel—unless it is an extremely large jewel, of the sort that nobles wear.

I quickly ran out onto the road, and began calling for the child. This caused a great commotion among the other travellers, who said to me, "What is wrong? How may we help you?"

I explained that my child had been stolen, and before long there were a hundred people, travellers, merchants, farmers, and even a group of hunters with dogs, all of them calling out for Dalit, and searching through bushes and ponds.

It was a moving scene, now I think back on it, for these good and honest folk of Saghena stood nothing to gain for their efforts, except the knowledge they had returned my child to me. They searched for two hours or more, with no sign of the child, until at last I was approached by a tall man in a yellow suit. He said, "Are you the man who has lost his child?"

I said, "I am."

He said, "Was the child about this big, with dark skin and brown eyes, a little ugly about the chin and forehead, and wearing a leather tunic?"

I said, "Indeed yes. Have you seen her?"

He said, "I believe I have. Early this morning, I was travelling west from Stanneck when I passed a fat man riding in a biddler's cart with his wife and a myrmidon. They were travelling fast back to the city. There was a little girl up there with them in the cart, and the woman was holding her very tight, and laughing in a curious way. The man, too, was laughing, and driving the donkeys at great speed. For truth, I thought them both mad."

I gave a groan then, for I had a terrible feeling the man in question was none other than Otter, the wicked carpenter, whose very life, it seemed, was devoted to bringing me misery.

My suspicions were confirmed when I checked my belongings, for I found the items stolen included everything I had righteously removed from Otter's house: the china spoon, the silver incense holder, the tray that had held the tarts, and even a number of my cakes, which, I suppose, was in retaliation for the loaf of bread I had taken, although anybody can tell you that fine cakes cost a good deal more than loaf of plain bread, so it was not a fair trade, even if you believe my requisitioning of Otter's things was unjust, which it was not.

Also, when I counted the money in my purse, I discovered ten arrans were missing, which, when I worked it out, was the same amount God had given to me from Otter's cash box.

When I tell this story, people always say the same thing, which is, "That man Otter cannot have been as bad as you say, or he would have taken all your money, not just a part of it." Such people think only in terms of material gain, and not in terms of pride or honour. For I knew what message he was leaving me by spurning the bulk of my gold. He was saying to me, "I have taken this sum of money, but I will take no more, because, although I am an unprincipled thief, your money is not good enough for me, for it has been soiled by your hand. There now, I have insulted you. Follow me and be rightfully avenged, if you dare, for I and my villainous friends will be waiting for you in Stanneck with our myrmidons at the ready."

What comfort is it to have gold, when your honour and your dignity have been bruised in such a way? Still, I did not wish to take him up on his challenge, for I am not such a fool that I would march back into a place I have fled in fear of my very life.

I called together all of those who had been searching for Dalit, and spoke to them. I said, "I thank you all for your tireless efforts, but I fear they were all in vain. My daughter has been stolen by an enemy of mine in Stanneck. The fellow is a rogue, and has many thieves and assassins among his friends, so I dare not take her back, but I will curse him now, before all of you."

Then I laid a terrible curse upon Otter. I said, "Otter, carpenter of Stanneck, may your business fail, may your ambitions fail, and may your health fail. May your wife desert you for a still less worthy man, if one exists. May your children be struck with skin blight. May my child, Dalit, grow tall and healthy despite your improper care, and may she abandon you to marry a wealthy man, yet may this match bring you no wealth and may her leaving break your evil heart so you die of sorrow. Also may your house burn down, and may your myrmidon be killed in battle."

Then the crowd said, "May all these things be," and they swore on the names of their various gods.

Many of them came to me afterwards, saying what a fierce and righteous curse I had made, and those who were going to Stanneck said they would seek out this man Otter for me, and would do mischief to him. So, in the end, I think I was at least partially avenged for his wrongs to me.

I then continued my travels west. (I was now travelling under the name of Yreth again, by the way, for I had become tired of people calling me Glissa.)

A group of merchants who had helped me in the search invited me to join with their company, and I gladly accepted. They were all very kind, and they consoled me as we walked the long road to Uot, saying what a terrible thing it was to lose a child. Of course, I spent much time talking about the raising of children, and how unfortunate it was that my child would not be raised in the way I had wished. Then I told them about the rules which I had written out.

In the evening, when we had made camp, one of my fellow travellers asked if he might see these rules I had talked about. I said yes, and I gave him the paper to peruse—merely so he might satisfy his interest, for I took him to be a merchant, just like the rest.

This man's name was Lophtha. He had a bald head and a wrinkled brow, and there was a look of great intelligence about him. As he read my words, he nodded and made approving noises, and then, at last, he turned to me and said, "You are truly an exceptional teacher and philosopher. The wisdom of your words is self-evident. If only all parents would raise their children in this way."

I said, "I believe the importance of these rules can hardly be understated. In our towns and cities today—not just here in America but also in other great kingdoms around the world—we see children running the streets like packs of dogs, shouting and throwing stones and fighting with each other. Who is advanced by these actions? Nobody, to be sure."

Lophtha asked me then, "Have you ever thought about publishing these words, so people everywhere might gain the benefit of them?"

I admitted I had not thought about it but it was certainly a good idea.

He said, "I own a good printing house. If you will come with me to Belpinian, I will print your wise words, and I dare say you will make a pretty penny from them."

I said, "That is a tempting offer, but I had thought to go to Uot, for I have heard it is a wealthy city."

He said, "Peh! Uot is a vile place, full of pestilence and foul smells. No, come with me. It is a long journey, but I promise you will not regret the choice, and perhaps, in some small way, the printing of your excellent treatise will give meaning to the terrible loss of your child."

Well, this fellow had a convincing tongue, and, since there was nothing specific waiting for me in Uot, I decided to accept his invitation and we travelled past that city, continuing on to the south-west for a good many weeks, and passing uneventfully through the kingdoms of Precia, Dakota, Great Meece, and Havolenko, until we finally came to the city of Belpinian, which does not lie in any kingdom as such, but is, rather, a free city under the immediate protection of the mighty Saskatoon Empire.

A Fifth Section Of The Eleventh Part

In Which I Tell Of The Things I Created In Belpinian

B ELPINIAN IS A FINE CITY. Not big, but pretty, with plenty of colours about the houses. The architecture in these parts is closer to the Cypriot style than that of East America and Manitario: tall towers built with plenty of strong cross-bindings. Some of the designs were perhaps a little too ornate for my own tastes, but they were well suited to the warm climate in those parts, and the overall impression upon the eye was one of cleanliness and wealth.

Lophtha's house was situated in the centre of Belpinian, overlooking the city square. I stayed there as a guest, sharing the place with his wife and his children (who, alas, were all grown up and beyond the useful influence of my four rules) and six slaves.

During the days, I worked with Lophtha in his printing house, helping him to assemble the print for my tract and for other books too. I found the printing machinery fascinating indeed.

In case you have never seen such equipment in operation, I will explain it, for such tools are surely among the wonders of our world. The machine is built like a loom, but in place of a shuttle, a large mechanism, called the tongue, slides back and forth across the frame. Upon this tongue is placed a strip of wooden blocks, glued at the back upon a loop of canvas, and upon the faces of these blocks are carved the letters which are to be printed. When the tongue dashes across the loom, a cog causes the loop of letters to turn, rubbing each letter block, one after the next, against a piece of inked wool, then against the paper, which is fastened to the frame. Because the blocks are placed in a circle, they can print upon up to five sheets of paper, one after the other, if the sheets are placed in a row upon the frame.

Each pass of the tongue prints a complete line of text, and the operator of the machine has only to pull the tongue across the sheets of paper, and to change the sheets with every pass, to have all his writing done for him quite automatically.

When enough sheets have been printed, the wooden blocks are removed from the tongue and a new loop of blocks, representing the next line of text, is placed inside it, then all the sheets of paper are replaced upon the frame, in lines of five sheets, and the printing continues. After the job is done, and every line has been printed on every sheet, slaves are brought in to glue patches over the edges of the sheets, in order to cover the various rips and snarls that occur during the natural course of the printing process.

The method is calculated to minimize waste. For example, after each loop of blocks is done with, it is soaked in hot water to remove the glue holding the blocks to the canvas, then both blocks and canvas are set out to dry in the sun, whereupon they may be glued together again in some different order and reused for printing a new document.

I was very impressed by this machine, but I quickly realized its efficiency might be improved upon if it printed more than one line with each pass, so I asked Lophtha for his permission to attempt this improvement.

He said, "Ah, three lines with one pass. That is every printer's dream. But I must say your idea is not a new one. It has been tried by many wise men, but the results are never good, for the letters come out patchy."

I said, "Let me try it anyway. I am sure I can make it work."

He said, "Very well, if you wish. But do not work with my good machine. Instead use this old one." Then he pointed me to an old printing machine, which was a little worn and which he no longer used because it was too small.

Well, I removed the base of the tongue, which is made of wood and resembles a large carpenter's plane. I set to work with a chisel then and widened the gap in the middle of the tongue so it would allow not one, but *three* loops of blocks to pass through at one go. I also placed a wider strip of inked wool inside the tongue, with two extra ink-droppers above it. Then I cut a good wide strip of canvas, and glued three lines of text to it. We gave it a go, and it did not work too well at first, for the printing was patchy, just as he had said.

I did not give up, though, but instead gave the matter some thought. I soon realized the patchy printing was because the pressure upon the letters was too light.

"A little extra weight will remedy that," I thought to myself. Then I took several pounds of ordinary oven lead and attached it to the top of the tongue. The modification worked perfectly, printing three clear lines of text with each pass, where it had formerly printed only one. Better still, because the strip of text was now wider, it seemed to tear the paper less with each pass than before, so there was less repair work for the slaves to do.

Lophtha was astounded that I had so quickly solved this problem which had vexed all others who had tackled it. He was delighted too, as you might well imagine, and he asked me to make the same changes to his large printing machine, which I did, and it worked just as well.

He said to me, "I should pay you for this work, for it will surely mean money in my pocket."

I said, "No no, I am your house guest, and that is payment enough. Besides, I take the greatest pleasure from solving problems of this sort."

Then he said, "How I wish I had your keen mind and skilful fingers! You are truly one of the most accomplished men of the modern age, and perhaps the *most* accomplished."

I shook my head in modesty at these words, but as I did, I heard the cooing of a dove up in the rafters.

Lophtha heard it too, and said, "You see? The dove, which is a holy bird, agrees with me."

I said then, "We shall see." Then I picked up a nail, and I said, "I will throw this into the rafters. If the bird is lying, may the nail pierce its heart, and may it fall to the ground dead. If the bird is telling the truth, may it be protected from the nail."

Then I threw the nail, good and hard, up into the rafters. A moment later, I heard it strike the ground again with a tinkle. I could see the bird was still up there, for its nose stuck out beyond the beam, so I was compelled—though unwillingly—to accept Lophtha's words as entirely true.

It took us only a few weeks to print my tract. I had made a few changes here and there, expanding my argument in certain places, and adding examples, so, instead of being one page in length, my manuscript now totalled around thirty pages, but the basic four rules were the same. We printed two hundred copies, all told, and the finished tracts, bound in pigskin, were given into the hands of Lophtha's merchant friends, who carried them to the various cities of the region in order to sell them. The work was titled *On the Proper Training of Infants*, but do not bother searching for it, for it has never been printed in Europe, and no library here holds it.

The sales of my tract were spectacular. In fact, Lophtha said he had seldom printed a book that sold so well, and, before the month was out, we were once again gluing blocks to canvas in order to print several hundred more copies. This gave me the opportunity to make further changes to the tract, for I had discovered parts where the arguments were not so clear as they might have been. We added pictures too (these were printed by hand using an ordinary hammer block, inked with a brush) so the length of the book increased a little more, to a total of sixty-seven pages.

I would say I earned an arran each week from my book, which is very good, when you consider it was just the result of setting down a few commonsense rules. The book also brought me much fame locally, which I found flattering, and there was hardly a place I would go without being pointed out by the citizens of Belpinian.

"There he goes," they would say, "the wise philosopher Yreth who taught us how to raise our children properly."

Often they would offer me gifts or food, so my expenses during my stay in the city were very small indeed.

I was in Belpinian for some months. When I was not working at Lophtha's fascinating machine, I spent many hours doing my own work in his dining hall, where I laid plans for a number of great buildings, including detailed plans for the cathedral in the shape of a pointing hand.

After a while, though, I began to find the dining hall dingy for my drawings and plans, and I started to become distracted by the bright sunlight and clear skies outside. I said to myself, "What I truly want is an outdoor workplace, for the weather here is certainly sweet enough to permit it."

I went for a few walks around the city, to see what places I might find. At last I came across an old house which seemed to be empty, together with a garden. The moment I laid eyes on it, I thought, "That would make a pretty spot for an ornamental garden, together with a table for my work, and a sliding roof, so I can continue my work even when it is raining."

I knocked on the door of the neighbours and asked them, "Who lives in that house?"

They said, "It belongs to a rich baker, but he has gone travelling for a time."

I said, "Is he a good man or a villain?"

They said, "Oh, he is a villain, everybody agrees with that, for how else could a baker win himself such riches? Moreover, why should an honest baker go travelling the land, unless it is to go thieving as a bandit?"

"In that case," I said, "I trust you will have no objection if I, an honest stonemage and philosopher, appropriate his land and put it to good use."

They said they certainly would have no objection to my plan. In fact, they said they would be honoured to have such a famous man as their neighbour, and said, indeed, if I wished, they would even lend me slaves to assist me in my work—an offer which I gratefully accepted.

With the help of two of these slaves, I spent the afternoon placing a fence around the house and garden, in order to claim it for myself, then I went home and sketched out a few plans.

I decided the theme of my ornamental garden should be "water and land," and it should have fish, waterfalls, and towers too. I sketched out a few plans that night, and the next day I went back to the site and removed all the furniture, pots and other belongings from the house. I gave these items to the neighbours as a gift for their kindness.

Then I set to work removing the bindings. I began at the roof, taking the point bindings off the shingles, and I worked my way steadily down, until by the end of the day the entire house was just a mass of rubble upon the ground. I had the slaves collect the stones together and place them in a neat pile, for I planned to use some of it for my ornamental garden. As Gibo says, "Waste nothing and you shall never be left wanting."

Over the course of the next week, I set the slaves to digging holes where I planned to place the rivers and pools which would make up this garden. When the holes were dug, I lined them with the stones from the house and fused them into smooth sheets, so the water would not escape when it was poured in. In colour, these channels were a deep blue, so the natural colour of the water would be enhanced.

I took the water from a nearby river. It was a little brown, though, so before I poured it in, I strained it through sheets of sacking cloth, using a large wooden funnel. This took some time, and required frequent scraping of the cloth, but the results were most satisfactory, and all the dirt and small creatures were very effectively removed from the water.

Once the waterways were finished, with water in them, I set to work building the garden towers. Each one was topped with the head of a different animal. One was a deer, one was a sparrow, one was a black lizard if I remember right, one was a rabbit, and one was a parson-snail. The purpose of these decorations was to attract wild animals from all around to this garden, so it might appear a natural paradise.

Of course, the towers themselves were only miniatures, each around twenty feet high and just two feet wide, but they looked very pretty there, reflected in the water.

Another tower was hollow at the top, so when it rained, it would collect water. I designed it to function as a waterfall. The water slowly drained from the top of the tower into a raised pool which I had placed directly below it. From there, the water tumbled down to a second, larger pool, and from there it fell to the stream which wound through the garden.

I also started work nearby on a kind of pump which I planned to harness to a goat or a donkey. As the animal walked in circles, water would be lifted up to the top of the hollow tower, and then released down the waterfall, even when it was not raining. I did not manage to complete this machine, but the plans were very innovative nonetheless, and even to this day I have not seen another waterfall driven by such a method.

In the very centre of the garden, I had built a circular pool with an island in the middle. I connected the island with the rest of the garden by means of an arched bridge, covered in ruby-glass.

I built a large stone table on the island, with a flat top suitable for writing. On either side of the table, I set up two posts, with a rope mechanism slung between them. The rope and pulleys were fixed to a wooden platform upon which I had attached numerous tiles. On fine days, the platform rested on the ground near the table, but if it started to rain, I had only to pull on the ropes to lift the platform into the air, directly over the table, keeping me and my work quite dry, and allowing me to watch the gentle play of rain upon the waters.

Unfortunately, small insects and slugs would often shelter beneath the platform while it was on the ground, and when it was lifted over my head, I found the cost of protecting myself from a shower of rain was exposing myself to a shower of these crawling creatures—but this annoyance was a minor one.

Once I had built the table, I used to spend a good portion of my days there, planning and overseeing the construction of the rest of the ornamental garden, and working on other plans too.

For the next stage of the garden, I intended to beautify the land, adding many paths and bushes and flowers and trees. The paths were easy, and I built them from rocks and sand, fused together, and, like the bridge, studded with pieces of coloured glass.

The plants, though, posed more of a problem for me. You see, although I like to look at plants occasionally, I do not like to grow them. It is a slow and tedious process, and I am impatient by nature, for my mind is very alert. And anyway, plants are fickle, and often choose not to grow in my care. So I decided to find plants and trees that were already grown and to place them in my garden. In the meantime, I told the slaves to sprinkle some grass seed around, for grass grows very quickly, and it looks better than plain earth.

It was around this time a visitor came to see me. I was sitting at my table, working, when a voice said, "Are you Yreth?"

Well, I was used to being recognized by then, so I thought nothing of this and said, "Yes I am," without even looking up.

Then the man said, "Honoured sir, I have been sent to bring you an offer of employment."

I looked up then and saw a very strange fellow. He wore long white robes, and his hair was also long, and he wore a gold comb in his hair marked with a crest of some kind.

I said, "Who has sent you?"

He said, "I cannot say, but you will find out if you accept the offer."

I said, "Ah, then it is some noble or other, for they often seek employees in this secretive way," but the man neither agreed nor commented upon my speculation. Then I said, "What is the nature of the work?"

He said, "Again, I cannot say. However, you may rest assured it lies within your field of expertise."

I said, "I have not seen you around the city. Is this work to be carried out here in Belpinian, or in some other place?"

He said, "In another place many days' journey from here, but I cannot tell you where."

"Very well, then, " I said, "what is the pay?"

He said, "I cannot give precise details, but I am told to tell you it is more than you have ever received before for your work."

Well, this pricked my curiosity, you may be sure. Still, it was all too secretive for my liking, and I feared the whole thing might be the work of my enemies, trying to trick me into an ambush. So I said, "I cannot possibly accept an offer of employment when the terms are so vague. Besides, I am busy with work at the moment. Come back to me in a month, and bring a sum of money with you representing one-tenth of my proposed fee. If the sum pleases me, I will leave with you and work for your mysterious master."

The man agreed to my terms and left then.

Later, over dinner, I told Lophtha about my strange visitor and the offer that had been made to me. When I described what the man had been wearing, and particularly the gold comb in his hair, he gasped and said, "That is the costume of a courtier of the emperor. It sounds to me as if the emperor himself wishes to employ you."

Lophtha's wife agreed with this, and said that, in her home town of Pos Croythorn, which is not far from the Imperial City of Saskatoon, she had often seen courtiers dressed as I had described going to and fro on official business. She was afraid for my safety then, and said, "You should not have declined the offer so, for the emperor will be offended and may try to have you killed."

I laughed at this, and said to her, "It is clear the emperor is very desperate for my building skills. If he kills me, my skills will be of little use to him. Besides, it is I who should be offended, for such a vague offer of employment should have had a little gold behind it in the first place—and I mean gold coins, not gold combs."

Then Lophtha said I was right, and I was a very brave fellow to look at it so, because most people would have been so choked up with fear they would not put the facts into perspective as I had done.

Then he said, "Let us drink a toast to our intrepid and successful guest." And Lophtha, his wife, his daughters and his son raised their glasses to me and drank in my honour.

I, for my part, resolved I would accept the emperor's offer if the money seemed reasonable, and prepared to leave Belpinian in a month.

I knew there would not be time for me to finish my ornamental garden, but I determined to do what I could before I left the city, for I did not know if I would ever return.

In the next few days, I purchased a quantity of colourful fish and octopuses from a merchant who imported such rare things, and I had them poured into the water. Most of the fish died, unfortunately, and although the octopuses looked very elegant when they were swimming around, they had a habit of crawling out of the water onto the land, so I was finally obliged to kill them by stamping on them. Still, those fish that did survive gave a charming, natural feel to the blue waters.

I made several trips into the countryside around Belpinian, looking for attractive bushes and plants. I had the slaves dig up some of the good ones, and we brought them back to the city on a cart, then placed them at certain positions around the garden. One of the bushes was a mulberry bush. Another was a bush with blue-green leaves. Another had yellow flowers. Another had broad leaves and rounded purple flowers and attracted the butterflies and bees.

As for ground-flowers, I found that those growing in the country were too leafy for my tastes, with not enough blooms on them, so we did not dig up too many of those. Instead, I went about the town by night with a handcart, looking in people's gardens for flowers of the most alluring and exquisite varieties. Whenever I saw some attractive plants, I pulled up a third of them, leaving enough so no injury was done and the missing plants would not be missed in any way. The next day, I had the slaves put the flowers in the rich beds I had set for them. They were few and far between at first, of course, but after a few weeks, my garden began to look very colourful.

I left the trees until the end, because I could not think how to dig one up. We tried digging up an oak, but we soon found the roots of an oak go very deep, and it really seemed to be more trouble than it was worth, applying all that work just to preserve a few roots that nobody would see in any case, once the tree was planted again.

Finally, as the month was drawing to a close, I had a better idea. I set out into the forest with my slaves and some axes, then I picked out some good trees and the slaves chopped them down. We brought them back to the town, laying them along two big carts I had borrowed. It was quite a sight, and all the city came out to watch.

When the trees were back at the ornamental garden, we dug holes in the ground wide enough to accommodate the trunks, and about ten feet in depth. Then, using ropes, we placed the tree trunks in the holes, padded them around with earth, and I fastened the trunks in place with several cross-bindings and a sheet binding.

I then told the slaves to pull on the ropes attached to the trees, and to try to topple them. They pulled as hard as they could, but the trees did not budge, for the bindings I had placed anchored them as firmly as any roots, and I knew they would hold the trees in place for as long as it took for new roots to grow.

We placed eight trees in all. Three were oaks, and the rest were great tall pine trees. They had been difficult to transport, but the end result was worth it, and my ornamental garden looked magnificent.

Finally, I put up a stone sign which said, "This ornamental garden is a gift from Yreth the stonemage to the generous people of Belpinian, given to them on the sole condition that I, Yreth, shall be allowed to work at the garden's table whenever I desire, and that those in the garden will not make loud noises when I am working."

Once the sign was in place, I ordered the slaves to remove the fence which had surrounded the garden until now. Soon afterwards, a great crowd was gathered there, staring in wonder at the beautiful wild place I had created in the heart of their city.

The next day was precisely one month after the man in the white robes had visited me. In the morning, I gave my farewells to Lophtha and his family, and I told them I would return to visit them again if I was able.

Lophtha asked me where he should send any future profits I had earned from my book. I replied he should not worry about that, and he might keep all the future profits if he wished, which was exceedingly generous of me when you think about it.

He was a gentleman, though, and he declined my offer, preferring instead to give me a sum of thirty arrans then and there, and promising, if my future profits exceeded that sum, he would search the ends of the earth in order to find me and give me my money.

Then I made my way to the ornamental garden, together with my pack, and I waited there for some hours, until, as promised, the man in the white robes returned. He laid before me a bag which looked to be full of coins. When I poured it out, though, I saw it contained not coins but jewels, and of the most delicate and valuable types. I guessed the value of this purse to be more than a thousand arrans, which meant, since this was only a tenth of the full payment, the total would be ten thousand, give or take. (You may calculate this for yourself if you use mathematics.)

I accepted the job on the spot, and within an hour I was walking along the road leading north and west from Belpinian.

A Sixth Section Of The Eleventh Part

In Which I Describe My Journey To The Imperial City Of Saskatoon And The Strange Employment I Found There

I CANNOT SAY THIS MAN IN robes was good company. In fact, he was exceedingly tiresome. He did not speak as he walked, nor did he sing along with the many entertaining ditties I sang.

That evening, as we made a camp in a cave among some rocks, I grew a little tired of his silent ways. I said to him, "Talk to me, for frankly I find your hushed manner disturbing."

He replied, "It is not my way to indulge in idle chatter."

I said, "That may be so, but if you do not entertain me in some way, I swear I shall turn around and walk back to Belpinian, and you will then have to explain the matter to your master."

He thought about this for a while, looking very displeased, and finally said, "Very well, then, what is it you wish me to talk about."

I said, "If I am to tell you what to say, I might as well talk to myself. Talk about whatever you please."

"May I tell stories?" he asked.

I said, "Yes, I like a good story."

This man (he never told me his name and I did not ask it) started telling stories then and there. They were all stories about a holy man named Boh, who did not eat, did not fight, did not enjoy the company of women, and did not value wealth in any form. Whenever Boh was threatened by any dangerous thing, he would turn into a kind of vapour, so nothing could hurt him, and when the danger was gone he would turn back into a man again and continue his travels until the next danger.

These stories soon bored me, and when I had listened for a few hours and grasped the tiresome pattern of them, I finally told the man in the white robes that, if he wished, he could remain silent once more. He stopped telling his stories, and we did not talk further for the remainder of the journey, except for such comments as "Beware of that snake," and "Give me that food there."

We travelled for several days across flat, arid desert plains, and in my head I spent much time trying to imagine what sort of work the emperor wanted from me. I was certain it would be something very important, and supposed either a palace or a great tower, for this is usually what such powerful persons ask for. As you will see, though, I was far from the mark.

The desert gradually came to an end, and we entered a region of many small lakes. As we travelled over this flat terrain, the land became increasingly green and lush. In the distance, upon a low hill, I could now see a great walled city. I asked my companion if this city was our destination. He said it was.

Our road joined another, which ran along a great river, and we took this lovely riverside path towards the city. The setting was so pretty it literally filled me with hunger, and even though it was mid-morning and I had eaten a few hours earlier, I was compelled to sit down by the riverbank and eat another meal. I ate two meaty buns and drank a cup of weak wine, as I took my fill of the scenery.

Of course, my miserable companion did not appreciate the delay and he paced and tutted the whole time.

When I was done my feast, we followed the road through the green lands, towards the fortified city. I saw other travellers upon the route, and, although they were far away, I could see many of them were wearing white robes, just like my dull companion. We reached the city gates half a day later, in the early evening.

I was awestruck at the tremendous height and thickness of the city walls. They towered two hundred feet above the ground, with wall towers extending that height by another hundred feet again in places. Even the gates seemed to have been built more for giants than men, for the arch of the gateway was at least eighty feet from the ground. The walls were made of strong fused stone, cast in brown and yellow. Also, there were thousands of arrow slits in the sides of the walls, and I could see myrmidons behind them.

Many other courtiers, also wearing white robes, were milling around the gate, chatting and laughing with each other. I greeted one or two of them and was surprised to receive a friendly response.

One said, "Ah, a new face! Welcome to the Imperial City of Saskatoon. You look as if you have had a tiring journey."

I said, "It has been more dreary than tiring."

Then he laughed and said, "Don't worry, for you will find entertainment enough in the city."

This greeting made me happy at first, but then it made me cross at the emperor, for I realized not all of these men were of the same gloomy disposition as my guide, and I suspected the emperor had sent a mindless and slow-witted servant to fetch me, while many of the others, who might have made better travelling companions, remained here, gossiping at the gates.

In any case, I was led through the first set of gates and past a large, armoured gate house. Then we went through a second set of gates which were no less impressive than the first, and were sheeted in iron. Beyond this was an open strip, with hundreds of myrmidons standing guard on either side.

We were stopped here, and the commander of the myrmidons came to see who we were. He recognized my companion, though, and let us pass with no questions.

We crossed this area and went through a third set of gates, a little lower than the first two, but very formidable nevertheless, for the gates were studded with sharp black spikes and were set into walls that were also covered in spikes.

"One thing is certain," I said to myself, "I have not been brought here to build fortifications, for no army in all the world could penetrate these defences."

Within the three sets of walls stood the city itself, which, apart from its fortifications, was much like any other city you might come across, with a market and houses and people coming and going. They were not all dressed in the white robes of courtiers. In fact, most people just wore the ordinary clothes of the region, which is to say a tunic and duffs, plus sandals or pigeon boots.

We made our way to the centre of the city, where a great domed palace stood. When we entered the palace building, a long entrance hallway stretched out before us, lined with tall columns, and pilasters upon the walls. There must have been a hundred myrmidons lining the route, and at the far end were two great red doors.

I began to go down the hallway, but my companion said, "No, not there. This way." Then he led me up a flight of stairs and down a corridor. I thought at first this was some secret route to the emperor's apartments, but then it struck me as unlikely, for there were no myrmidons here, and it seemed inconceivable to me that any route to the emperor, secret or otherwise, would go unguarded.

My suspicions were confirmed a few moments later when we entered a chamber which led off the corridor. Here I was brought before the person who had summoned me, and it was not the emperor at all, but a woman, sitting in a chair shaped like a giant seashell. Looking at her face, it seemed to me she was young, although there was a good deal of grey in her hair. She wore a dark green gown studded with gems, and had a tiara of emeralds about her head. Several slaves stood around her, and also two other women, wearing clothes that were also very fine, though not so fine as hers.

My companion stepped forward and said, "Here is the man Yreth."

She said to the courtier, "Good. You may go now: your punishment is over. But the next time it is your turn to dine at my table, you will eat what is put before you."

The courtier gave a grunt and left us, then the lady turned to me and said, matter-of-factly, "Thank you for accepting my invitation. Your help is sorely needed here. Do you wish to start work immediately?"

Well I was still in a foul mood about the company I had been forced to endure, and my mood was made worse when I realized it was not the emperor who had summoned me, but some other person, obviously of lesser rank.

I said to her, "I will not cast a single binding until I am told exactly who you are, what your relationship is to the emperor, and the exact nature of the work you wish me to do. Also, I want your guarantee, before these witnesses, that I will receive ten thousand arrans for my labours."

She was startled by my brusque tone, and I think she was on the verge of becoming angry with me, for she said, "You would do well not to speak to me in that way."

But I said, "Come come, none of that! I am a man of great wealth and power, and I will not be treated as a common servant. State your business with me and be quick about it!"

She was even more taken aback then, and did not seem to know what to say. Her eyes flashed fury, but her lip trembled as if she would weep. For a moment, I regretted my angry words.

But then she seemed to gain control of herself, and she said, in a less arrogant way, "Yes, of course. You have a right to know these things. I am the Imperial Aunt Diaphrone, the daughter of the eighth youngest sister of the emperor's paternal grandfather."

I said, "Eighth youngest?" for I wondered how many sisters the emperor's grandfather had.

She smiled and said, "Yes, indeed! The eighth. We have long felt this a fortuitous placement within the family structure and I am glad to see you are similarly impressed by it." Then she leaned towards me and said, "I have asked you here, Yreth, in order to entrust you with the care of my child, for he is badly behaved and I cannot control him. Moreover, I fear that his conduct may impair his future advancement in the eyes of the emperor. I have tried to follow the excellent advice in your book, but with little effect, and I suspect your own masterly touch is required. As to your fees, I will gladly pay your ten thousand arrans, if you can successfully train my dear child."

Now it was my turn to be surprised, for I had blindly assumed I was being summoned about some matter of building, forgetting how, in this part of the world, I was now much better known as a philosopher on the education of children. Still, I did not let my surprise show too much, and although my mouth was agape, I covered for this by quickly picking at my teeth.

Finally, I said, "I will accept the offer. Moreover, I will begin my work immediately, just as soon as I have bathed and eaten. Note, however, the prompt commencement of my work is not because you have asked it—for, as must now be clear, I will not be given orders—but because I am an enthusiastic worker in everything I tackle, and I am keen to make a start."

Now, you might wonder whether it was wise to take such a strong stand against this woman who, after all, was possessed of considerable rank. However, I quickly perceived that my angry outburst, which might have been a disaster for me, had instead been a stroke of good fortune. It had come purely from the mood of the moment, but I had gained the high ground over the Imperial Aunt and it set us off on the right foot.

One of the women who had been standing by the Imperial Aunt led me out of the bower and showed me my quarters, which included a large pool for bathing. As I inspected it, the woman said to me, "You certainly have a way about you! I have never seen the Imperial Aunt so meek and agreeable."

It was clear the foul mood I had felt, and the firm hand I took as a result, had been the influence of Heaven upon me, helping me to make my way around these powerful people, so I might be raised to new heights.

Later, in a large hall, I was introduced to Diaphrone's son. His name was Pandrick, and he was the vilest little toad I have ever met. He was about nine years old, I should say, with a sour, disagreeable expression upon his face, and an upturned nose which reminded me of a bat. He did not nod or take my hand when I came up to greet him, but instead gave a scowl.

I turned to all those present then, for there were dozens of them turned out to see me at work, and I said, "Well, it seems he knows *his* place in the world, and mine too."

This got a good laugh, and I could see they thought me an excellent fellow for being so pleasant about the boy's rudeness.

Then I said to the observers, "Let us see if we may win his love by satisfying his natural appetites." I took a tray of cakes, which I had requested for the occasion, and held it before the child, saying softly, "There you are, dear Pandrick. Take one of these for yourself."

The child did not take one of the cakes though. Instead, he kicked up at the tray, sending all the cakes flying. All those present gasped in horror at his rude behaviour. Then the Imperial Aunt said, "He is fond of cheese. Try the plate of cheese."

It was clear to me, however, I would have no more luck with the cheese than I had had with the cakes, for I now perceived exactly what kind of child I was faced with. Although he was the son of an Imperial Aunt, I had seen his like often enough, playing in rat-infested alleys and splashing in gutters. I knew, too, how to deal with such a child, so I turned to the Imperial Aunt and said, "It is very difficult to work, with so many people around, for the child can see he has an audience, and it makes his behaviour worse. Is there a place, somewhere very quiet, where I might be alone with the child for a time and reason with him?"

She said yes, indeed, there was such a place, and I was taken to a fencing room on one of the lower floors of the palace. I asked then that I might be left quite alone with the boy, with no people around, and no slaves, and no myrmidons. Nothing, in fact, that might distract him. I also asked for another tray of cakes, and some of his favourite cheeses. These, however, were a deception, and I had not the slightest intention of using them.

When we were alone, I looked out of the doorway to make sure there was nobody in the corridor beyond. Then I gave a great shout, crying "Help!" in as loud a voice as I could muster.

I waited for a short time, then I called help again. When no help came, I turned to the boy and said, "You see? Nobody can hear you here."

He said, "I don't care." Then he ran at me, and butted me with his head. Well, almost without thinking, I seized him by the hair and pulled him over backwards, then pulled my throwing-razor from my boot and held its point at his throat.

I said, "Don't trifle with me child, or I will have your life!" And I meant it, too, for he had made me angry.

He was startled for a moment, but instead of staying that way, he narrowed his eyes, looked up at me in defiance and said, "Make your cut, then, if you will, but remember, the emperor will put you to death for it."

I said, "Perhaps I will not kill you. Perhaps I will simply slice off your ear."

He said, "Kill me or injure me, it will make little difference to your punishment."

He was right, of course, and I saw I could not inflict any visible hurt upon this child.

I thought on this problem for a moment or two, keeping the child in my grasp, and, as I pondered, I glanced this way and that around the room, looking at the various swords and equipment which were hung up here. Suddenly my eyes fell upon a leather training gauntlet which lay upon a table.

Now, in case you do not know, a training gauntlet is a huge thick glove, with heavy padding upon the palm. It is used by those swordsmen who favour the use of a gauntlet in the left hand instead of a shield or a dagger. For practising, they do not like to use a metal gauntlet, for it damages the opponent's blade, so they use a leather one in its place.

I put my throwing-razor back in my boot and dropped the child. Then I went over to where the training gauntlet rested. The brat ran up behind me, kicking at the backs of my legs and calling me names, but I did not respond, and instead deliberately let the anger well up inside me. When I put the glove on my hand, the child began to see what I was about, and tried to escape from me. Well, I quickly swatted out with the glove, and gave him a solid blow on the shoulder which sent him sprawling to the carpet, yet without putting any bruise upon him!

I said then, "I am now going to teach you how to nod politely to your visitors. In this way, you will appear noble, and you will come to be loved and respected."

He responded by spitting at me, but his expression of contempt instantly changed to one of alarm and astonishment as I snatched him from the ground and gave him a very hard blow across the back.

He ran from me then, jumping and twisting like a little ape, and trying with all his heart to reach the door. I was fast, though, and I blocked his every attempt to pass me, swiping at him with the useful glove.

Next he threatened me with magic. He said, "I know a powerful spell. If you strike me again, I will use it upon you, and you will burst open like a grape."

I called him a liar and struck him a good number of times, saying, "Very well then, use your magic. Burst me open!"

Of course, he did not, because he did not know any magic.

Finally, some of the spirit began to go out of him, although there was still a hatred within his eyes. When he had regained his breath, he said, "You have hurt me. You will be put to death."

I said, "Show me the bruises and cuts that will be evidence of your claims."

Well, he looked at his arms and waist, but he could find no bruises or cuts, because, as I have said, the glove did a good job in cushioning all my blows.

Then he said, "I will tell the Imperial Aunt, my mother, what you have done, and she will take me to see the emperor. I will tell him you hurt me without bruising me, using that evil glove."

I said, "Then I am truly afraid, for I know the emperor will believe your word. That is, unless you are the kind of child who often tells lies, for in this case neither your mother nor the emperor will believe you, and I need fear nothing." I knew, you see, this was a child who was in the habit of telling lies. Then I said, "Better than that, I will have for myself the great pleasure of bringing you back here the next day and beating you all the harder for trying to have me punished."

He immediately understood the truth of my arguments, as well as the threat behind them, and he fell silent.

I said, "Now you can see the value of honesty, for if you had been honest in the past, you would not now be in so desperate a position, and would not be left without any official protection from my attacks. However, I rather fancy that if you had been honest and good, your mother would not have seen the need to summon me in the first place. Your sorry plight, then, is one you have brought upon yourself."

Then I pulled him to his feet and said, "Now, let us begin your training in manners. We will pretend I am a visitor just arrived. Give me a polite nod."

He would not do it, though, and instead he tried to give me a polite kick. I quickly grabbed his ankle and pulled him over again. Another series of tussles followed, as he, once again, divided his efforts between escaping the room and attacking his teacher. Of course, he came away from the fight very much worse off than I did, and when I next asked him to show me how he should nod to visitors, he gave me a proper nod. We practised these nods for some time.

Eventually, I was satisfied he had learned how to greet his guests, and I said, "We will now return to your mother, and you will remain silent until you are spoken to, whereupon you may answer either 'Yes, dear Yreth,' or 'No, dear Yreth.' Do you understand?"

He did not answer me, so I slapped him with the glove a few times until he finally agreed to my terms. Then he added, very cheekily, "Since I am compelled, I will do as you ask. But if you wish me to be honest, you should not have me call you 'dear Yreth' for you are not dear to me, and there will be no truth to my saying you are."

I replied, "Indeed there is truth to it, for until that time when I am *dear* to you, you will *dear*ly rue the day you met me." It was a very clever turn of phrase, and I chuckled as I thought about it afterwards.

I took the child back to its mother then, and she was delighted with my rapid progress. He was surly, as you might expect, but he did what I had told him, even when there were people watching.

Later, I explained to the Imperial Aunt that his lack of smiles was because he was feeling sad. After all, changing one's nature is always a difficult thing, even when the change is a great improvement.

During the following weeks and months, young Pandrick and I paid many visits to the fencing room, and, gradually, he began to see the value of the lessons I taught him, for he saw that even the slaves treated him better when he assumed a manner more appropriate to his high rank. In time, this noble behaviour started to come more naturally to him, and he began to look more like a cousin to the emperor, and less like a common street sparrow..

Still, I did not want him to behave well in front of others and to be a demon in secret, so I took elaborate steps to spy on him. At first, I watched him from behind windows, and around corners, but he sometimes saw me, so I became more sophisticated in my methods. I made a careful study of the plans of the palace and found a number of places where I might watch him without his knowledge.

For example, he often played in the courtyard, and when he did

I would go to one of the cellars, for I had made a discreet crack there, high in the wall, so I might look out over most of the courtyard. If I saw him attacking the other children, I would make a note of it and punish him later.

He played in the garden too, so I secretly had a number of pits dug there, connected by a series of underground tunnels. The pits were covered with sacking, which I made rigid with sheet bindings, then earth and grass was placed on top of this. It looked very solid from above, because the sacking was brown, and the space below it was dark. When I was inside the pit, though, I could easily see out through the holes in the sacking, and if the child moved out of the sight lines of one pit, it was an easy thing for me to scurry underground to a better pit. From this excellent hide, I watched him in all manner of wicked activities. I noted everything, even the most minor infractions, and later on, during my sessions with him, I would tell him of his deeds and seek recompense with the padded gauntlet.

I even spied upon him at night, although I risked my life in doing so, because my hiding place in this instance was high above the ground. You see, I had set a rope along the outside of the palace, running through a number of rings which I had stuck to the wall with point bindings. Each night, I left my room through the window, carefully made my way along the wall, walking upon the rope, then climbed around a corner tower and along another wall to a certain point outside the boy's room.

This was a dangerous journey, not only because of the risk of falling, but also because of the myrmidons who patrolled the area below. I had told their commander of my nightly excursions, of course, but even so I ran the risk of having some poorly trained myrmidon mistake me for a thief and throw a spear into my back. Still, when I do a job, I try to do it well, and I care little for any danger it might bring me. After all, is not every moment in life fraught with dangers of some kind or another? We have all heard stories of those who flee a war in one town only to die of plague in the next. There are also reliable tales, told by honest men, of people who are sitting at home, in clear and beautiful weather, when suddenly a stray bolt of lightning flashes through the window and strike them dead. Life is innately dangerous and beyond our control, so it is important we accept the fact and take pleasure from its perils.

In any case, once I was outside the boy's room, I climbed a piece of ornamental tubing up into an old bartizan inhabited chiefly by pigeons. This overhang opened into a small nook above the boy's room. I had made a hole in the floor of this nook which opened up into a cunningly concealed slit in his ceiling, and from this station I could not only watch him but also hear him talking in his sleep. Later, during our sessions in the fencing room, I would confront him with the wicked things he had said in his dreams, and I would punish him for those words. He was truly astonished at me then, for he surely thought I could read all the secrets of his soul. It was this, I think, which brought me my final victory over the child, and after that he became very docile and easy to teach, not only for me, but also for the other tutors the Imperial Aunt had employed.

Now, you must not imagine I spent my every waking hour peeping through cracks to spy on this child. In fact, my duties as a teacher, both open and furtive, took up no more than a few hours of each day. The rest of the time I wandered freely around the Imperial City of Saskatoon, learning about the place and meeting its people.

I discovered the city was a very ancient one. It had been the seat of the American emperors for centuries, even in those days when the emperor ruled the whole North American continent, and Brazil besides. In saying this, I do not wish to belittle the power of the Emperor in our own times. Even today, his dominion is vast indeed, including the kingdoms of America from Manitario west to the Pacific ocean, and south as far as the wastes of Mexico.

Saskatoon is also a great centre of learning. It is said to have been the birthplace of the great engineer and architect Tuno Peefe (or, if you prefer, Tunotric). I spent many long hours in the great libraries of the city searching for ancient manuscripts by this great man, hoping I would uncover some valuable lost secret. In fact, I did succeed in finding several ancient works he had written, but, alas, none of them contained anything useful, and they were really of no more than historical interest. Some of his theories on building were quite wrong, or at the very least simplistic, so, in the interest of those who might come after me, I scratched out the various mistaken passages and wrote in my corrections before returning the documents to their shelves in the library. If only more people would do this, it is my belief that the growth of human knowledge would be accelerated.

Aside from its extraordinary fortifications, the architecture of Saskatoon was competent but unremarkable in its styling. Even the emperor's palace was not especially innovative or beautiful, merely very large. But one aspect of that building intrigued me: I could see the top of a tall triangular structure within the palace walls. It was like a ramp of some kind, and I observed people climbing it and descending it, but I could not discern its function. When I asked around, people told me it was the emperor's *luma*, but they did not know what it was for, or if they did know, they did not wish to tell me. I was very intrigued, but any further investigation was impossible: the *luma* was not on the plans for the palace, and it was situated in one of the emperor's private gardens, making it quite inaccessible to me.

I rarely caught a glimpse the emperor himself in those days. He lived in the central part of the palace, which was completely shut off from the area occupied by the Imperial Aunt and her son. He kept himself hidden away most of the time, almost like a prisoner, despite his unimaginable wealth and power. In fact, compared to him, even a wealthy woman like the Imperial Aunt Diaphrone was insignificant, for she was merely one of dozens of Imperial Aunts and Imperial Uncles, and cousins and nephews, none of whom might even set eyes upon the emperor unless they had first made an appointment through his courtiers, many months ahead of time.

After six months or so, I had brought Pandrick to a level of behaviour I deemed appropriate to his age and position. I went to the boy's mother then and said, "I consider my work to be complete. The rest of the boy's training may easily be completed by ordinary tutors."

She said, "Oh, you have done a wonderful job with Pandrick. He is so sweet-natured now that I am even tempted to hug him myself, and everyone around the palace speaks of how much he is improved over what he once was."

I said, "Then I trust you will be gracious enough to pay the fee we agreed on."

She said, "Certainly. What amount did we say?"

I said, "Ten thousand arrans, of which one thousand have already been paid."

She gasped then, and said, "Is that all? I cannot believe we agreed to so little."

I said, "No, ten thousand arrans was the sum, and I am content with this amount."

She said, "Come, let me pay you more. Will you take sixteen thousand?"

It was like my conversation with Gavor Hercules. And, just as I had said to him, I told her I wanted only the sum we had first agreed on and nothing more, for this is my way, as a man of honour. "And if you deem my work was worth more," I added, "then I am flattered by your praise and pleased you consider my work to have been of such good value to you."

She was touched at my words, and she said, "Very well, I will pay you the sum you ask. But let me arrange other employment for you. Stay with us and teach young Pandrick further. Or, if you wish, I will arrange for you to train other children within the Imperial family, for there are many who could use your loving guidance."

I said, "If you wish, I will stay on as an occasional teacher to Pandrick, however I do not wish to train other children, for I feel my talents in that direction are subordinate to my true calling."

She asked me then, "What do you consider your true calling to be?"

I said, "I am a stonemage by profession."

She said, "A stonemage? Surely not!"

You see, like so many others I had met in that region of America, she considered the art of the stonemage to be a lowly one and did not realize the stonemage is the king of mages.

I said, "I am not just any stonemage, but the world's finest."

"Yes," she said, "but it is a profession of rocks and mud."

I said, "Is not teaching also a humble profession? Yet you have seen for yourself what wonders I have worked in this area. And I assure you, I am a hundred times better as a stonemage than I am as a teacher."

My words pricked her curiosity. She said, "If this is true, what kind of marvels do you build?"

I said, "Wait, and I shall show you." Then I ran to my chambers and took the various plans I had been working on. I quickly returned to the Imperial Aunt and rolled out the plans before her, with the topmost plan being the one for the cathedral shaped like a hand.

She said, "What is this? A drawing?"

I said, "No, it is the plan for a cathedral. See here, I have drawn a little person upon the ground, so you can see the great size of it."

She gasped then, and spent a minute or so silently studying at my plan. Then she looked at some of the other plans. There were a number of fine towers, and a great bridge designed to span a lake or a small sea, and an arena, and a large printing shop with a tower on it styled to look like a bird in flight.

At last she said, "I am no authority on buildings, but these plans strike me as truly remarkable. You are clearly an architect and stonemage without equal, for you transform plain buildings into spectacular works of art."

I said, "I would like to receive the funds and assistance to create all these structures. How would you advise me to proceed?"

She said, "This is the Imperial City, and only the emperor may commission great works such as these. Of course, I could speak to him, but he knows I am no expert in this discipline, and my words will carry little weight. No, if you will take my advice, you will approach the emperor through his closest courtiers, for these are the men and women who execute all the emperor's plans, and they are also the ones with the real influence over him. Buy them wine and expensive gifts. You will win their friendship that way, and they will do you favours to aid you in your worthy cause."

I asked her then which courtiers would have most influence in matters of architecture, but she could not advise me. "You are a clever fellow, though," she said. "Make a study of them. I am certain you will quickly determine who can give you the best service in return for your gifts."

I thanked her gladly for her sound advice and resolved I would follow it to the letter. So I spent some gold around the town in exchange for detailed insights into the makeup of the emperor's court.

I discovered there were various ranks of courtier. All wore identical white robes, but, if you looked carefully, you could tell them apart by the combs in their long hair.

Those who served the various members of the emperor's family, like the tedious man who escorted me from Belpinian, were of the lowest rank. They were known as the Imperial Service, and they wore gold combs stamped with the mark of the family member they served.

Next up were the Imperial Bearers. These men and women, and there were hundreds of them, were courtiers who served the emperor in some minor capacity, for example, by purchasing food, or overseeing the numerous garden slaves. They wore gold combs stamped with the emperor's mark.

Above these in rank were the Imperial Attendants. There were only about fifty, and they worked much more closely with the emperor. They too wore combs stamped with the emperor's mark, but the combs were a little thicker and heavier, and contained more gold.

Highest of all in rank were the Imperial Advisors. These were six in number, five of them women and all of them old, and they wore combs with coloured gems along the top.

To add to the confusion, there were subtle distinctions within these four broad divisions. For example, among the Imperial Bearers, some bore special additional markings upon their comb. If they had balls there, it indicated they worked within the household. If they had tweaks, it showed they held a favoured position, and the more tweaks they had, the higher the degree of favour. There were numerous other markings, too: horses, leaves, rope, and so on, all indicating subtle differences in status.

At first, all these combs looked very much the same to me, but after a time I became so adept at recognizing the different markings that I wondered how anyone could think they were alike, and I chided myself for my blindness in not seeing the differences from the beginning.

As for the other citizens of Saskatoon, they did not wear combs at all, nor did they wear white robes. In fact, to do so, if you were not a courtier, was considered a very grave crime, and in the market you would often hear people complaining about how unfair it was that they were not allowed to wear a gold comb or white robes even in the privacy of their own homes. For myself, though, I could not see why anybody should want to wear such a ridiculous outfit, and if a man walked the streets of Piapa wearing such garments, he would be the laughing stock of Cyprus. Still, the people of Saskatoon thought the costume a very fine one, which just goes to show that foreign folk are very strange.

I made a number of friends among the courtiers. I did not try to win the friendship of the high-ranking Imperial Advisors, for these people constantly received lavish gifts from members of the emperor's family who wanted this or that, and I knew I could not compete against such great wealth. I therefore took a different strategy. I sought out those courtiers who were of low rank (and therefore cheap to impress), but who were likely to attract the emperor's attention in some way.

For example, I discovered that one of the new courtiers, an Imperial Bearer by the name of Sooni, was an attractive young man, and highly skilled as a dancer. I said to myself, "I will warrant he dances sometimes for the emperor, and that, on these occasions, the emperor chats with him in a friendly tone. If the emperor hears good words about me from a man such as this, it will be at such a time when he has been well entertained and is in a receptive mood, and such reports are likely to be far more influential than those coming from those ugly old Imperial Advisors."

So, I sought the acquaintance of this man Sooni, and, for the cost of just a few arrans spent on fine meals, I made him my friend.

There were others too, of course. In the ranks of the courtiers I found two other male dancers, a man who played the harp, a woman who sang, a husband and wife who performed poetry, and also several women who possessed no special performing skills, but who struck me as unusually charming and beautiful: I had heard, you see, that the emperor has an eye for lovely women, and I was sure these women would catch his eye in a particularly favourable way.

An added advantage to my plan was that the new friends I made were very interesting and delightful people to be around, and were accomplished in many fields, so my time with them was always well spent.

I asked no difficult favours of my courtier friends, but I showed them my building plans, which impressed them greatly, then I said, "Do not make any bold overtures on my behalf, for you might risk offending the emperor. However, if, by chance, the emperor happens to strike up a conversation with you, then I would be much obliged if you would try to mention my name in a casual way, reflecting, perhaps upon my successes in training the formerly incorrigible Pandrick, or praising my skills as a stonemage."

And I suggested to the musicians that they might write a song in my honour, and said to the dancers that they should name a dance after me. I also asked the poetic couple if they would write a poem about me, but they said they only performed ancient works. Still, they assured me they would mention me to the emperor as a great patron of the poetic arts.

This, in any case, was my plan, and it very soon started to work. Several of my courtier friends told me they had been approached by the emperor, and they all managed to drop my name subtly into the conversation.

However, it was not these ingenious ploys which finally gained me the emperor's attention, but rather a very remarkable feat of mine. I will tell of this next.

A Seventh Section Of The Eleventh Part

In Which I Describe How I Achieved Further Fame In Saskatoon

ONE DAY, NOT LONG AFTER I had received my money for training Pandrick, I was enjoying a fine meal in Dochi's pie shop, which is situated not far from the palace. Dochi, like me, was originally from Cyprus, although he was from the western side of the island, from the town of Limmerhat in the Duchy of Bayon. We had little in common, really, he being a cook and I a stonemage, but we always gave each other a friendly greeting, and occasionally we would sing some of the old songs together.

I was sitting, talking pleasantly with one of Pandrick's other tutors. Her name was Hanna, and she was an older woman who was an expert in geometry and a great admirer of my building plans.

Suddenly our pleasant conversation was interrupted by a commotion. Three of the emperor's minor courtiers burst into the place, carrying light hunting spears and a big yellow hare they had killed. They were staggering, and it was clear they were the worse for wine.

One of them slammed the animal down upon the counter and said to the owner, "Here, Dochi, cook this up for us, and make it into a pie, will you."

Well, Dochi was a quiet, pleasant fellow, and he said he would do his best, but it would take some time to cook the meat.

"How long?" said the courtier.

"Two hours," said Dochi.

His answer did not please them at all. "We have been hunting all afternoon and we are hungry," they said. "We will not wait. Bake us our pie immediately!"

Of course, Dochi said he could not, for these things take time, but his reasonable words made them angry, and they started to curse at him, smashing his plates and calling him a fool. They said then that all Cypriots were fools.

Well, this was more than I could bear. I stood and called out to them, saying, "Hoi! You there! Stop at once."

They looked over to me then and spoke a few words among themselves. Then the ring leader said, "Who are you to speak to the emperor's own courtiers like that?"

I said, "My name is Yreth, and it so happens I am one of those Cypriots you are so quick to insult."

He shook his spear then, taunting me, so I snatched out my throwing-razor, and I would have sent it through his skull on the spot had Hanna not quickly grabbed my wrist. She whispered to me, "Take care, Yreth. Do not strike at them, for any blow they receive is a blow against the emperor, and you will be put to death for it."

Well, these words cooled me off a little, so I put the throwing-razor upon the table, then I slowly wiped my mouth with a cloth while I thought what to say, all the while keeping my eyes on those drunken courtiers with their spears.

Finally, I said, "In the first place, you would do well to remember your manners. Good Dochi has said your pie will take two hours. If that is too long for you to wait, go and cook it yourselves. In the second place, Cypriots are not fools."

The ring leader said, "Indeed, they are fools. The world knows that Cyprus produces the greatest fools that were ever born."

I knew he was trying to goad me, but I was determined not to be provoked. Besides, a much better plan was entering my head, for I thought to challenge them in some way, although I did not wish to be too obvious about it.

I started by saying to them, "As to the question of folly, I am no expert, and therefore I will bow to your own superior experience in this matter."

The ring leader smirked at my words, for he did not see how cleverly I was insulting him.

Then I said, "I will say this, though: we Cypriots are better cooks than you Americans. And do not deny it, either, for you could have taken your animal to any cook in the city, yet you brought it here, to the oven of a Cypriot. Moreover, I will say that we Cypriots are better hunters than you Americans, for it took all three of you to catch just one hare. I will wager I could outdo your success, even hunting alone."

They grew interested then, as I knew they would, and said, "How much will you wager?"

I said, "If I lose, I will pay you ten thousand arrans."

They did not believe I possessed so much gold, but I assured them that indeed I did, and they had only to check with the courtiers who served the Imperial Aunt Diaphrone to find out my claims were true.

Then they said, "And what if we lose?"

I said, "If you lose, I want your gold combs as trophies of my victory."

Everyone in the room was at eyebrows-and-tongues when I made this challenge, for, as I have said, these combs are the mark of a courtier's rank, and if these men were to surrender them, they would also lose their favoured positions.

The three courtiers talked among themselves for a few minutes, considering my wager, although I harried them as they talked, saying, "Come then, what is it to be? Is it yes or no? Do not be all day about it!" This, you see, was my way of getting back at them for interrupting my conversation with Hanna by their din.

Finally, they said, "We will accept the wager, on two conditions."

I said, "State them."

They said, "First, we will determine the animal you are to hunt."

I said, "Can the animal can be found within this region?"

They said, "It can."

I said, "Is the animal truly a wild animal, and not the property of some person?"

They said, "No no, it is wild, and it is nobody's property."

I said, "In that case, your first condition is acceptable to me. What is the second?"

They said, "You must not kill or injure the animal, but must instead capture it, and bring it back to the Imperial City."

Well, that was a challenge indeed, especially if they meant me to hunt a ferocious animal, such a sand cat. Still, a number of clever plans for capturing a fierce animal popped into my head even as I stood there, so I was quite sure that, with sufficient thought, I could come up with something.

"Very well," I said. "The terms of your wager are acceptable to me. Now, what animal do you wish me to capture?"

Then the ring leader grinned at me and said, "The Pulsiter."

At once, there was a great reaction from the others present. Some people laughed, while others cried out that the wager was unfair. For myself, I did not know what a Pulsiter might be, but I knew trickery of some sort was involved. Still, I also knew I had agreed to their terms for the wager, so I said, "I will bring the Pulsiter to the Imperial City before six weeks have passed. Now, please be so good as to leave this place in peace."

They laughed, saying, "In six weeks we will be rich men." Then they left the shop, taking their hare with them.

Now, I soon found out the Pulsiter is a unique magical creature. Just as the chameleon can change its colour, so the Pulsiter can change its form, taking on the appearance and attributes of any living thing, large or small, that pleases it at that moment. For example, if the Pulsiter is travelling over land, it may take the form of horse and gallop along. If it comes to an ocean, it will change into a fish and swim across. If a hawk plucks it from the waves, it will change into a lion and eat the bird, then change back into a fish upon the instant it strikes the water once more.

I talked to many people about the Pulsiter, and some said it did not exist. However, the older folk I talked to assured me that it did exist, for they remembered it was kept captive in Saskatoon many years earlier, and would have been there still if an enemy of the previous emperor had not opened the door of the enclosure and allowed it to escape.

I searched through the libraries next, looking for more detailed information about the Pulsiter. I discovered many eyewitness accounts of those who had met the Pulsiter in the wild. Some had been attacked by it, and they wrote of how it changed from the form of a tree into the form of a wolf, all in the twinkling of an eye. As might be expected, many of these accounts were confused or contradictory, for doubtless the writers were very afraid when they met the Pulsiter and did not have the time to make exact observations. Nevertheless, I noticed two important facts which virtually all of the experts mentioned, and I took careful note of these, for I knew, if everyone agreed on some facts, it was very likely these facts at least were true.

The first fact was that the Pulsiter has an unusual love of areas near rivers or lakes or other bodies of water. Once I had made this observation, I was struck by its perfect sense, for such locations would allow the creature to change into a water creature, such as a fish or a frog, if a danger should approach by land, and to change into a land animal, such as a gazelle, in the event a danger should come from the water.

The second fact I noted was that the Pulsiter seemed to be attracted by music. Many of the observers wrote of how they were casually walking along, whistling or singing, before they encountered the creature. Clearly, then, it was this whistling or singing which had drawn the creature to them.

Using these two facts, I formulated my plan to catch the beast. I decided I would buy a musical instrument of some kind, something easy to learn, and I would then go to all those places in the region which were close to lakes or rivers and play the instrument. This would draw the creature to me.

Here, however, a problem arose. How would I capture the Pulsiter once it had come to hear my music? I thought hard upon this question, but I could think of no good answer. After all, if the Pulsiter had assumed the form of a bird and I tried to catch it with a net, it had only to change into some large, strong animal to tear itself free. On the other hand, if I designed a trap for a strong animal, perhaps a cage of some kind, the Pulsiter might easily change to a flea and crawl through the bars.

I examined the place where the Pulsiter had been kept when it was a prisoner in the city. I found its enclosure was a sealed area of stone and glass set into one of the side walls of the palace. The chamber was precisely crafted, with no spaces the creature could have used for escape, only a grid of very tiny holes to give the creature air. It was a good design to be sure, but not the sort of thing I might lift up and take on a hunting expedition, and so I was no closer to finding a workable plan.

One evening, I was explaining my problem to a friend of mine who was both a courtier and an artist and went by the name of Bitian Teppel. I had won this man's friendship not by means of gold, but because of my taming of the boy Pandrick. The boy, you see, had formerly been in the habit of pulling Bitian's ladder over as he painted, and the artist had suffered several grievous injuries as a result. Thanks to me, however, he could now do his painting work in safety, and he swore he would be eternally grateful to me because of it.

In any event, I told him all about the difficulties of catching such a creature as the Pulsiter. I had worked myself into such a pitch over the matter that I finally threw up my hands and said, "It is all quite futile, for no cage will hold the beast securely."

Well, Bitian was a very witty man, and he responded by saying, "Then why not use no-cage, since you say it will hold the beast securely."

This was a joke, you see, and he said it to cheer me up. It did cheer me up, too, when I caught the cleverness of it, and we laughed for a good few minutes.

Later on, after Bitian had left, I had another chuckle over his joke. Then, suddenly, I thought to myself, "I wonder if I could use no-cage? Perhaps there are more brains than feathers to his witty words."

Well, I thought upon this for a bit, and I said to myself, "How might I take the creature to the city without confining it in any way?" I realized the music which first summoned the creature might also be used to keep it my prisoner. "Perhaps," I thought, "I could simply continue to play my beautiful music and walk back to the city. If the Pulsiter is as fond of music as I suspect, it will follow me on my journey. Then I have only to lead it into the old enclosure and close the door, and it will be captured.

Of course, I had my doubts about this plan at first, for it seemed almost too simple to be workable. Yet, when I considered the matter, I realized that all those who had tried to catch the Pulsiter in the past had failed precisely because they had used clever nets and traps and cages, so there was some wisdom in my no-cage idea.

The next day, I looked around the market for a musical instrument of some kind. Most of them did not please me, for, while they looked easy to play, they were actually very difficult.

Take the pipe, for example. There are only eight holes upon a pipe, and, since eight is a low number, I reasoned the manipulation of these holes should not be too taxing. But the truth is that the holes are placed with a subtle unevenness, barely perceptible to the eye, which causes one's fingers to become confused and tangled as they move over them.

The horn is impossibly difficult, and when I tried one I found I could not get any sound out of it at all except by humming into its mouthpiece, but the man told me this was wrong.

I said to him, "Why should this be wrong? At least it produces a sound that is in some way musical, whereas when I employ your method I can produce no sound at all."

He had no good answer to this, however, reinforcing an opinion I have held for many years that those who play upon the horn are generally halfwitted.

The various stringed instruments, both those played with the fingers and those played with a bow, were easier to get a sound from, but the sound did not seem musical to my ears, and I quickly discovered that to play these instruments correctly required the tiresome memorization of a great many combinations of finger positions.

Eventually, though, as I scoured the market, I came across an instrument called the rare-bellows. I had not heard of it before that time, and I have seen it only once or twice since, so I will explain how it works. In appearance, it is like a rounded box, with a pair of bellows set underneath it, and a stick down one side, connected to a wheel at the bottom. To play it, one has only to pump the bellows and push the wheel over the ground. The movement of the wheel is transmitted, by means of a strong thread, to a mechanism inside the box. As the mechanism turns, it plays beautiful music, sounding a like a troupe of highly skilled pipers.

I knew at once this was exactly the instrument I had been looking for, and I purchased it on the spot, even though it was expensive. I also received a number of wooden cylinders with pegs attached. The woman who sold me the instrument showed me how the top of the box could be opened up and the cylinder within replaced by one of these others. Once this was done, the rare-bellows would play a different tune, for it was the placing of the pegs upon the cylinder that determined the melody. The cylinders she gave me played *Ein's Lament*, *The Pack of Wolves*, *Trickle down the Fountain*, *Poultry Boys* and *The Weaver's Angry Slave*. All these are American songs, of course, but they are good melodies nonetheless.

"And if you wish," she said, "you can pull the pegs from the cylinders and place them in different holes, thereby creating your own tunes."

I found later this claim might be true in theory, but the process was so difficult I would have been better off simply learning all the finger positions required for the viol or the guitar!

There was also a kind of pipe attached to the front of the instrument which could be played with one hand in time to the music. I experimented with this for a while, but soon found that this pipe was just as badly designed as every two-handed pipe, and, besides, the rest of the instrument sounded very beautiful even without the accompaniment. Therefore, I removed the appendage and threw it away, plugging up the hole with a cork.

Later the same week, I placed food and water into a pack, together with a map of the region I had copied, and I walked off into the wilderness, pushing my rare-bellows ahead of me.

I travelled east for a day or so, following the road which led, so my map told me, to the town of Eight Trees, which lies upon the river, and is close to a number of small lakes.

With so much water about, this appeared to be ideal territory for the Pulsiter, so I wandered around the riverbanks and lake shores for five days playing my rare-bellows. I tried each of the cylinders in the instrument, but no animals came near me, and I came to the conclusion that the Pulsiter must be elsewhere.

I moved on then, following the river to the south and into a region of swamps. I wandered the swamps for a couple of days, keeping to the dry patches and playing my instrument. I also smiled at any unusual looking trees I came across, just in case one of them was the Pulsiter in disguise. My efforts were entirely unsuccessful in locating the creature, although I did come across several ancient buildings. I searched them, too, but there were no treasures within, just decaying timbers and a small crocodile which looked as if it had been dead for some time.

I continued my wanderings for weeks, still concentrating on the areas closest to lakes or rivers or streams. I played my rare-bellows with a will (I was becoming a very talented musician by this point) but still my mysterious quarry did not appear. Then I began to regret I had so rashly given myself only six weeks to find the beast, because the region was large, and there were numerous places I would have liked to examine more thoroughly.

I searched for as long as I could, but the time trotted away, and I had still seen no sign of the Pulsiter. Regretfully, I turned around once more, heading back towards Saskatoon.

Of the original six weeks, only three days now remained, and it would take me that long to make the journey to the city gates. I imagined I was beaten, and I hung my head very low.

Now, I had been walking along the road for a little over a day, my eyes fixed upon the ground in my dejection and woe, when I observed a curious thing. Upon the earth at the side of the road I saw the footprints of a small animal—a cat or a fox. The footprints went only for a short way, however, before they disappeared. A little further on, I saw the footprints had changed to those of a bird. Then they vanished again, and later still they changed back to the footprints of the small animal again and headed away from the road.

The meaning of these footprints was obvious to me, as I am sure it is to you. Clearly, these were the tracks of the Pulsiter, travelling, perhaps, as a fox for a time, then transforming into a bird, and flying over the sand for a short distance, then landing upon the ground, and walking with its bird's feet, then flying a little further, and then finally changing back into a fox.

I immediately knelt down and gave thanks to God for leading me, in my despair, to the trail of my quarry. I said to God, "Now, let me capture the animal, and I will ensure the great cathedral I have been planning is the next thing I build, and it will be built right here in this very place."

I heard a voice speaking to me then, in tones that seemed faint and faraway, yet also deep and powerful. The voice, which I knew to be that of God, said, "No, build me five cathedrals."

I responded, "Five is a great many. Will you take three?"

For three, you see, is the number of the Holy Trinity, and it seemed a good number to me.

God did not reply, and I took this to mean He approved of this number, so we settled upon three, and I immediately left the road and went off in the direction of the tracks, in pursuit of the Pulsiter.

After a time trudging over through the bush, I saw a body of water ahead. I crept forward, examining the ground and plants around to see if they were hiding some small creature which might be the Pulsiter in disguise. But I need not have checked so closely, for this noble beast has no need to be timid. As I came around from behind a clump of trees, I gasped, for there I saw a cow. It was just standing by the water, eating the grass.

The cow was of the black-and-white kind—the sort you might often see in a farmer's fields. But I was far from any farm. The cow looked up at me, then continued with its eating, feigning innocence.

I looked carefully at the ground around its feet and saw, just as I had suspected, that there were not so many hoofprints as there should have been if the cow had been there for a long time. Also, I saw numerous bird tracks, and the footprints of other animals, although it was clear none of these animals were present. There could be only one explanation for all this: I was face to face with the Pulsiter!

I knew I must go very carefully, for the Pulsiter can be a dangerous foe, especially if it decides to transform into a lion or a mud dragon. I approached cautiously, and when I was just a few yards from its tail, I started to play the rare-bellows, marching back and forth and doing my best to push the wheel through the mud and long grass.

The Pulsiter tried to ignore my alluring tune, and it pretended it was just an ordinary cow eating grass, but I could see the tip of its tail twitching in time to the music, and I knew it was falling under my spell. When I had played for a few minutes, I walked around to stand in front of the animal. It raised its head, and, even though it was in a trance from my music, I immediately saw the great intelligence and wisdom in the creature's eyes, signifying more plainly than ever that this was no ordinary cow, but the one true Pulsiter.

I turned away then, pushing my rare-bellows ahead of me and hoping the Pulsiter would follow. However, it did not follow. It was in such an ecstatic blur from my music that it could do no more than stand and chew.

I said to it, "Come along, do not just stop there, for I have enchanted you and you are compelled to follow my tune." So saying, I broke off a branch from one of the bushes, and I whipped it against the creature's rump, which brought the Pulsiter out of its dazed rumination. Then I pushed the rare-bellows off once more, and we went off. I pumped at the bellows with one hand, and whipped at the Pulsiter with the other. In this manner, I led the creature out of the wilderness towards the Imperial City.

When we finally arrived at the city gates, I was exhausted. I had not slept in two days, for I had needed to keep the Pulsiter entertained with music day and night during the long walk. My efforts were well rewarded, however, for the creature made no attempt to transform into some other animal and escape.

My good friend Bitian Teppel was waiting for me outside the gates, and he supported me at the elbow, keeping me from falling as we went past the guards. Naturally, I had no sooner entered the city, than a great crowd began to gather, for word of my quest had spread. How they cheered to see I had brought the Pulsiter back to the Imperial City once again, although there were three men present who were not cheering at the sight, and I think you can guess who they were.

We moved quickly then, and placed the Pulsiter in its old enclosure, together with a trough of water and a sheaf of long grass cut fresh in the city's gardens. In spite of my fatigue, I turned to the great crowd waiting there, and I told them the story of my great search for the Pulsiter, and of the miraculous events which had finally led me to it.

No sooner had I finished my story, though, than the three courtiers came forward. They were angry at my success. One of them said, "How do we know that this is truly the Pulsiter, and not just a cow?"

The crowd hissed at them for this, but I raised my hands to quieten the assembly. I said, "No, it is a fair question. Listen, then, I have stopped playing my music now. I invite any one of you three brave courtiers to enter the enclosure and touch the Pulsiter. If, as you suspect, it is nothing more than a cow, you will certainly have nothing to fear, for a common cow cannot change to a bear and tear you limb from limb."

Of course, they declined my offer, for they knew very well that this animal was the true Pulsiter. They were clever, though, and they said, "We have no doubt in our own minds that this is the Pulsiter, and therefore we do not choose to enter the enclosure. Nevertheless, we also represent the emperor, and for his sake we desire more certain proof."

"As you wish," I said. Then I knocked on the glass of the enclosure and called to the Pulsiter, saying, "Pulsiter, change your form! Become an eagle, so everyone may see your magic!"

The Pulsiter, though, was angry at being imprisoned, and, being of a vindictive and churlish disposition, it refused to change its form.

Then the three courtiers cried out, "See! It is not the real Pulsiter!"

Things might have turned against me then, but, as luck would have it, an old woman stepped out of the crowd to make a case for me.

She said, "You cannot ask the Pulsiter to change its form at your whim. It is a noble creature, and, like our own emperor, it does not take commands from any man."

Then she said, "When I was a young girl, my father was appointed with the care of the Pulsiter, and on several occasions I was allowed close to it, for it liked me. Let me in there now. I will soon tell you if that is the real Pulsiter."

We carefully opened the door to the enclosure and let the brave woman in. She walked up to the powerful creature, took its head in her arms, and looked into its eyes. She gazed at it for a long time, and we were all very tense and excited as we waited to hear what she would say. At last, we saw her smile, and she smoothed the creature's head. Then we let her out of the enclosure to pronounce her verdict. She said, "There is no doubt in my mind. This, indeed, is the one true Pulsiter."

Everybody cheered then, both at my bravery in capturing the creature, and at hers in proving its identity to the world.

As for the three courtiers, they handed over their golden combs on the spot, although they did so in very poor grace, and one of them simply threw his comb at my feet, which the crowd did not care for. Since it was unlawful for me to wear the combs in my hair, I fixed them to my belt, wearing them like a tally of the courtiers I had bested.

A few days later, two of the men left Saskatoon, and they did not return. The third remained there, but was obliged to find work as a common scribe in order to pay his bills.

An Eighth Section Of The Eleventh Part

In Which I Describe My Meeting With The Emperor And The Things That Came Of It

I SPENT SEVERAL DAYS RECUPERATING FROM my trying journey, and during this time many of my friends called upon me to give me their congratulations and tell me the latest news. Of course, the whole town was talking about my remarkable catch, and there was a constant crowd around the enclosure for many weeks. In fact, I heard that the emperor himself, with all his myrmidons and courtiers around him, had stepped outside the palace to see the Pulsiter the day after it was captured. I was sorry I had missed the spectacle—for I had slept right through that day—but it made me proud to think my efforts had brought me such fame.

My friends also told me the emperor had heard the story surrounding the capture and found it fascinating. They said it was likely he would invite me to come before him, so I might tell the tale in my own words, for he was astonished by the bravery, cleverness and selflessness I had shown in securing the Pulsiter for his city. It goes without saying that this was a very exciting prospect for me, and I spent a good many hours thinking about how I would present the story to him.

The invitation came a few days later, and a group of four big myrmidons and two Imperial Attendants escorted me as I went to see him. When I came across the emperor, he was in one of his private gardens, shooting arrows at a carcass. I was a little nervous, but I need not have been, because he was the most agreeable man you can imagine. He did not wear jewelled robes, but just a simple brown tunic and a wide leather hat. He was so powerful, you see, he did not need to make a show of it.

I walked across the garden with his myrmidons around me, and no sooner had he set eyes on me than he said, "Ah, Yreth! I have heard so much about you. Will you join me in setting off a few arrows?"

His tone was so friendly and relaxed that I did not know whether to bow or to take his hand. In the end I did both, first making a deep and respectful bow, then taking his hand, then giving him a close hug for good measure.

I took up a bow and we took turns shooting arrows at the target. I scored nine hits and twelve misses, while he scored sixteen hits and five misses, so you can see he was an excellent marksman. Even so, he was very kind about it and said I had a good eye myself.

I said, "You are very generous with your words, but I fear this is not really my weapon."

He said, with great interest, "Oh? What do you favour, then?"

I said I liked the throwing-razor, for it was good for fighting in close as well as far away. I showed him my own weapon then, the new silver one, and he admired it, saying he used to have a similar blade himself.

"However," he said, "you could not use this little blade against a target as far away as that goat carcass."

I was indignant at this, and I said, "Indeed I could! In fact, I will warrant I could hit it even if it were another thirty feet further on."

He found this incredible, but I assured him I could do it.

He said, "Very well, let me see." And he instructed the slaves to remove the arrows from the carcass and to pull it back another thirty feet. Then he said, "Take your shot."

I said, "First, let us see how your arrows perform at this range."

The emperor agreed to this, and he fired a single arrow, which struck the carcass near to the leg. Then I took my shot. Of course, over such a range, I knew I could not throw in the normal manner, for it is impossible to calculate the tumbles, and even if the weapon finds its mark, it is as likely to hit with the handle as with the point. So instead I took a run up and threw the blade barbarian-style, which is a much more difficult throw, for it involves holding the blade facing out, keeping the wrist straight, and using the elbow to impart the twist. This way, the tumbles are much fewer, and therefore easier to guess at over a long distance.

I took careful aim and threw the blade as hard as I was able, but even so, it seemed to miss the carcass by a hair, striking the ground. This brought a chuckle from the courtiers who stood around.

However, when I went to retrieve my blade, I called out, "Here, you emperor, look at this!"

For, you see, his arrow, which had seemed to strike the leg of the carcass, had actually flown cleanly between the legs, striking the ground just behind. Moreover, when I took a close look at my blade I saw that it had pierced the skin of the carcass before entering the ground. My throw, therefore, was a hit. Not a good hit, perhaps, but certainly a better hit than his.

When the emperor took a look at the carcass, he was very much amused, and slapped me on the back. Then he turned to his courtiers and said, "You see! You laughed at this man's throw, but now you can see he is the kind of fellow who will have the laugh on you in the end. In fact, I declare that he is a bubble."

And they all said, "A bubble? What is the meaning of that? He is not round and does not fly."

To which he replied, "No, but he must be a bubble nevertheless, for he *always rises to the top!*"

Well, we all gave a great roar of laughter when we heard this, for it was a wonderfully funny joke.

I laughed louder and longer than all the others there, and I shouted out, "Oh! A bubble! That is a splendid joke! A bubble! Oh, my!" until my sides and belly were sore from the effort of it, for I knew the joke contained a profound truth to it, and it made the humour even richer and more enjoyable for me.

The emperor took great pleasure in my laughter and said, "I see you are a bubble in another way, too, for you are light in your heart!" which tickled me even more, so I could hardly control my mirth.

At last he said, "But enough of this merriment. Let us take dinner now. Yreth, would you care to join us, and tell us your tale of hunting the Pulsiter."

I said, "I would be honoured. However, I will come only on the condition that you restrain your ceaseless flow of exceedingly funny comments, emperor, for otherwise I fear I shall choke upon my food."

He was very well pleased by my answer, and agreed he would try to be on his best behaviour. We all made our way then to a great dining hall with walls of gold, and there I partook of a superb array of fruits and meats, while telling my story of the Pulsiter, as I have already told it here.

I made a good job of the tale, I think, because the emperor attended to my every word, stopping me only to clarify certain points, such as "Did you say a *dead* crocodile?" and ask certain intelligent questions, such as, "How did you know that the crocodile was not in fact the Pulsiter?"

Actually, he seemed to take uncommon interest in the matter of the dead crocodile I had found, and he briefly interrupted my story to tell me of a time when he had gone hunting and had tried to shoot a great crocodile with his arrows, but the creature's skin was so tough it turned them all.

I quickly brought the conversation back to the subject at hand, however, and continued with my tale. I ended it by saying, "All of this was done by my hand, of course, but my hand was guided by another, greater hand, this being the hand of God. Therefore, I intend to keep the promise I made to Him to return to that wilderness and to build three great cathedrals, using my skills as a stonemage, which surpass even my skills as a hunter. You may be certain, then, that once I can find some great person who is willing to be a patron to this project, these wonderful structures will be built."

I said no more than this, for I felt it was best to be very soft and subtle in my dealings with the emperor. Such great men, you see, do not like to feel they are at the service of others. That is why I did not say, "if you, emperor, will be patron to the project," but instead said, "if I can find some great person," as if to imply that any great person would do, and that I did not presume upon his generosity to take that role. There are stonemages today who could learn much from my tact and discretion.

It was still light after we had finished eating, and the emperor asked me if I wished to join him in shooting off some more arrows.

I said yes, so we went back into the garden, and we sent off a good many shafts, this time into a pig carcass.

He said, "Is this not excellent good fun?"

I said, "There can be no doubt of it. I have heard it said that archery is the king of sports, but now I know the truth, and I see it is the emperor of sports, and is, moreover, the sport of emperors."

He said, "You and I are agreed on that point! I spend, I should say, two hours each day upon this graceful art, and I take a great delight in every moment."

I found out after this that he was being modest, for one of his courtiers, and one who was in a good position to know, said he spent closer to five hours a day with the bow in his hands, practising in the various private gardens within the palace walls.

After a time, I said to the emperor, "I tire a little of shooting at this pig. Let us change targets. What do you say to a moving goat."

He said, "How is that? A live animal, do you mean?"

I said, "No no, a goat carcass, like before, but with a slave in armour beneath it, carrying it around him like a cloak. Have you never encountered this method?"

He said he never had.

I said, "Well, then, you must certainly try it, for it is a far more diverting sport than any fixed carcass."

The emperor was willing, so I took one of his slaves, a short one, and had the other slaves fetch a good mail coat for him to wear, in case the arrows should go through the meat. We got the goat carcass and placed it over the little slave, then I told him to walk back and forth, not too fast, while we shot our arrows.

When the emperor tried shooting at this target, and saw how well it worked, he was delighted beyond measure, and with every hit he gave a loud exclamation of pleasure, saying, "Ho! I caught you there!" and "I have you now, you strange, vertical goat."

We had a long contest then, which went late into the night, until we were playing by torchlight. My shots were much improved over my earlier efforts, for a moving target quickens my pulse and makes my aim truer, but I let the emperor win in the final tally.

When it was time for me to go, I thanked the emperor for his kindness, and he said, on the contrary, he would long remember the entertainment I had given him.

Then, as I left, I pulled my clothes straight, and as I did so I pretended to make a fumble, letting fall a piece of paper I had been carrying. This paper contained a drawing of the cathedral I planned to build, the one in the shape of a pointing hand. As I picked it up from the ground, I shook the paper a little—not in an obvious way, but just very slightly—so the paper unfolded and revealed the drawing.

The emperor said, "Well, what is this?"

I said, "Oh, it is nothing, merely a sketch of the great cathedral I mentioned."

He said to a slave, "Bring me that light." Then he took a closer look and said, "No, it is a hand."

I said, just as I had said to the Imperial Aunt, "Forgive me, but it is a cathedral, although it is in the shape of a hand pointing up to heaven. See, I have drawn a little fellow walking by down here at the bottom. You can see, then, how large the structure will be."

He looked at the little man I had drawn and whistled with amazement. Then he said, "Will you make me a gift of this drawing? I wish to look at it further on my own, and to think upon it."

I said, in a carefree way, "If you want it, it is yours to do as you will with," although, in fact, as you will probably guess, I had drawn this copy with the sole intention of giving it to the emperor.

At last, I left, knowing I had made a good impression upon the emperor, and confident he would ask me to built these cathedrals.

A week or so later, I was invited to see the emperor again. He was in his court this time, surrounded, as usual, by his white-robed courtiers, and also by a number of visitors—kings, lords and high officials from his dominions across America.

He talked to these visitors for a time before he noticed me there, but when he did see me he was very pleased and pointed me out to the other powerful persons present, saying, "This is my excellent friend Yreth."

You may think I exaggerate when I say "excellent friend," but those were precisely the words he used, although, for myself, I could hardly believe it when I heard them coming from his lips.

Then he said, "He has shown me a fine new way of practising my archery upon a moving target, and I owe him a great debt because of it. What do you say, Yreth?"

I said, "Emperor, I do not know what to say, for I am at a loss for words when I hear your high praise. Moreover, even if I did know what words I might properly speak now, I fear I would still remain mute, for my tongue is paralyzed with joy when I hear you hold me, your humble servant, in such favourable regard."

They all clapped their hands at my words, and the emperor said it was very nobly spoken.

"But now to the matter at hand," he said. "This same good Yreth is also a stonemage of great skill and ability, therefore I have decided to reward him for his services to me by giving to him a great commission, and one which is very close to my heart, for I intend to have him increase the height of my *luma*, so it will be twice as tall as it was."

All the nobles there clapped again, and all eyes were upon me to see how I would take this news. I did my best to smile and bow, of course, but my heart was not in it, for I had my ambitions set upon my cathedral, and I did not even know what his *luma* was yet.

I think the emperor read my thoughts, for he said, "Does this commission not please you, Yreth?"

I considered this for a moment, then I said, "Emperor, you may be certain that any favour you bestow upon me is received with a degree of gratitude and ecstasy lying at the utmost limits of human capability. Moreover, I am supremely honoured that you would grant to me the enviable task of increasing the height of so important a structure as a *luma*. I must confess, though, amidst my rejoicing, there is a dark shadow over my heart."

He said, "Show me the shadow, dear Yreth. Perhaps I may cast light upon it."

I thought again and then said, "If I build this *luma*, I fear it would bring down the wrath of another great lord."

He said angrily, "Any lord who threatens my subjects gives offence to me. Tell me his name, and I will go to war with him and shoot arrows through his heart."

I said, "I fear you would not be able, emperor, for the lord I speak of is the one great God. I swore to him that the next buildings I created would be three cathedrals to Him, and I fear that if I do not hold to my word, He will strike me dead. Worse yet, though, I fear He would also wreak His vengeance upon you, emperor, and I would be loath to induce such a terrible calamity."

The emperor turned to one of his visitors, who was the Bishop of Pos Tangrove, and said, "Do you think Yreth's appraisal of our God's nature is correct?"

She replied, "Oh, he is certainly correct. Countless kings and emperors have been struck dead because they, or one of their servants, committed some offence against God. But what are these cathedrals he speaks of?"

Well, I had brought my plans with me, so I unrolled them and showed everyone present the sketch of the cathedral, as well as a large plan showing the binding scheme. They were all transfixed by the beauty of it and thought it was unutterably magnificent, and the Bishop of Pos Tangrove praised it more, even, than any of the others.

And do not think this woman was low in rank, for I know I have spoken earlier of my dealings with bishops and archbishops and cardinals and bishopas. There, however, I spoke of the Eastern Gnostic Church, where a bishop is one of the intermediate ranks, just as it is in Cyprus. However, in the Saskatoon Empire, the older Canadian Heterodox Church is dominant, and within the Canadian hierarchy a bishop is the highest clerical rank.

Unfortunately, the Canadians and the Gnostics hate each other bitterly, so my previous rank of archbishop meant nothing here. For this reason, I had not told anyone about my old post, and, indeed, I thought it best to keep it a secret.

After she had finished admiring my plans, the wise Bishop of Pos Tangrove said, "If you will take my advice, emperor, you will see to it that Yreth builds these cathedrals without delay, for not to do so would insult God, whereas to build them would bring you the rewards of His love, and would besides increase still further your reputation in the world as a patron of beautiful things."

The emperor looked glum then and said, "I fear it will be years before these cathedrals are finished, and I will have to wait that long for improvements to my *luma*, for I will trust none but Yreth with this valuable commission."

Then one of the Imperial Advisors, a woman called Paos, said, "Emperor, I have an idea. Why not have Yreth begin work on these cathedrals at once in order to satisfy the dictates of his powerful God. But let his work be of a very preliminary nature, so it will not take much time. Then, when this part is done, he may turn his attention to your *luma*, and complete it, before returning to the arduous task of finishing the cathedrals."

This seemed like a good plan, and the Bishop of Pos Tangrove said she would go to pray upon it, to see if God liked the sound of it. When she returned, we were all delighted to hear that it met with the complete approval of God, although He had added the condition that she should help me with the work, and that, when the cathedrals were finished, she should be set in charge of them.

It was all settled, then, and to the complete satisfaction of all those present, both human and divine. The emperor said he would pay me generously for my labours, and this was no idle boast, for I received a truly magnificent stipend of one thousand arrans each month while the work was in progress, in addition to lavish gifts from many of the emperor's family and other citizens of the town, who, knowing how close I was with the emperor, hoped I would speak well of them to him.

Soon after, I went out into the wilderness again to find the most suitable sites for my cathedrals. I decided to situate them in a great triangle around the city, with each cathedral standing at a distance of three miles from the city walls.

I worried at first that the Bishop of Pos Tangrove would interfere with my work, but as it turned out her taste in architecture was impeccable, and she had a great many useful ideas for me. For example, I had wanted to name the cathedrals after the Holy Trinity—one after God, one after Christ, and one after the Holy Ghost. The bishop, though, had a better idea.

She said to me, "You would be better to name the cathedrals after the great cities of the region, for that is the way we do things here, and it draws the people in very well. If you call your building the Cathedral of God, you may be sure that God is the only one who will be inside it, which would be hollow praise to Him indeed."

I saw the wisdom of this, and so we decided to name the cathedrals the Cathedral of Pos Tangrove, the Cathedral of Pos Vindwater, and the Cathedral of Ichic, and within them they contained numerous smaller chapels, such as the Chapel of Belpinian, the Chapel of Entric, the Chapel of Pos Croythorn and Pos Pola, the Chapel of Great Tasker, and so on, in order that the cathedrals might draw in pilgrims from all across the Saskatoon Empire—which, when they were finally built, they did.

On another occasion, I had been feeling uneasy about some aspect of the three cathedrals, but I could not say what it was. Strange things started happening to me then: one of my shoes went missing; I cut my arm; a large bird landed in front of me and pecked at a dead mouse. I was disturbed by these omens and felt God was somehow displeased with my designs.

Then the Bishop of Pos Tangrove, quite unexpectedly, seemed to echo my thoughts, saying, "You know, I feel uncomfortable with these cathedrals being all so very much alike. It seems to me it might be impious to have three fingers pointing up to God in such a way."

I realized at once that she was right, and this was the very thing troubling me. I decided on the spot that only one of the cathedrals would take the original form I had envisioned, which is to say, a fist with the first finger pointing upward. For the other two cathedrals, I would vary the designs slightly, so each construction pointed to heaven with a different digit. I changed the designs then so one was a fist pointing to heaven with the second finger, and the other was a fist on its side, pointing skyward with the thumb.

In any case, once I had revised the designs, I went out into the wilderness with a few slaves to the sites I had selected and we hammered large wooden stakes into the ground, with signs upon them bearing the words: "This will be a great cathedral."

Then, with the preliminary part of my constructions begun, I returned to Saskatoon and spent six months working on the emperor's accursed *luma*.

I am sure, by now, you are feverish with the desire to know what a *luma* might be. It has amused me to keep the secret to this point, while several times mentioning the mysterious structure here and there, and knowing you will be puzzled by the reference. Still, it is now time for my amusement to curtail itself, and for me to tell you what the *luma* is all about.

A *luma*, simply put, is a kind of artificial mountain. It is constructed in the shape of a square-edged triangle, with the square edge upon the ground, so you might climb up the sloping edge to the top, then peer over the sheer drop, drawing a sense of excitement and danger from the great distance to the ground. This is the whole purpose of the structure, and for all its great size, it contains no rooms or doors or windows. It is merely a thing you climb.

I should add that advocates of the *luma* do not treat its climbing as a mere amusement. Indeed, to them, the sensation of danger which they feel as they peer over the summit is spiritually moving, and they believe, through the experience, they are brought closer to the knowledge of death, and, therefore, to God.

I tried the *luma* for myself, and found it a very terrifying sensation. It is not that it was so very high, for I have built and climbed many towers higher than the *luma*. No, the *luma*'s curious terror comes from the fact that the drop is so sharp and precipitous, and, together with the sloping floor at your feet, and lack of support, it gives one a precarious, giddy feeling.

I was dining with the emperor regularly by then, and I said to him one evening, "I cannot imagine why you would want the *luma* any higher. It seems to me it is already high enough to serve the function, and its height surely filled me with dread."

He said, "When I first ascended the *luma*, my reaction was the same as yours, but since that time I have climbed its slope on thousands of occasions, and, gradually, its terror has diminished to my senses. These days, when I climb to the top, I can happily sit upon the edge, or jump about, or hop, or shoot arrows to the ground, or even do a handstand, just as I please, and with no dizzying sensation at all. You can see, then, the great *luma* has lost its spiritual power for me, and I find this fact disturbing."

I said, "Then you are saying it is not the *luma*'s height that gives it this spiritual power over you, but the sensation of danger it imparts, a sensation you no longer feel?"

He said, "Yes, you have defined the problem exactly. What a clear mind you have!"

After hearing these comments, I started to find the problem of the *luma* more interesting, and I realized that, despite the emperor's request, there was more to be done than just making the *luma* higher. Even if it were to go to the moon, its height would eventually lose its blow upon the nerves of its climbers, for people become accustomed to such things.

Then a wonderful idea came to me. I thought to myself, "Suppose the top of the *luma* were not quite so solid and sturdy, but instead swayed and creaked like an old bridge, as though it might give way. That would certainly be terrifying." Then I thought, "No, for even this is something the climbers would eventually find tiresome. What is needed here is not the illusion but the reality of danger."

At once, I knew exactly how the new *luma* would be built. It would be tall, that was certain—I had already planned to increase the height of the *luma* by three times through the addition of two stages—but now I decided to make an ingenious alteration to the peak of the topmost section, which is the place where people peer over the edge. It would appear very solid when people walked upon it, but in actual fact it would be set upon a delicately balanced pivot, held in place by a mechanical latch. The latch was to be of a temperamental nature, and when people walked up to the edge of the *luma* it would, on occasion, fall away, sending them tumbling to their deaths.

This latch, which sounds so simple in theory, was actually a very difficult thing to construct. The first latch I built would either give way too easily or else would refuse to budge at all, depending upon how well it was greased. Then I built another latch that gave way whenever the weight of more than two people, or one fat person, was placed upon it, but would remain firm under a lighter weight. This did not please me, though, for it was too predictable, and I knew people would soon discover the secret to survival.

Eventually I built a more complex mechanism. It used a cage

containing a number of desert rats. The cage's pathways were partially blocked by several wooden paddles, attached to stiff wires.
The other end of each wire went into a hole in a vertical sliding
rod. As the rats moved through their enclosure, they pushed
against the paddles, extracting the wires from the holes. When
all the wires were pulled at the same moment, the rod dropped
onto a trigger plate, tripping the latch mechanism and releasing
the luma's pivoting platform. In this way, the random movements
of small animals controlled a structure weighing many tons.

If, at that moment, people were standing on the edge of the pivot, looking down at the terrible drop, the entire top ten feet of the
luma would abruptly tip beneath them, sending the unfortunate
observers to their deaths. Once the weight of these people was
gone, of course, the pivot slowly returned, and the mechanism
locked once more. A lever pushed the rod back into place, and, assuming the rats were no longer pressing on the paddles, the wires
would keep it there.

It took me about eight months to construct the luma, of which a
month was spent installing the mechanism at the summit. I placed
a secret door partway up the third section, by means of which a
slave might crawl through to feed and water the rats, or, if necessary, replace them.

During this time, I used to have my luncheon in the Courtiers'
Hall, where I would talk with the various courtiers on this subject
or that. One of them was a very rude fellow by the name of Lambic
Staid who loved to pick arguments with others and to cause all
manner of trouble. Unfortunately, he was also a favoured Imperial
Attendant, with eight tweaks upon his comb, and many of the other courtiers were afraid of his influence with the emperor.

One day, he sat himself down at my table, although I had not
invited him there, and he said, "I hear you are from the sea."

I said, "I was not born under the waves, if that is what you mean,
but I have lived by the sea, and I know my way around a ship."

He said, "Tell me this, then: what manner of creature is a seal?
Is it a doglike fish, or is it a fishlike dog?"

Well, I knew this man's reputation, and I had seen his argumentative ways in action, but I was not afraid to take him on, so I said, "It is a doglike fish, although I am quite certain you will think differently."

He tapped his fat nose and said, "Indeed I do, my friend, for I have been an important courtier for a good many years now, and in all that time I have learned a thing or two. A seal is a fishlike dog."

I said, "That is not so. It spends its days swimming in the sea, and so we know, in its heart, it is a fish, not a dog."

He said, "Ah, such amusing folly. Can you not see that its love of swimming is the very thing that makes it fishlike. Since it is not a fishlike fish, it follows that it must be a fishlike dog. Moreover, some months back I had the opportunity to taste the meat of a seal which a merchant had brought here for the emperor's table. I dine with him at least once a month, you know. I was struck by the fact that the meat tasted nothing like fish, but in many ways quite similar to dog. Do not feel ashamed, however, for you could not have known these things."

I said, "If the meat of the seal tastes like dog, then it shows that its taste is one of the doglike aspects to its fishy nature. It is, therefore, a doglike fish, and you are wrong. Nevertheless, I must say I find your arguments delightful, and childlike in their simple naivety. I will be sure to report them to the emperor for his amusement, for I dine with him at least three times every week."

The other courtiers around gave a chuckle there, for they saw Lambic Staid had met his match in me. But instead of being done with the discussion, as he should have, he started to chide me, saying I did not know what I said, and I knew nothing about the true nature of the seal, and so on.

Well, I started to get angry. I said, "Who are you, a man who lives thousands of miles from the ocean, to talk to me about seals? I have seen a thousand seals in my life. I have hunted them in boats, I have eaten them for dinner, and I even kept one as a pet for a time. Do not tell me they are dogs, for they are fish, as any fool can tell you."

He said, "You bluster thus, but you cannot prove it."

I said, "Indeed I can, for there is one sure way to know the nature of a creature, and that is to observe the company it keeps. If you place a seal among fish, they will swim together in the most cordial and agreeable manner. But place a seal among dogs and they will quarrel. The seal will bite at the dogs, and the dogs will bite at the seals, until, at length, the seal lies in pieces, or else, if it is a fierce seal, the dogs do."

He said, "You do not know this. The story is clearly fabulous."

I said, "No, it is true, and I have won many bets on such contests." Then I said, "A seal is not a dog and can no more live peacefully among dogs than a foolish old hypocrite with eight tweaks on his comb can live among wise and worthy courtiers."

The other courtiers roared with laughter at my sharp retort, but old Lambic was furious.

He said, "You will apologize for those words, or, as I stand here, you will risk the emperor's displeasure."

I said, "And you will leave my table or risk mine."

He did not know where to turn then, so he picked up his plate of stew and threw it into my lap, whereupon I jumped to my feet and snatched the comb out of his hair. Then, on a sudden impulse, I took from my belt one of the inferior combs I had won in my wager over the Pulsiter, and I stuck it in his hair in place of his old comb.

"There," I said, "I have demoted you for your rudeness. Now, take that back to the emperor, if you will." Then I pushed him and kicked him until he was out of the Courtiers' Hall.

All the other courtiers gathered around me then, and said how excellent and just it was that I had treated Lambic in this way, and how he had deserved this punishment for many years.

When the anger had left me, though, I thought to myself, "What have I done? Treating that courtier so may have been a very dangerous act, and although the man is a fool, he is vindictive and might find some way to turn the emperor against me."

I need not have worried though, for later I heard exactly what had happened. Lambic Staid had stormed straight back to the emperor and told him everything I had done, showing him the new comb I had given him. He thought, by repeating what I had said and telling the emperor how I had treated one of his courtiers, he would make the emperor angry at me.

Instead, however, the emperor was amused and entertained by the incident, because he knew this courtier had a habit of being too proud and officious. The emperor said, "This man Yreth is as bold in his debating as he is in his hunting."

Then he had me brought before him, and he told me to return Lambic's comb, which I did, after taking back the comb I had given to Lambic in its place.

Lambic said, "Is there to be no further punishment for this man, emperor?"

The emperor said, "No. Be at peace, you two. The matter is at an end."

Lambic was furious at this, but there was nothing he could do about it, so he merely nodded and smiled at the emperor, as if all was new tulips in his garden. I knew, though, he was secretly angry. Later on he came to me in a corridor and said, in a very spiteful tone, "You got off too lightly there, that is certain, but I swear by the emperor's name that I will be avenged against you."

I said, "Be counselled by me and drop your plans, for I swear by God's name that any actions you take against me will bring about your own undoing."

He scoffed at my words, but as you will soon see, I had spoken prophetically.

When the *luma* was complete, a special celebration was organized within the palace. Fine foods were laid out in the courtyard, and all the courtiers and the Imperial Family were allowed there. They stared in amazement at the *luma* and said it was the most wonderful thing they had ever seen, especially when viewed from below like this. Until now, you see, many of them had not been allowed into the courtyard, and had seen only the upper part of the *luma* over the palace walls.

After everyone was well fed, the emperor ascended the *luma* with me at his side, and a number of the most prominent courtiers following on behind. We reached the first stage, and the emperor stopped there to look down and to wave to the people below. Then we went up to the next stage, and he stopped again to wave. Even though this stage was twice the height of the first, he showed absolutely no fear, and he walked back and forth balancing on the edge for a time before continuing up.

Finally we reached the summit. I stopped short of the pivot, of course, but I told the emperor to go on without me if he wished. He did this and peered over the edge, accompanied by a number of his important courtiers.

He stood there for a short time, then he walked back to me. He said, "Ah, you have done a fine job for me there. What a height that is!" But it was clear to me he was secretly disappointed, for otherwise why would he have stayed there for so short a time?

The emperor politely asked me a number of questions about the *luma* and the details of its construction. Most of the other courtiers were gathered around to hear what was said.

I said, "Its structure is simple enough," then I winked and said, "although it also has its secrets."

Now, as I talked with the emperor, Lambic Staid remained upon the edge of the precipice along with Vepilla, a young Imperial Bearer who held a great admiration for Lambic and tried to ape his manner.

Lambic said, in a loud voice, "What do you say, Vepilla? I do not think this new *luma* is such a wondrous thing."

"No," said Vepilla. "It is tall, but it is not as frightening as it might be. And I fancy the quality of the construction does not even wet the stick."

"What is worse," said Lambic, "this new *luma* fails to move the soul in the way the original did. But really, what can you expect of this simple man Yreth. After all he knows nothing about spiritual matters."

"They say he will build cathedrals next," said Vepilla.

"If I were the emperor," said Lambic, "the work I have seen here would give me cause to think twice on that score."

As I have said, he spoke in a loud voice, for he hoped the emperor would hear his words and I would be discredited. Still, the emperor was very courteous, and he pretended not to hear, talking to me instead.

Suddenly, to my enormous surprise and pleasure, the edge of the *luma* gave way, and Lambic and Vepilla were sent plunging to the ground.

The emperor gave a cry and said, "Oh! What is this? The *luma* is breaking apart!"

"No," I said, "it is not breaking apart. Watch and you will see the edge rise up again."

So he watched, and the edge slowly rose up again, and as it did so, I explained how I had placed a trick latch inside, so such catastrophic events as we had just witnessed might occur from time to time.

The emperor reacted very strangely to the news. First he grew pale as if he would faint, for he realized the danger he had been in just moments before. Then he became angry, and I thought for a moment that he would have me killed on the spot. However, that emotion too soon faded from his features, and it was replaced by a look of the utmost joy and spiritual fulfilment.

"You have done it!" he said. "You have regained for me the trepidation I felt on my first ascent of my *luma*. Oh, my dear Yreth! How can I thank you enough! I must try it once more, this time with the full knowledge of this peak's danger."

Then he walked to the edge again, together with one or two of the braver courtiers and they looked nervously over the edge, down upon the bodies of Lambic Staid and Vepilla so far below. When they came back, they all appeared very frightened and exhilarated.

You can see, then, my prophecy to Lambic Staid was not merely an idle threat but was rather the product of my close relationship with God, for it had pleased Him, in His omniscient wisdom, to toss Lambic Staid from the *luma* even as the old fool was trying to discredit me with his critical words. And what a bitter irony it was for Lambic Staid that his own death should have astonished the emperor so, raising my reputation to new heights.

A Ninth Section Of The Eleventh Part

In Which I Briefly Describe The Passage Of Many Years

After my triumph with the *luma*, the emperor was overflowing with gratitude to me, and he insisted I complete the cathedrals without delay, for he knew it was my dearest wish to build them. He put hundreds of slaves and myrmidons under my command to help with the task.

I worked at great speed, but even then it took me five years to complete the three great buildings. When they were finished, they were the wonder of the land.

There is much I could tell about the years I spent building the cathedrals, as well as the years which followed. I remained in the emperor's service, as his principal stonemage, his dearest friend, and eventually his treasurer. All told, I served him for almost eighteen years, and in that time I built many other wonderful buildings and had numerous exciting adventures.

The events of my life during those years would make a tale of unsurpassed excellence, for there were many brave fights and battles, incredible accomplishments, astonishing travels, and passionate romances.

Still, I think I will not tell those tales here, for I fear they would take up a great many pages, whereas I am growing tired of all this writing and anxious to come to the real meat of my story. And besides, I did not say I would set out my whole life in this book, so if I choose to tell of some parts and not of others, you can have little reason to complain, even if some of the parts I leave out are more interesting than the parts I put in.

Moreover, it strikes me now that my adventures during those eighteen years were of such exceptional interest that I would be a fool to throw them all into just one book. Instead, I would do much better to wait a year or two, and, if the interest is still there, perhaps I will write a second book, describing those fascinating years, for you may be sure they were so rich in event they easily merit a book of their own, and might even be made into two books, or even twenty books, although the events then described would be of a more minute and trivial nature, describing the various walks I took, and the conversations I had, and the meals I ate, and so on.

Let us take those years as dealt with, then.

Now, you will remember Pandrick, the boy I had trained with the leather glove. Well, he had grew into manhood, and became a skilled general, and (thanks to my training) he was much favoured by the emperor for his wit and manners. You would think Pandrick would be grateful to me for opening the happy gates of fortune to him, but this was not the case and he held a stubborn and deep-seated grudge against me. As the emperor grew older and more feeble, Pandrick assumed more power, and—spoilt child!—he resolved to kill me.

While the weather was turning stormy in the Imperial City, I heard news that the birds were singing in Cyprus. This was because King Bellay was now dead, meaning the bounty which had been on my head was lifted.

Clearly, the time had come to leave Saskatoon and return at last to Cyprus, and so I bade farewell to all my closest friends. They wept like children to hear I was leaving, and said I was the finest fellow they had ever known.

Moreover, my dear friend Bitian Teppel, who had become a prominent courtier by that point, as well as attaining great fame as an artist (thanks to my favourable recommendations to the emperor), said to me, "I swore I would be your friend for all eternity, and therefore I must accompany you on your travels."

I said, "You have already given me an eternity's worth of your splendid friendship. I declare your promise is fully satisfied."

He would hear none of this though, and he insisted he must come with me. Since none of my reasoning would shake him, I was obliged to accept Bitian Teppel as my travelling companion.

As for the emperor, he did not fully understand my meaning at first when I told him the sad news, for he had become simple in his mind and could not conceive of me being absent from his court. At length, though, his ears seemed to hear my words true, and he said, "If you are off to catch me another Pulsiter, you will need some money for your purse. Go to my treasury, and take any trinket that strikes your fancy. Do it right away, though, or I will send a sharp arrow through your heart, you rogue."

Faced with such a threat, you may be sure I went to the treasury at that very moment! I chose a gift for myself which I considered worthy of my talents and long service to the emperor, then, with the assistance of twenty of the treasury guards, I loaded the gift into various sturdy boxes.

The following night, Bitian and I made a discreet departure from Saskatoon. I carried my wealth on fifteen large ox-wagons. These were principally loaded with gold coins, expensive clothes, and treasures of all kind. I also had a chest as high as your knee and filled with gemstones, all of them large and of the highest quality. I had earned a portion of this great wealth through my building work. The rest was the magnanimous gift the emperor had given me.

We made our way overland across the wild plains, a journey of many weeks, until we reached the Hesperian Mountains. More weeks passed as we wound through the mountain paths and tunnels. It was long distance, surely, but my heart was so light with thoughts of Cyprus I was not fatigued in the least, and rode or walked with a song constantly on my lips.

At last, we arrived at Great Tasker. My old ship, the *Moray*, was waiting there in the harbour, together with most of the original crew and all twelve of the original myrmidons, who, as you will remember, I had placed upon the ship to guard it when it sailed from Quebec.

(Actually, for many years I had assumed the ship had been lost at sea, for it did not arrive at Great Tasker. However, during my travels in the emperor's service among the wild lands of the utmost south, I was led, as if by a divine hand, to the very place where the ship was stranded! I knew from this divine intervention that the *Moray*, which had brought me to America, was destined someday to take me home again. I saw to it the ship was always well maintained and ready to sail with just a few days' notice.)

When all my treasure was loaded aboard, we set sail to the west, following the route to Cyprus that had been explained to me so many years before by the ghost of Saint Elifax. As the land diminished behind us, I bade farewell to the Saskatoon Empire, knowing my eye would never again behold its lovely walls and towers. Unless I choose to return there one day.

A Tenth Section Of The Eleventh Part

In Which I Tell Of My Voyage Across The Pacific Ocean

WE HAD BEEN AT SEA for no more than a week when the head slave told me a group of ships were approaching us from the southwest.

"That is not so strange," I said. "There are many ships which travel these waters, carrying goods for trade."

"These ships do not look like trading ships," replied the head slave. "Indeed, it is clear they are warships, for I can make out the great spears upon their prows."

I took a look for myself then, and could see the ships plainly enough, although I could not make out their prows. Still, slaves have good eyesight, and it is best to trust them in such matters.

I said, "They are probably pirate ships. Tell those slaves upon the sails to give us all the speed they can give us, by hoisting such sails and pulling upon such ropes as will accomplish this. And tell those upon the rudder to turn our ship to the southwest."

The head slave said, "Sire, forgive my question, but do you not mean for us to turn to the northeast, for the warships lie to the southwest?"

I said, "Did I not say 'northeast'?"

He said, "No, sire. You said 'southwest.'"

"That is very strange," I said. "I meant to say 'turn to the southwest,' and indeed, I thought I had said so, but somehow my words came out differently."

The head slave looked puzzled then, and said, "Sire, if you meant to say 'southwest,' then your words came out precisely as you intended, for you said 'southwest.'"

I suddenly realized he was right, and I had made the mistake for a second time. Still, such mistakes happen now and then, and I thought little enough of it, so I said to the head slave, "A mere slip of the tongue. My meaning, however, should be clear enough, since you cannot imagine I would wish us to sail towards those warships. Therefore, and mark me this time, go to the slave upon the rudder and have him set our course to the southwest."

"Northeast," said the slave.

I instantly realized I had made the same mistake for a third time.

Well, that struck me as very strange indeed, for I am ordinarily very careful in my speech, especially when the matter at hand is an urgent one.

They say "Spirits speak through tripping tongues," and I shuddered now as I realized God's spirit had been taking possession of my lips as I spoke, and had told me, three times, to sail to the southwest, towards the warships, even though common sense would have told me to fear those ships.

I spoke to my head slave then, saying, "Listen to me well, for God is speaking through my very lips, and I do not wish to offend Him by speaking more than I must. We must sail to the southwest, towards those fearsome warships."

The head slave said, "Shall I bring the myrmidons upon deck, with spears at the ready."

I said, "No. We shall sail towards those ships showing not fear, but enthusiasm, and we shall see what Providence places in our hands."

Well, we sailed to those ships, and they sailed to us, and at length our vessels came together. I stood on deck and waved to the warships, and you may be sure the folk aboard those terrible vessels were astonished to see us approach so fearlessly. After a time, their myrmidons raised spears, and I thought they would strike, but then their weapons were lowered again, and we were allowed us to draw close.

Their ships were very huge, and they rose up over mine like a great wall jutting out of the ocean, even though the *Moray* was nevertheless a fair size of ship.

I heard a voice shouting, then, and I looked up to see a woman was hailing me. She said, "Accept my apologies. We took you at first to be a trader or a fishing vessel."

I did not take her meaning, but I knew God was guiding my journey, so I replied, "The mistake was a natural one to make. Think nothing of it."

Then she said, "Stand back. We will lower nets."

Well, they lowered nets then, and, since they made no move to climb down the nets, I climbed up them, onto the deck of their ship.

I had no sooner boarded the vessel than I was struck by its awesome size and beauty. I saw huge ballistas placed there, covered in patterns of gold and jewels. The lookout cabins were as large as mansions, and covered with statues and paintings of fearsome animals. As for the decks, they were so wide it would take a man a hundred paces to cross them. In the centre of the craft, a great rectangular opening looked down upon the lower decks. On those decks I saw not only myrmidons, but also such animals as horses and pigs, and food gardens too.

The woman who had hailed me hugged me in greeting. She was in her fifties, I should say, but with dark and weathered skin and short grey hair. Her features were not like those of any American, nor yet were they like those of a Cypriot, or a Kennian, or a Chinese, or any other race I knew. She had a long, narrow nose, a thin face, jutting cheekbones, and narrow lips. An emerald, or some green gem like it, was set into one of her teeth.

There were other men and women there too, who stood behind the captain, dressed in fine clothes, and with many jewels to decorate their persons.

The captain said then, "Welcome. I am Captain Da Qua Yansh."

I said, "Excellent. I am Yreth."

"That is a strange name," she said.

I said, "I find it serves me well when I am travelling in such parts as these."

She tugged upon her nostril then, saying, "I understand perfectly." Then she asked, "Do you bring a message from the Ucher Tad?"

I replied, "I bring a message of unsurpassed urgency." And this was quite true, although she took my meaning to be that the message I brought her was from Ucher Tad, whereas, I knew that, when I delivered the message, it would just be off the top of my own head.

She said, "Tell me the message, friend Yreth."

I did not to wish to speak too rashly just yet, so I employed a clever ruse to find out more information about this woman and these warships.

I said, "Before I speak, let me say this. Spies are a constant danger in this world, and it is often difficult to know who is truly a friend and who an enemy. I feel in my heart you are indeed the same brave Captain Da Qua Yansh to whom I must deliver my message, but it occurs to me now you might be some imposter, who has commandeered this vessel through the violent disposal of its famous captain."

She said, "Ah, you are very wise to consider this. All too often, folk are tricked by first impressions, and, seeing a great ship or a fine uniform, assume without question that all is as it seems. But how may we settle this matter in order to put your mind at rest?"

I said, "I will ask you a number of questions. If you are who you claim, you will certainly know the answers. If your replies satisfy me, I will deliver my secret message."

She said, "An excellent plan. Ask your questions."

Well, I thought for a moment, then I said, "What is the extent of your command?"

She said, "These five great warships, of course."

"And how many myrmidons do you carry?"

"Twelve thousand, upon these ships, although, naturally, there are many more on the entire fleet."

My ears pricked up at this. "How large is this fleet you speak of?" I asked.

"Why, two hundred ships," she said. "Surely, though, this fact would be known to any spy who had managed to take my place."

"Yes, indeed," I said, "but I fancy only the real captain would be puzzled by my asking the question."

She said, "Ah, yes. You are very clever. I had not considered that. Have you now heard all you need to hear?"

I said, "No, not quite." Then I asked, "Are all the ships within the fleet as large as this one?"

She said, a little impatiently, it seemed to me, "Some are as large, others are a little smaller, still others are a great deal larger."

"And what is your mission?" I said.

She said, "To spearhead the raids along the coast of America, and to destroy those cities which are within the realm of the emperor, for the Ucher Tad has heard this wicked emperor is an eater of goat flesh."

I was alarmed to hear of this plan, for the emperor had shown me nothing but kindness. I resolved on the spot to do all I could to avert this attack, and I realized I might do so by means of issuing false orders.

"Good, good," I said. "I am now completely satisfied you are indeed who you claim, which is to say, the noble and fearsome Captain Da Qua Yansh. I will now deliver to you my message, which comes directly from the person of Ucher Tad."

But before I could give my orders, she interrupted me. "First," she said, "perhaps you should allow me to ask a few questions of you, again, just to determine that you, too, are who you say, for it strikes me now you do not look like a Tulvuki, and your ship's design is strange."

Now, I will confess I was afraid at these words, especially since the captain then waved her hands and called myrmidons to surround me with spears. Still, I was determined I should not let my fear show, and it was well I made this decision, for her next words to the myrmidons were: "I will ask him questions. If he shows fear, or hesitates with his replies, then run him through instantly."

Then she said to me, "How many toldics decorate the Ucher's mask?"

I laughed carelessly, and said, "The question is preposterous!"

She said, "Why is it preposterous, good Yreth?" Then she leaned forward, with some unusual interest, it seemed to me.

I thought to myself, "Ah, there is a trick to the question, and while I do not know what a toldic might be, I will warrant there are either none of them on the Ucher's mask, or that the Ucher does not wear a mask."

So I took a chance then, and said, "There are no toldics on the Ucher's mask, and I pray there never will be!"

She gave a great smile at this, and all the men and women around her cheered, saying, "Well said! The Ucher will never be reduced to wearing toldics."

Then one of the men, a young fellow with blue eyes, said, "Let me ask a question, captain. I have a good one."

She gave her assent, and he turned to me, saying, "Do you *enjoy* eating the flesh of the cow during the moon's half phases?"

Well, from the way he asked the question, it was so obviously a trick I did not even take any time to think about it, but instead pretended to grow angry, saying, "How dare you accuse me of such a vile act! The Ucher will certainly hear of this!"

He looked scared then, and said, "But it was merely a question to test you."

Then I said, "It seems to me anyone who would ask such a question must have thought about committing the act himself. There can be no other explanation for thinking upon such depravity."

"I would never do such things!" he said.

But the captain said, "Are you sure, Tin Mik? I find Yreth's argument compelling. I will be watching your behaviour carefully from now on."

Then another man asked me a question. He narrowed his eyes and said, "What shade of red may a warship be painted?"

I suspected yet another trick question, and so I said, "No shade of red. A warship should never be painted red."

Once again, my answer pleased them.

Then one of the women said, "What building lies in the centre of Pior's Lake?"

But all the others objected to this question, saying, "No no, it is too easy. All the world knows the great Mathematical Dome lies in the centre of Pior's Lake. Ask him something harder. Try to trick him."

The woman retracted her question, and instead asked me how many times deer had been seen in the Forests of Lid. I replied that deer had never been seen there, for the Forests of Lid contained no deer. They laughed then, saying "Of course! How could they? The deer would drown in Old Lid's watery kingdom."

Their interrogation continued in this way for some time. They asked question after question, each trying to outdo the other in the sophistication of their trickery. However, because I knew each question was a trick question, I had merely to discover the nature of the trick in order to deduce the correct answer. This was fortunate for me: if they had asked me an ordinary question, like the one about Pior's Lake, or even a question like "What is the name of the country we come from?" I would certainly have been exposed.

Finally they were satisfied I was who I claimed, and the captain apologized to me for the rigour of the test.

"We had to be certain," she said, "for there is much about your appearance that is unusual."

"It enables me to blend easily with others in these parts," I said.

"I can see that," the Captain replied. "But on to our business. Do you prefer to give me the Ucher's order here and now, or would you rather rest for a few hours and tell me over dinner."

I said, "That depends on the dinner. What do you plan to have served?"

She replied, "In your honour, we will serve fine spadge, naturally."

Then I said, "How do you prepare your spadge?" I wanted to find out what sort of food it was, you see.

Her reply was not helpful, though. She said, "Oh, in the normal way."

So I said, "No, I mean, in what order are the ingredients added?"

"Ah, an excellent question!" she said. Then she called for the slave who supervised the cooking. When he arrived, she said, "Tell this man in what order the ingredients are added to the spadge."

The slave said, "First goes the brine, with the seaweed in it. When this is heated, I add the black beans, then the yellow beans. The fire onions are thrown in next, and the mixture is stirred until it forms a thick paste. Only then do I add the cabbage leaves, cloves and scraps of bone marrow."

Then the captain said, "Although he is but a slave, he is a master of the spadge."

Well, whether he was a master or no, the concoction did not sound tasty to my ear, so I told the captain I had remembered other urgent tasks I needed to perform aboard my own ship, so I would not be able to attend the dinner.

Then the captain asked me for the new orders I had brought.

I said, "Here are your orders. In the first place, you must not attack the coast of America."

She said, "That is strange, for we were given very specific orders, even down to the ports we should attack. But perhaps this was merely a ruse on the Ucher's part, in order to foil spies."

I said, "The Ucher is ever mysterious, and spies may be anywhere, therefore your speculation seems to have merit."

The captain said, "But if we are not to journey to the coast of America, where are we to go?"

I said, "Go west."

"To what land?"

I thought for a moment and remembered a story I had once heard about the foul and crude people of Poagh. They live upon a rocky island and sew their clothes from sackcloth. They are in the habit of drinking too much strong wine, and when they do, they shout loud insults at each other and sing disagreeable songs.

Perhaps the people of Poagh did not deserve to be slaughtered for the sake of these habits, but neither, as it seemed to me, did the kind folk of America, and if it was a choice between one or the other—as it clearly was—the people of Poagh were obviously less worthy to survive. So, faced with two violent and disagreeable options, I did what I had to do, and what any reasonable person would have done, and picked the one less disagreeable to me.

I said to the captain, "Find the island of Poagh and lay waste to its towns and villages."

The captain said, "With rockets or with myrmidons?"

I said, "First unleash all your rockets upon their towns, then send in the myrmidons to kill all the inhabitants."

She nodded and said she would do as I had asked.

Then I said, "Do you have some way of contacting the other ships in the fleet?"

She said, "Certainly. We have trained certain large seabirds to search out our ships. By means of these birds, which we carry aboard in cages, we can send messages to the main body of the fleet. Do you wish me to relay the Ucher's message to them?"

I said, "Yes. Send the message. Let all the ships in the fleet unleash their fury upon the wicked inhabitants of Poagh. I, for my part, will return to my ship and travel on ahead of you."

I returned to my ship and we sailed off. Even though my ship was heavily laden with treasure, it was faster than the great warships, and, by late the next day, they were no longer visible behind us.

I was very satisfied with the work I had done, and I knew in sparing the cities of America from the enemy fleet, I had handsomely repaid all the kindness the emperor had given to me over the years. What I did not yet realize, though, was that my actions would also bring salvation to our own dear land of Cyprus in its time of need. You will hear how a little later, but remember this story!

We continued to sail west for a month or so, plying our way across the Pacific Ocean. I had made sure I had plenty of water and food for the journey, along with a number of interesting books, not to mention the excellent company of Bitian Teppel, whose skills in philosophy and reasoning were almost as keen as my own.

There were dangers, of course. Several times the weather turned foul, and on one occasion the wind lifted the waves up like mountains, and they towered three times higher than my ship's masts. Oh, we were cruelly tossed! Although I am normally of a sturdy constitution, and not prone to seasickness, I became very seasick then, I will tell you, and things went even worse for Bitian Teppel, who was not used to the sea and would become sick even when things were only a little choppy. Still I was not afraid when these great storms lashed at us, and I prayed hard to God despite my sickness. Sure enough, within a day or so the storms had gone and my sickness with it.

On another occasion, a number of large whales appeared near the ship and swam alongside us for a time. I saw the cruel eyes of these monstrous fish and knew they had only one purpose: to sink my ship and eat its crew. Still, they did not attack us immediately, for I rather fancy they sensed something unusual about this ship, and they said to each other, "I feel within my brutish heart there is one aboard this vessel who is protected by God."

I went out onto the deck then and waved to the whales with both arms, shouting, "Begone, you murderous fish!" Then I said to them, "I am Yreth, and I swear by God that any injury you visit on me will be visited upon you tenfold."

Well, the fish thought on my words for a time and, I am sure, discussed it among themselves. At length, they seemed to decide it was not worth the risk to attack me, and they turned away to seek some other victim, which proves that, on occasion, a fish can be more intelligent than a man, for I had given a similar warning to the courtier Lambic Staid, but he had ignored it and suffered the consequences.

Eventually we sighted land. It did not seem we had been travelling very long, so I thought this was just some island in the middle of the ocean, but, as it turned out, it was the land of Sira Tereen, close to the Western Extremity. I had heard of this place, and, because I am of an inquisitive nature, we put in there for a time, at a port called Iacho, so I might see what kind of folk lived there.

I will tell you about this, because it well illustrates the dangers of travelling to far lands, dangers which derive, very often, not from savage animals, but from the curious customs found in various parts of the world.

I knew Sira Tereen was a land with strange ways, so I decided to go about the town with some care. I did not dock the ship where its cargo might easily be seized, but instead anchored it out in the bay and lowered the rowing boat from the deck.

Bitian Teppel wanted to come with me, but I had qualms about this, for he was not so resourceful as I, so I said, "No, stay here for the present. If all is safe, I will return for you."

He said, "Will you take myrmidons?"

I said, "No, for then I will appear like a warrior, and this may provoke an attack. Instead, I will go as a merchant, for all the world loves merchants." Then I put on a merchant's robes, and took a large bag, as if I had wares to sell. I also carried a solid staff, for this is a good weapon, but it does not look so threatening as a sword or a spear.

I rowed to the dock, climbed up from my boat, and walked into the town. I looked around for some person whom I might befriend and employ as my guide to this place. When I approach strangers in foreign parts, I have learned always to proceed with the utmost caution. I do not approach those with scars or wild hair, for these features indicate a quarrelsome disposition. Neither do I speak with those who snarl or curse or bang hirdy stones upon the walls, for these are the traits of assassins and thieves. Rather, I look for a person of light build, well dressed, and with a small mouth tilted slightly upwards at the edges. I always seek out a man rather than a woman since, unfortunately, my own attractive appearance makes women weak in the hips and incapable of giving useful advice.

After a few minutes of casual searching, I spotted a fellow who met my standards. He was standing by a merchant's stall, sharing a dish of creamed bacon with his two children. I nodded to him, then addressed him, saying, "The weather, you will note, is not in an extreme state today."

I had carefully chosen this remark for its four merits: it was unlikely to give offence; it was undeniably true; it was interesting in itself; and it demonstrated what Vanseefe calls "a delight in the moderate," which shows a refined nature.

Well, the fellow agreed the weather was very much as I had described it, and, since there was little more to discuss on that topic, I moved on to greater ones. I explained I had travelled to his island from across the ocean. He said he had seen my ship in the bay and assumed something of the sort.

I was about to tell him more when I noticed a small dog sniffing near his children. Without considering the matter, I kicked the dog away, so it might not bite them. Instead of showing gratitude, though, the man became ferocious. He shouted, "What? You would kick a dog!"

I said to him, "These are my boots, and I kick them where I will."

He pushed at me then, and I pushed him back. Then he struck at my face with his hand and waited for my response.

I knew I must be careful then, for if I struck at his face in return, he would likely strike me again, upon the body, whereupon I would strike him upon the body. Then he might kick at me, and I would kick back. And where would this lead? Before I knew it, we would both have drawn weapons, and we would be fighting like a couple of bandits. And yet I had not come to this place to begin a fight, and now that a fight seemed to be starting I wished only to end it quickly. Therefore, I lifted up my staff and brought it suddenly down upon the ingrate's head, to his great alarm and instant stupefaction. The fight was efficiently finished, with my adversary flat upon the ground.

There were people watching, and many gasped to see my skill. But one argumentative old man pushed forward and shook his finger in my face.

"How dare you commit such an outrage!" he said.

I said, firmly, but without anger, "The outrage was committed against me. The matter is now settled."

He said, "Not so! Not by any means! A man lies insensible. Stand where you are, while the impositors are summoned." Then he waved to a boy to fetch these impositors of his.

I said, "Peh! Do you think I will remain here at your whim? It is clear you are either demented or the worse for drink. Begone."

I made to leave, but old Grandfather would see and hear no reason. He pulled out a spillot, which is a weapon like a flat-sword but with a spoonlike tip, and thrust it towards me. I brushed it away with my arm, but he brought the blade around and swung hard at me, and I had to move swiftly to avoid the blow.

I could see this dotard meant to kill me, so I fought back with a will, parrying his blows with my staff and taking a few swings of my own. We fought only a minute or so, and finally, having knocked the spillot from his grasp, I took his legs under my arms, spun him around, and swung his head against a wall, which, alas, brought about the death of the old fellow.

You might think the business would have ended there, but this was a violent land, and no sooner had I picked up my staff than four young men came running, their leader blowing upon a whistle, and all of them clutching swords. Well, I was in a foul mood now, so I stepped forward to give them my warrior's handshake. I brought my staff down sidelong into the leader's face, which brought a quick end to his annoying whistle-blowing, then I pulled my silver throwing-razor from my right boot and stabbed him with it. It was a perfectly placed blow and struck him directly in the heart, so he fell instantly dead. I made a run for it then, with the other youths chasing after me.

One of the three was a swift runner, and as I ran back to the dock, he grabbed at my legs, sending us both to the ground. I turned on him with a vengeance, though, and gave him some good deep cuts with my weapon, until his pain from the injuries became a matter more pressing to him than the seizing of poor Yreth.

By this time, the other two youths were almost upon me. I scrambled for the long ladder which led down to the boat but instantly realized that, if I were so foolish as to climb down, the youths would catch me as I climbed, and swing their swords down upon me. I did not dare jump into the boat, either, for the dock was high up from the water, and I would certainly have capsized the boat, or broken the timbers in its belly.

I could see my ship anchored off the coast. I shouted for help, and waved furiously. As luck would have it, one of the myrmidons had his eye on the dock, and he hurled his spear at my pursuers. The huge weapon clattered to the ground at their feet. It did them no harm, but they were startled for a few seconds and looked around to see where the thrower was standing. By the time they had gathered their wits again, I had climbed down the ladder, cut the mooring rope, pushed off and was rowing back towards my ship, while my myrmidons covered my escape by throwing more spears.

Now, consider the tally of my visit to the town of Iacho. I had been forced to leave one man insensible, one injured, and two dead. And for what? The well intentioned kicking of a dog! As you may well suppose, we quickly departed that dangerous and capricious land, and continued our voyage west.

We were now very close to the Western Extremity of the world.

I was, naturally, excited at the prospect of reaching this unusual location and of seeing what it would be like to be instantaneously transported to a point thousands of miles away, so I stayed awake during the next night so I might enjoy the magical moment of transference.

The event occurred in the early hours of the morning. I was sitting upon the deck in a chair looking out at the stars, and almost on the verge of sleeping despite my best efforts to stay awake. Suddenly, I felt a strange sensation. I cannot quite describe it—it was a little as if someone had suddenly spun me around, although it was far more subtle. At once, I was jolted into wakefulness, and I said, "What? What was that?"

A slave was standing nearby, and he said, "I saw nothing, sire."

I said, "Did you feel a strange sensation just now?"

He said, "No, sire."

I knew I had felt the instantaneous motion of the ship to the Eastern Extremity, a motion too sublime to make itself known to a slave, but one which my heightened sensitivities were capable of detecting.

I shouted then, saying, "Haha! We have left the Pacific Ocean behind us. We are in the Great Eastern Sea now, and beyond the horizon lies Dranseet and Cyprus."

Then I woke Bitian Teppel, and, even though we had only slaves and myrmidons for company, we made a fine celebration. Bitian Teppel instructed all the slaves in the art of dancing and making merry, and I brought out a cask of sweet wine which Bitian and I drank with the utmost pleasure.

After another six weeks, we sighted the coast of Dranseet. Navigation became easy then, for we had only to follow the coastline until we reached the great towers at the entrance to the Asta. This leg of the journey took two months, and I used the time to write a book about the coastline of the east. I wrote down all I knew about the regions we passed, while Bitian Teppel made sketches of the lands we sailed past. Later I had the book printed. It is called *The Various Lands of the East as Viewed from the Sea*, and it is not only fascinating to read, but also contains some very pretty pictures. I urge you to find a copy and buy it, no matter what it may cost, for it is a book every refined and knowledgeable person should own.

We sailed through the Asta and up the Red Sea, where we passed a great many Indian warships, all painted in black, and travelling in the opposite direction.

I thought to myself, "How strange that so many warships should be gathered together here."

Still, I thought nothing more of it, and as I passed the ships I waved to them.

They waved back to me, then, seeing the myrmidons upon the deck of my ship, they shouted, "Where are you headed with those myrmidons?"

I said, "Cyprus."

When they heard this, the officers upon the ships gave a great cheer, and they waved their cloaks in salute of me as I sailed away.

I was puzzled by this, but dismissed it as the friendly ways of the Indian officers.

A day or two later, we passed a group of islands. I spotted a group of people standing upon the beach, shouting and jumping and waving their arms. It seemed as if they needed help, so I sent out a slave with the rowing boat to see what they wanted. He talked with them for a while, then they climbed into the boat and returned with him.

We took them aboard—there was a woman and five men, and they were in a piteous state, all covered with wounds, their clothes in tatters, and so thin they appeared as skeletons. One of the men had a terrible gash which went from his neck down to his waist. I gave him to the care of one of my slaves, who knew a little about herbs and such, but the wound had already become rank, and the man did not live to the next day.

As for the others, though, they improved rapidly once they were fed. They told me they were from Minyad and had been sailing to Relina on a little two-masted plait when they were attacked by Indian ships. Their ship was boarded by myrmidons, then sunk, and, of sixty passengers, they were the only survivors, having been carried by the waves to the islands.

I said, "Why should Indian ships wish to attack you? Did they take you for pirates?"

Then one of them, a physician called Ciren, said, "No, it was because of the war."

"What war is this?" I asked.

He said, "Don't tell me you do not know of the war. Did you not say you were from Cyprus?"

I said, "Indeed I am, but I have been in America for many years and am only now returning."

He said, "Well then, you have picked a fine time to return, for our great land has been at bloody war with India these past two years."

I said, "Surely not. I passed some Indian ships just a few days ago, and they greeted me very civilly."

He said, "How is that? And they did not try to sink you?"

I said, "No. In fact, they saluted me." Then I told him precisely what had happened when I had met the ships.

Ciren nodded then and said, "Surely God smiles upon you and keeps your soul safely cupped within His hand. My friend, those ships, and others like them, have been sinking every Cypriot vessel they find. But you, it seems, were saved by your innocence, for I am sure when the Indian ships saw you coming on so fearlessly, they took you for one of their own, bravely carrying myrmidons into the war."

I realized at once that this man was speaking truly, and I fell to my knees and gave thanks to God for his protection.

Then I said, "I have heard King Bellay is dead. Tell me, then, who rules our great land of Cyprus now?"

Ciren said, "It is Queen Sarla. She is just a young stick of a girl, but she is furious and warlike, and has already proved herself a mighty leader of armies."

I said, "Sarla? I do not know that name. Who is she, a daughter of Bellay?"

He laughed then, and said, "By no means." Then he leaned in and said, "Her true name is not Sarla, but Loryne, and she was nothing more than a common hunter before she became queen."

I said, "Surely not! How could a common hunter achieve such a station?"

He said, "Hear and I will tell you. Bellay took it into his head to marry this woman, his previous wife having died, and she was brought to his palace, with Bellay spreading it about that she was a noble from a far land. However, there were some in the palace who recognized the girl, and the king paid them handsomely to keep quiet about the matter. Later on, she did marry him, but within a month the old king was dead. Now, the word as you will hear it through the common talk is that he died on the battlefield, having killed a hundred enemy nobles. I will tell you different, though: he died in his bed, from poison. Moreover, it was poison delivered by Sarla's hand, for she hated Bellay, and married him only so she could kill him."

I said, "How do you know this?"

He said, "I have a good friend whose son is an officer in the castle. If you talk to those fellows, you will soon learn the truth, for there is nothing that escapes their attention. They saw all the evil Bellay did, and the hatred they bore towards him was so great that they did not punish Sarla for his murder, but instead made her their queen."

"And a good thing too," I said, "for Bellay richly deserved to die, and anyone who kills a such a king deserves a fine reward."

Ciren said I was absolutely right, and Bellay had earned his murder many times over.

On talking with my guests further I learned more about the war, and all the terrible things the Indian myrmidons had done, and all the great eastern cities of the Cypriot Empire which the Indians had captured. Of course, I do not need to go into further detail here, because I am sure everyone reading these words will be well aware of the wicked deeds of the Indians. When I heard what had been going on, I prayed to God a second time, and I swore to Him I would attack the next group of Indian ships I came upon, no matter what the danger might be to me.

As it happened, though, I met no more Indian ships on the voyage, and a few days later we had sailed through the Diplenian Canal and into the familiar waters of the Mediterranean. When we reached Cyprus, I let my passengers off at Relina, their intended destination, then sailed on up the Horn.

An Eleventh Section Of The Eleventh Part

In Which I Describe My Glorious And Triumphant Return To My Homeland

IT WAS NEARLY DAWN WHEN we arrived at the port of Rowel, my birthplace and the town where most of my family still lived.

Now, I had not visited my homeland for close to twenty-five years, and I decided I would attire myself in a manner befitting a returning hero. Therefore, I donned a very fat and splendid armoured robe, of gold and red and black, which I had bought upon my travels when I was in the emperor's service.

(To be more precise, I did not buy the robe, but rather won it in a wager with a certain high-ranking person, but this achievement, and the devious method I used to accomplish it, is of no importance here.)

In my hand, I carried my old archbishop's staff, which I had been delighted to find in my ship's hold during the voyage, and upon my head I wore a magnificent stuffed eagle, such as American generals wear, with its great black wings folded around to form the crown of the hat, and gold inlayed upon its beak.

I left my ship in the hands of Bitian Teppel and the myrmidons and walked quickly through the streets, which were deserted because of the early hour. I made my way directly to my parents' house then knocked upon the door.

You would think, given my long absence and my magnificent garb, my arrival at the door would be cause for the greatest astonishment and delight. Yet, when the door was opened to me, and my father looked out, he merely paused a moment, then said "Oh, it is you, Yreth. Come in then. I was going to make some honeyed milk. You may as well share the meal." Whereupon I entered the house and ate breakfast with my aged father and my brother Hendell, who also lived there, together with his lovely young wife, Yeppa, and their two children. It was all so very comfortable I felt as if I had been away for a few hours instead of a quarter-century.

After the meal was finished, we sat over the oven and talked, while warming our hands and feet, I asked where my mother was. My father said she had died of the sneezing fever a few years earlier, along with my brother Putren, but I should not be saddened, for no others from our family were stricken, (save for my cousin Oelo, whom I had never cared for) and further, four of my brothers and all seven of my sisters had married, and I now had more than forty nieces and nephews! To be sure, the loss of two is trivial compared to the gain of forty, and, in the main, I was very gratified.

"But tell me," I said, "what has become of my brother Urlem, who is my favourite?"

"He is unmarried," said Hendell, "and in that regard he is a great disappointment to us all. Yet he has achieved much in another field, for he is the senior commander to the Earl of Seopa, by whom he is exceedingly well regarded, and he has more than sixty myrmidons under his command."

Then my father said, "And what of you, my son? Has the world treated you well?"

"That it has," I said. "I have a good ship of my own, and some fine myrmidons, and so much wealth it would fill a deep pit or spill over a shallow one."

At this he was wonderstruck, and then doubtful, saying he thought my words a jest, but I told him of my many travels, and the great and powerful people I had met, and the many good things that had come to me.

"Ho," said Hendell, when I was done, "this is well timed indeed, for I have many debts and could use a few arrans."

"You shall have a few *hundred* arrans," I said, "for you have always been one to accumulate debts. And you shall also have such jewels as take your fancy. But not today, for I fear bringing you into such sudden wealth would cause talk, and I do not wish people to know I am rich until I have placed my gold in a safe place."

And Hendell nodded, for he saw how wise I was in protecting the people of these parts from the temptation of stealing, and thereby keeping Rowel a good and honest place.

Still, I could not resist the temptation of showing my gold to my father and my brother, and I invited them to come with me to my ship, where they might view my wealth away from prying eyes.

So the three of us went to the docks. It was now afternoon and we had been talking for many hours. A great multitude were standing around by the water, looking at the magnificent new ship at their docks and speculating as to who might own it.

As I walked towards the ships with my father, many people turned to look at my splendid dress. Then an old man, who had been a shopkeeper when I was young, cried out, "I know that face—it is Valuable Yreth! I never thought you would attain such worth!"

Hendell had warned me about this nickname: I was valuable not for my skills or virtues, but for the bounty of six hundred arrans King Bellay had put on my head.

I should have told them all on the spot that Bellay was dead and the bounty was lifted, but I felt so slighted I instead said: "So you think I am valuable because of a bounty of six hundred arrans? Why, my wealth is far beyond your puny imaginings! I could pay my own bounty a hundred times over if I chose."

Those who heard my words gasped, thinking, "Oh, how wrong we were about Yreth, and how ignorant of us to mock him when he was young! What a noble figure he has become, and how handsome."

Others, however, tried to seize me, and one of them said, "You may keep your great wealth, but we will keep you, and the six hundred arrans you will earn us."

Here, I drew my throwing-razor, and my brother drew his knife, and we set upon the treacherous hounds, so, for their trouble, they received not gold in their hands, but steel in their throats.

There were others of my friends and relatives in the crowd, and when they realized who I was and what was happening, they too joined the fight, which quickly grew in size, for friends and relatives of our assailants also came for a cut or two.

I fought like a hero. I killed three—wicked men all—and sliced open the arm of another. I did not even think to summon the myrmidons on my ship, for I was so caught up in the excitement of the moment that I felt as if I was in my youth once more, getting up to mischief in the streets, and my speed and fury in combat astonished all those who saw it.

When the fight was over, I climbed upon the deck of my ship and addressed the crowd.

I said, "I have been in foreign lands for many years, and in those places I achieved high rank and earned great wealth. In my heart, though, I knew there was only one land where I wanted to be, and that is my homeland, Cyprus. And in all of Cyprus, there is no part sweeter to me than the town of Rowel."

Then Bitian Teppel, who had been listening to my words from the cabin of the ship, stepped out onto the deck beside me. He said, "This man Yreth is the greatest hero the world has ever known. You should be proud to live in the town of his birth, for, by his fearless deeds, he has made the town famous in every land."

These words won them over, one and all, and they cheered me very soundly for making the town so famous, and they said I was a very honest fellow for returning to their midst, what with all the big cities and other grand places I might have gone to.

Then I had my slaves bring one of the boxes up from the hold, which contained dried carrots from America. These carrots were handed freely among the crowd, and everyone was most grateful at receiving such a fine gift.

A Twelfth Section Of The Eleventh Part

In Which I Tell Of How I Fought The Indians At Sea

I STAYED AT ROWEL FOR A good many weeks, and I spent the time well, being reunited with all my friends and relatives, and wandering all around the area, taking in the sights I had missed for so long.

One afternoon, I was out walking. Bitian Teppel was with me, and so were three lovely girls, who were distant relatives of mine and had been entranced by my striking appearance and fine manners. We walked up into the hills and followed a steep path to a little group of caves. The caves looked down upon the town and the sea beyond.

I said to Bitian Teppel, "When I was a child, I would hide up here and play at robbers. The other children would try to attack me here, but I would always beat them back and push them down the slope, for it is very steep around here."

He said, "Perhaps you should place your gold here. It would surely be an easy place for the myrmidons to defend."

I instantly saw he was right, for in such a place as this, twelve myrmidons might defend against a hundred. That very evening I moved all my treasure from the ship up into the caves. The people of Rowel were astonished as they watched the myrmidons carrying all that treasure through the town, for they had not imagined how much gold I possessed.

I had the myrmidons place the gold in a tall pile near the mouth of the cave, so everyone in the town might see it shining up there and take pleasure in its beauty. Then I placed the myrmidons around the mouth of the cave with their spears, as a dire warning to anyone who might think of stealing from my hoard.

It was an excellent idea, too, for all the merchants who came to the town saw the gold and asked about it, and when they heard my name mentioned, they quickly spread my fame to other towns and cities. Soon, certain merchants were coming to Rowel just to visit me, and to sell me their richest wares.

It was a good life I was living, and I knew it. But I knew too that the war with India was still raging, and I was playing no useful part in it. Well, I am not one to shrink from a fight, especially when the Indians were doing such evil deeds greedily invading lands rightfully conquered by good Cypriot folk, so I determined to take my share of the battle and fight it with a will.

I spent a good sum and bought myself a fine ballista from an arms merchant. I fixed the weapon upon the deck of my ship, next to with a great many special bolts that could be set alight and sent flying into enemy ships to burn them. My plan was to sail east, following the merchant routes, and to destroy any Indian ships we found.

I decided I would not take any myrmidons with me, for they were better left around the cave, guarding my money from thieves, and from any enemy who might attack the town.

My brother Hendell remarked that, for all its excellent protection, it was still possible my gold might somehow be stolen. He urged me to take a small portion of my wealth and bury it in a secret place as an additional precaution. This seemed a wise idea to me, so we filled a chest with gold and jewels to the value of several thousand arrans. We two secretly took it from the cave and buried it by a tree not far from the town.

When the ship was all prepared, I boarded and prepared for war. I took with me four men—Bitian Teppel, two cousins of mine named Basotel and Tiat Hammers, and a friend of theirs, Tiat Pode. They were brave men, and excellent seafarers too.

Hundreds of my friends and relatives turned out to see me off and to wish me well, and, just before we cast off, I opened another box of gold I had brought down from my cave. Then I made a gift of one hundred arrans to my father and the same to every one of my brothers and sisters, and a gift of twenty-two arrans each to all my father's brothers and my dead mother's sisters, and a gift of ten arrans each to all my cousins, and a gift of two arrans each to all my nephews and nieces, excepting only those whose behaviour or appearance displeased me.

We cast off, and sailed out to seek the enemy. With the weight of the treasure removed from the hold, the *Moray* was a fast ship once more, and I made at least another third the distance each day I had previously done on the way home.

We were all impatient to sink Indian ships, but all we found were Cypriot fishing boats. Finally, after four days at sea, we spotted an Indian warship. It was a three-masted beak, painted in black like the Indian ships I had seen on my voyage to Cyprus, but perhaps half of the size.

He turned towards us, thinking we would be easy prey and he might ram us and sink us, as he had doubtless done to the other innocent Cypriot vessels he had encountered.

Well, that Indian warship soon learned he was dealing with a different manner of vessel than he was used to and faced not terrified fishermen or merchants but fierce warriors. As soon as he was in range I started shooting off the fiery ballista bolts. The first few shots were shy of the mark, but I quickly began to gain an expert understanding of the weapon, and I scored several good hits on the deck of the ship, and another on the top sail of the foremast. I watched the Indians scrambling with buckets to put out the fires, which was an amusing sight, to be sure.

We shouted a few insults back and forth then.

I said, "The proud *Moray* will soon put an end to your murderous voyage."

They replied, "No, for rather the mighty *Flame* will sink your ship too and add her to our tally.

Then I said, "*Flame* is a good name for your ship, for it will soon sink in flames."

They said, "Not so. But *Moray* is a good name for your ship, for it will soon be swimming at the bottom of the sea."

I said, "No no, for our *Moray* will splash its powerful tail about and douse your *Flame*."

They said, "That may be your dream, but when you wake from it you will find breakfast ready, for our hot *Flame* will have cooked your *Moray*."

I said, "No, I will awake to find a fine thrashing *Moray* in the pot, for no fish would cook over such a sorry *Flame*."

They had no response to my last riposte, but came in close with their ram towards us. Of course, I did not let the *Flame* use his ram upon us, instead ordering the head slave to manoeuvre the *Moray* so we were circling him. Then, as we circled, I fired numerous ballista bolts, while he tried in vain to turn his wicked prow upon us.

Over the next few hours, I must have fired a hundred bolts at the Indian ship. Unfortunately, the Indians quickly saw I meant to sink them with fire, and they doused the sail and the decks with so much water that even a solid hit no longer started any honest burning.

In the meantime, the Indians had produced several bows and were firing arrows back at us. Poor Tiat Pode was struck in the chest and died soon afterwards.

We avenged his death, though, for Tiat Hammers had brought

his duckbow with him, and, being an excellent shot with his little weapon, he struck down at least six of the enemy before he finally ran out of arrows.

I tried the same thing with the ballista, aiming at the crew rather than the ship. The ballista is a big weapon, and exceedingly difficult to aim accurately, but even so I scored one hit upon a man on the deck, and it struck him so hard it killed him instantly, with the bolt going right through his body and sticking it to the wooden deck. Another of my shots smashed through their ship's rowing boat.

Basotel did not have his bow with him, because he had forgotten it at the dock, so I told him, if he wished, he could take some ballista bolts, strip the volatile padding from their tips, and throw them at the enemy like spears. He quickly set about doing just this, although I do not think he hit anyone. Still, I had a great many ballista bolts, and the waste of a few was of little importance.

As for Bitian Teppel, he did not care to throw anything at the enemy. He said, "No, instead I will set about the work I am best at: I will draw a picture of this great battle, so we will be inspired by it and fight all the more furiously."

I said it was an excellent plan.

He began the drawing immediately, and kept at it while our two ships turned and evaded and traded arrows with each other.

A few hours later, Bitian Teppel had finished his drawing, and when there was a pause in the fighting he showed it to us. It was magnificent. In the centre, it showed the two ships circling each other, and the likeness of the drawings to the real ships was so perfect it was as if you could reach out and touch them.

The *Moray* was drawn very small, and shining white, while the *Flame* was shown as a fat black monster.

In the top left corner, which artists call the symbol corner, he had placed a fierce little weasel stalking a fat rabbit. In the right corner, which is where the dead are shown, were all those who had been killed in the battle so far. The Indians who had died were shown as dark figures with arrows through them, while the brave

Tiat Pode was drawn as a colossus, towering over them, still waving his sword in battle even as the deadly arrow pierced his heart.

In the sea beneath the ships were all the old gods and angels of the deep, gazing in astonishment at the great battle which was being fought above them. They were drawn so perfectly you could read the very words from their lips: they were all saying "Ooooh" to each other. At the bottom of the ocean, bordering the lower edge of the drawing, was a great eel, which I recognized as a moray eel. He had his head tilted back to watch the battle, and there was a smile on his proud lips as he watched the ship that was his namesake fight its brave fight.

Basotel, who did not know as much about art as I did, said, "It is a good picture, it is true, but the ships need more work. I see the *Moray* is drawn smaller than our opponent, whereas, in fact, she is larger."

Bitian Teppel smiled at his words, of course, and I explained to Basotel that this drawing was a great work of art, in the old style made famous by the immortal Tybalt. Then I showed Basotel the weasel and the rabbit in the symbol corner, and I showed him how Bitian Teppel had drawn our ship to resemble the lithe and violent weasel, whereas the *Flame* was drawn like the huge and lumbering rabbit who will soon fall prey to its tiny foe.

Then Bitian Teppel showed us some of the other features of the drawing, and identified the various sea gods for us.

We all thought the drawing was very fine, and it truly did inspire us to fight more furiously. However, I started to get frustrated, for no matter what manner of arrows and bolts we sent flying at our enemy, we could not sink their ship. Instead, our two ships were circling, moving in and out, each unable to defeat the other. It was clear a new strategy was required.

I thought to myself, "If I can measure the sea at this point, I might sink the *Flame* using the Struts of Atlas, just as I sank those ships at the Duck Islands so many years earlier." I quickly went to my cabin and found a measuring line with a leaden bob at one end, then tried to measure the depth of the sea where we circled.

Alas, the sea was very deep, and even the full length of the line did not reach the bottom.

It was beginning to get dark now, and another plan entered my head, for Bitian Teppel's excellent drawing had sharpened my mind as well as honing my warrior's spirit. I said to Tiat Hammers, "Take over for me at the ballista. I am going to attack the *Flame* in the rowing boat."

Tiat Hammers said, "No, I want to come too, for I have brought my good sword along and I mean to use it."

Then Basotel came over and asked us what it was we were discussing.

Tiat Hammers said, "Our brave friend Yreth means to board the enemy ship. Will we let him go alone?"

And Basotel said, "Indeed we will not!"

But I raised my hands then and said, "Cousins, I do not plan to go to that ship so I might fight hand to hand. Rather, I plan to sink it through the prudent application of stealth and cunning. If you wish to be a part of my battle, then I urge you to stay here and to distract the crew of the *Flame* from the progress of my rowing boat. In this way, we will attack the enemy from two directions, a strategy which guarantees victory. Also, keep the *Moray* on this side of the *Flame*, for I will be working on the far side, and I do not wish their crew to notice me."

They agreed they would do this, and Bitian Teppel said, "I do not know what you are about, but I will warrant it will make a very fine drawing."

I said it certainly would, and he should set about it right away, which he did. Then I took his old drawing, folded it up, and put it in my belt pouch for luck.

The slaves lowered my rowing boat into the sea, placing it on the side of my ship which was furthest from the *Flame* so the Indians would not see my actions. I then rowed the boat quietly around and made for the enemy vessel under cover of darkness.

My plan was simple in theory. I had brought along a mallet and a chisel, and I intended to come alongside the *Flame*, then to chip a hole in the enemy vessel and sink it. Of course, anyone who knows ships will tell you this is a very difficult thing to accomplish. In the first place, a rowing boat is slow and cannot easily catch a fast-moving warship. In the second place, if you wish to make a hole to sink a ship, it must be made below the waterline, so you must work beneath (or at least partially beneath) the water. Naturally, however, I had clever solutions to both these problems, which you will learn of almost immediately.

I rowed for a few minutes in the general direction of the *Flame*, taking great care to go quietly, without drawing attention to myself, then I pulled in the oars and crouched down in my boat. I knew, you see, with these two ships circling each other, I had no need to chase my enemy. I had only to set my boat adrift between them and the enemy would eventually come to me. Sure enough, after a short time had passed, the *Flame* passed so close to me that I was able to seize onto the hull with my hands. I pulled my boat in then, and fastened it to the Indian ship with a couple of Peregrine Clasps. Once my boat was firmly secured, I set to work with my chisel, boring two or three feet *above* the waterline.

Now, it took me only a few minutes to make a small hole in the side of the ship. The boards were not thick, and I fancy they were a little rotten too, which will tell you what kind of mariners the Indians are!

I peered through the hole to see if there were people within, but all was dark, so I knew this was a safe place to continue chiselling. I then set about widening the hole as best as I was able, trying to work around the many nails which dotted the hull. This task was more difficult than it might sound, for the ship was moving this way and that, on a choppy sea, and the light for my work was very poor. In addition, I had to work quietly, for if I had been discovered by the ship's crew, it would surely have been the end of me. Still, even working in these conditions, I made a fine job of it, and only twice did I strike my chisel against a nail. At last, the hole was as large as I wanted.

Now, you will perhaps think I did not know what I was about

when I made the hole, for, as I have already said, if you want to sink a ship, it is best to make a hole below the waterline, not above it as I had done. However, the hole I had made was not for sinking the ship, but was just a hole I could climb through to the inside of the ship, there to carve a larger and lower hole.

I climbed within, staying clear of the protruding nails, then slowly lowered myself into the darkness until my foot touched the floor. It was a surprisingly long drop—nearly seven feet, I should say. Once inside, I crouched down as close to the floor as I was able, so I was perhaps four feet below the waterline. I then set to work with my chisel again, working in total darkness now, cutting into the side of the ship, carving a V-shaped groove in the outline of a large rectangle. The groove almost penetrated the boards, but not quite. In this way, I ensured no seawater would come in prematurely to interfere with my work. It was a slow business, and exceptionally difficult too, working blind as I was, but I did a masterful job, cutting until I was just a nail-white from the other side, and letting in only a little trickle of water. When the rectangle was complete, I stood and gave the chiselled area a kick with my boot. At once I heard a loud crack and the boards gave way, whereupon, the sea came rushing in with tremendous force, knocking me to the floor.

I tried to stand and pull myself back up to the hole by which I had entered, but I was knocked to my feet again by the rushing water. I tried a second time, grabbing a beam for support. With some effort, I managed to stand—the water was already halfway to my knees—but when I tried to jump to the hole above me, the water knocked my feet from under me, and again I fell back, with water all around me. After I had made several more futile attempts to reach the hole by jumping, I decided to apply my intelligence, perceptiveness and ingenuity to the problem at hand. I instantly realized that the lower hole, which was doing such a masterful job of bringing water into this ship, might also be usefully employed as my own exit. Without a moment's hesitation, I ducked down under the water, groped around for the hole, and crawled through it, pushing with all my great strength against the powerful flow of water. Moments later, I was bobbing in the sea, a few feet from my rowing boat.

I reboarded my boat, dismissed the Peregrine Clasps, releasing the boat from the *Flame*, and rowed back into the darkness, crouching down so I might safely observe the sinking of my enemy. After just a few minutes I could see the ship was listing badly, and I chuckled to see the crew running this way and that trying to discover the source of their misfortune.

Meanwhile, my comrades, observing my success, had brought the *Moray* in much closer. They fired arrows and flaming bolts at the *Flame* with a renewed vigour, which was a spectacular sight you may be sure, and reminded me a little of the flaming bolts I had seen against the night sky when I escaped from Quebec.

A warlike fever filled my blood then, and I became anxious to join the battle, so I picked up my oars and started rowing for my ship. Suddenly I heard a great crash, as loud as thunder. I turned to look (for I was facing backwards in my rowing boat) and saw the *Moray* had ventured too close to the enemy, and the *Flame*, in its death throes, had managed to turn directly into the hull of my ship, ramming a great hole there. Moreover, it seemed the two ships were now stuck together, for the chank hull of my ship was much stronger than the ordinary wooden hulls the *Flame*'s ram was designed for, and once the sharp beak had pierced the hull, the boards did not give way enough to let it pull out again.

I instantly knew the situation was dire for both ships and I must rescue my companions. I cared nothing for stealth now: I rowed with tremendous speed and strength, spurred on by the sounds of shouts and skirmish which I could hear from the ships, for now that the ships were locked together, everyone was fighting hand to hand. When I caught up with them just a few minutes later, the *Moray* was so low in the water that the deck was almost level with my little boat. Alas, in those short minutes, the Indian pirates had won the fight—for the dead bodies of my cousins lay upon the deck. I saw too that the Indians had killed my slaves, which was a very cowardly act, for slaves are timid by nature and do not fight well. I pulled my rowing boat back then, for it was clear where things were headed. As I moved through the water, though, I saw a body floating there, which I recognized as Bitian Teppel. I pulled him onto my rowing boat, but he was in a bad way, having been stabbed through the belly then thrown into the sea. His heart was still beating, though, and when I pressed his eye he blinked a little, so I knew he was not yet dead.

Now, it is a fact that one must always listen to the words of a dying friend, for they can be very instructive and are often prophetic, so I tried to rouse Bitian from his unconscious state to see what he might say to me. I splashed water against his face and tapped his cheeks and shook him. But it was all to no avail, and I had almost given up when suddenly his eyes opened wide and he said, "Tah! He has put the wrong pigment in the mix!"

I said, "What do you mean, Bitian Teppel? Explain yourself?"

He did not answer me, but his face assumed the strangest expression, as if he was seeing something very wonderful and remarkable. Then his eyes closed again, and a few minutes later he died.

I was annoyed, for it was clear, whatever visions were before Bitian Teppel at that moment, he could not be bothered to share them with me, who was probably his closest friend upon the earth, but rather chose to enjoy them for himself. That is what these artists are like—particularly painters. I am sure if it were me dying, I would not hesitate to provide any onlookers with as much useful information as I could glean.

A strange thing though: Bitian Teppel's last breaths exactly coincided with the moment the deck of the *Moray* went under the waves. I took this to mean he wished to be buried at sea with my ship, and so I pushed his body back into the water and let it float off on its way.

By then, the bow of the *Flame* was completely submerged, although the stern was lifted right out of the water. The Indian sailors had lost their rowing boat earlier, thanks to my fine work with the ballista, and now they leaped from their ship into the water.

I watched the *Flame* sink, feeling great pleasure at the sight. When the show was done, I made my way back to where the ships had been and rowed around for a time, searching for those of my enemies who were floating in the darkness. When I found them, I struck each upon the head with an oar, saying, "You see, the *Moray* still has a little bite in her!"

I killed a dozen of those warlike Indian sailors this way. When I could find no more, I turned my boat around and made for land.

A Thirteenth Section Of The Eleventh Part

In Which I Tell Of How I Fought The Indians On Land

T HE LOSS OF MY SHIP did not discourage me one grain from my mission, and I decided, since I could no longer fight at sea, I would join up with some army and fight on the land.

As for the deaths of my friends, I did not feel too much sadness, for they had all died bravely, and I had avenged them well. I was a little sorry, though, that all my slaves had died, for they were a good crew.

Still, I was near to the battlefields now, and, after I had made my way to shore, I continued on foot, wandering across the country until I found an encampment where the tents bore the crest of Cyprus.

The army here was led by a commander called Raella. I present-ed myself to this man without delay and asked him how the land was set out here.

He said, "A large Indian army lies a short way to the east occupying the town of Chonia."

I said, "Chonia, is it? That is an important town. I will warrant that a victory for us in Chonia might send waves of despair throughout the Indian army, perhaps yielding us much greater victories throughout the length and breadth of our domains."

He said, "As to that, I cannot say." He was no more than a field commander, you see, and lacked my grander perspective.

I said, "I have some experience commanding myrmidons. Is there some way I can make myself useful?"

He said, "Yes, indeed. Take five slaves and scout out the areas to the north. If I wore the enemy's boots, I would attack from that direction."

Well, directing slaves was not the kind of job I was looking for, so I said to him, "I have a much better idea, which will make a more profitable use of my various talents. You and I will enter Chonia as spies. Then I will find the commander of the Indian myrmidons and learn from him, using clever and subtle questioning, many facts which will aid you in your battle plans."

Raella did not care for my plan, and he said he would rest easier knowing there were no troops massing to attack from the north.

I scoffed at his views, for they were timid. "Besides," I said, "a spying expedition will be a great adventure, such as befits intrepid fellows like us, whereas even the most inexperienced of your officers could carry out the simple scouting mission you have described."

He said, "No no, it is not a good idea," and then told me all the dangers spying would present.

Well, I spoke frankly to him then, saying, "This is no way for a commander to talk! Still, if the job is not suited to your own timorous disposition, then you can wait behind, and I will go alone!"

He said I was free to do as I pleased, provided I did not interfere with his own plans, and he added that he hoped I would be hanged when the Indians caught me.

I said, "I will not be *hanged*, you may be certain of that, but you will *hang* your head in shame when you think back on your callous words. I will be back before long, and with much useful knowledge in my head." Then I left him, and went into a nearby village, so I might set myself up for spying.

For my purpose, I carefully assumed the appearance of a herb merchant, taking care to wear only such humble garments as a poor merchant might wear, and placing various leaves and herbs in my hat and belt. It was an excellent disguise, and when I looked at my reflection in a puddle I was astonished at how exactly like a herb merchant I looked.

The next day, a couple of hours before dawn, I left the village. I did not march straight for the enemy, but instead marched around in a great circle, so I entered Chonia from the east side. I reasoned, you see, that if the enemy myrmidons saw me coming from the west, they might suspect I had come from Raella's army.

I arrived in the town about mid-morning. It was a small place, and it was not difficult to find the enemy commander, for I saw a group of myrmidons on guard outside a mealhouse. So, I entered the place, as if I was hungry and looking for my breakfast—although in actual fact I had eaten well on my long walk.

The commander was sitting at a table, playing at chess with a person from the town, while others stood around and watched, commenting upon the cleverness of the commander's moves.

Now, I saw a great opportunity in this, for chess is a game I am very good at, and I always win. I decided, then, to play a game against the commander, so I could enter into conversation with him. When he had beaten the man he was playing, I asked if I might try my hand. He said yes, and I sat down at the board.

This commander's name was Tary. He was around my age at that time, which is to say, close to his sixtieth year. He was tall and fat, with a round, foolish face. He spoke in an amusing way, panting, as if he was short of breath, after he had spoken just a few words.

In any case, I had hardly sat upon the bench when this fellow began to set up the pieces and said, "Let us begin, then. Shall we play with bishops-out, or do you prefer pawns-ready."

I said, "Not so fast. Let us first decide upon the stakes. I propose three arrans."

He said three arrans was too rich for his blood, and suggested four grotecs.

"That hardly makes the game worth the playing," I said. "Let us settle upon a single arran."

He agreed to this, even though it was a large sum, for I could see he had every expectation of winning, and he placed his money upon the table, as I did.

Then I said, as I always say, "And let us agree now that if either player should withdraw from the game before it is resolved, then he will have forfeited his stake, and it will go to the other."

"Yes, yes," said Tary, who was all ready to make his first move. "Now, let us begin. Did you say you favoured bishops-out?"

I never begin a game in such haste, for I find it is in the negotiation over the terms of the game where I achieve half my victories. So, I like to ensure the negotiation preceding the first move is a drawn-out and complicated affair, in order to make my opponents tired and angry. I always begin by making demands which are somewhat in my favour.

Therefore, I said to Tary, "No, I do not care for bishops-out—it makes for a dull game. Let us have more exciting terms. I propose you shall lose all your pawns save only for the centre ones, and, further, you shall play without queens or rooks."

"And your terms shall be the same?" he asked.

"No," I said. "That would make the game predictable, for we could mirror each other's moves. Rather, I propose that I shall take a penalty which is identical in value to your own, but different in form. Specifically, I shall lose the two pawns which stand before the rooks, and in the place of these pieces I shall have two dragons, and you may not capture either of them with any of your pieces until they have made a single capture of their own. Further, I shall sacrifice the movement of my knights, for I find the hopping ways a distraction and difficult to calculate, and instead they shall move and capture exactly as a queen does."

Tary did not care for these terms in the least, and he said he did not care to start the game with dragons, for they are too powerful. In this he was quite correct: they spoil the skill of the game, and I would never allow my opponent to have the use of one; although if I were permitted the use of dragons, and my opponent were not, then I should surely accept the terms, for a dragon is very difficult to capture by any other piece.

He also said I had substituted my knights for queens at no cost at all. There was something to what he said, of course, but even so, I refuted his words with great passion, pointing out that although my knights might move and capture as queens, their horselike heads showed they were still obviously knights, as any observer could plainly see.

Then he said my terms were ridiculous, and unfair to him,

I responded that, on the contrary, my side was now so powerful that I would certainly become lazy as I played, making dangerous mistakes, whereas he, being constantly on guard for further depletions to his puny force, would inevitably play the more skilful game.

He dismissed these arguments, however, suggesting instead that we start with crescent layouts, which I flatly rejected as being too symmetrical.

Then he suggested my crescent layout against his pawns-ready, but I rejected this too, saying it was unfair to me.

Then he offered me the pawns-ready layout, with the crescent for himself, but I rejected that on the grounds it was unfair to him, and I wished to take my money honestly.

He said I should take my turn once more at suggesting the terms, since his were clearly disagreeable to me, whereupon I made some other outlandish suggestion. I do not remember what it was.

Then he made other proposals, which I rejected, until at last he said, in his panting way, the thing my opponents always say:

"Since you will not be reasonable in setting the terms to the game, I will not play against you."

I picked up the money and said, "If you wish to walk from the game, then you may do so. I will pocket my winnings, for, as we agreed, your withdrawal carries the cost of forfeiture."

But he gripped my wrist, making me drop the arrans, and said he did not wish to withdraw just yet.

So we returned to this obstinate haggling, and we continued for half an hour or so. When he had grown very bored and frustrated from the debate, and angry too, so he was on the verge of coming to blows with me, I finally made a proposal that was reasonable, this being that he should lose his king's rook and the five phalanx pawns (which is to say, those in front of the rooks, bishops and queen) in exchange for a second queen in the rook's square. For myself, I would keep my full complement of pawns, and my king would have not only its natural movement, but also the movement of a knight.

These, incidentally, are the final terms I always insist on for myself, and, provided I get them, I will agree to any of the common terms for my opponent, though, as I have said, I do not permit dragons, and neither do I permit phantoms, for, if there is to be a piece upon the board, I want to see it, and not to trust upon the reliability of some third person, who may, after all, be in league with my opponent. I sometimes permit my opponent rockets, if he is willing to lose enough pawns for the privilege, because they really do not offer so great an advantage as people think.

In any case, we began our game, and I began to hum a little tune, while moving each of my pawns one square forward, starting at the leftmost pawn, and going to the rightmost, while he moved various pieces into play. I pretended I was paying little attention to the board. I looked around the room, and I ate bread, and I called out flattering words to a pretty young girl who sometimes walked through the room carrying dishes.

I moved chiefly my pawns, using a strategy which I call the Creeping Wall, for the pawns advance up the board like a wall. I moved the other pieces only when it was necessary to defend a part of the wall. But still, I hummed tunes, and pretended to care little for the game.

At first, Tary scoffed at my tactics, for he was one of those who relies on planning and predicting, so they will say, "If he advances the knight to the sixth rank, next to the bishop, then I shall be checked and in danger of losing my queen. Therefore I must place a pawn forward to defend the spot. But, if I do this, the protection will be gone from the other pawn, next to my queen..." and so on. This style of play merely taxes the mind, making one irritable and sucking all pleasure from the game. It is the way men play when they have studied the game from books, and the use of the technique is easily discovered, for such people make small movements with their fingers when looking at the board, pointing to the places where they imagine pieces will be.

Soon, though, he began to take my moves more seriously, for he saw how relentlessly my pawn-wall was approaching. Moreover, as the game progressed, I began to change my humming, so the tune was the *Lullaby of Skulls*. I sang a little louder each time the pawn-wall moved forward.

Although chess is but a game, most players will start to become fearful at this sight, for the pawns approach like a well trained army, marching to my music, moving steadily onward, fearless of any danger, and blind even to destruction within their ranks.

Well, Tary tried the best he could to ignore my marching pawns, and he set himself upon killing my king. He threw a good many pieces into the attack, bishops and knights, and his queen too (for he had sacrificed his second queen by now for the sake of gaining a good position to strike against my king). But when he finally let the sword fall, saying, "It is checkmate for you," I turned to him and said, "Not at all, for as you will surely remember, my king can leap to safety like a knight." So saying, I moved my king away from his attacks.

Now he saw it was his king and not mine which was in danger, for he had been so intent upon setting his pieces against my king that he had not protected himself from the great storm clouds floating towards his camp in the form of the dreaded pawn-wall.

As it happened, his king managed to escape the wrath of my pawns, but this did not help him for long, because my little wooden army proceeded boldly onward to the eighth square, and once they are there, as you will know if you have studied the game as thoroughly as I have, the pawns may be transmuted to become any other piece.

Tary said, "What will you have for your pawn, then? A queen?"

I said, "No, not a queen, a dragon."

He protested then, saying I had prohibited dragons from the game.

"Not so," I replied. "I did not prohibit them from the game but merely from the starting terms."

He appealed to those who were watching the game, but they all agreed with me, for they were eager to see the dragons turned loose upon Tary's pieces.

Well, in just a few moves, I had three dragons on my side, and they flew around the board with a fury, killing all his men. I left his king until the end, and then, just to make the victory sweeter for me, I killed the old fellow not with a dragon, but with my own king, using its knightlike movement to strike the final blow.

Tary was angry at the result, of course, but I had won fair and square, and he let me pocket my winnings without a fight. Then he rose from his seat and said, "I have had enough chess for this day, I think."

I said, "Wait, will you not have a second game for double stakes, for I sense my luck is now on the wane, and I am sure you will come out the better for it."

He said, "I think I will not." Then he walked for the door and took his cloak from the hook.

I could see he would talk carelessly now, so I shouted after him, "I surely hope you have more luck with your myrmidons than you do with your chess pieces."

He said, "I will. You shall see that for yourself soon enough, for I have a fine attack planned against the Cypriots."

I said, "Ah, that will be a hard battle. There must be four hundred myrmidons in the Cypriot encampment, whereas they say you have only one hundred."

He was walking through the doorway right then, but my words made him indignant. He turned and said, "One hundred? I will have you know I command nearly five hundred. I am a man of importance, and as such I must go now. Goodbye."

He left then, and I made a note of this valuable information. Then, after I had played a few more games of chess—and won every game!—I went back to Raella's camp by the same circuitous route I had taken to get to Chonia in the first place.

That evening, I presented Raella with the information I had gathered: not just how many myrmidons Tary commanded, but also what manner of man he was, and the way he approached the game of chess, which is very telling of a commander's style in war. Raella was envious of my bravery, though, and, instead of thanking me from the bottom of his heart, he tried to belittle my accomplishment, saying, "I already knew the number of his myrmidons. My scouts have counted them from a hill overlooking the town."

I said, "What are the vague reports of scouts compared to my information, which comes directly from the enemy commander. And besides, if it were not for me, how would you have gained the detailed insights into Tary's character which I have given you."

He said, "As for that information, it is as solid as vapour."

"Ho, these are your words now," I said, "but I will warrant you use the facts well enough when you plan your attacks. Mark my words, this man Tary is fierce in battle, but he is reckless. Take my advice: present an obstinate defence which is like the shell of the leathery turtle, and then, when his forces are rebuffed, deliver a swift counterattack with the speed and fury of the blacksnake."

Well, as I have said, Raella pretended to dismiss my words. Since his good opinion meant little to me, I left the place without further comment.

Now, mark this. A few days later the two armies met in battle outside Chonia. I watched from the hills above, together with many of the citizens of that city. As we sat with our drinks and pies, we saw Tary's army deliver a furious attack, exactly as I had predicted. Raella's troops resisted these attacks, then delivered a counterattack, driving straight through the heart of the Indian force to divide it, then soundly defeating each half.

All around me, folk were saying, "Oh, see how they fight! He is a great strategist, that Raella." Of course, I smiled at these words, for I knew this great strategist was merely following, to the letter, the precise instructions I had given him. I rebuked my companions then, saying, "If credit is to be apportioned fairly, it must go to me. Why, the battle we are watching conforms so closely to my own plans that I might as well be directing our troops myself." They did not believe me at first, but when I explained my story to them, they were awestruck to think that the real general in charge of their forces had been sitting with them on the hillside all along.

A Fourteenth Section of the Eleventh Part

In Which I Reveal At Last How It Was I Who Won The War

AFTER THE FIGHT WAS DONE and Chonia was saved, I decided to stay there for a time, so I might bask in the warmth of victory. Raella stayed there too, and was considered a hero by the townsfolk; but after I spread the word of my involvement in the battle, they thought me a much greater hero, for he had merely pointed to myrmidons and barked commands, whereas I had ventured alone into the heart of the enemy's camp. This turnabout in public opinion irked Raella bitterly, compounding my satisfaction.

While I was there, the news started to come in that the Indian armies occupying certain other towns and cities in Veoth and Syria were also on the run. I explained to everyone that I had carefully chosen Chonia as my arena, and my victory there had inevitably led to other victories for us, because Chonia was located near the centre of the Indian vanguard, and to weaken the centre is to pierce the heart.

As the months passed, it became clear that Indian forces everywhere were withdrawing, and victory was at hand. The townsfolk bought me gifts of food and fine wine, saying, "Ah, Yreth, how right you were. See, the wave of despair you predicted surges through the Indian forces, driving their armies from all our empire's lands."

Well, I took the gifts and thanked them, but I was sorely puzzled. The battle in Chonia was important, to be sure, but was it truly possible that this single action had led to the winning of the war? No, it seemed to me there were even more significant events at work, and I had a strange feeling that, whatever those events were, I had been their cause.

I asked many of the commanders for their opinions, for by now they were returning from the wars. "What events," I said, "precipitated the sudden retreat of our enemies?"

One of them, a ship's captain, said, "It was the work of our navies, who launched a deadly attack on Maybo, the capital of India, and also upon other towns and cities on the Indian coast. After these attacks, the Indians knew they were no match for us."

I said, "What is your evidence for this claim?"

He said, "Before my return, I talked to some Indian men. They told me what a grievous and demoralizing blow it was to them to discover their greatest cities had been laid waste."

Another captain explained to me that, yes, it was the navies that were responsible, but the key victory was the sinking of a certain sacred ship which, according to Indian superstition, brought them good fortune in battle.

Later, a commander, a shrewd man named Demeth, said to me, "I will tell you the truth of the matter, although it is a great secret. This victory of ours had less to do with our work upon the battlefield, and more with events in the Indian court."

I said, "Your words intrigue me. Explain yourself."

He said, "No, for this is a great secret, and if I told you, you would think me a traitor."

I said, "Perhaps your words would be disagreeable to some, but I for one would rather hear the honest truth than a patriotic lie."

He said, "Ah, you are a rare and perceptive fellow, I can see that. Well, then, I will tell you. The truth is that the king of India had already lost much of his will to fight, for many of his commanders had died in the battlefield, and some were very dear to him. The final blow, according to my sources, who are spies working in India, came one night when a dark and sinister figure crept into the palace and took the lives of his two brave sons."

I asked, "Who was this assassin?"

He said, "Oh, some enemy of his, I am sure. Their country is racked from within by such murderous hatreds. The king was so dismayed by the loss that he put an end to his warlike ways."

One thing at least was clear to me: all these explanations were typical of the simple-minded gossip one hears upon battlefields everywhere. And yet, phrases spoken by these commanders lit fiery beacons in my mind: *a great naval attack upon Indian cities*, and *dark and sinister figures killing the Indian princes*, and the *sinking of a sacred ship*. I knew there was a nugget of truth within these stories, but each was only part of the story—and it was a story only I might understand fully.

Let me then share with you my own hypothesis, which, when you consider it fairly, does a more perfect job than these soldiers' tales of explaining why the Indians so abruptly removed their myrmidons from our lands and made peace with us once again.

You remember, while I was sailing the Pacific, I had sent a fleet of great ships to lay waste to the barbaric peoples of Poagh. Well, later on I thought about this, and I asked myself, what would have happened if those ships had, through some error in navigation, sailed past Poagh? It would be an easy mistake to make, certainly, for Poagh is a very small island, and could be easily missed. If this happened, where would those powerful ships have sailed?

The answer to this question is obvious: they would finally arrive at Dranseet, just as I did. Moreover, if they followed the coast west, they would come, after a month or two, to the coastal cities of India, and they would lay waste to those cities believing them to be the islands that had so offended their ruler.

When I thought it through, I knew this was precisely what had happened, for the logic of it made so much sense. The great ships had sailed all that distance and attacked. They launched ten thousand rockets upon those Indian cities, then they let their thousands of myrmidons loose, killing every man, woman and child in those places.

Of course, the cities of India called upon their own puny warships to fight these invading giants. Their best efforts, however, were useless against such powerful craft, and, very soon, all those Indian warships lay on the bottom of the harbour, with rocket holes through their hulls.

Wave upon wave of the giant ships made their attacks, for there were two hundred of them in the whole fleet, you remember, until at last the people of India cried out for mercy.

"Who is it that unleashes such destruction upon our towns and cities?" they said.

Then others replied, "Why, who else but our enemies in Cyprus! How strong they are, and how foolish we were to declare war upon them."

But it does not end there. If you cast your mind back, you will also remember how, many years earlier, in America, I had given a final order to my Behemoths, telling them to strike at the princes and kings who commanded the enemy armies. The Behemoths, mistaking my instructions, ran from the battlefield and away into the distance.

In their brutish minds, they reasoned thus: "Yreth is a Cypriot and has asked us to attack the kings and princes of his enemies. By this, he surely means not these armies before us now, but the enemies of his people, the Cypriots. Let us travel hence to Cyprus and see who those enemies might be." So they fled the battlefield, seeking Cyprus. The journey surely took them many long years, for I fancy no ship would have those brutes as passengers and probably they were obliged to swim across the vast ocean.

At last, though, the Behemoths completed their great journey, arriving in Cypriot lands. Once there, they quickly understood who were the enemies to our people and they travelled far and wide, seeking out the tents of Indian commanders, nobles and princes all, and killing them without mercy. Then they travelled to India itself, and slew the princes in their royal palace, much to the king's dismay.

The description of the "dark and sinister" assassins perfectly matches a Behemoth, for they were exceedingly sinister to behind, and their hides were black, which is certainly a dark colour. Moreover, who but the Behemoths could creep into a heavily guarded palace and murder princes with such ease?

It is easy to guess what must have happened next. The king of India, beside himself with grief, said, "Enough! I will call back all my myrmidons who are so wrongfully occupying the cities of the Cypriot Empire. Perhaps then these terrible fleets and fearsome black assassin myrmidons, which I believe to be from Cyprus, will cease their attacks upon my lands and my family."

But his counsellors, many of whom were surely naval men, just as they are here, said, "No, king. Let us fight on. Our sacred ship will yet bring us victory at sea, and a great naval victory would be a fitting revenge against the Cypriots and their powerful forces."

The king agreed, and, in order that the sacred ship should not be sunk, he commanded that it should be sent away from Indian waters and instead travel to the Mediterranean, there to sink a few of the weaker Cypriot craft.

"The Cypriots will not think to look for it there," he said, "and besides, all their warships are busy attacking India."

I think you will now guess the thrust of my argument. That sacred ship was none other than the *Flame*, the craft I defeated with my proud *Moray*. This explained the small size of the Indian ship, for it was an ancient vessel, and warships are built larger today. Also, it is why there were no slaves or myrmidons aboard, for the Indians would not suffer such folk to step upon their holiest ship. Finally, it explained the name of the craft, which, I must confess, had puzzled me from the first, for what does a flame have to do with the sea? Why, nothing, to be sure, but it bears an intimate connection with temples and holiness and all manner of sacred things.

Well, once the king of India heard his sacred ship was gone, the rope had frayed its final strand. Despairing utterly, he gave the orders for his armies to retreat, and they quickly obeyed. However, when our commanders saw the movement, they did not stop to wonder at what miracle might have brought it about. No, they merely quaffed their ale, saying, "Ho! We are clever fellows indeed! We have outsmarted the Indian armies, and they are retreating in terror before our troops."

Now, you may say all this hypothesis is groundless, a mere flight of fancy. However, a few years ago, I overheard a man talking of his travels, and I heard him mention that he had been to the rocky island of Poagh. Excited, I quickly interrupted his conversation and asked him whether the people of Poagh still lived.

He said, "They live, yes. But it is a barbaric, simple life."

I said, "In your time among them, did you hear tales of a terrible attack upon their island, laying waste to their towns and killing most of their number."

He said, "No, I heard of *no such attack.*"

There you have it, then. It is the proof of my hypothesis, and now you can see why the war came to such a rapid end. It was not the strength of the Cypriot armies which drove off the invaders, but rather the results of my own actions, guided by the hand of God.

A Fifteenth Section Of The Eleventh Part

In Which I Describe My Second Triumphant Return To My Homeland And Events Concerning My Treasure

I RETURNED TO ROWEL, ON FOOT this time, two months after my spying expedition. When I told everyone about my adventures at the war, they held a great celebration in my honour which lasted for two full weeks and cost me a thousand arrans in food and drink.

Still, the expenses were nothing to me, for, as near as I could calculate, there was so much gold in my cave I could have spent *two hundred arrans a day* for the rest of my days, and I would still have enough left over for a grand funeral, and I could have done all this without doing another stroke of work, if I had been of a lazy disposition. As you will know by now, though, I am very active by nature, and easily bored by too much rest, so instead I used my hours productively, working on all manner of imaginative new designs for buildings of all sorts.

I also made plans for a new house for myself, since none of the houses in Rowel suited my new station in life. The house was to be round, with a high wall around it, and a tall tower in its centre which I intended to use for an observatory. I made meticulous drawings of the building and invented a host of novel features.

In the meantime, I lived with my father, my brother and his family in the old home, sleeping at night in the bedroom that we boys had occupied when we were young. Thanks to my great wealth, we lived like princes, with all sorts of exotic food and drink. One night it was spicy udder drenched in orange juice, the next it was tower-of-beef, the next it was mariner's delight, which is to say fresh sea snake wrapped around a fat horsefish.

The money did not give me any worries either, despite what they say about a rich man's hair, for I had twelve good myrmidons protecting my fortune in a safe place. I knew I would never be at risk from common thieves, and I imagined I would be wealthy forever.

What I did not realize was that when you have such vast sums as I had, it is not the common thieves who are the danger. Rather, it is the noble thieves. A common thief, after all, may take your purse, but a noble thief will try to take all you have. And when I say a noble thief, I do not mean an arrogant prig who wears a colourful coat and walks the street with an ivory stick, but the kind who lives in a castle and has a fine title to his name.

I had not been back in Rowel long before Luro, the new Duke of Oaster, came to visit me. Luro was the only son of the old duke, Huriband. He had been but a child when I worked for the duke, and I barely remembered him (I chiefly had eyes for his older sisters!) but looking at him now I could see he resembled his father in appearance, although his hair was lighter.

I was honoured by the visit, of course, and I made sure the duke was made very welcome at our house. I insisted he stay with us there for the night, and I gave him my father's room to sleep in, which is a good large one, with a fine view of the vegetable garden.

We placed rabbit cages in there too, for the breeding of rabbits was my father's livelihood, and he was so proud of his animals he wanted the duke to be able to see them as he lay in bed.

The duke had brought several advisors with him, and I put them into my brother's room, which is as good a room as any you will find in a king's palace, for it had a water basin set right into the wall. The bed is so large that four might easily share it, which meant there was plenty of room for the three of them. As for my brother, he shared my room, with me upon the bed and him on the floor with his wife, while my father slept in the kitchen with the two children.

I spent great sums of gold on the very best foods for my noble guest. To impress him further, I brought some of my treasure into the house and set it about the dining room. I had nailed a gold chain over the fireplace, and hung an American gold-and-silver shield upon the wall, and I had also scattered coins all over the floor, so the tiles chinked as you walked upon them. Everywhere was gold and jewels, and it looked very lovely, you may be sure.

The first evening was most cordial, and my father was delighted to have such rich company. Unlike me, you see, he was not used to meeting with noble persons, and he could hardly believe his good fortune in having one as a guest under his own roof.

The next day, I showed the duke around our neighbourhood, taking him to the places where I used to play as a child, and telling him entertaining stories of my youthful misadventures. I took him up to the caves, too, where all that gold was piled up. Even if you were standing in the town square, you could often see it shining as brightly as the sun itself, with my myrmidons standing bravely around it.

The duke was impressed by everything he saw, and he talked to me as if we were old friends, although in fact he had been but a young lad when I had worked for his father. Still, all was not quite right to me, and it struck me that, while the duke Luro was very much like the old duke, still there was something about him which did not seem quite so noble.

In the evening—which is to say, the second evening the duke was with us—we all sat down to dinner together, eating duck and octopus and all manner of good things, and talking about this and that.

The duke asked me a little about my adventures, and I told the tales as well as I was able, which is to say, exceedingly well. Then he said, "So, then, now you are a man of wealth and power. How do you plan to put your gold to work for the good of all?"

I said, "What do you mean by that? You may ask anyone in this town and you will find I am charitable enough with my money. All the merchants hereabout have gained business from me."

He said, "No, that is not my meaning. Such wealth as you have is not for free spending. Rather it carries with it many responsibilities. It must be used wisely."

I said, "Well, I do not think I have ever been one to spend money foolishly: I am always careful to buy only the things I like, and I never purchase things I hate or despise. But perhaps you would like to give me some advice."

He said, "Indeed I would. I will speak plainly, my friend: it is not right or proper that a man like you, without noble rank, should have such treasure for yourself. I would like you to give this gold to me. I am in a much better position to use it wisely than you are. Moreover, you may rest assured that I will look well upon you for the gift."

Well, this was such a shock to me that I barely knew what to say. Still, I have a quick mind, so I said, "A gift is like a compliment. I do not believe in grandiose compliments, for such words do not come from the heart. In the same way, such a lavish gift would not show my respect for you, duke, because respect is not measured in gold, but in love and in blood." Then I picked up a beautiful little pearl which was sitting in a box of treasures upon the table, and I gave this to the duke, saying, "Let me give you instead this gift, which is smaller in size, it is true, but shows a more sincere, heartfelt love."

He took the pearl, and looked at it, but he did not seem to relish the gift, or the great love and loyalty which it represented. Then he placed the pearl back in the treasure box it had come from, as if to spurn my offering, which is certainly something the old duke would never have done.

He said, "Remember this, Yreth. I am the duke of this region, and I have the duty of protecting those within my lands. This, as you may suppose, is a considerable expense. When these expenses are not paid for, the degree of protection afforded must quite naturally suffer."

I pretended I did not understand his threat, and I said, "Oh, you need not fear for me on that account: I have twelve good myrmidons of my own, and I have set them to guard over my treasure."

He became sour then, and said, "Tell me now, will you give me the gold or no?"

I knew I would have to appease him, so I said, "Duke, I served your father when I was young. He was an excellent lord, and he treated me well. In return, I loved him and gave him everything it was in my power to give, for I believed I owed him no less. But now he is dead, and you are the duke, and I swear, by my father who sits at this table, that I will give you all I owe you. Tomorrow morning, you may go to the caves up in the hills and help yourself to all the gold there."

The duke was pleased then, and we continued our feast in good spirits. You see, he took my words to mean I would give him all my gold, but in fact I had said only that he could take all the gold he found in the caves the next morning, and I vowed to myself that, when sunrise came, not a single coin should remain there.

We continued to dine for some hours, until, at length, the food and the wine and the lateness of the hour had got the better of everyone, and we were all ready for bed.

But although I dressed for bed, and lay beneath the sheets, I did not allow myself to slumber. Instead, I waited quietly for an hour or so, until I was sure everybody else in the house was sleeping. Then I silently rose again, and I crept out of the house and went up into the hills.

When I reached the caves, I told my myrmidons to take all my great wealth of gold and jewels and pack it back in its chests and boxes, then bring it all to the western crossroad. While they did this, I gathered all the treasure I had laid about the dining room and placed it in a sack, then I carried the sack to the crossroad too.

It took many trips to carry all my wealth from those caves, for there was far too much of it to manage it one go. While the gold was being moved, I sent one of the myrmidons to scout around the local farms looking for donkeys. We rounded up about thirty of these animals, leaving gold coins behind to pay a fair price for them.

You may think, "Donkeys? Why did Yreth not use ox-carts, as he had done in America?"

Well, I would very gladly have used ox-carts, if there had been any. However, those who have been to the Horn of Cyprus will know it is a dry, rocky place, and oxen do not like the grass that grows there. So, donkeys it was, and they were good enough, because they are strong animals, for all their small size, and each one carried a good weight of gold.

Before I left, I had second thoughts about my plan to leave the cave completely empty, for I knew the duke, in his greed, would think I was like him and cared only for wealth, whereas I wished to show him there were higher principles at issue here.

So here is what I did: I took another pearl from my treasure. It was small and pretty, and it looked very much like the one I had given to the duke. In fact, it may even have been the same one for all I know. I took that pearl, and I went back to the cave, which was now entirely empty, then took a sheet of purple silk, which I placed upon a big rock there, and I placed the pearl on top of the silk, so the duke would be sure to see it when he went there the next morning.

I knew when he saw this pearl, he would be racked with guilt and anguish, for he would see I had given him what I owed him, which is to say a token of my loyalty and devotion, despite the fact he had overstepped the limits of his authority by trying to steal from me, and take what was rightfully mine.

I had already decided exactly where to go with my donkeys: I travelled east, to the royal palace of the queen, which is to say, the fortress at Ithron. I reasoned that, if I were under her protection, I would have nothing to fear from the Duke of Oaster if he were still angry at me, and my gold would be safe from his greed.

The journey took about two weeks, and we were waylaid by robbers only once. They attacked us on a remote stretch of road, sending arrows down at us. One of my donkeys was killed by an arrow, and another was slightly wounded. Then the robbers came running down the hills waving swords and shouting and doubtless thinking they looked a fearsome sight. I kept a cool head though, and waited until they were very close before I gave my myrmidons the order to charge. Then my strong friends went to it with a will, furiously repulsing the attack, and killing at least six of the robbers before those rascals finally saw what kind of opponent they were up against and fled in terror.

At last we arrived at the royal fortress, which is very magnificent to behold, and every bit as grand as it appears in the paintings. I found the man who commanded the gate-guards, informing him I wished to see the queen.

He said, "That is not possible. Nobody may see the queen except for those she has summoned before her."

Then I opened one of my treasure boxes and took out a large topaz, and also a lovely ruby which had been carved into a cheerful face. I said to him, "Take this ruby to the queen and tell her it is a gift from the stonemage Yreth, who begs to appear before her. As for the topaz, you may keep that for yourself, in payment for your help."

Well, his tone changed instantly. He bowed to me and went quickly off to deliver the message. He returned just a few minutes later, and he said, "The queen asks if you are the same Yreth who owns a mountain filled with gold."

Well, I did not own a mountain filled with gold, but I had owned a cave filled with gold, and I know well enough how the rumour-mongers will see a cow and say a herd, so I said, "Yes, I am the same Yreth."

Then he said, "In that case, I am instructed to take you before her with the greatest cordiality." Then he led me into the palace. I left the donkeys, together with my myrmidons, in one of the interior courtyards, where there was plenty of good green grass for them to chew on. As for me, I went into the throne room and I met with the new queen.

The queen was not at all as I had expected. In the first place, she was young, having seen no more than twenty years. Her clothes were very grand, of course, but her skin was as brown as a nut, and she sat on her throne in an undignified way, with one foot on the seat and her knee up in front of her. I knew, when I saw this, that the story I had heard from the physician, telling of how she had been a hunter, was true.

I would not say she was beautiful to look at. In fact, to speak frankly, she was plain. Her lips were thin and pinched, her nose was large, and her ears stuck out a little, so you would almost think someone was pushing them from behind as a joke. Also, she was as skinny as a pole, and her breasts were small.

Still, I bowed very low when I met her, for she was the queen and deserved my utmost respect. Moreover, I knew this was the same resourceful young girl who had rid the world of Bellay, and, if it had not been for her, I would still have been in exile for a good many years longer.

Standing around the queen were a number of her young commanders, famous men, all of them. Yunte the Bee was there, and Briss Corniman, and even the Earl of Tarphonay in his wide blue hat.

I talked with the queen for a good long time, and everyone there was impressed by the intelligence of my conversation. When the queen found out I truly was as wealthy as she had heard, or at least close to it, her eyes lit up with delight.

She said to me, "Yreth, you must serve as one of my advisors, for I will wager a good five grotecs that any man with the wits to gather such a great fortune about him as you have will also have much good advice for a queen." Then she laughed loudly and said, "Am I right? Am I right?" and, still sitting at her throne, she kicked around at my rear, which I did not think an appropriate action for a queen.

Still, I maintained my good humour and said, "You may rely upon my good advice at any time."

Then she said, "Hah! Good then. Now attend to this: you will live here at the palace, in one of the apartments which is behind the south wall, for those are the finest apartments there are, and they are kept for the use of such important persons as yourself."

I said, "Queen, you are very generous."

Then the famous Briss Corniman said, "Friend Yreth, you are right about the queen's generosity. Do you know, this queen is so liberal she gave me a gift of five thousand arrans for recapturing the town of Esper."

I could scarcely believe my ears. Five thousand arrans for re-capturing little Esper! I said then, "If Esper is worth five thousand arrans, it would be difficult to calculate a worthy reward for me, for I saved all Europe by my actions."

They all laughed then, thinking I was making a joke, but I said, "No, truly, it is so."

The queen said, "Explain yourself. And make it a good story too, for I am bored today and sorely in need of amusement."

I said, "My story is so fascinating by its own merit that it barely requires a good telling, although as luck would have it, I happen to be an excellent storyteller, when the mood takes me."

I then told the story of the giant ships I had met upon the ocean, and I explained how I had commanded those ships to sail west, and how they had attacked all the Indian cities. I said, "Above all else, it was these attacks, ordered by me, which gave us our victory in the war."

Of course, none of the commanders would admit they believed my story, and they scoffed, saying I knew nothing about military matters and the ways of warfare and so on.

I replied, without malice, "Of course you would say my story is not true, for it makes all your accomplishments seem puny by comparison. Still, I will give you evidence of my claims."

Then I produced Bitian Teppel's superb drawing of my sea battle against the *Flame*. It had been soaked in the sea when I fled from the Indian ship, but in the months since, I had carefully repaired the water damage and coloured his drawing with paint, so it might look even more beautiful and lifelike.

The queen said, "Is this one of the great ships you spoke of?"

I said, "No, but the picture shows an Indian warship which I fought, and it also shows my ship, which I lost in the fight."

Yunte the Bee, who was well known for his insolence, said, "This picture does nothing to prove your claims about the giant ships."

I said, "Indeed it does. In the first place, it shows I possessed a ship capable of crossing the ocean—you can see it here most accurately portrayed. In the second place, it shows I am an accomplished warrior, well able to distinguish between an enemy I might defeat, such as this Indian ship, and an enemy with whom I must negotiate, such as the giant ships I mentioned. In the third place, it shows my love of fine art, which, as all the philosophers agree, goes hip to hip with the love of truth."

Yunte was an ignorant man, though, knowing little about philosophy. He said, "That is no proof at all."

I said, "Well, then, I will soon show you something that will force you to believe me."

Then I went out to the courtyard and I brought in my donkeys, with their valuable burdens, and my myrmidons too. I opened every box the animals were carrying, and I poured out all my gold and jewels onto the floor.

"There!" I said. "Would a man who is as wealthy as I am have reason to lie?"

The queen said, "By my socks! What a treasure that is! It is obvious now you spoke truly, a suckling calf could see it!"

The others agreed with her—even Yunte the Bee—saying my story must be true. You see, they had never seen such wealth as I had placed before them. Then the queen said I deserved a reward for my services to Cyprus, and she asked me what I would like.

I said, "Well, not money, certainly. I have so much gold I hardly know what to do with it all. But there is a favour of a different kind you could grant me."

She said, "What, then?"

I said, "Now this war is at an end, and many of our cities are in ruins, there will be much building to be done. Let me provide the designs for these huge commissions, and give me the authority to carry those designs through to completion."

I knew, you see, such works would be a wonderful opportunity to further my fame as a stonemage. Many of the stonemages of antiquity had achieved fame in this way—most especially Henry Eagles and Illipton—and I believed, by following their example, my name too would live on.

She said, "Ah, that is true. Now I think of it, there will certainly be building to be done. You have your wits about you in realizing that." She talked with some of her advisors for a few moments, and then said, "Well, Yreth, the post is yours. You are now the Queen's Own Builder. Go the ruined cities and do all the building you like."

I was very pleased at this, and I asked her then if she would like to see some of the plans and sketches I had made. I said, "They show my ideas for a marvellous castle which might be built at Drantellie, and for a great harbour building which would sit well at Neppo, and for a lord's mansion which I will construct in Carping or some similar place, as well as other plans for entire streets in these places, with fountains, and parks, and waterfalls."

She said, "No, I do not need to see these things, for I find papers and plans very tiresome. I am sure you know what you are about. Do as you wish in those places—it is all the same to me."

She had no real appreciation for the art of building, you see. I think she liked gold, though, because the moment she had finished speaking to me, she stepped down from her throne and began rummaging through my pile of treasure, picking out objects that struck her fancy, and saying things such as "That is a fine ring. I will try it on, I think," and "This gold pot would suit my bed chamber very well," as if it were her own treasure rather than mine.

She gathered together the things she liked best and said to me, "I would like these for my own. Will you give them to me?"

I looked over the objects she had selected, which were brightly coloured, though only of intermediate worth, and then I magnanimously said, "You may take these things for your own."

She turned to my myrmidons next and examined them closely. She said, "These are good myrmidons, I can see. Will you give me those too?"

I said, "No, for they are mine, and I need them."

Then the Earl of Tarphonay said, "Do you think it is appropriate that, in your new role as Queen's Own Builder, you should have such a force about you?"

I said, "I think it most appropriate, for they do an excellent job of protecting my treasure. Moreover, I think they will help me to earn the respect of those stonemages who might differ with my views."

"That is true, as far as it goes," he said. "And yet, I fear many people will think it is these myrmidons who have won you the post of Queen's Own Builder by their fearsome ways, and not realize you have earned it by your own talents as a stonemage."

I became worried at this, for it seemed to me the earl was right, and it is the way of people to gossip so. Then he suggested the queen might buy the myrmidons from me, at five hundred arrans apiece (which seemed to me a very good price).

I said, "Yes, but who will guard all my treasure then?"

The queen said, "That is simple enough. Place it in my treasury."

And the earl added, "Yes indeed. We will place it in the treasury. It will be much safer there than it would ever be surrounded by your myrmidons, and whenever you want to take some, why, you will be free to do so. You may trust my word in this, too, for I supervise the treasury."

Well, this seemed like an excellent plan to me, for I knew that keeping treasure with a king or queen is something many of the wealthiest persons do. When I was treasurer for the Emperor, all manner of wealthy citizens would come to me, giving me their jewels and gold for guarding. I also knew the earl would be an honest, forthright custodian of my gold, because his grandmother came from Rowel, and her brother was married to the sister-in-law of my own great grandfather.

So I accepted the queen's offer.

Then the queen said, "And I think, as long as the treasure is there, I shall make occasional use of it too, for a queen needs gold, and plenty of it."

I raised my fist in fury and said, "If that is your plan, you would do well to think again, for it is my money, and I will not have it taken from me, not even by the queen!"

But the Earl of Tarphonay said, "You misunderstand the queen. She well knows it is your wealth, and she would never presume to take it from you. No, she merely wishes to borrow from it occasionally. I would ensure all is scrupulously accounted for, and you may rest assured that the full value of the amount borrowed would be speedily returned to you, together with, let us say, an additional one-fifth for each year the money was outside the treasury."

I said, "In that case, it would be my honour and my privilege to give you the use of my wealth, according to the terms you have just stated."

Then the queen said, in her blunt way, "Well, there is no point waiting about for it. We must stash this gold in my treasury right away." And she set her slaves to work collecting up all the gold and placing it into one of the treasury rooms.

As they worked, I told everyone of how the Duke of Oaster had tried to steal my treasure, and I explained this had been the reason for my angry outburst. They were all shocked at the news, and the queen said the duke was a rogue to behave in such a way to a hero like me.

She said, "Now you are dealing with me, and I will make sure you get what is rightfully yours."

I put this to the test on the spot and asked her when I would receive my additional money for my myrmidons.

The earl replied for her, showing me a little book filled with numbers, where he had already made a note for the value of my myrmidons. He said, "Do not worry. You may be sure all it will be entered into the accounting, and the figuring will be scrupulous and exact, to the last grotec. Nothing will be forgotten."

This put my mind at ease, and the earl and I went off together to see my new apartment, leaving the queen to sift through all my fine gold things.

It was a magnificent apartment, too. I was so delighted when I saw it that I turned to the earl and made him a gift of my donkeys, for I was done with them in any case, and they were a bother to feed.

A Sixteenth Section Of The Eleventh Part

In Which I Describe My Plans For Rebuilding Many Cities And An Injury That Befell Me

THE TASK OF REBUILDING WHICH I had chosen for myself was vast in scale—a hundred times larger than any job I had done previously. I knew I would never be able to do all the building alone, so, using my new powers as Queen's Own Builder, I summoned all the important principal stonemages from all the eastern regions of the Cypriot Empire, and I told them to bring maps of their towns and cities, so they might show me the extent of the damage.

I spent some weeks talking with these stonemages and working with maps of the various towns and cities I had decided to rebuild, but I soon realized, if I was to do the job properly, I would have to visit these places. So, I packed up my plans, together with a good supply of food and some travelling clothes, and I spent three months touring the eastern regions of our empire, where the Indian armies had done the most damage.

My tastes had become expensive by now, and I spent a great deal of money during my travels. This worried me not at all, though, because the Earl of Tarphonay was as good as his word and kept a very precise account for me, so whenever I was in need of more money, I had only to send a message to him, and he would promptly have a satchel full of gold delivered to me, wherever I was, by means of a fast runner.

I made many plans and sketches during those days. With every hour that passed, I thought of another wonderful idea for improving this town or that city, especially when I was travelling on the road between each place. I will describe a few of these now, so you can see how fresh and original my conceptions really were.

My Ideas for the Improvement of Peasmond:

I talked to the people of Peasmond, and also to the Earlina of Livy who lives there, and I learned this town is subject to frequent floods, due to its location near the river.

This set my mind humming, and I considered various ways to hold the water back with improved flood walls and so on. But then I thought, "Why fight nature? It is better for people to grow accustomed to it." At once, my ideas took a new direction. I decided that all the roads of Peasmond should be dug up, and ditches should be put in their place, so the water might flow there from the river. There would be no streets, but only streams and pools, with every house designed so the water flowed right into it.

Children born into this environment would quickly become so accustomed to the water they would swim around like fish, holding their breath for long periods, and never fearing the effects of future floods. Furthermore, these people would be most useful in any future war, for they could swim out to the enemy ships and attack them from below.

As for those residents of Peasmond who were sick, or old, and therefore unable to hold their breath, they could easily get around the town using rowing boats.

My Ideas for the Improvement of Treedle:

Treedle's two great industries are leather and cheese, both of which send unpleasant smells about the town. This is a shame, because in many ways Treedle is a beautiful town, all set in the hills as it is.

My plan for this place was to mask the odour with the sweet smell of roses, and to this end I made sketches of the houses and other buildings which might be constructed here. Outside the window of each house, I planned to put a large flower box, as big as a wagon and filled with earth. Into this earth would be planted the roses, thanks to whose fragrant blooms it would be possible to open the windows wide and smell the sweet air once more.

"Yes, very clever," you will say, "but what about those who must walk upon the street? They will still be subject to the evil odours."

For those persons, I had a simple solution, which I designed in my head. It involved taking petals from roses and other fragrant flowers, placing them in a silk pocket, then sewing it shut to make a pouch. This pouch would be tied around the nose and mouth, so those upon the street would think, from the smell of the place, they were in some beautiful garden, even though, in fact, the air on the street would be as foul as ever.

My Ideas for the Improvement of Savercass:

If you have been to Savercass, you will surely know its worst failing: the city is so large and contains so many twisting streets that you can hardly walk fifty paces without becoming hopelessly lost.

My plan was to eliminate this problem entirely by stripping away all the buildings and roads, then building them along a new pattern. The city would have a single road, spiralling inwards, and covering the entire area of the city. In this way, it would be impossible to get lost in the city, for no matter where you were, there would only be two directions you might travel: towards the centre, or towards the exterior.

To make things even easier, I planned to build a large tower in the centre of the city, so people might see at a glance which way they were travelling. If the tower was to their left, they were travelling outwards; if to their right, inwards.

My Plans for the Improvement of Beacon:

I had a wonderful idea for Beacon. I said to myself, "Since the town is called Beacon, I shall build it a beacon—the biggest and brightest in all the world." As I envisioned it, the beacon would be contained in a great glass bowl as big as a mansion, supported at the junction of three vast leaning towers. The glass bowl would be filled with wood from the nearby forests, then, every night, it would be set alight, so it would shed its warm beams down upon the town as brightly as the sun.

If you have read that fine philosophical work of Ducambe Aletto's entitled *On the Necessity of Sleep*, you will know sleep is induced by the debilitating effects of darkness. Aletto explains that, if the sun were to be in the sky during the night as well as the day, we would all have no need to sleep at all, and, moreover, we would never age.

My great beacon, then, simulates this state of constant daylight, thereby conferring everlasting life and wakefulness on the fortunate people of Beacon, who would happily work and play all the day long, hardly noticing as one day crept into the next, and the next, and so on.

Of course, not all my plans were as original as those I have described above, and in such towns as Zoam and Redwall and Dresh-by-Sea, and many others besides, my ideas followed more conventional lines, with rolling walls and fine towers and wide roads. After all, let us never forget that the true aim of building is not to create some vainglorious bauble to please the stonemage, but to serve the real needs of those who must live their lives in the place.

Even so, every one of my drawings, even those I considered

relatively ordinary, was met with the utmost astonishment by the nobles of these places, and they all said my designs were the finest they had ever seen.

I would say, "You realize, of course, these constructions will be very expensive. Just because the queen has chosen me as her own builder does not mean you must accept my designs."

But they said, "No, but we will accept them, for this is what we truly wish, whatever your position with the queen might be." They cared not a flea for the price, either, for my plans were so lovely that thoughts of gold dissolved from their minds, and they thought only of eternal beauty.

The Earl of Omerlind, whose regions included the towns of Carping and Treedle, said the sketches were more like the work of God than of man.

Then I said to him, "Perhaps that is because I became an archbishop when I was in America, and, indeed, since the post was never taken from me, I can only say I still hold it today."

And he said, "It certainly explains everything. But how did it happen that you gained such a rank in that far-off land?"

Whereupon, I told him of my adventures, and he said my stories were astonishing in the extreme and must be recorded for future generations.

Upon thinking this over, I saw he was right. But at the time I was too busy with my plans for buildings, and I did not take my labours in this new direction until recently.

I was received by more than thirty great nobles, and to see the cordial manner in which they greeted me, you would think I was a great noble myself. Although, artistically speaking, I suppose it was true I possessed a kind of nobility which made me greater in rank than any of my hosts.

Wherever I went, I would summon all the local stonemages before me and give them words of advice on how the first stages of the reconstruction should be dealt with.

I said to them, "I am the Queen's Own Builder now, so you must not build anything, or even draw any plans, until you have first presented the idea to me for my approval. In that way, my own good taste will be reflected upon your entire city."

Many of the younger stonemages used to follow me from city to city, watching how I appraised each place, and listening to me lecture about how each place should ideally be laid out. Oh yes, I was a popular fellow in those days, and much admired by all who met me.

Now, an unfortunate thing happened to me during my travels. I was travelling on my way from Teodrick to the little town of Mian Staff. Since it was just to be a quick visit, I travelled alone, without my usual accompaniment of junior stonemages. It was getting dark on the road, and I knew Mian Staff was still a good few miles on, so I stopped at a little village on the road and went into an inn there.

That night, I got to talking with a number of men. They saw my fine clothes and asked who I was and where I was from.

I said, "I am Yreth, the Queen's Own Builder, and I now live in the palace at Ithron."

They said, "No, you are joking with us. Prove that you are who you say."

I said, "How shall I prove it?"

Well, they thought about this, and then one of the men, a big farmer, said, "I know. Tell us where the queen comes from. That is to say, tell us who she was before she was queen."

I said, "That is easy enough." Then I told them the story the physician had told to me, that she was a hunter who had poisoned King Bellay after he had married her.

The farmer said, "Wrong."

I said, "What do you mean, wrong?"

He said, "I have heard the true tale, from a very wise traveller, and if you were really from Ithron, you would have heard it too." Then he told me the story as he believed it. He said, "The fact is, before Queen Sarla was queen of Cyprus, she was a warrior queen from a far-northern tribe. One day, though, she wandered too far south, and, from a high mountain in the Deyern range, she caught a glimpse of the glittering cities of Cyprus, saying to her followers, 'I will have those lands for my own.' Then she marched forward, but on the way she met the mighty Bellay with his armies. He said, 'Where are you going?' and she said, 'I mean to have these lands for my own.' Then he said to his followers, 'And I mean to have this woman for my own!' He did, too, and they were married until he died a hero's death."

Well, I had heard this foolish story before, and I knew very well how to show it up as the nonsense it was.

I said, "What you say cannot be, for I have talked to travellers who have visited the Deyern Mountains and climbed their peaks, and they say, from these high points, they saw only mountains and forests stretching to the horizon. The cities of Cyprus are simply too far away to be visible from the mountains."

He said, "Perhaps those travellers lied to you."

I said, "No, for I am an excellent judge of such things as whether a person is lying or telling the truth. Moreover, if you approach the matter in another way, you will realize that, if it were possible to see the cities from the mountains, it would also be possible to see the mountains from the cities. But everybody knows this is not so, and even if you climb the tall towers of Eopan, you will not see the Deyern Mountains, just as you will not see America."

Well, he had no answer to that, so it seemed I had proved my point. Just then, though, an old falconer, all in black, spoke to us from across the room.

He said, "I have been listening to you fine fellows discussing the queen, and I will tell you that you do not even know what it is you are saying."

Then the farmer said, "Well, Mild Lestic, if you are so wise, then tell us the truth of the matter."

Mild Lestic said, "I will, though you must swear you will keep this tale a secret, for I had to swear the same when the tale was told to me."

We all swore we would not tell another soul.

Then he said, "The truth is that Sarla was a princess, the daughter of King Yreth [after whom I was named, incidentally]. When she was just a tiny baby, a passing eagle spotted her lying upon her bed, and Vush! it swooped down and stole her away. Yet the eagle, breaking with its savage nature—for it is the king of all birds, you know—did not eat the child, but raised her as its own. So, when the king's family were slaughtered by Bellay, she alone escaped. Later, Sarla swore she would be avenged against King Bellay. And do you know how she did this? Well, I will tell you: she carved a monster from the very rocks of the mountain, and she said to it, 'Go! Go and kill Bellay.'"

I said, "Come now! You cannot believe such a tale."

He said, "You cannot prove it false!"

I said, "Indeed I can, for how did the eagle teach Sarla to speak? Moreover, is it not the habit of eagles to toss their young from their nests, in order that they might learn to fly?"

He said, "You know much about these great birds, for what you say is correct."

I said, "Well, then, since Sarla does not have wings, she could not possibly have survived the ordeal. But most of all, if the child was stolen before King Yreth's family were slaughtered, then why did she harbour such a burning desire for revenge against King Bellay? She could not have known of the slaughter—unless perhaps she was told of it by a passing dove."

Then Mild Lestic said, "Yes, perhaps that is how it happened," for he was such a fool he did not even realize I was making a joke with my comment about the dove.

Well, then somebody else said we were all wrong, and Queen Sarla was the child of a demon. A woman denied this, saying the queen was not a demon, but a goddess in human form. A young fellow replied that, according to what he had heard, the queen was actually a man in disguise.

The farmer laughed at this last story and said, "Well, I think we can all be agreed upon the falsehood of that tale, for, no matter how he was disguised, a man could never make himself to be as beautiful as we know the queen to be."

I said, "How do you know she is so beautiful? Have you ever seen her?"

He said, "Yes, for her portrait is upon the new coins, and she is certainly very lovely to behold."

Well, I knew the man who had engraved those coins, and I knew too that he had not even used the queen for a model, but instead had copied an old engraving of Malina the Radiant, who once ruled Pheyos.

I said, "There is no doubt the lady on the coins is lovely. But I will tell you this: she is as much like Queen Sarla as a butterfly is like a clod of earth."

For some reason, this comment of mine, which was no more than a statement of fact, made the farmer very angry, and he struck me a powerful blow across the face with his hand. It came so unexpectedly I was knocked straight to the ground.

Well, I was not taking any of that, especially with my high station and all, so, the moment I came to my senses, I pulled out my throwing-razor—the old one, not the silver one—and I ran at him, intending to cut his throat, but I was no more than halfway to him when one of his friends, standing by the door, lunged out with a fishing spear, sending its point straight through my right leg, a little below the knee, which brought the fight to an end before it had even really started.

The conversation in the inn took a new direction then, and, instead of talking about the queen, they were all talking about leg wounds. Everyone gave his or her opinion on how the spear should be removed, for it was the sort with a barbed metal point, and if you pull it back out, it will do even more damage than it did going in. We discussed this for some time, with them all gathered around me in a big circle, as I lay upon the floor with the spear through me.

At length, it was decided to cut the tip of the spear near the point it entered my leg, so the tip and the piece of the shaft attached to it, could be pushed through to the other side of my leg and then out. This was done, albeit painfully for me, and then they put dandelion leaves on the wound and wrapped bandages around my leg.

The man who had thrown the spear said he was sorry he had injured my leg, and the farmer said he was sorry for hitting me, so I did not stay angry at them, for I thought, "Ah well, it is a wound, but it will heal soon enough."

We all sat around singing songs for a time, and I stayed there the night. The next day, the farmer took me to Mian Staff, with me riding on his cart. When we arrived, the earl there, which is to say, the Earl of Mian Staff, received me with great honour, and said, in full view of the farmer, "You must stay with me until your leg is healed."

Then I turned to the farmer and said, "You see, I am just as important as I said I was."

The farmer bowed to me then, and he went off on his cart looking very shamefaced at the terrible wrong he had done to such a powerful person as myself.

My leg felt a little better the next day, so I was able to walk around with the help of a stick. But the day after, it grew suddenly worse. It oozed and changed colour and was very unpleasant to look upon. Then I became sick, and the earl brought physicians to look at me.

They said, "This is a very serious wound. There is a small piece of the spear still inside you. We will have to remove it, or you will die."

They set to work with their knives and needles, trying to find the piece of spear remaining inside my leg. They had made me drink a whole cup of wormsblood to lessen my senses, but even so, having those gentlemen prod and cut at my leg was almost more pain than I could bare, and, brave as I am, I begged them to stop and let me die instead. Of course, they did not, for they were experienced physicians and well used to ignoring such pleadings.

They worked for an hour or so, but they could not find the piece of spear which was lodged inside me, and at last they gave up and told the earl I was doomed.

Fortunately for me, that excellent earl quickly sent a messenger to the royal palace, giving details of what had happened. The message was received by my friend the Earl of Tarphonay, who instantly sent the queen's physician, Joesken Tesk, to my aid.

Now, Joesken Tesk was from Germany, and he was the finest physician in all the world. When he arrived and took a look at my leg, he told me I would not die, providing the leg was cut off.

I said, "Go ahead and cut it, for it is surely no use to me in its current state."

Then he gave me some wormsblood, but this time I received only a very small amount.

I thought he had made some mistake, and I said, "Is this all I am to get? It does not seem much."

He said, "It is all you will need, for I work as swiftly as the wind."

This was no exaggeration either, for, the moment the wormsblood had taken effect on me, he took my injured limb in one hand and a tiny little knife in the other, and, with just a few deft cuts, the job was done, having taken no more than the count of thirty.

He had hardly finished stitching up the wound than I felt my illness begin to lift, and I knew I would quickly be well again, which, indeed, I soon was.

I felt a little sorry for myself at first, of course, for I imagined it would be a miserable thing to have only one leg. In fact, though, quite the opposite was true. You see, with my leg gone, my vital essence was concentrated into a smaller volume, which made my mind sharper than it had ever been and left the rest of my body very much stronger. So then, far from being an unhappy change, I found the loss of my leg was one of the best things ever to happen to me.

Since then, whenever lame or injured people have come to me asking for my advice, I always urge them to have the afflicted arm or leg cut off without delay, even if the injury is quite a minor one, for the experience is so invigorating in the long term, it is well worth the aches and pains that go along with it. You may be sure all those who took my advice were very pleased with the outcome and thanked me wholeheartedly afterwards, except for a few ungrateful souls who I will not speak of here.

I remained in Mian Staff for a month or so. For a time, it was a problem getting around, for I had to use crutches, and they were very slow. But then my newly heightened faculties struck upon a unique solution to the problem: I designed for myself a kind of false leg, which I might strap upon the remainder of my real one. I had the device constructed by a fine engineer who was indentured to the Earl of Mian Staff. The leg was jointed at the knee, and it had a little ring attached just above the ankle, into which I could insert an ordinary walking stick. Holding the walking stick in my right hand, I could lift the leg and move it forward. Moreover, as the ring rotated through this motion, a simple but ingenious mechanism caused the knee joint of the artifice alternately to stiffen and to bend, so I could walk very well using the device, despite the loss of my leg.

The false leg was made of wood and iron, and I designed it to be precisely the same size and shape as my real leg, so I could pull an ordinary leather boot over it and it would be a perfect fit. When we had finished making it, I hired a goldsmith to cover it with gold leaf and precious gems. He did a masterly job it, so it was a lovely thing to look at, and certainly better than any real leg.

I tried the artifice out and it was a great success. With just a little practice, I soon found I could walk just as fast as before, and it looked so natural in its movement that, if I had worn leggings on it, nobody would have been able to tell it was not my real leg. As it was such a beautiful thing to look at, though, I usually wore it uncovered, except for a leather boot over the foot, so everyone could see the decorations in all their glory and take pleasure from their colourful glitter.

While I was practising with this device, I received a written message from the queen, in the hand of her First Scribe, which meant the message was an account of the queen's own words. She said how sorry she was to hear of the terrible tragedy that had befallen me, and then she wrote, "When you feel you are well enough to move once more, return here to Ithron. You will be well looked after here, with servants to come and go for you, and to carry you around, and to feed you and bathe you and supply all your needs. Certainly we will never laugh at your piteous state nor hide you away in a cellar. In fact, we shall have you sit about the throne room constantly, so all who visit may see the wounds my loyal Yreth won in my service, and, as I have heard it told, defending my honour."

When I read this, I thought of an excellent joke I might play upon the queen, so I wrote back, in a deliberately shaky hand, saying I thought I was just barely able to move now, but I hoped to head back soon, and to arrive in Ithron on Saint Emlough's day, "assuming I do not die on the journey first."

I sent this letter back with the queen's messenger, and the next day, I gave my thanks to the Earl of Mian Staff for all he had done for me. I also gave him a large and valuable diamond as a host-gift. Then I returned to Ithron on foot, going at a leisurely pace and enjoying the sights and sounds of the country.

When I finally arrived at Ithron, I wandered the streets for a time, until I found an old beggar who had no legs at all, was missing his left arm, and who also had scars all over his face. I said to him, "I will give you two arrans if you will do as I say."

He said, "I'll take your kind offer, providing you do not want me to do something unnatural."

I roared with laughter at his wit, then I called a couple of strong lads, gave them each an arran, and told them to carry the beggar into the castle to the throne room.

I said, "When they stop you to ask your business, tell them this is Yreth the Stonemage you are carrying."

Then I placed my travelling hat upon the beggar's head and let them go on their way, while I followed at a discreet distance.

They got inside easily enough, and I watched them being escorted by myrmidons to the throne room.

I took a different route there so nobody would discover the trick, and when I arrived I saw the queen bending over the old beggar. There were two beautiful girls beside her, and she said,

"You have suffered horribly, I can see that. But now these two girls will care for you."

Then the old beggar said, "These girls are a fine gift, but there is something I would like even more."

She said, "What is that, dear Yreth?"

Then the old scoundrel said, "A kiss from your own dear lips, good queen."

Just as she was bending down to kiss him, I said from the corridor, "Well! Here is a pretty picture. I have walked all the way from Mian Staff at my queen's request, only to find she is bestowing her favours on a filthy beggar."

Everybody looked towards me then, and they were astounded, for they saw that Yreth was not the helpless cripple they had imagined, but was a tall proud figure, with a fine walking stick in his hand and a magnificent golden leg.

Then I walked forward and grabbed the beggar by his collar, saying, "It is time for you to leave, my friend, for I have returned to the queen's court, and I mean to raise the standard of the courtiers."

I turned to the two youths I had hired to bring the beggar in, and said, "You lads, throw this rogue into the street where he belongs."

They hauled him off at once, while he shouted foul imprecations at us all. We certainly laughed to watch that entertainment! When he was gone, everyone congratulated me. They all agreed it was an excellent joke I had played, and it had fooled them all very well.

The queen said, "I had intended to give you these two servant girls, together with your own seat in the throne room, in consolation for your injury. But now I think I shall give you these things in reward for your wit, and for the beauty of your new leg."

Then everyone admired my leg, and I showed them how it worked, and described all the gems that were placed into it, saying what sort of stone each one was and how much I paid for it. Later, when those present had left the throne room, they talked about my leg to others, who then told others, and very soon my leg was the talk of all Ithron.

In fact, the news soon spread across the land, and I know for a fact that many of the nobles who came to the palace in the following months did so not to see the queen, but to catch a glimpse of my astonishing leg.

After a month or two, I realized it was very selfish of me to keep my leg hidden away in the palace, where only the rich and powerful could see it. "What of the common people?" I thought to myself. "Do they not also have a right to delight in this beautiful leg I am wearing?" Well, of course, I knew they did, so I decided to show my leg to the people of Ithron. I immediately left the palace and went on a long walk through the streets. Wherever I wandered, people pointed at my leg in amazement, saying, "Look at that! It is certainly a strange leg."

Although the admiration I received brought me great pleasure, I also knew it was a hollow praise, for the people saw only the gold and jewels which decorated the leg, and did not fully appreciate the ingenuity of its design. Therefore, I decided to organize a race, where I might show my leg in action. I placed notices about the town, calling upon all those men who were missing a leg or two to assemble, on a certain day, outside the Three Trestles, where a great race would be held. The winner was to receive a hundred arrans. (The Three Trestles, I might add, is an inn at the foot of Tinder Street.)

When the time came, there were more than eighty men outside the inn, all of them crippled to a greater or lesser degree. Some were missing one leg at the knee, others were missing both legs at the hips. (Such injuries were common at that time, thanks to the war.) There were hundreds of onlookers too, curious to see what sort of a spectacle this would be.

I lined everyone up outside the door of the inn, then I told them they were all to race up the street to the orange orchard. Then I said "Go!" and we started running—they with their crutches and pegs, and I with my Golden Wonder.

The race began. It was splendid fun, and I won the race by a long way. In fact, I was so fleet that, when the race was done, many of my rivals in the race refused to believe my leg was a false one. I quickly silenced those objections, though, for I removed my boot and waved my stump around, bringing cheers from the delighted onlookers.

It was a successful event to be sure—in fact, it was so successful I decided to repeat the event every week, for a larger purse. These races became very popular among the people of Ithron, and folk would place wagers upon the winner. However, all those who wagered against me were sure to lose their winnings, for I always won the race.

Now, because of the races, I spent much more time in Ithron than I had done before. On any day, most of my hours were spent in the palace, working on my designs, but I also used to travel the town, talking with people and hearing the news and so forth. I had many friends in the city—important merchants, and poets, and philosophers, and other learned people.

One afternoon, I went to a soup house looking for some conversation, for this particular soup house was popular with certain of my intelligent friends. Unfortunately, none of them were there that day, only an old woman called Peacock. (This was a joke name people had given her because she always dressed in brown from head to toe.) She had worked in the palace as a servant since she was a girl and knew all the gossip.

Well, I bought myself some soup, and, since I had no one else to sit with, I sat with old Peacock, and we talked about this and that, until she suddenly said to me: "I think it is very shameful about the queen. Do you not agree?"

I said, "What is shameful?"

She said, "That she surrounds herself by so many military men."

I said, "It is because the queen loves to hear tales of the war."

She said, "Is that so? Then why does she never keep any of our famous military women around her, such as Besset Wise-Eyes, or Myressa the Thrower? Do they have no tales to tell?"

I said, "No, I am certain they must have some fine tales."

She said, "There you are, then: the queen cares nothing for tales.

The true reason she has those men around her is that she has lust-ful designs on them, for they are all very young and handsome, and they flatter her with their sweet words. But that is not the whole story, oh my, no."

I said, "What do you mean?"

She said, "Every night, our good queen brings dozens of these handsome men to her room, and she takes them all to herself, one after the other."

I said, "I can scarcely believe this to be true!"

She said, "Well, I assure you it is true, for I heard it directly from a very reliable source."

I said, "Then your source is not so reliable as you think, for I can assure you our queen does not do such things, despite her humble background."

Then she laughed and poked me in the side, saying, "Hah! I know why you are denying it! It is because you are one of those men the queen uses. You are handsome enough, that much is cer-tain. Tell me now, I am right? I will wager I am."

I said, "And I will wager you are wrong. I would not participate in such things even if the queen invited me. Besides, I have two young servant girls of my own. They are much prettier than the queen, as well as being supremely talented in their nightly man-ners."

She whispered, "Well, that may be, but I have heard that what the queen lacks in talent, she makes up for in variety. Oh yes, you would surely be astonished to hear of the scandalous acts that oc-cur in the queen's chamber at night. It is the shame of all the king-dom."

Well, I had finished my soup by then, so I told Peacock once more that she was wrong in what she said, and then I left. Her words troubled me, though, and I thought the matter over, and prayed upon it too. And when no clear answer came to me by these methods, I cast dice to settle the matter. I cast two dice, and they came up a seven, which is the number for sin. Then I cast them again, and they came up a seven again. Then I cast them for a third time, and they came up a four, which is principally the number for food, but is also the number for a wilderness, such as one where Queen Sarla would have spent her time when she was a hunter.

Then I knew, in my heart, that what the old gossip had said was true. After all, why should a young queen surround herself by such men as those commanders were if it was not so she could indulge her lustful passions with each and every one of them?

I said to myself, "This is the shame of all the kingdom, and no good will come of it!" Then I thought, "Ah, but it is not the queen herself who is to blame, for she is but a foolish young girl. No, the core of this evil comes from those worthless commanders and their false praise. In believing such praise, the queen thinks herself to be perfect, and nobody may scold perfection." Then I said, "I pray to God that her eyes may be open to her folly, so she may be made to see her imperfections." And I added, "I also pray to God that God listens to my prayer."

This double prayer brought me God's attention, and about two weeks afterwards He gave to me the perfect opportunity to do for myself the things I had asked.

I was in the throne room discreetly drawing plans—for, as you will remember, the queen had said I should be around the throne room constantly. This, then, was where I did my work, at a table in one corner. The queen had a number of her favourite young commanders about her, and they were very arrogant and boast-ful, swaggering around with their swords. Even though I called myself a stonemage, and they called themselves warriors, what they knew about warfare did not make up one fingernail of what I know about it.

In any case, the queen was having these young bucks compete, to see who could speak the best compliment about her. And there was no doubt in my mind that the prize in this contest was an evening of intimate favours from the queen.

One of them said, "Your eyes are diamonds, and they are set in the brooch of my soul."

Then another said, "Your lips are as red as burning coals, and, like those coals, they set aflame all they touch."

And another said, "The daggers of war are fearsome, but the daggers of your beauty are more terrible still, for I cannot fend them off, and they strike me in my heart."

All this went on for an hour or more, and was very boring to listen to, until one of these fellows, who thought himself very witty, said, "Let us give Yreth a turn. We shall see how his compliments compare to ours."

I put my sketches down and said, "I do not wish to play your game."

Then the queen said, "Why is that, then? Do you have nothing good to say about me?"

I replied, "Queen, if I were to bestow a compliment upon you, you may be sure it would be a hundred times better than anything these champions of yours have to offer. That is because my compliments are truthful, and come from the heart, unlike these casual lies you are used to hearing."

In saying this, I meant to show her how foolish her game was, but instead, my words had just the opposite effect, for they made her determined to hear what kind of excellent compliment I would give her. At first, I declined to give a compliment, but she kept on and on at me about it, until at last I said, "Very well, I shall give you the praise you ask for. It will be in the form of a poem, and I will present it to you one week from now."

She was delighted at this and said she would look forward to hearing my poem. She said, moreover, that she would invite many others to the event, for she wished them all to hear praise from the lips of a master.

I was glad I had given myself a full week before I presented the poem, for it took me all that time to write it. As I had promised, I made my words beautifully honest, for there are no words more flattering than honest ones. It was hard, though, for I knew I must blend compliments with loving criticism, gentle correction, and moral guidance. Her commanders might describe her to be a better person than she was, but I must outdo them and truly make her so.

It was a beautiful poem, and I put so much passion into it that I would often weep as I put pen to paper.

When the day arrived, I went to the throne room. A great evening feast had been set out on highboards, and all manner of people were talking and eating and walking about. There must have been at least three hundred people there, not only champions and commanders this time, but also many nobles too, and priests, and important merchants.

When I entered the hall, a great cheer went up, and people shouted, "Behold! The great poet is here!" Then the queen asked me if I was ready with my poem. I said that I was, and the whole place fell quiet as they listened to me read it to her.

I had titled the poem "A Very True Praise Indeed" and I remember the words to this day. They went as follows:

> Now, flattery's an ugly thing,
>   when taken to excess
> For words that strive to move the heart
>   oft smack of hollowness.
> But plain and simple, honest words,
>   undecorated by
> The artful poet's flow'ry verse,
>   his sweetly worded lie,
> Bestow, without such gushing praise,
>   a greater compliment,
> And, coming from a truthful heart,
>   are the more permanent.
>
> And so, I ask you, hear me now,
>   as, in this noble cause,
> I itemize, with candour, both
>   your virtues and your flaws.

To start: your head, the organ most
      deserving reverence,
The seat, in man, of Reason, and,
      in woman, of Good Sense,
Seems adequately gifted with
      the faculties of thought,
And certainly you would be wise,
      if you had just been taught.

Your lusty ways spring merely from
      a wilful female pride—
And what young girl is not this way,
      before she is a bride?
In time you'll learn to serve a caring
      husband as you should.
You'll learn that tending hearth and home
      is, for a woman, good.

Your ways could bear improvement: you
      are arrogant and vain;
You often giggle, fuss, and nag,
      and whimper, and complain.
Your behaviour in public lacks
      propriety and grace,
Yet your visage remains cheerful—and
      this brings me to your face.

Your cheeks are adequately fair,
      and lack both scars and warts.
Your nose, while large, is sensitive
      to odours of all sorts.
The set of teeth behind your smile
      will stand you in good stead,
Remaining white and straight until
      long after you are dead.

Your eyes are two in number, which
is as it ought to be.
Your hair is fixed upon your head—
a fact that pleases me.
Your neck is tough and sturdy, while
your arms are sleek and long.
Continued exercise will keep
them muscular and strong.

Your thighs greet every groping hand—
at least that is the talk.
Your legs are straight, and I would say
they aid you when you walk.
In short, I find that all your parts—
your ears, your feet, your hands—
Meet or exceed the standards that
a gentleman demands.

So, having meditated for
considerable time
Upon your pros and cons, which I
have stated here in rhyme,
I come to the conclusion, after
thinking matters through,
That I will give, without a qualm,
my best regards to you.

Then I bowed to her and said, "My *very* best regards to you, my queen—for being my queen, you deserve nothing less, whatever your faults."

The queen, of course, had become accustomed to hearing false praise, and the impact of my truthful words moved her deeply, for her face was flushed like a shy maiden. She stared at me a few seconds, then at the great assembly who sat in tense expectation of her comments. But she had no comments. She was so moved by the simple beauty of my poem that she merely rose and left the room without a word. Neither need she have said a word, for the poem was a spiritual message which said more than any common words could express, and, when such messages are presented, no further word is necessary.

After she was gone, some of those young bucks were angry at me, thinking the queen was upset. They shouted insults at me, telling me how my poem lacked in sensitivity, and was, furthermore, deficient in praise. But the truth of the matter was that these men saw how much better my poem was than any of theirs, and they were envious of my skill.

The throne room is not a place for fights, so I ignored their rude invectives and left the place, with my throwing-razor in my hand to discourage attacks upon me.

I could quite easily have killed them all, if I had wanted to, but there is little pleasure in snuffing out such young lives, and I knew it was their youthful folly that made them so brash.

In any case, that is how I raised myself higher in the queen's estimation than any other man living. I imagined my actions had won me her permanent favour and lifelong admiration.

But the world is not so simple a place as that, my friend, and I soon found out that those who occupy such high and exalted ranks as mine are in constant danger from the ambition of those below them. I will tell of this next.

THE PENULTIMATE SECTION OF THE ELEVENTH PART

In Which I Tell Of How The Actions Of Others Did Great Harm To My Standing

I SPENT THE NEXT DAY WANDERING the beautiful grounds of the fortress. In my head, I made plans to place a maze upon the lawn. It was to be a very remarkable maze, and so complex that a map would be required in order to negotiate it safely. Further, remembering the lessons I had learned while building the *luma*, I thought of placing small biting animals at certain points in the maze, together with trapdoors, so those taking a wrong turn would quickly pay a painful price, thereby increasing the entertaining properties of the structure.

I did not see the queen that day, because I knew those accursed commanders would also be there with her in the throne room, and if they provoked me again, I would surely draw their blood this time.

In the evening, I drew a few preliminary sketches for the maze, then I kept company with my girls for a time, took a fine dinner in my room, and afterwards slept very soundly.

The next day it rained, so I remained indoors, working on my plans for the maze. I was so pleased with these that, in the evening, I found the Principal Secretary, who was a greasy young man by the name of Toteel, and said I would very much like to join the queen for a private dinner.

He said, in an indifferent tone, "I will see what I can do, but she is very busy and does not have the time for everyone who may wish to see her."

At this, I said to Toteel, "Look here, I am a very close friend of the queen, and you had better watch how you treat me."

He did not like this, and he left, saying he would speak to the queen on my behalf. I do not think he could have done so, for I received no invitation to dinner with the queen, but instead was forced to dine in my room. The food I received, moreover, was poor in flavour, and cold too, which put me in a foul temper.

The day after, I waited, but no invitation arrived. I sent another message to Toteel, but received no reply. On the fourth day, there was still no reply.

On the fifth day, I met Toteel in the corridors, and I gave him a severe dressing-down for withholding my messages from the queen. I said to him, "You are walking upon a very soft bog if you trifle with me. Now, give her my messages without delay, or it will be the worse for you."

He said, "I have already given her every message, and it is none of my affair if she does not choose to answer them. I think she is angry with you."

I said, "Oh, you envious, bitter youth! Why do you try such lies upon me, when I know the queen now holds me in higher regard than anyone else in the world? Go! Deliver my messages, and let us have no more of your courtier's tricks, for I am well acquainted with the way things work in palaces, and if you give me such poor service, I will pay you the grotec you have earned, which is not a silver grotec, but another, very unusual kind."

Then he said, "Oh really? And what kind of grotec is it that you will pay me?"

And I said, "This kind!" Then I punched him twice in the face and kicked him in his private parts with my versatile golden leg. You see, although he was much younger than I, he was scrawny and weak, whereas I was still powerful and strong.

He gasped for breath, saying, "You will rue the day you treated me so," and took his leave.

I laughed at his threat, for he looked a sorry sight with his bloody nose and broken teeth. However, I should have taken other measures on the spot, because he was true to his word.

As for me, I decided I would pay a visit upon the throne room the next day and talk to the queen in person, and if those bellicose commanders provoked me again, I would give them the fight they deserved.

Later that evening, a strange thing happened. I was lying upon my bed, looking at the walls of my chamber. They were covered with a ten-brush pattern. And if you do not know what this is like, for it is out of fashion today and not often seen, a ten-brush is a fat brush, made of a great many small brushes which clip together. Each small brush is daubed with a different colour, so, when assembled, the ten-brush paints a rainbow effect, and, if the paint is wet enough, can produce strange swirls where the colours run together.

I was looking at the patterns on the wall to see what they might resemble. There was one part which looked much like a man's head, but with long pointed hair. There was another which looked like a ladder with many people on it. And there was another that looked like a round, comical pig, although this was a hard one to find, because it would sometimes seem to disappear, even though I knew it was beneath the window, next to the hook. But surely I do not need to explain this game of mine, for it is a commonplace one, and I have seen children playing it as they looked at clouds or flames.

As I was looking, a strange and light-headed feeling came over me. Then, suddenly, my eye fell upon a pattern I had not seen before, and I pointed this out to one of my girls, saying, "Look at that pattern. It looks very much like a mouth."

She said, "Where? I do not see a mouth."

I said, "There, above where you saw the snail, and a little to the right of the winged bottle. And see, behind the mouth is a book that contains all the knowledge of the world."

But even though I described the location of the pattern in the most accurate way, she was unable to see it.

At once, I realized God was speaking to me through these patterns. The mouth was His mouth, and the book was His wisdom, and He obviously wanted to tell me something important.

I studied the wall some more, and I saw a part which looked like a hill with a group of trees on top of it. After some thinking, I realized the meaning of this: that I must leave this fortress, and take a journey across the country.

Then I noticed a pattern which resembled a man clutching a shovel with a very large blade, although the girls thought it was like an old woman pulling bread from an oven, which I too could see. The man, I knew, represented hard work, and the meaning of it was that, after my journey, I would set upon some great task of building, greater even than the one I had already been given. And the image of the old woman indicated I would earn so much money from this work that my previous wealth would seem like a widow's savings.

I thought, "What kind of wonderful task can this be? I have already been entrusted with the rebuilding of one-third of this great domain. Can it be that all of Cyprus's great empire will soon be mine to sculpt? Truly, there seems to be no other explanation, as incredible as it seems."

Now, perhaps you will think my conclusion sounds far-fetched, for, you will say to yourself, "This man Yreth, while clearly very wise in all things, and skilled in both building and battle, is no trained augur. How, then, can he speak with such certainty upon the matter?"

However, the mother of one of my girls, who also worked in the fortress as a maid, was widely renowned as a great seer, and an augur too, and she was so talented that she charged five arrans for a single hour of private advice and prophecy. When I consulted her, she said my interpretation of the divine message was exactly correct in every detail. Moreover, she said I had hidden abilities as a seer myself, and I should always follow my visions in any difficult matter. And I knew she was correct in saying this, too, for there have been very many times when I have had troubles of various kinds, and often the answer would come to me in the form of some obscure vision, or some supernatural event.

I said to myself, "I will leave this palace soon, then, to set out on my profitable journey. Perhaps in another month."

The next day, I went into Ithron to buy some fine new clothes before I paid my call upon the queen. I found a very fine cloak with jewels upon it, but the tailor had heard I was wealthy and insisted on receiving a hundred arrans for it, whereas I was carrying only eighty. This, incidentally, is one of the problems of being very rich: all the best merchants will inflate their prices by ten or twenty times.

I was not in the mood to haggle that day, so I went back to the palace to get some more money from the Earl of Tarphonay. I had got no further than the gates, however, when I was stopped by the guards. They said, now I had left the palace, I was not permitted to return.

I called for the gate commander, who eventually came, and I said to him, "What is the meaning of this? In the past I have always gone freely back and forth through these gates."

He said, "That was the past, and it is so called because it has passed by. I have new orders now."

I said, "Oh yes? And who gave you those orders?"

He said, "That is none of your concern."

I said, "No, but it will soon be your concern, and the concern of the Principal Secretary too, for men are apt to become very concerned when they are being tortured to death for the crime of treason."

I knew, you see, that the Principal Secretary, Toteel, was behind this, because he was responsible for the important messages that went to and fro within the fortress, including to the guards.

The gate commander said then, "There is no use discussing it, for I will not let you pass. If you wish, though, you may write a letter to the queen, and I will take it for you."

I said, "No, for I know all too well where such a letter will end up." (Which is to say, on the Principal Secretary's desk, where he might mock it, and, when he was done mocking, place it in his fireplace.) Then I said, "But please send a message to the Principal Secretary from me. Tell him I am leaving Ithron for a secret destination. There I will forge a great hammer, and, in a few weeks, that hammer will fall upon his head."

Then, after buying some food for my journey, together with some cheap leggings to hide my golden leg from thieves, I left the city of Ithron and took the road to Beacon to begin some of my building work.

The journey took about a week. Along the way, I did indeed meet a group of thieves, who robbed me of the money I was carrying, which was about eighty arrans, together with some fine jewels I was wearing, worth more than five hundred arrans. Because I had covered up my golden leg, though, they did not steal it. I also met an angry stag, but I stood my ground against his fierce horns, throwing rocks at him until he wandered off.

When I reached Beacon, I was welcomed by the earl there, whose name was Elliel, and I was made an honoured guest.

We talked once more of the many plans I had made, and the earl expressed his enthusiasm for my project, saying he could barely wait for the work to begin, and was very honoured that the Queen's Own Builder would come personally to oversee the work, to which I responded that I would start the detailed plans without delay.

He said, "I will see you are well paid for your speed, yet do not go so fast that any important detail might be overlooked."

I assured him I would overlook nothing, for I was, by nature, an exceptionally fast worker, and, also a very diligent one.

Then I said to him, "Will you permit me a favour?"

He said, "State it."

I said, "I wish to send a message to the queen, but, for various reasons, I wish to conceal the identity of its sender until it is in front of her. Perhaps, when you next send a letter to the queen, you will permit me to enclose a letter of my own inside the package."

He said, "I will be happy to serve you in this way, good Yreth. Moreover, your request is exceptionally well timed, for I have just finished a letter to the queen, and I plan to send it this very afternoon."

This was excellent news, to be sure, and I quickly called a scribe and dictated a short letter to him, with a second copy for my records. It went as follows:

> My Dear Queen,
>
> I have left Ithron because of the rude treatment I have received at the hand of your Principal Secretary. I do not think I will return while he still lives. It is a shame, too, for I was planning to write a second poem, even more heartfelt than the first.
>
> I am your honest subject,
>
> Yreth.

Then I wrote another letter, this time to the Earl of Tarphonay. It read:

> My Good Earl,
>
> Alas, I was set upon by thieves on my journey here. Please send a large satchel of gold to me here at Beacon. Also, please see to it that the Principal Secretary is put to death, for he has committed treacherous acts.
>
> I thank you for your trouble,

Yreth.

I enclosed these letters into the envelope containing the Earl of Beacon's own letter, then watched as it was securely sewn shut, and a good measure of the earl's wax was dripped along the thread.

Now, letters sent by nobles are treated differently from letters that other important persons have sent. Only the queen herself may open the envelopes containing such letters, and Toteel would not dare to interfere with the delivery of such a package, even if he knew that a letter from me was also inside. But, since I had told nobody where I was, he would not know even this. So, by sending my letter in this way, I could be certain it would be delivered directly into the hands of the queen.

I was very pleased by my plan, and I imagined Toteel proudly taking the package to the queen, little realizing that the message inside it would, within a few minutes, bring him face to face with the executioner's sword.

During the following weeks, I spent many hours thinking about my great project in Beacon. As you will remember, I wished to build for Beacon a kind of artificial sun, bathing the town in life-prolonging light from a fire in a great glass bowl. But I talked to glassmakers, and they said there was no glass in the world that would withstand such fire. Of course, the glass might be protected by a layer of magic, but I wanted to avoid this, for I reasoned that light shining through a magic sheet might lose its health-giving character.

Then they said, "Quartz might work."

I said, "Excellent, for I can create a giant bowl of quartz very easily, using my stonemage skills upon certain common rocks."

However, when I used my spells of fire and furnace, I found it was difficult to create the clear quartz I needed. In fact, the best I could manage was to create slabs of coloured quartz, which were very beautiful to look at, but were opaque, or only partially translucent.

I set upon a different strategy then: I decided to construct the bowl from a great many natural quartz crystals, held together by a delicate lattice created from my coloured quartz. Of course, I knew the quartz crystals required would be very expensive, for, although quartz is not a precious stone, I would need a vast number of good crystals for my beacon-bowl.

I went to the earl with this news, but he said, "Build it anyway—I care nothing for the cost. This is a thing of beauty you are creating, good Yreth, and the value of it is greater than any coin." Then he asked if he might look once again at the other plans I had made for the town. I brought the plans out and he admired them for some time, saying, "Oh, this is very beautiful," and "How I like the shape of these houses," and so on.

Within two days of this discussion, I received strange news. The earl called me to him and said, "What is all this I hear? It seems you are no longer the Queen's Own Builder."

I said, "Where did you hear that lie?"

He said, "From the queen herself." Then he showed me a letter, written in the hand of her First Scribe, which said I was no longer the Queen's Own Builder, and that the post had been given to another man, by the pretentious name of Defiance Wages.

Now, the meaning of all this was clear to me: that scoundrel Toteel, for the sake of a few well deserved blows, had spoken ill of me to the queen, perhaps claiming I had insulted her or poked fun at her base origins, so the queen's friendship for me had dissolved into nothing.

Moreover, since I still had not received my money, I knew Toteel had told similar lies to the Earl of Tarphonay, so the earl would be lax about sending me the money which was rightfully mine.

I explained this to the Earl of Beacon, of course, and said, "No matter what post I hold, or fail to hold, you may be certain my work will be of the highest quality. Moreover, the high cost of this project will be offset by the gold you may earn by it, for folk will come from all around to benefit from the life-prolonging rays of this beacon, and I will warrant you could levy a good tax on those persons who wish to visit the town.

He said, "Yes, that is very true. People will pay me well to win more years for themselves. Very well, then. We will continue as before."

Then I went off to further my work on the beacon, and I was sure the earl and I were still the best of friends.

Now, over the next week or two, I noticed a change in the earl's manner towards me. It seemed to me he had grown less friendly, and more lordly, so I became worried I had displeased him in some way. Yet, when I pressed him upon this point, he denied it, saying "Your work is of the quality it ever was, and you have said nothing that offends my honour." But even this reassurance was said in such tones that I was certain there was something upon his mind.

Then, another couple of weeks further on, I was called before him. It was the afternoon, and there was no food on the table, so I knew he had summoned me on matters of business.

He said, very bluntly, "The beacon is too expensive a venture for my liking. Discontinue your work on it, and do not purchase any more crystals of Angel-bone." (By which he meant quartz.)

I said, "We discussed this before, and we agreed you would earn far more from the beacon than it might cost you."

He said, "If it worked, yes. But I now know this beacon will not have the effects you claim."

I said, "What makes you say so?"

He said, "These past few nights, I have placed seventy candles in my room, so it might be brightly lit even in times of darkness. But instead of making me wakeful throughout the night hours, these candles merely made me hot and irritable, and these unhappy states were compounded with the most irresistible fatigue."

I said, "That proves nothing! The light from the beacon will be far brighter than seventy candles, or even than seventy times one hundred candles. The beacon will rival the sun in its brilliance, for only in this way, with such a bright light, can the deleterious effects of darkness be nullified."

But the earl was no philosopher, and being very simple-minded, did not understand what I said. He said, "I do not care about your objections. I have decided this beacon will not be built, and that is that."

I contained my annoyance and said, "Very well, then, I shall turn to other matters around the town, for there is plenty of work to be done here."

He said, "As to that, I have reconsidered. On looking over your designs, I find they do not please me as much as I first thought. The shapes lack smoothness, the colours are too brash, and the total aspect is worn and old-fashioned."

When I heard these words, I felt my anger rise, for I did not care to be lectured on architecture by a man such as this, whose business was all taxes and myrmidons. Still, I kept my courtesy, saying, "Noble sire, if there is any part of my designs that displeases you, you may be certain I will have no rest until I have changed it."

Then he said, "I'll wager you would, for there is good money in such work. But I have it in my mind to give the commission to a younger fellow, and one who will be less fond of tasteless and archaic styles."

Now, by archaic styles, he referred to the great classical designs, and in calling them tasteless he showed only that it was he who was lacking in taste, for such designs are timeless, and do not fade with the years, as the designs of the modern school will.

I told him this, without mincing my words. My voice was stern, but I did not yet show my anger, for I wished him to see that the advice I gave was not merely some ploy to keep the commission for myself, but consisted of pure, unbiased fact.

Then he accused me of being unreceptive to the new aesthetic, and he showed me other plans which had been prepared for him, without my knowledge, by a stonemage working under Defiance Wages. One showed a house with a door that occupied half of the front wall, and windows jutting from the roof. Another showed plans for a new temple; it was ruddy brown in colour, with neither tubing nor gadroons to ornament it. It had a dozen functionless columns along the front, with the architrave out of all proportion to the frieze . A third showed plans for a feast hall with a central abber dome, and this building had so many steps leading up to its entrance that it would take a man all afternoon to climb them. Moreover, lancet arches had been placed in the walls, which I thought most inappropriate for a feast hall.

All of these designs, of course, were in the fashion of the new school, which people of real taste do not care for in the least, for the colours are too drab, and there are too many elements, so the buildings confuse the eye and possess no unity.

I explained the profound flaws of the buildings to the earl, of course, but he said, "To my eye, these plans are very fine indeed, and it is my desire they should be built, so you had better resign yourself to the fact. Still, you are a good stonemage, in your way, and, if you wish, you may help this fine young architect with his construction."

Well, here I said to the earl that he was an idiot, and a drunkard too, and I said I would no more assist his lackey on such a task than I would eat my dinner off his fat rump, for both actions promised to leave a foul taste in my mouth.

Then he grew angry at me, and tried to have me tossed out by his myrmidons. However, I was still very fleet, thanks to my special leg, and I escaped into the street without being caught.

Later, I began to wonder why the earl's tastes had become so changed in the short time I had been with him. Well, of course, once I set to thinking about this, the truth of the matter became quite obvious, and I saw that, once again, that scoundrel Toteel had been up to his mischief. Once he found out where I was staying, he sent messages to the earl, claiming the queen was displeased with me, and requesting that the earl should not give me the commission I deserved, but should try to allay my suspicions by offering me a lesser one.

These views were confirmed in my mind when I went once more to Neppo, and to Carping. I quickly found that the nobles at these places too had curiously developed a taste for the new school which they had lacked before, and they offered me work of a much smaller scope than I had planned. Of course, I flatly rejected their insulting offers, even though the Earl of Tarphonay had still not sent me my gold, and I was in need of money.

The Earl of Mian Staff, though, remembered the fine diamond I had given him some months earlier, and he treated me with great courtesy on my visit. When he heard the cruel tricks the Earl of Tarphonay was playing upon me, he gave me two hundred arrans as a gift. Then I asked him whether there were buildings I might work on in Mian Staff, for there had been some damage in that city too, though not so much as in the other three places I have mentioned.

But the earl said, "I fear not, good Yreth, for the works have already been assigned to other stonemages."

Then I asked to look at the plans. They were not the plans I had penned, but were signed instead with the name Defiance Wages, and, as you may suppose, all were marked with the brush of the new school, employing strange shapes, and many steps, and columns, and parapets.

I asked the earl then, very frankly, whether he had received instructions from the Principal Secretary not to employ my skills, for I was sure there was a conspiracy against me.

He said, "No, that is not so. Tastes have merely changed in a new direction, and you, alas, are left behind them."

Now, from these words alone you would read nothing, but he spoke them with a slight twinkle in his eye, and I noticed too a little movement of one hand, so that I knew that he was thinking, "Ah, Yreth, you have hit upon it! You are right to suspect such plots against you, but understand that I can say nothing, for the queen believes the Principal Secretary's lies, and I fear her wrath. You will find it hard indeed to secure any work in all her lands."

I soon found that the Earl of Mian Staff was quite correct: the queen's power, coupled with the constant subversive efforts of my enemy, the Principal Secretary, made it very difficult for me to find any commission at all which I might want to put my hand to. In fact, after a year of paying futile visits upon various nobles

I decided Cyprus no longer suited me, and I longed for my old lifestyle back in America, where the people still appreciate good architecture.

I made my way to Neppo then, and I found a trading ship which was headed to America. The merchantwoman who owned the ship asked thirty arrans to pay for passage.

I said, "That is far too much! Ten is the correct price."

She said, "My price is thirty, and if you do not like it, you may take another ship. Although I do not think you will find another ship, for it is late in the season."

Well, I knew she was right, so I paid over my thirty arrans. But as I did so, I said, "I curse you and your damned ship."

We sailed the next day, and the weather was fair. However, before two days had passed, my curse took hold, and a freak storm came up. Nobody aboard was killed, but the ship was tossed against rocks and sank, and we were forced to make our escape in boats. When we got to land, I found I was only a few miles from my homeland of Rowel.

I said to the merchantwoman, "You see now what comes of asking a passenger to pay too much!"

All the other passengers agreed she had done wrong by me, and that my righteous curse was certainly the cause of the ship's sinking.

The merchantwoman said, "Then I curse you in return, Yreth."

I said, "You cannot curse me, for your curse is not righteous and God will not hear it."

She answered, very sinfully, "Then I curse you in the name of the Devil."

Some might have scoffed at that curse, but I tell you, such words are a serious business. And if you do not believe me, hear this: when I returned to Rowel, I remembered the treasure I had buried against such dark times as these. But when I went to dig the money up, it had vanished! It is impossible such a lonely spot would be dug up accidentally, and Hendell and I were both quite certain we were not followed when we went to bury it, so I knew the loss was because of that evil curse, and it well shows the potency of such curses.

Hendell said: "You are wise, Yreth, to accept this fate as you have, for perhaps your lost wealth is a sign to follow some new path." I agreed, for this followed exactly my own philosophy about prophecies and omens. Hendell himself took the principle to heart and started paying closer attention to his own dreams and visions. He was rewarded by earning a great fortune in trade, so he, who used to have many debts, is now much wealthier than I am!

Fortunately, I knew the nature of the curse, and I prayed a long prayer to God, asking Him to lift the Devil's curse from me. I think it must have been a strong curse, for it took Him several hours of work before I felt it was all gone.

My life quickly improved then, and I found that all the people of Rowel treated me very well, remembering how generous I had been to them when I was rich. I had given them money in their time of need and now they returned the favour, giving me constant encouragement, and urging me to try to get my money back from the queen, which is the thing I will tell of next.

As for the message God had sent to me in the form of those ten-brush patterns, I believe now that it was not truly a promise of wealth or of a great building commission, but merely one of His little jokes which He plays from time to time on his most dearly beloved, for, instead of receiving the great work I was promised, I lost almost everything I owned.

The Final Section Of The Eleventh Part

In Which I Document My Attempts To Win Back My Money From Our Thieving Queen

OVER THE FOLLOWING MONTHS AND years, I sent many letters to the queen, asking for my money—and also to other nobles, asking them to plead the case on my behalf—but I received no prize from my efforts.

I even sent a letter to the Duke of Oaster, reminding him of the lovely pearl I had given him and asking him to help me in the matter, but he wrote a rude letter in reply, saying, "Now that you are back in Rowel, I will send myrmidons and have you thrashed, for it is what you deserve." This was an empty threat, though, because he knew how popular I was in the town, and he knew what people would think of him if he mistreated me.

My friends and relatives, who knew the whole story by now, told me I should write to Toteel, the Principal Secretary. They said,

"Apologize to him. It is foolish to have such pride when so much gold is at stake."

I said, "No, I will not bend so low to kiss a flop of dung."

Later, though, I reconsidered, and I did send a letter to Toteel. It was a long one, and very cunningly worded, for it sounded apologetic in tone, but it actually carried other meanings which I knew Toteel would not understand.

I have a copy of it here somewhere, but I have looked for an hour and I cannot find it. Still, I remember some of the phrases in it. I wrote:

"It was wrong of me to have kicked you once with my leg." (Yes, for I should rather have kicked you thirty times!)

And "Now I look back at my actions, I wish I had done something different," (Like stuck a dagger in your belly perhaps. Ha!)

And "Be so kind as to retract the lies you have told to the queen, and I will give you a reward to fit your actions." (Yes, I will torture you, you rogue!)

The whole letter was written in this vein, appearing to be very penitent in tone, although anyone who knew me well would understand its true meaning.

Unfortunately, I did not receive a reply to my letter. It may be that Toteel recognized my hand and did not bother to read it, although I like to think that one of my many friends in the castle had heard of my sufferings at his hand and had already avenged me, killing him in the night.

In any case, that letter was the last one I wrote to the Queen, because a week or so after I had sent it off, my father, who was one of the oldest men in Rowel, caught the same disease that had recently been killing so many of his rabbits. He died just a few weeks later, having seen ninety-two years. At the funeral, the augur examined his feet and his hands to see what message was there for all of us. The message she discovered was: "Forget the losses of the past, and look to the future."

I said to myself, "Yes, it is folly to spend my own old age worrying about that money. I will never get it back now, for it is too well guarded."

Then I resolved to make a gift to the future. I would start my own school of building. So I sold the gems which I had so wisely placed upon my special leg as decoration, replacing them with imitations of much lesser value, then used the proceeds to buy an area of land on the western side of Rowel. On this site, working alone, I built a very fine school, with three towers and a small but beautiful abber dome. It took me three years to finish the structure, although you must not draw anything from that, for, if I had had a few slaves working for me, I could easily have completed it in three months.

I lived very pleasantly for a few years, earning my keep by teaching the occasional student in my school, and carrying out a few building repairs about the town. I lived in my father's old house, which I had to myself now, for, as I mentioned, Hendell had unexpectedly flourished in his business and bought a larger house for himself. It was a very lavish place, and he lived there with his family, which now comprised a wife and six children.

I imagined I would live on in this slow, peaceful lifestyle until I died, but, of course, this was not to be.

About five years ago, a judge was travelling through Rowel and the surrounding area, settling cases for a fee. He pulled a cart behind him, full of books and papers, and he would say, "Come to me, for there is no case I cannot resolve fairly."

My brother Hendell had seen this man in the town and was much impressed by his claims. He said to me, "Why not see if the judge can settle your dispute with the queen regarding your treasure."

I said, "Come, do you think such a man as that will have authority over the queen?"

Hendell said, "Who knows, he might."

I said, "Very well, then, we shall try. It will be an amusing thing to test this judge's abilities."

Then we went to look for the judge. We found him coming back along the south road where he had been settling the quarrels which the Gammon brothers had picked for each other.

We stopped the judge on the road, and I said, "The queen has taken possession of a great fortune which belongs to me, and she will not give it back."

He said, "Do not play games at my expense. I am a judge and very important."

I said, "This is no game, and if you are as important as you say, then you will help me resolve a great injustice which was committed against me." I then told him the facts of the matter.

When he had heard it all, he said, "Ho! That is an unusual case." He sat down on a grassy bank and looked in a book for a time, and then another book, and finally he said, "I cannot settle the case."

I said, "Why not?"

He said, "If you give me an arran, I will tell you."

I said no.

He said, "Very well then, give me an arran, and I will also tell you how you can regain your wealth."

Well, that was a tempting offer indeed, so I looked in my purse to see what I had, which was just a few grotecs, for I had not done any building repairs in some weeks. Then I asked Hendell if he had any money upon him. He had a few more grotecs. It was not quite an arran, but the judge said, "It will suffice," and took the money anyway.

Then he said, "I cannot resolve this case, and neither can any judge, even those in the Great Courts, for all judges are in the service of the queen, and we may not be used to settle a score against her."

I said, "Then how is it possible for me to seek redress?"

He said, "There is but one way. You may do so through the Holy Court."

"The Holy Court? What is that?"

He said, "In the normal way, the Holy Court is a place where decisions are made upon points of theology. However, few people know that this court may also be used to bring to trial those of royal rank."

Well, this was news to me, for I had always thought kings and queens were accountable to no one. I said, "How may I proceed against the queen in this Holy Court. That is to say, what person should I make my dealings with?"

He said, "I cannot tell you that, but perhaps a priest will know."

The next day, I talked to several of the priests in Rowel. Some knew a little about the Holy Court, but only of its role as arbitrator upon church doctrine; they had never heard it could be used for settling a dispute with a monarch. They said, "Go to Balcorn and talk to the bishop there, if he will see you. He knows about the Holy Court."

I did as they advised and made the journey to Balcorn, which is about a day's travel by sea. The bishop received me at once, without even knowing who I was, for he was a very jolly man, and he loved to have visitors.

I asked him my question about the Holy Court, and he was most perplexed. "I have served at the Holy Court several times, in a variety of capacities," he said, "but I have never heard of it being used to even a score with a queen."

Still, he was intrigued by the idea, so he consulted a number of ancient books and documents for a good many hours. At last, he found a book which suited him and said, "Ah! You are quite correct! The Holy Court may indeed be used to bring monarchs and nobles to trial under the justice of God, although the last time the court was used in this way was three hundred years ago."

I asked, "How should I proceed in this matter?"

He said, "You should proceed in the same way I would, if I wished to have some theological argument resolved. I will tell you this, though, it is a cumbersome process, and very slow."

He was not exaggerating there, either. In the year that followed, I had to make at least twenty journeys, to all parts of the region, in order to set my case in motion. I will not describe these visits, for most of them were very tedious.

When this was done, it was another two years before the case was heard. I used this time wisely, finding what I could about the customs and procedures of the Holy Court, so I might present my views in the most persuasive way.

My suit was to the tune of 27,882,000 arrans, and for some months the case was the talk of the whole kingdom, for there is no earl in the land who has so much gold, and I believe the amount would have put an impossible burden even upon the queen's treasury. Still, it was a figure fairly arrived at, estimating the value of all my treasure, as well as all the towns and cities I saved by my actions during the war, not to mention my myrmidons, for which the queen had promised me five hundred arrans apiece.

When the day finally came, I travelled to Meadric for the trial, which was held in a large room beneath the cathedral there. I went in the company of nearly two hundred friends and relatives, who, as I had planned it, would serve as witnesses for me.

I had said to these people, "Come with me to Meadric and serve as my witnesses. If I win the case, I will reward you all handsomely."

Of course, they were all nervous, and said, "What is it we must say?"

But I said, "Simply speak the truth: say I am an honest man. That is all."

The queen herself was not at the court but was represented by a man named Isenna, who is widely known as a cunning speaker. (The queen's absence, incidentally, shows how very seriously she took the case, for she was afraid even to show her face there, and so was the Earl of Tarphonay, who held all my money in her treasury.)

The judge for the case was none other than Agrator, the Bishop of Meadric, who, at first, seemed to me to be a wise gentleman. He said, "Yreth, I have seen some of your old buildings in Oaster. They are very fine."

I said, "Your words are high praise, especially coming from a person of such excellent judgement."

He chuckled at this, saying it was a fine play on words, what with him being a church judge and making judgements all the time. Then he greeted Isenna, in a cool way as it seemed to me, and we each sat down and gathered our papers together.

Before I describe the trial, I must first tell you a thing or two about the Holy Court. Matters brought before this body are resolved according to an unusual timetable. Like cases in a Great Court, the procedure begins at dawn and must be resolved by nightfall. However, instead of taking place in a large chamber with a round table, it is held at a long table, with food upon it. The judge sits in the middle of the table, and the two parties, with their helpers, if they have any, sit on opposite sides of him.

The procedure follows exactly that of the first Holy Court, which is to say the Last Supper, where Judas was tried before his friends, with Christ as the judge, and sentenced to be hanged, and to pay a fine of thirty pieces of silver. (If you do not know this story, you may read about it in the Fifth Testament, in the Book of Exploits.)

The trial is divided into nine segments, with the first eight named after the principal food served. The sections are Broth, Lentils, Cheese, First Figs, Fish, Flesh, Second Figs, Bread-and-Wine, and Judgement.

We began with Broth, and little bowls of broth were placed before us. It was a poor sort of broth, no better than a shepherd would eat, with too many oats and not enough meat.

Agrator said, "Well, then, let us get this extraordinary matter underway. Yreth, you claim to be the wronged party. You may begin, if you wish."

I thanked him and stood to speak. I knew the first task at hand was to show my claims were reasonable and honourable, and not impertinent, for I knew that many people who did not know me were saying, "Who does this man Yreth think he is? He is not even a noble, and yet he brings the queen to trial."

To settle objections or prejudices of this sort, I had prepared a very eloquent speech, which told everything I knew about the queen—her origins as a hunter and a murderess (albeit the murderess of a wicked king). The speech also told what kind of a person I was—the great armies I have led; my unsurpassed skill in building; my carefree, generous ways; and so on. The speech, as I had written it, showed how I was very much loved by God, while the queen was very sinful in His sight, which is the sort of argument I knew would be well suited to the Holy Court.

Alas, I had hardly spoken two words of my excellent speech when Isenna interrupted me, saying, "I do apologize, but how should I properly address you during the course of this trial—as plain Yreth, or as Archbishop Yreth."

At this, old Agrator asked him his meaning, whereupon I explained that I had been made an archbishop in America, and, since I had never had this post taken from me, I could only say I was an archbishop still.

But I went on to say, "This is a technicality only, for I no longer carry out the duties of that post, and I do not expect to be treated or addressed as archbishop by any in the court." Then I made another little joke, saying, "And you, bishop, need not be intimidated by the fact that my standing is higher than your own, because the days when I had disagreeable clerics tossed from the cliffs are very far behind me."

The bishop was very angry at my amusing and reasonable words, and he rebuked me with great venom, telling me that an archbishop in America is by no means the same as an archbishop here in Cyprus.

Then, in a friendly way, I told him that, as it seemed to me, there was little difference between the church in America and the church here, and that, since I had lived both in Cyprus and in America, while he had lived only in Cyprus, I was in a better position to compare the two than he was. "And if there is a reason why this is not so," I said, "let me hear what it is."

Well, the bishop took my challenge to heart, and he gave many reasons why what I said was not so. He talked on and on for so long that I thought I would die of boredom. Yet my polite yawns and drooping eyes did nothing to bring his speech to a quick end, for he was a very rude fellow, and, seeing he had an captive audience, was determined to have the final say upon this matter, which, after all, had little to do with the case at hand.

Unfortunately, the bishop took so long about it that he exhausted all the time that had been apportioned for Broth, and so that part of the trial was completely wasted.

I found out afterwards that Agrator had long hoped for an archbishopric himself, but he had been overlooked for the position many times, despite the fact he had served twenty-five long years as a bishop. This, of course, was why Isenna had raised the matter: he knew it would make the bishop brood resentfully over my archbishop title from the very start of the trial, and the case would be biased against me, which it was.

We then began Lentils, which was conducted while each of us sat facing our own little mound of lentils. I cannot bear lentils in any form, so I did not touch them. However, I noticed that Isenna was eating his greedily, so I spoke in a loud voice to one of the priests standing around, saying, "I do not think I should eat this while there are poor people who have nothing to eat. Please, take these lentils and give them to a beggar."

Agrator was still angry at me, though, and instead of saying, "What a charitable action! Here is a truly good man," he said "What, you do not like your lentils?" which made me cross.

Since I had, technically, been the first to speak at Broth, it was now Isenna's turn. At Lentils, each party must show how the resolution of the case in their favour will augment and magnify the glory of God.

Isenna said the queen's position in the kingdom was like God's position in Heaven. He said, "This proves God must love our queen, for, although all of us are made in His image, God has also made our queen like Him in rank, although her post is of finite, rather than infinite scope."

Then he told a little story. He said, "A drunken merchant, fat and wealthy, came into this very cathedral here at Meadric many years ago. He had a purse full of gold coins, and he tossed one these coins upon the altar, saying, 'There is my offering to God, for He made me rich.' Later, when the wine was worn off, the merchant came back to the cathedral and said, 'Where is my gold coin?' A priest told him, 'It was accepted as an offering and has gone to pay for a fine jewel for the bishop. It cannot be returned.' Then the merchant pulled out a club and beat the priest to death."

Isenna turned to me then and said, "Did the merchant do right?"

Well, I was outraged to hear the facts of this story. I said, "No! That merchant should have been knifed for his crime, or smashed open with his own club."

He said, "Yes, for the merchant had made his gift to God and, once made, it should not have been retracted. In the same way, Yreth, your gift to the queen must also remain where it is."

You can see from this what a crafty speaker Isenna was. However, I am a good speaker myself, and I knew how to deal with these charges.

I said, "I heard recently of a priest who had gone begging. He collected a good sum of gold, then made his way to his home town to place the donation in the church. On his way, though, he was ambushed by thieves. They stole his money from him. He said, 'Do not take that money, for it is God's.' But they replied, 'It is ours now.' Then they killed the priest. Tell me, Isenna, were the thieves right or wrong."

He said, "Wrong, of course, for the money had been given, as a gift, to the monarch of heaven, and, as I have said, such gifts should not be taken from that monarch, or from any monarch."

"Yes," I said, "and I too would very likely have given my gold to God, or at least a portion of it, but now I cannot, for it all lies in the queen's treasury. Answer me this, Isenna: What is more important—a gift for God or a gift for a queen?"

I hoped he would say "A gift for God," for this would mean I should get my money back, so I could donate some of it to the church.

But instead, he said, "In making a gift to the queen, we also flatter God, for the queen serves God, just as the nobles serve the queen, and we serve the nobles. This is the proper order of things."

I said, "Yes, but whom do you serve foremost—the queen or

God?"

Then the sly fox said, "Whom do you most aim to please, the Duke of Oaster, or your queen?"

I knew if I said, "My queen," then he would say I should please her by letting her keep my gold, whereas if I said "My duke," then I would support his argument about the proper order of things. So I said, "I aim to please neither, for I serve only God."

He said, "I fear that answer smacks of treason, which is a thing that pleases neither the queen nor God."

And Isenna had no sooner spoken those words than Agrator declared Lentils to be at an end, for he had just finished his plate and was hungry for cheese.

Cheese was next, then, and plates of soft cheese were placed before each of us. It was a good cheese, made from goat's milk, or possibly from sheep's milk.

During Cheese, it is the judge who asks the questions, clarifying the various points which have been established in the case so far. As I have said, though, he was very biased in his approach, and he asked me only two questions, about my birthplace and my profession, before turning his attention to Isenna.

Isenna then told all manner of lies about me, and the judge asked for details, which Isenna dutifully invented. According to the rules of Cheese, I was not permitted to speak unless the judge first spoke to me, so you can imagine how infuriating the whole thing was. Still, I soon realized that, although I was prohibited from speaking, there was no reason I could not laugh, and so, whenever Isenna told one of his lies, I gave a laugh—either a gentle snort, or a chuckle, or a loud roar of mirth, depending upon the extremity of the lie. This did a fine job of distracting Isenna.

Agrator glared at me several times, but I merely shrugged and pointed to my lips, to remind him I was not speaking. And of course he could not criticize me for what I was doing, for he would have to speak to me to do so, and then I could respond to Isenna's outrageous falsehoods.

We then moved into First Figs. This is a short break, where

those in the courtroom may wander around, talk to others at their pleasure, and eat from the trays of figs and other fruit which are placed upon the table. I talked at length with a very pretty young priest who was impressed by my keen wit. She said, "You may have set off on the wrong foot, but I think you will yet take the day."

I said, "When my foot offends me in that way, I simply pluck it out." Then I pulled off my golden leg, which amused her very much indeed.

When First Figs was done with, we began Fish. This is the most important part of the trial, for it is the time both parties may bring in the witnesses who will support their claims.

Isenna went first, and he brought in six of the military men I talked about earlier, the young courtiers. As I have said, they were envious of all my skills, and so they said many wicked things about me. I will not repeat their words here, for it was all lies and you do not want to hear it.

It was then my turn, and I called upon my two hundred witnesses, one or two at a time.

They did very well at their appointed task, coming forward, one after another, and saying, "Yreth is an honest man," and "There never was such an honest man as Yreth," and "I declare that Yreth is the most honest man in all the world," and "Yreth's honesty is so great that I weep to think of it."

I had given a few of them additional things to say. My sister Wegnir said, "Thank you, Yreth, for all you have done in spreading the word of God around the world."

And my brother Hendrick held up a robe and said, "I have brought your second cloak, Yreth, in case you are cold on the long walk home."

To which I replied, "I have a cloak already. Give it instead to someone who has no cloak at all. Perhaps to an old blind priest."

In this way, I showed Agrator my virtue and my reputation for honesty, so he would know my claims were all true, and the words of Isenna and his commanders were lies of the basest sort.

That was Fish, anyway. And, in case you are wondering, the fish served was perch, covered in a sauce made from olives and onions. It was very good.

It was now early evening, and time for Flesh, where each side may speak at length upon the case.

I spoke first, saying, "It pains me exceedingly to have to bring such a case as this against the queen, even though she is a vulgar sort of queen who was once a hunter then married Bellay and murdered him and now lives her life ruled by lustful passions."

You will see how I incorporated, as part of my address at Flesh, many of the points I had intended to make in Broth.

Then I said, "This matter may be divided into two important questions. The first of these is: 'Does the queen owe me a large sum of money?' The second is: 'How much does she owe me?' I will deal with these questions in the precise order I have asked them."

Then I repeated the first question, for those who may not have heard it properly. I said, "Does the queen owe me a large sum of money? My friends, the answer to that question is yes. I assure you, upon my honour, and upon my dead father's honour, and upon the holy name of the one true God, that the queen does owe me a large sum of money. As proof of this, I offer nothing more nor less than my own statement of the fact, supported as it is by the testimony of two hundred witnesses, people who know me well, and have confirmed that I am exceedingly honest."

Then Isenna said, "Yes, but we have also heard from my witnesses, fine commanders all, who claimed you are a liar and a rogue."

I replied, "Yes, we heard from six of your witnesses. But what are the opinions of six compared to the opinions of two hundred? Especially when these two hundred know me well, while your six barely know me at all."

I saw Isenna cringe then, for he had not thought of that, and all the other priests there murmured to themselves saying, "Yes, this is the argument of an godly man, for, like Christ before Pharaoh, he offers no papers or documents as his evidence, but simply his own honest words."

I said, "We come then to the second question. How much does the queen owe me. We can divide the sum into four parts. In the first place there is the money and the treasure which I placed into her treasury, under the care of the Earl of Tarphonay. I estimate the value of this gold and treasure at a little over five million arrans.

"In the second place, there is the interest which is payable to me over the time the money was unavailable to me, which comes, at a rate of one-fifth per year, to another five million arrans.

"Thirdly, there is the money which the queen agreed to pay me for my twelve myrmidons. This comes to five hundred arrans per myrmidon, for a total of sixty thousand arrans.

"Fourthly, there is the reward the queen said she would pay me for my heroic actions in saving Cyprus. She gave me the post of Queen's Own Builder for this service, but since she saw fit to take the post away again, I will insist upon a golden payment instead. I have calculated a fair reward, in line with the sums the other commanders were paid for their victories, and it comes to seventeen million arrans or so.

Then I said, "As must surely be clear, each of these sums lends weight and validity to all the others. My claim is thus self-reinforcing in each of its parts, and quadruply so in its total, which, having being calculated for me by an excellent priest and mathematician, exactly matches the amount of my claim—specifically 27,882,000 arrans."

Then Isenna rose. While he spoke, I turned my attention to the meat before me, which was goat and ham, cut into delicate slices.

Isenna said, "I will not speak further on the subject of Yreth's honesty. Enough has been said about that." I was pleased at this, for I sensed he was half beaten, and I waved a piece of ham in his direction to annoy him. Then he said, "I will turn instead to his extravagant claim for compensation." He then launched into an speech which was remarkable for its blatant fraudulence. It was such a foolish and desperate argument that, for most of the time he spoke, I did not even bother to dispute him, but merely ate my meat, shaking my head at his sorry efforts.

He said, "In the first place, the gold which was placed into the queen's treasury had been earned overseas, in America, and once brought into Cyprus, it was subject to a great many tariffs and fines. His failure to pay these fines promptly rendered the sum subject to confiscation."

He then brought out various documents showing the Laws of Tariff, and letters, and all manner of tiresome things, thereby wasting a good deal of time.

He said, "Moreover, most of the gold within this hoard was in the form of American arrans, a currency which is not recognized here as having any legitimate value at all."

As evidence of this claim, he brought out more ancient papers and passed them around. I did not lower myself by looking at them.

"Thirdly," he said, "in transporting gold to Cyprus, Yreth passed through enemy waters without sinking enemy ships, rendering him subject to still further penalties. I could list other infractions too, but I am sure I do not need to, for it must certainly be clear that, whatever sum was initially placed within the treasury, it was subject to so many fines, taxes, penalties and tariffs that its value is reduced to nought.

"It follows that the interest owed to Yreth must also be of no worth, for one cannot earn interest on nothing."

I said, "Your tedious arguments have not dealt with the matter of my myrmidons."

He said, "Under the law, the possession of myrmidons by anyone other than a noble is a grave crime. In promising you such a generous sum for the myrmidons, the queen was simply trying to offset the fines which you surely owed for your offences. Her calculations were precise, and you will be pleased to hear that the sum you must pay for possessing the myrmidons is exactly negated by the amount the queen owes you for buying them. This matter, then, is settled equitably."

I objected to this line of reasoning, saying that, at one point while I was in the service of the Emperor of Saskatoon, I held the rank of a duke (which is absolutely true, although I have not told of the event here). I was, therefore, a noble of sorts and entitled under the law to own myrmidons.

But the bishop said, "We have heard enough of your past ranks, and we care nothing for them. At present, you are merely Yreth, a stonemage of some repute, and I will acknowledge no higher claim."

I said, "What of my bounty, then? Am I not owed a generous reward for my actions in lifting the blight of war from Cyprus? I should say seventeen million arrans was a very modest price to pay for such a happy transformation."

Isenna replied, "In the first place, there is no proof that these giant ships and great black myrmidons you have spoken of actually laid waste to the lands of India, or that they existed at all. But even if their existence and actions were to be proven beyond doubt, the payment of a victory bounty is not an obligation. If the queen wishes to pay one, or to grant some boon, whether for real or imagined victories, she is at liberty to pay it. But no person may compel her to do so."

I said to Agrator, "I have heard enough. Now, let me give you my opinion of this man's words."

Unfortunately, the judge would not allow this, claiming the time for Flesh had elapsed, and we must now move into Second Figs, which, like First Figs, is another break from the debate.

During Second Figs, Isenna was in a jolly mood, and he demonstrated a silly hopping dance to the judge, saying it was greatly enjoyed by the queen.

For myself, I talked further with the pretty young priest, who had been winking at me throughout Flesh. After a time, though, I became annoyed at Isenna's prancings, and I shouted out, "Ho, there! Your bland steps are no way for a man to dance. Watch this."

Then I hauled myself up onto the table and performed a magnificent quafe, stamping and marching in a very rousing manner, despite my leg. I sang a song too, which was *The Murderous*

Whore, and all the priests around clapped heartily at my fine performance.

After Second Figs came Bread-and-Wine. The bread served was just plain loaves, but the wine was that very rich, strong variety, which is known as bloodwine. I do not normally take such things, but I made an exception here, for this was holy wine. It tasted so delicious I drank three full goblets, and it went to my head very powerfully.

Isenna then gave a summary of his arguments in the case, for the general purpose of Bread-and-Wine is to render the past arguments into a brief form. He was a fine speaker, certainly, but his arguments sounded no more plausible when stated concisely than they had done when stated at length. I knew though, that the judge would be impressed by Isenna's words. The weather had been foul for me ever since the trial had begun, thanks to Isenna's comments about my archbishop's post. I also knew I would not get a fair hearing, no matter how cleverly I spoke my piece.

When it was my turn, I said, to Agrator, "I will not summarize my arguments, for they are so simple they need no summary. My case rests upon the words of an honest man, which is to say, me. Instead of more talk, let me challenge Isenna to a form of combat. We will throw knives at each other and see who is the first to die. The one whom God chooses to survive will win all the gold at stake in this case."

Agrator replied, "That method of determination would not be appropriate. Moreover, since you do not wish to summarize your arguments, I declare Bread-and-Wine to be at an end."

Judgement followed immediately. Agrator said Isenna's arguments were compelling in every respect (which should tell you all you need to know about that judge's wisdom!) and I should be paid nothing by the queen.

Truly, I expected no less, for I knew Isenna and Agrator were conspiring against me. Moreover, when we left the court, I saw Isenna and Agrator go off together, doubtless to indulge in some unnatural act.

Still, I was not angry, as you might think, for in my heart I felt justice would yet be done. Later, when I returned to the inn where I was staying, I had a strange and vivid dream, brought on by the holy wine. In this dream, I saw myself standing upon a hill, which I knew to be one of the hills of Heaven. Before me was my pile of treasure, exactly as it had appeared when it was in the caves above Rowel. A voice said, "Here, Yreth, your treasure is waiting for you."

Then I saw five more piles of treasure, identical to the first, floating in the sky all around my treasure. I knew then that I was seeing the future. These five piles were my rightful interest, and the amount of it indicated the passage of twenty-five years, meaning I would live another twenty years before I died and was reunited with my treasure. (You see, five years had already elapsed since the money was taken, and twenty-five less five is twenty.)

Then my old friend the Holy Ghost came before me, assuming a visible form. He had the appearance of a hanging lamp, with a cosy red flame on his wick, and a gentle smile upon his base, but no eyes or ears.

I said, "Holy Ghost, where is Queen Sarla?"

His lips moved and he said, "She is in Heaven, but she lives in poverty, no better than a street dog." Then he showed me a vision of Queen Sarla, dressed in rags, with dry leaves around her in the place of gold.

Then I said, "And where are Isenna and Agrator, the Bishop of Meadric?"

He said, "Those sinners are burning very nicely in the flames of Hell."

I said, "Ah, I am glad of that, for they were unjust."

He said, "Yes, you must forget about them. There are great new battles for you to fight, my friend. Return to your own palace of learning, Yreth's School of Stonemagery and Architectural Knowledge, and make it your fortress in a great war. It will be a war not of soldiers, but of aesthetics, and your opponent will be the loathsome new style of building."

I said, "Will you guide me in this war?"

The Holy Ghost replied, "Not in a pigeon's ear! No, God has decreed that this is the last time we will speak together while you are alive. But when you are dead, we will chat again. I have a fine joke to tell you."

Then the vision vanished, and I awoke feeling unspeakably serene and tranquil, and ready to emerge triumphant from the great struggle that lay before me. In the next part I will tell of my fight against the new style of building, and of the wonderful victories I have achieved in it so far.

The Twelfth Part

In Which I Explain The Meaning Of The Term "My Name Is Writ In Stones"

ENRY EAGLES, THE GREAT STONEMAGE, was once asked why he did not place upon his buildings a cornerstone bearing his name. This, you see, was the fashion in those days, and all his contemporaries did it. It is said that he replied by gesturing to the great tower he had built and said, "My name is writ in stones."

I have followed his wise principles. I never inscribe my name on any building I have created. Instead, I let the building's stones speak for themselves—although usually I add a frieze or pattern which cunningly contains my name repeated over and over in its swirls. In fact, you can visit any of the buildings I have described in this book, and if you study their decorations carefully, you will find my name written into the stones somewhere, just as Eagles recommends.

The fame of Henry Eagles became so great that he founded the school at Eopan, and I have followed his guiding star in this too, for I too have founded a school, where I teach others to become stonemages, so my wisdom and experience can be passed onto them, and my name will be written in the stones my students work.

Although my school is very small, its reputation is spread over the continent—and even beyond, to America, I am certain—for I teach many things, not merely stonemage techniques, but also how to deal in matters of business, and also in such day-to-day skills as how to eat at the table of a noble and how to handle a weapon.

I leave out no field of study which might benefit my students, teaching them even of the True Religion, for God can be a greater ally than any king, except at those times when He plays His jokes.

Mine is the only school in Cyprus where the classical techniques are still taught in their pure form, unsullied by the vile methods of the Piatian stonemages which have become so popular.

Even at the school in Eopan, where I learned my craft, students now ape the new style, throwing down a dozen bindings where they should use one, and filling every open area with a hundred steps.

When I learned they were teaching this rubbish at Eopan, I was horrified. I said then, and I say still, that to pass on such methods is a terrible betrayal of a great heritage in building, which has been handed down for centuries from the skilful hands of the great Henry Eagles.

To date, twelve students have learned the craft of building under my instruction. This is a small number, it is true, but I think it is better to teach a handful well than it is to teach a multitude badly, although my skills in teaching are now so refined, after ten years of practice, that I rather fancy I could teach a multitude well. And you may rest assured I certainly would be teaching multitudes, if I had been willing to make certain compromises in my principles, and to embrace the aesthetics of the new school. But I am proud to say I did not compromise my beliefs in this way, though it meant the loss of students—and well paying students too, from families of the noblest rank.

Earls, and dukes, and even princes have said to me, "Here, take my sons and daughters and teach them the ways of the stonemage, for it is the finest calling in all the world, and we know you are its greatest living practitioner, whatever prejudices the queen may have against you."

To which I say, "I will take them gladly, providing you realize I will teach them nothing of the new school, for the styles of that camp are detestable to me."

Then they say, "They are detestable to us also, but the world at large loves them, therefore we pray you to teach a little of this style."

And I say, "Ptoy! The world at large may be damned for its bad taste, but I will have no part of it. Here my students learn only the great techniques which have survived the ages."

And they reply, "If you will not teach as we ask, then our children must study elsewhere, for we wish them to learn the innovative new techniques. But we respect you greatly and admire you for your high principles."

I have heard these exact words more times than I care to count, yet I do not take it much to heart, for I know these nobles are ignorant about architecture and judge by appearances only, thinking, since my school is humble in appearance, while the school in Piatia has many huge and tasteless halls, it must follow that the skill of building according to the Piatian style is a valuable one to have. Yet, if these nobles truly wished their children to learn innovative techniques, they would certainly be better off sending them to me, for the great structures I built in America were more innovative than anything the new school has ever produced, but these designs of mine were also firmly rooted in the ancient stonemage traditions.

I wish the queen had given me the money she owed me, for then I would buy a great plot of land and buy slaves and build the largest school you have ever seen, with great halls and towers cast in every colour of the rainbow. The nobles would come flocking back to me, you may be sure of that, and I would say to them, "The queen is little better than a whore."

And they would say, "What? Are you not afraid of her?"

And I would reply, "Who, that little stick? She does not dare to show anger to such an important stonemage as me."

As it is, of course, the queen hates me bitterly for having brought the trial against her, and she would gladly see me dead. I know she has tried many times to have me done away with, but her agents are afraid to strike at me by day, for any would-be murderer would quickly find himself set upon by my allies.

At night, though, I often hear the sounds of assassins creeping around in the streets below—and I know they mean me ill, for they slip into their hiding places when I look out of my window. To protect myself from their daggers, I bought myself a large dog, called Wing, who is very ferocious and who lives with me in my house. Also, once each week, I smear the doors and windows with a little goat's cheese, which, I have discovered, is a thing all assassins fear. I give a little cheese also to the dog, to make the smell of his breath the more terrifying to them.

I also say a prayer each night, which goes as follows:

> *O, protect me, God,*
> *And keep me from the knives of murderers.*
> *And, should one enter my house,*
> *In the dark hours,*
> *Let me wake,*
> *And give me strength to seize his weapon,*
> *Driving it into his own wicked heart.*

If scrupulously followed, my methods offer complete protection from the night attacks of assassins, and I recommend them to everyone who must deal with such things.

Still, I have strayed a little from my story, which, at this stage, is about my fine school, and the students there.

I was sitting in the Statue Square, talking to the renowned musician Olag Moon, who is a very good friend of mine, when I saw a girl by the name of Lepic. Now, this Lepic had been one of my students, and a good one too, so I waved my staff at her and called her over.

"How are you progressing at your craft, young Lepic," I said. "Are you building great castles to further your reputation?"

I said this only in jest, for such is the prejudice against classically trained stonemages these days that none of my students has received any major commissions, and those who have found paid work do only occasional repairs, or must earn a wage by commanding myrmidons (which is another skill I teach at my school).

But her reply surprised me, for she said, "No, I have been offered no castles, only a little water stall near to the Trader's Arms, yet I do not think I will even submit a design for this task, for it is a lowly structure, and you taught us to build only great things."

"By that," I said, "I meant only that you should build things which show your skill to be very great. This water stall would give you every opportunity to do so."

But she said the water stall was a base and degrading thing to build, and would be a place of foul smells and grunts.

I quickly set her mind right on this score, however, for I employed my keen mind and logical reasoning. I asked her, "Suppose, then, you had been offered a great new feast hall for your commission. Would you take the job?"

"Of course," she said. "It would be a wonderful thing indeed, and I would be a fool for declining the chance to build so glorious a thing as a feast hall."

"If a feast hall is glorious," I said, "which is, after all, merely a place where people eat their food and drink their drink, then it follows that a water stall must share the glory, for what is that but a place where these same people deposit their food and spill their drink after their bodies have taken their fill of its goodness."

She instantly saw the truth of this, and said I was very much wiser than she. And Olag Moon said I was wise also, and he said, "I have heard many times of your keen mind and precision in the ways of argument. What a rare honour it is to see these skills at combat in the field."

I asked her then how many pots were to be in these water stalls. She said "There are to be ten—six for the women, and four for the men. And also there must be four pissing walls for the men."

Olag Moon said, "Ten pots and four pissing walls. That is certainly a reasonable size of water stall!"

I agreed, and I told Lepic that, if she could win the commission, it would bring great credit to her, and also to me.

She said then that she would set upon the designs without delay. Yet I saw from her face that she was still uncertain, so I asked her to speak of what troubled her.

She said, "I worry I shall do the design poorly, for I do not like the smell of the water stalls, nor the noise from them either, and so I have never been inside one."

I said, "Great God, my girl, what then do you do when you are in the street and feel the need to relieve yourself? Do you just squat down in the park, upon the lawn?"

To which she replied, "Oh, no, not upon the lawn!" Then she added, in her innocence, "It is among the trees that I squat."

At this, I burst out laughing, and Olag Moon did too, for it was the funniest thing we had heard all month. I laughed so hard that the tears rolled down my cheeks, and I could make no noise for it tickled me so. The girl Lepic began to cry then, for she was just a simple country girl at heart and was ashamed of her ignorance. Therefore, I comforted her, and said I would help her with her designs, for it would be both of us who would benefit from the piece. Then she was most happy with the situation, and agreed her naive ways must indeed seem comical to us refined townsfolk.

After that, we spent a good week working upon the design. In truth, it was I who did most of the work, for she was inexperienced, and slow about reckoning even the simplest bindings. I settled upon a crescent shape for the building. On the inside of the crescent were the four pissing walls, with a good wide entrance to them. On the outside of the crescent were many doors, which each opened upon a stall with a pot. The crescent was covered by a circular roof, with pieces of glass set in the place of certain tiles so the interior might be well lit.

The design had some clever twists too. For example, I placed a number of pipes within the wall of each stall, so each patron might carry on a conversation with the occupants of other stalls, for the pipes carried the sound so well that you might think you were talking with somebody sitting a few inches away rather than forty feet.

Also, I placed perfume receptacles in the stalls intended for the women. The receptacles were filled with a perfumed liquid, and, just above the liquid, was placed a stick, and, glued to the underside of the stick, a great black beetle. The beetles were positioned so that, as they tried in vain to fly away, their wingbeats would splash the surface of the liquid and send it showering down upon the patrons in a fragrant, soothing mist.

Some people, on hearing of this device, have said the idea is ridiculous, and could not work. But they are wrong, for we had the receptacles made, and they did work, and very well too. Indeed, they would be working today if the man who oversees the water stall would periodically replace the beetles, for the creatures die after just a few days, and he is too squeamish to stick a new one in place. He does not admit this, of course, but instead claims the beetles pull themselves loose and fall upon the women who sit below, but this is a lie, and he says it only to hide his fear.

In any case, the design was completed, and Lepic took it to the Baker's Guild, which is responsible for maintaining the water stalls here in Rowel. The bakers looked over the design, and they said it was very good, but they would not give her the commission upon the spot. Lepic asked them the reason for this, and they said they were also considering a second design, which came from a stonemage of the new school. Now, she is a clever girl, and did not grow angry at this news, but instead feigned a great interest in her opponent, asking to see his plans, and, while admiring them, taking note of the signature, which bore the name Ghymlan.

She brought the news back to me, describing the plans she had seen, which, as far as I could make out, were exceedingly tasteless, for this Ghymlan had surrounded his water stall with columns, and, atop each column, was a loaf of bread carved in stone. Of course, this motif was a very pleasing one to the bakers, but to everyone else it would have been laughable, for there is no bread to be bought within the building.

Still, I knew well how to deal with such a competitor, and I asked my friends in the Statue Square whether they had heard tell of a Ghymlan who had come to the town. I quickly learned that the fellow had arrived two months before from the mainland and had a room in a farmhouse owned by one of my distant cousins.

Then I summoned together all my old students—there were twelve, just as there were twelve disciples of Christ—and I asked them to pray with me. I said:

"God, although this man Ghymlan has done no wrong to me, it would serve us all very well if some accident should befall him, so the commission for the water stall might go to a student of my school, whose style is so beloved by you. God, we pray to you, send your spirit to the my cousin's farmhouse by the river, the farm where the donkeys and pigs are all in the same field, and wreak your judgement upon Ghymlan."

And they all said, "May these things all happen. Amen."

Well, as luck would have it, an accident did befall our fine friend Ghymlan a few days later, because his hands were crushed under a heavy stone! As a result of this event, he was unable to practise his trade further, for a stonemage needs a delicate touch, and Ghymlan had certainly lost his.

It was, therefore, Lepic who received the commission. She was paid twenty arrans for the work. I took fifteen arrans from this sum, though, for fifteen-twentieths of the work had been my own.

You will think it was a cruel and unhappy thing that befell poor Ghymlan, and you are right in thinking so. But then, this world is a cruel and unhappy place to us all, and if the unhappiness we bring to others through our prayers can relieve our own misery for a short time, then it is proper we should ask God to inflict unhappiness, for, were the positions reversed, our enemies should surely do so to us.

This is a lesson which I learned only very late in life, yet I practise what I learn, and, as a result of other heartfelt prayers, two more stonemages who came to this town seeking work have left with their arms in bandages, so I think the next great structure which goes up here in Rowel will be solidly in the classical style.

Until then, however, I take much delight in the water stall which I helped build. It is a lovely sight, and brings admiring glances from all who chance upon it. And within are further enhancements, which I created as I built, and which were not in the plans. If you come to Rowel, I urge you to visit the building, which is near the Trader's Arms, just off the Harbour Road, and please sit upon the pots there, for, when you gaze down at the floor, you will see glazed images of the various buildings I have mentioned in my tale.

And, if you are a man, you must also pay a call upon the pissing walls, for there you will discover, to your utmost delight and pleasure, that the black walls are crafted, in places, of stones that become very dark when wet, so as you relieve yourself, you will see a word forming before you. And this word is none other than the name of your humble and unworthy narrator, which is to say

Yreth.

Index

About the Author

Duncan McKenzie was born in Plymouth, England, but now lives in Oakville, Canada. He occasionally works as a TV writer and producer, and helps run an improv theatre. He has four children, one wife, and no knowledge of architecture or magic.